PASSAGES

Also by Laurel Wanrow

The Windborne Series - for young adults
The Witch of the Meadows
Guardian of the Pines
Lost Whisperer of the Seas
Keepers of the Sea Cliffs

The Luminated Threads Series - for ages 15 & up
The Unraveling, Volume One
The Twisting, Volume Two
The Binding, Volume Three
The Luminated Threads Volumes 1-3 Box Set

Science Fiction Romance - for adults
Passages

PASSAGES

LAUREL WANROW

Sprouting Star Press

Laurel Wanrow/Sprouting Star Press
P. O. Box 2311
Reston, VA 20195
www.laurelwanrow.com

Copy Edit by Joyce Lamb
Cover Artwork © 2016 Danielle Fine
Book Layout ©2017 BookDesignTemplates.com

Wanrow, Laurel
  Passages/ Laurel Wanrow. ~ 1st ed.
  ISBN 978-1-943469-08-6

First Edition: January 2017

Dedicated to my fellow writers sharing the journey.
You have changed my world.

"The best proof of love is trust."
~Dr. Joyce Brothers

ONE

QUINN

The city of Cavvert, Aarde

Another morning, another motel room, and another day my brother was still missing.

I slung my travel pack over my shoulder and shoved the lapels of my field jacket together against the chill mountain air. My cheeks stung beneath my beard, and my eyes watered, reminding me I'd best brace for both another search of another town *and* the cold. I strode the length of the old motel building to the street, where my grandmother waited, bundled in her tan jacket over travel clothes.

"Morning," I called. "What backwater town are we off to today?"

Graen wasn't listening. I followed her gaze past the quaint eateries and shops surrounding the snow-patched green. Across the town square, a line of people waited alongside flatbeds of shipping boxes at the Conducer station.

Four helmeted Blackguards emerged from the station's door. A fifth waved the travelers aside while the guards in their black polymer armor marched to the nearest flatbed. Each hoisted a box and carried it back inside, their stun swords swinging from their weapon belts.

My gut twisted at the sight of so many electorg guards. "They've requisitioned this passenger station for cargo transport." I shook my head. "Trust a 'torg to put equipment before the needs of the natives."

"Quinn, hush," hissed Graen. "We've got to get past those people."

I dropped my glare from the Blackguard barring the transporter station's entrance. "*Electronic* humanoids aren't people. Not anymore."

"Of course they are, and when we get to the head of that line, you treat them as such." The snap of Graen's words matched the midwinter morning. "Or at least pretend to, so we can move on."

I let it go. The search for my brother was difficult enough without today's challenge. Though it didn't appear the electorg guards were turning anyone away, just holding up the line.

Lifting her long gray braid aside, Graen hoisted her pack. She linked her arm with mine, and we crossed the street. Sticky situations didn't bother my take-charge grandmother. *She* remembered her past, giving her plenty of material to fabricate stories for the alien electorg authorities on this volcanic planet.

I patted Graen's hand. "We'll find him. We've got two weeks yet to cover the remaining inhabitable regions."

Her green-eyed gaze darted up at me. "Our list is down to the rural spots I didn't think Quil would be, but—" She shrugged. "If it takes scouring every pumice barren and mud pot, I'll do it before I leave Aarde without your brother."

"Where to, then?"

She wiped a hand across her brow. "Remember the island I pointed out on the map? Zeffir?"

"Yep, I recall the coordinates. Remote."

"I'll request it, claiming an ill sister needs my help. We should be able to search its small town and leave again more easily than from a populated area. Plus, it's not a hazardous Spore Zone."

We joined the line.

At regular intervals, the elite Blackguards—more 'torgs than I'd seen in any one place during our weeks here—returned and collected their heavy boxes. After they disappeared, the remaining Blackguard allowed one or two impatient groups to depart. A regular station operator stood mid-line asking for identification, another new policy. I met Graen's gaze and silently extracted my ID. We shuffled closer, until at last the conversations reached us.

"*Home?* What do you mean I have to return to my place of residence? We're on *holiday.*"

"Travel has been canceled across the planet," intoned the operator. "You must return to the location designated on your ID." His porta-scan spit out a slip of paper. He handed it over. "Next."

Graen offered up her ID with a grandmotherly "Hello."

I kept my lips pressed together as I showed my card

with its matching, false address.

The operator eyed us. "Just the two of you traveling? Related?"

I stiffened, but my steady Graenie wrapped an arm around my waist. "My grandson was kind enough to take me shopping in your lovely resort. Quite boring for a young man. Quinn is happy to head home."

"He's one of the few natives who is." The operator tapped his porta-scan. "Next."

We accepted the slip of paper bearing the coordinates to Stranaar, though it wasn't home. Nor were we natives. But we matched their humanoid looks, and despite their machine components, so did the 'torgs.

As the queue advanced and the operator moved from earshot, I dared a glance at Graen. She stared toward the nearby mountains, deep creases marring her fine-lined forehead.

"They're toeing a hard line," I murmured.

She raised her worried gaze to mine. "Something's up... Something besides a spore evacuation. I just wish I knew what." Her pressure on my arm increased, and I bent closer. "Do a cross-leap," she whispered.

I'd be hacking a Conducer in front of witnesses. I briefly closed my eyes and steeled myself before nodding. The skills of our people came easily to me. Remembering how I knew them did not.

And then it was our turn. We hefted our travel packs and entered the small limestone station. The plates of the particle accelerator hummed along the thirty-foot corridor, making the air ripple between the five sets of wall-mounted gray rectangles.

Graen offered our verification paper to the operator perched at the console, then pulled it back at the last instant. "Did he get it right?" she asked with false concern. "Stranaar? On the coast?"

I slid behind her, peering at the paper she held to me while edging closer to the raised line of yellow stones bisecting the slate floor, the actual Conducer entrance. I needed extra time between the first set of plates to start the leap. Afterward, all we had to do was reach the end. Together.

"Did he get our town entered right?" Graen waved the slip and fidgeted from foot to foot, effectively positioning us at the yellow threshold.

I stepped across. Energy flowed over my body. With a thought, I connected to it.

Graen said, "Young man, check this, would you?"

"Yes." The operator snatched the paper and studied it. He repeated an impatient "yes" and bent to input the destination that would lock us into going to the Stranaar station.

Graen clasped my hand. We walked, each step dissolving us as I hijacked the power we'd need for our cross-leap, a method our people used to make direct connections to a particular destination. Six steps, seven, eight—

"Stop!"

My adrenaline spiked, but we couldn't stop. Wouldn't. Nine steps, ten. Halfway through the array of plates, halfway dissolved. Graen faltered, then slipped from my grasp. *What the—?*

I shoved my molasses-dense particles into solidity and turned around.

Between the third and fourth sets of plates, a Black-guard blocked Graen, his sword waving in one out-stretched hand, the other batting at her loosely collected figure. An untimely déjà vu hit me, muddling my mind and breaking my concentration. *This has happened before, in another place, in another leap more urgent than this one.*

Graen solidified and shot me a panicked look.

The guard grabbed her arm. "What do you think you're doing?"

No! I knocked him aside.

He stumbled upright and came at me. The stun sword flared to life.

Damn. With the energy I'd amassed on my body, I couldn't risk a hit of current. I retreated, hands aloft.

"Get back to the entrance. Now." He brandished the sword, reaching with the electrified blade to provide me with a tap of incentive.

"Quinn!"

Graen's call startled the guard, giving me time to jerk aside. He swung his sword. Heart thudding, I instinctively dodged into Lacuna, the gap between molecules.

The surreal feel of his slicing sword jostled my dissolved particles. A muffled burst of curses sounded through the thin but stable barrier walls of the gap space. I held myself intact, panting for the seconds of eternity it took for him to move away. Then I darted out, ducked and rammed the guard. He fell into Graen, arms and sword flailing.

She shoved him off and straightened.

I grabbed her hand. The Conducer's energy swirled around us, ready, but a raw slice below her ear oozed with blood. "You're cut!"

"Keep going. Do the cross-leap," she gasped, "even if I black out."

Hell. What else could I do? With the guard cursing behind us, I flung an arm around her shoulder and trotted along the corridor. We dissolved.

Fully immersed in the accelerator's energy, I could make connections to any destination once I visualized it...but my mind jumbled. No image came. *Do the cross-leap.* I mind-linked with Graen. Her trips appeared and I snatched the vision of the island. West of here at fifteen degrees longitude. North, sixty degrees latitude. No direct course between this Conducer and another, but that made it harder to trace. I merged two segments...shortened another, and in a split second my mind cranked out the jumps. Our molecules flew apart.

We hurtled through space on a trajectory manipulated from a map's coordinates, and I held to the transference as if our lives depended on it—because, judging from the Blackguard's shouts, they did.

The tingling in my body ebbed. I collapsed with Graen into the leaves at the edge of a wood. Frigid air surrounded us under a sky speckled with starlight. Aarde's golden moon, Roamer, hung on the horizon, about to set. Behind a rocky outcrop on the adjacent hilltop, the faint glow of pink meant Misha, the red moon, was rising. It was at least an hour before the dawn we'd left behind on the mainland.

Graen hadn't moved, but neither had I. I tightened my arm around her and applied pressure to her bleeding neck. Her steady breathing comforted me as I listened to the stillness. Had the 'torg guard followed? We'd never had witnesses to what I could do before. According to Graen, our people's way of rearranging particles for movement—into the near space gaps of Lacuna, or far space travel like cross-leaping—marked us as aliens on this well-secured planet.

And Aarde banned outsiders. If the Docga's 'torg minions discovered us, it'd land us beds in jail until we could be deported to an off-planet detention center.

"Graenie? Do you think the guard'll figure it out?"

No answer. I called her name and rubbed her hands, but couldn't rouse her. If she never—*no!* Had a jolt from the guard's stun sword hurt her more than the cut? I took a deep breath, dismissed the wave of foreboding and squeezed her hand. I would deal with her wound.

Her bleeding had stopped. Under the green tint of my night vision, the edges of the scrape had darkened. Graen healed fast. She'd be over this quickly. I dabbed her skin with antiseptic from my pack and covered it with a bandage.

That done, I calmed my mind. Nothing annoyed Graen more than when I charged into a mind-link, another of our skills. Now was not the time to get on her nerves. I laid a hand upon her cheek and sought her out. Within our linkage, images rose and fell in a murky haze, unlike her strong projections that had helped me cross-leap. Not good.

I sent her a message—the vision of the island, and us.

My portrayal flickered, and swirling clouds obscured the land. A roaring wind cut in and moved them—Graen attempting to communicate. I struggled to maintain my image. The fog cleared, and the view of central mountains, rolling lowlands and blue sea shifted. In a series of jerks, the coast magnified. A smudge of gray resolved into buildings—the town.

Through the howling wind, one word repeated: *Passages...passages...passages...*

Passages? I asked.

The wind dropped and died. *Yes. Find me...help in...passages.* The image went black.

"Passages?" What the hell, or where in it, was passages?

Graen heaved a sigh, but her eyes remained closed. She wasn't going to be any help.

Think, Quinn, think.

A bitter breeze picked at the bare branches around us. Best to let her sleep and recover. For that, she needed someplace warm, especially if I had to go for help.

Along with practicing our particle transference, Graen had drilled me in survival techniques as part of my recovery. She figured we might need it after running for our lives when I injured my head and lost my memory. Ten weeks of urgent searching for Quil had sharpened my skills, so when I cast my gaze around the woodland, a plan snapped into place. I shrugged out of my coat, positioned Graen on it beside a fallen log and wrapped her in a compact, emergency sleeping bag from our supplies. I tented a second bag over her using our packs, and then stuffed every crevice with insulating leaves. By the time the sky had lightened, the low shelter was warm.

Graen would be proud, if... Damn it all. She still *slept*. I bit back a sigh and asked anyway, "So, Graenie, ready to shake this off?"

Her breathing and heartbeat were normal, but she was dead to the world. What would I do if she didn't revive?

"Blast it. So I'm supposed to get help...in passages. What on Aarde is 'passages'?"

TWO

EVE

Zeffir Island

"Eve!" Evard bellowed, shattering the early morning peace of our bookshop before I'd even taken two bites of toast, let alone a swallow of coffee.

I glanced in the direction of our office, where my coworker had headed after finishing his breakfast. He was prone to theatrics, but...

Across the kitchen my gaze met the eyes of the local girl who cooked for us. Mylta shrugged and, without missing a beat, slid eggs onto a plate, added potatoes and brought them to the table.

As usual, the portion seemed huge, a far more elaborate meal than the barley bread that served to break the fast in my organic years. But with Evard starting this early, I'd need it. My fingers flexed around my steaming mug, and I dipped my nose to inhale the roast's aroma, a luxury we certainly never had in sixteenth-century England. Maybe Evangeline, the third in our electorg triad, would respond.

"Eve!"

Or maybe not.

"You best see what the problem is, Miss Eve." Mylta

handed me the morning's notes from community members, requests of our triad or thanks for past help.

I took a sip for staying power before rising. With the folds of my local-styled woolen skirt catching at my legs, I pushed through the swinging door into the bookshop and strode to the back hall. Evard filled the door of our combination office and lab, his fingers raking quick strokes through his blond goatee.

"What's wrong?" I asked.

He jabbed a thumb toward our message board. "No travel. Just when that cute little 'torg from the trade ship has agreed to a hop to Palmmani's beaches. Her ship arrived overnight, and those new ministers suspended travel at dawn. Can you believe it?"

I rolled my eyes. Yes, I could believe Evard was upset at this hitch in his plans. But he'd make others. Few electorg women in the Biosphere Corps had refused the gregarious man's invitations. Our family-like triad arrangement made me more a sister than a potential target, so he had no problem regaling me with his romantic entanglements.

Shooting me a frown, he pulled a pocket watch from his coral surcoat, a copy of one he'd worn in his organic life ruling a mushroom-growing collective on his home planet of Tarne. "You busy today?"

Why the change of topic? "What do you really want? All that shouting couldn't have been over canceled travel with your"—I had no idea what status this one had reached, if any—"girlfriend."

"Date." At least he had the grace to look a little

sheepish, trying to cover it by releasing the cord on his long hair and re-sweeping the blond locks into place. "Even if we can't leave, I'd still like to see her."

He made it sound like the meeting wasn't happening, unheard of for—wait a second. I shot a look to our Post roster. "Aha. *You're* on Post Duty."

His hands dropped onto my shoulders. "Take it for me. Please?"

"Why? You're due to assume the lead position in another few months, even with this transfer they've thrown at us. May as well get in some practice." I shrugged him off and snatched up my porta from a workstation. I tapped into the schedule drawn up by our current lead—Evangeline. Where was she? Her assignment read "preparing status reports." She should've been here.

"Then do the fungal level tests for me," Evard said.

"What? You haven't done them yet?"

He groaned and flopped into a swivel chair. "Kind of slipped my mind."

"I bet." Besides my daily update with Zeffir's leader, I had four counseling sessions listed with community members...and the first note from Mylta requested another. Hmm, unusual. But I'd rather have my responsibilities keeping harmony among the Zeffirites, than managing Evard's social engagements.

"Evy, please." He took the porta and notes from me. "I can't possibly run around and collect data from a dozen farmers and still placate my date, now can I?"

I crossed my arms. He'd never try this on our lead.

But then again, he'd learned our run-mate didn't understand his emotional needs. Now if he were one of her beloved goats... "Don't tell me Evangeline is allowing a late submission."

His long nose wrinkled, and with a roll of his eyes, Evard gestured to the whiteboard.

I'd thought she must be on a husbandry call, but Evangeline's neat printing read: *I've left to report to Dome by 0600 per a blanket broadcast to all leads.*

"Dome?" I said stupidly. There was only one reason our lead would be called to the Corps headquarters on the mainland. A twist of dread knotted my stomach. "Evangeline's received the transfer orders," I choked out.

"No, not that. Finish reading her note." Evard rose, threw an arm around my shoulders and hugged me to his side while reading: "*Apparently, this meeting is to announce a new protocol, not the transfer assignments. Because all leads are attending, they closed the Conducer to other B-run travel. Evard, complete those test results on the pending compost shipments—today. Evangeline.*" His hold on me tightened. "New protocol," he repeated in his big-brother manner. "Not the transfer."

Blessed Waters, I'd jumped to the wrong conclusion, letting the weight of the move taint my thoughts. I buried my face against Evard's burly chest until my heartbeat leveled out.

"A protocol announcement. That's all," I whispered to myself.

"Ah, you poor nymph." He patted my back. "I'm not

looking forward to the day we leave Zeffir any more than you are. The people here have been most welcoming—ah, *bloody hyphae.*" He sucked a breath. "They're not just natives, they're friends and..." He cleared his throat. "Once they give us the transfer location, I'll set up another of my Conducer shortcuts so you can visit here easily."

I wiped my fingertips over my eyes. "Thanks for the offer, but I'd rather not risk your *illegal* shortcuts."

"Illegal doesn't mean impossible, and if it's possible, it's permissible." His blue eyes sparkled. "Why would Basic-runs like us be equipped with the same hardware as the Elite-run ministers if not to use the circuits?"

Not this again. I pushed off of Evard's chest before he launched into his favorite topic of restricted electronics. "The Docga limit our use of them, same as they've allowed this new batch of ministers to place us B-runs at their beck and call. What's the point of settling into a home and career in my so-called second life if I'm forced to leave?" I poked him in the shoulder. "Can you focus on something else, please? Like the 'new protocol'? What's that about?"

"Rather vague, I agree. And why ban travel? Previous ministers didn't when the leads traveled for those ridiculous morale-boosting seminars." He snapped his fingers. "Bet it relates to the rampant hornwort growth over on the La'adir mainland. Minneri Pools isn't too far from Dome. The ministers have *finally* come to their senses and set up a field excursion to get the leads' input on the situation. Or at least inform them. 'Bout time they got us official word, before releasing the news to the masses."

I leaned on a work counter and cocked a brow at him. "If it's yet to be released, then why have I heard about the hornworts' advancing sporophyte stage every time you return from one of your covert visits to Dome?"

"I have my sources," he replied smugly.

Yes, and I knew who she was. Who his stylist's sources were, was another matter. I shifted back to our immediate problem. Our lead did a splendid job with the Zeffir livestock and managing her administrative tasks, but she didn't grasp the subtleties of interacting with her fellow humanoids. "Do you think Evangeline will get the information straight?"

Evard met my gaze with a shake of his head. "She'll never ask the right questions. You should go after Evangeline, make sure she gets the scoop."

"Scoop? Where do you learn these terms? What if you go ask your stylist? Surely she knows what's happening."

"Love to, but"—he pointed to the whiteboard—leads only."

That was reason enough. Every 'torg stationed at Dome knew Evard on sight—a man who towered over most everyone and drew attention just by being himself.

He shrugged. "If *I* could use the Conducer, I'd be going to Palmmani."

I let him ramble about his ruined plans while I considered the situation. I *could* make the trip. Although I was tall compared to women of my time, I was more average in height and brown-haired looks, so I didn't stand out among 'torgs or Aardites.

Yet, the very reason the Docga chose me for a position with the Biosphere Corps, my empathic gift, caused my reluctance to mingle in populated areas. I hated the confusion of the urban live-work setting for our administrative 'torgs. The enclosed space seemed busier than some city-states on Aarde, or G47 as the Docga called the planet. I'd managed to avoid trips to Dome all but half a dozen times in the nearly fifty years I'd been a 'torg.

I straightened from the counter. "Unlike you, I know no one there to ask. Let's wait and see what information Evangeline brings back. If it's not enough, you go get a trim when the travel ban is lifted."

"I'll be happy to."

With a trip postponed—hopefully permanently—I could resume my day. I opened one of the community notes, then the rest. *What?* Another two Zeffirites wanted to talk to me. I shoved the papers at Evard. "Look here. You haven't been blabbing about the hornwort status, have you?"

He raised his hands. "Not me. They have *their* sources. We just...confer. Work talk." But he studied the names, his frown growing. "Only half these people are my hires for the fungal project, and they know we're well stockpiled to mitigate a spore release. It's got to be some other complaint."

I pinched my suddenly aching forehead. Zeffir was safe, far from the thermal areas where the hornworts grew, and our elders had emergency plans. So what was causing this level of community panic?

Evard blew out a breath and dropped into a chair at a monitor. "I'll check the news, but I suspect it's those bloody new ministers and their damned 'don't worry' stance. That only promotes worry. And not just over the hornworts. I didn't want to get your hopes up, but my hires plan to approach the Docga when they arrive in two weeks. They're in a positive tizzy about that idiotic decision to transfer us—*Great Grünmann*, that's it! The new protocol. Someone's heard something."

I groaned. "What could be worse than a transfer?"

THREE

QUINN

Zeffir Island

With the rising sun visible through the tree trunks, I left Graen in the shelter to start my search for her baffling "passages" and medical help. A stream meandered through boulders littering the plateau, forming dozens of shallow pools. I paused for a drink and found the water warm on my frozen fingers. The liquid had a distinctive yet pleasant taste, which I chalked up to minerals.

The bleating of goats led me down the hillside. Far below lay the town, a village really, spread at the bottom of a gentle slope on the edge of the sea, just as Graen's image had shown.

In between, terraced crop fields exhibited the modern—for the natives—agricultural practices the Corps encouraged: contour plowing, irrigation and crop rotation. Goat pastures and an unusual number of greenhouses dotted the outlying hills, long, mounded compost heaps alongside each.

Compared to what we'd seen in our travels, this island was an agricultural mecca. Small steps for the year 2092, yet steps in the right direction. My opinion of the freezing, windy Zeffir rose, though I doubted we'd find

Quil. The rural lifestyle didn't fit what Graen told of my brother's avant-garde tastes.

I entered town on a cobbled street, passing stone houses with shake roofs and then modest shops. The villagers eyed me. I averted my gaze, the only thing I could do in a small community where everyone knew everyone else. A few children scurried by with tablets and pencils, but most everyone was in his or her twenties, like me. They probably would have said hello if I'd given them half a chance, but no conversation was our rule.

I lengthened my strides. A butcher shop. A tailor's. Dry goods store. Where was the Docga-sponsored medical clinic, opened in every last municipality to catch early signs of lung damage from the spore inhalation? Maybe they didn't have one, since Zeffir was far from the equatorial volcanic zones and protected by its own Bounded Winds.

Along the docks, the pungent odor of the fish stalls assaulted me. An alley dead-ended with a barn where a ringing hammer proclaimed a blacksmith shop. On the main thoroughfare, I dodged the tempting smell of fresh bread, while my gnawing stomach protested.

I'd decided to question the next friendly face, when I happened across a side street with a half-dozen shops on each side. Partway down, a sign caught my eye.

Passages.

I stumbled to a halt on the worn cobbles. Had Graen meant a place *named* Passages? This store matched the others, a two-story stone building where the owners lived above. The green door and trim were a bit weather-beaten, but not nearly as neglected as some. Yet, the lines of books in the display window sapped my excitement.

A bookstore. My gaze darted again to the carved wooden signboard, still trying to puzzle out what Graen could have meant by sending me here—if she had. I walked past, but my mind wouldn't let go of the shop. Perhaps they had a volume on healing. I stopped and rolled my face skyward. My options had disappeared. I was going to screw this up somehow, but using a book might prevent exposing our situation. I turned back.

The door opened. Out rushed a couple in the midst of an argument.

"Evard, I need more information to reassure people," said a woman with an English accent. "Not to mention, you're in charge, and she'll pitch a fit if that report isn't complete when she returns."

A broad back encased in an orange coat blocked my view of her. The man topped me by a good half foot and spanned twice my bulk. The back began to shake with laughter.

"Ah, my fair nymph, you can't say when that might be," the blond man replied in a rich but strangely accented baritone. "Besides, I'm not leaving the *Post*, merely taking a break until that other source comes through. Let loose a bit and let me have my fun."

"Oh, I can't stop you, so do what you want. And don't call me your fair nymph."

"Aw, I try not to, but when you look like that, all in a

snit, I revert to my past. Forgive me, my girl, and just remember you yourself have enjoyed many transgressions over the years. Here." He pulled a palm-sized, leather-bound book from his side pocket. "Borrow my handbook and look them up. I shan't be."

The man thrust the black book at her and strode toward the center of town, leaving the girl scowling on the stoop. She stood as tall as I, about five-foot-nine, with a fit weight. A little younger than I, perhaps. Dressed in a sort of old-world outfit—a long brown skirt and vest over a long-sleeved tan blouse. Definitely a local Aardite.

She saw me and gasped. Her full pink lips opened as wide as her gray eyes, surprise evident in every creamy feature.

"I beg your pardon," I said. "Didn't mean to startle you, but the door opened and I didn't want to interrupt... Sorry."

The pretty girl released her breath, and a slight smile transformed her features. "That's quite all right. Is there something I can help you with?" She stepped aside and gestured me in while clasping a pile of books, including the little black one.

Despite my need for medical information, I found myself not caring much about books.

Watch it, Quinn. Graen would give me hell for befriending an Aardite, although she'd never frowned on casual interactions with the native people. In contrast, we kept our distance from the electorg workforce. If my hazy memory of a cross-leap incident resulting in our current situation hadn't supported that, the ordeal at Cavvert certainly did.

The girl's welcoming smile was slipping.

I didn't want that to happen. "Thanks, there might be." I walked inside.

The store was a rabbit's warren of bookshelves. Taller than my arm's reach, they lined the walls and projected into the room to form library-like stacks with a wide corridor down the middle. I searched for labels, particularly one denoting medical help, but couldn't find any.

"Are you looking for a particular book?" She dropped her armload of volumes onto a table with a *thud.*

"Yes." I drew out the word to stall while her gaze bored into mine.

Her light brown hair fell beyond her shoulders, thick and straight, unlike my snarl of curls. Both my hair and the beard Graen hated probably harbored leaves from my shelter construction. The shelter—Graen. She still lay unconscious a half mile away. How could I solicit medical help discreetly? Asking for first aid for a simple cut might lead—

"Or perhaps you wish to browse a topic?" The girl rubbed her hands together, covering a ring with a thick, yellow stone.

All of a sudden, I had no qualms about telling this lovely girl what I needed. "Could you point me to the medical section, please?" My words came out as a whisper, but thankfully she didn't seem to notice.

"This way." She wove between the stacks. I followed.

We cut through a sitting area. A gentleman in a suit was ensconced before a roaring fire, books with time-worn leather bindings open on the table, but he was holding a porta. He glanced my way and did a double take.

My clothes. That must be it. Graen had fashioned them to blend with the planet's typical dress, but this place remained decades behind the rest of Aarde.

"Healing, medicine and first aid fill these facing stacks." She pointed down a row. "The collection covers scientific and folk, traditional and alternative, but I'm afraid they're mixed together. If you don't find what you need, call me. My name is Eve." With that, she disappeared.

After several false starts, I found a medical encyclopedia and used the index. The information under abrasions didn't cover unconsciousness. Under coma, the entry suggested Graen needed a hospital and life support. Shock fell somewhere in the middle, but didn't fit either, as her skin hadn't felt cold or clammy. Should I pick one and hope for the best? No, I knew my limits—I'd never find anything to help Graen.

I pressed fingertips to my eyes. If she didn't...

I couldn't remember a life without my grandmother. My only memories were of the two and a half months we'd spent on Aarde. Not much, not even how we came to be here. But Graen knew my past. If I lost her, I lost my guide. Getting back to our people, as she wished to do, didn't mean as much to me since I couldn't remember them, but losing Graen—I couldn't. Without Quil, she was the sole person on this alien planet like me, the only one with whom I shared a history and skills. She'd cautioned me to keep them secret, making anything I did with my cursed memory a risk to us both.

As a testament to that problem, the man with the porta passed my aisle and peered in twice while the pile of books around me grew. If I had to talk to someone, I wanted it to be Eve.

She had a self-assured air, one I wished I possessed. Confidence was hard to carry off when you couldn't remember beyond a few months, or get a straight answer about yourself from your only known relative. Even asking, "How old am I?" the closest I'd narrowed Graen to was the range of twenty to twenty-five. At times, I did feel twenty-five, but in my current circumstances, twenty was all I could manage.

At the central aisle, I looked both ways. No one in sight. The place was quiet, not even a clock ticking. I could call Eve's name, but that felt foolish. Instead, I angled my way through the smaller aisles in the direction she'd taken. I passed the packed shelves and glanced at the book bindings. Some titles stood out. A few seemed to glow and then fade.

An uneasy feeling came over me, but I searched for another title with that brightened lettering...

"*The Mirror of Her Dreams*," I whispered, and in uttering the words, I knew. I'd done this before. Flashes of déjà vu were my friends. Graen always said follow these leads, and by doing so I'd brought back skills of our people. Not just the particle-transference abilities to use Lacuna, cross-leaping and mind-linking, but also my mechanical and electrical aptitude.

I walked a few paces, looking for the next glowing title. "*Roadmarks.*"

Another old Earth book. The memory became clearer. Reading these titles would turn the key—no, not quite right. Open the door. Lead me to...what? I shuffled forward.

"*Journey to the Center of the Earth.*"

How did I control this phenomenon? I should stop. If I disappeared through the Conducer, Graen would die. No one would find her in the camouflaged shelter.

But I had no say. Titles appeared before my glazed eyes. Compelled, I read them, my nerves humming beneath my skin. The next was just ahead, glowing its call to me.

"*The Lion, the Witch and the—*"

A hand slapped over my mouth.

FOUR

EVE

I kept my hand over the young man's mouth. He'd accessed Evard's shortcut to Dome. No one else knew about the illegal connection—or could know. Absolutely not, under no circumstances...no.

I swallowed, unable to catch my breath. If a Blackguard caught an Aardite in the 'torg-only facility, saying he'd come via Zeffir, unaccompanied, and without a pass slip! All that on top of today's no-use mandate, we'd be hauled in for review. Attention I didn't need if I petitioned to stay on Zeffir.

D'dair. *Eve, you've got to calm down.* Though if ever there was an occasion for swearing, this was it, especially the Aardites' curse of the Dead Air plaguing their planet.

I rubbed my thumb across the inch-long crystal in my ring, liquefying part of the yellow stone with the friction. The goud—an element properly named goudrogen—washed over me, spreading comfort like a warm fire. Nothing had happened to warrant a reprimand. My position at the remotest Post on G47 was safe, as were those of my triad run-mates. For now.

What business could this youth, obviously an Aarde native, have at Dome? He'd made a mistake, that was all. I never should have left him alone in the shop. I lowered my hand, ready to slap it up again if so much as a syllable came out of his mouth.

It didn't.

He held fingers to his temple, dazed. His soft brown eyes weren't focusing, and his lips had paled amid the unruly curls of his beard. That wavy brown hair needed cutting, but he was good-looking. He had a long straight nose, high cheekbones and tanned skin. That, his rugged clothing and his physique—slim and muscular—told me he spent a lot of time outdoors.

He could be a real catch for some Aardite woman, though I found it hard to tell with him in this state. I steered him through a side aisle and left the Conducer to close down of its own accord. Unusual that Cyrem, our resident academic, hadn't heard him and alerted me. Though the trade ship was in port, this man stood out from the few visitors Zeffir received. Mud smeared his sturdy canvas trousers, and his shirt sported a few rents. Why didn't he wear a jacket?

Safely in the back hall, I squeezed his solid shoulder and murmured, "You don't look well."

He stared, unseeing, his face drawn. His insensibility decided matters for me. Though he wasn't Zeffirite and under my care as island counselor, I unfurled my gift and reached to sense his emotions.

I couldn't get a good reading. Odd.

"Come to the kitchen and sit." I urged him through the swinging door and into a chair at the wide-plank table. "You look like you could use a cup of tea." After putting on the kettle, I sat beside him and tried again. "Is the healing information for you?"

"No, my grandmother," he said flatly. Then he blinked.

Shock flashed over his sharp features, until he noticed me watching, then his expression shifted to blank. But his emotions had opened and created a current of change in the air. The message was as clear—to me—as if he'd spoken: a whiff of annoyance, not directed at me, but at himself.

He shook his head. "I've got to get back to her. She's hurt and..."

Ah, now I understood. He was distraught. He couldn't resolve this situation. "What kind of injury did she sustain?"

He jerked, and his gaze shot to me in surprise. His emotions wavered, on the fence, unsure, vacillating...

I used my gift. I forced sympathy from my pores and sent it across the space between us to wrap him.

"A cut. It seemed little more than a scrape, but she's unconscious, and at her age—"

"Unconscious?" I jumped to my feet. "For the love of life! Why didn't you say so sooner?" I grabbed the medical bag from the cupboard and crossed to the coat pegs at the back door. Where had this happened? And why had no one in town come to fetch one of us? A Post's 'torgs helped everyone, even if they were visitors. I threw my cloak over one shoulder and yanked open the door. "Where is she?"

My visitor rose, but not agreeably. The tenor of

emotion around him had changed. His narrowed eyes fixed on me in a hard stare, accompanied by a slight twist of his mouth.

I'd lost him, but if this Aardite woman was unconscious, I had to try. I gestured to the doorway. "Shall we go?"

"I appreciate the offer, but I think this situation is out of your skill set."

"I can help."

He snorted, eyebrows quirking. "My grandmother needs a doctor. Just point me to someone old enough to have a medical degree, and I'll be on my way."

Old enough, indeed.

Protesting would do no good. Why, if the know-it-all thought that age equaled experience, nothing I said about my training would change his mind. Damn mainlanders. We were mandated to assist all Aardites, and may the Waters preserve any electorg remotely involved in one of their deaths. Well, I wasn't losing my position because of his doubts.

I dropped my things on the table and spared a few seconds to glare at him from a distance that was probably too close. "I'll get my mother. Wait here."

With our combined fury inundating me, I raced up the stairs, unbuttoning my vest as I went, and called, "Mother!" for dramatic effect. In my room, I dropped my skirt, kicked off my short boots and pulled on the trousers I'd worn yesterday. Feet back in the boots, I yanked a thick angora sweater over my head. Should I leave my ring? Though large and identifiable, I hadn't

taken it off in years. Could I function without it? Well...
I left it on and stepped to the mirror.

I scrunched up my twenty-year-old face in concentration. My reflection wavered, my features reshaped.
There? No, this young man thought wiser meant older.
I must shift more. My face settled into a near copy of
Evangeline's, a woman of about forty. With a snarl, I
aged up *an additional* ten years and darted from the
room, only to return to grab up a ribbon and hairpin. I
swept my hair into a horse's tail, tied it off and wound
the length into a bun I secured with the pin as I hurried
down the hall, at a walk this time. More befitting my
age.

Humph. Apparent age. Here I was, presenting myself as a sage. Learned, judicious, prudent. But still Eve.

Back in the kitchen, I reintroduced myself, this time
as Evangeline, a healer. I started to pick up my cloak,
but at the last second shifted my hand to the bag and
handed it to the visitor, flooding him with consolation
emotes again, a product of the rising urgency inside me.

Scarcely any Aardites remained on G47. Just a few
thousand had survived after the Dead Air Years deci-
mated the populations in the thermal regions of all
three continents. While the humanitarian mission of
the Biosphere Corps had restored order, pinpointed the
airborne hornwort spores as the cause and isolated the
Spore Zones by installing Conducers to ensure clean
travel, the planet's population had only gradually increased. Every life was precious.

Taking Evard's oilskin duster, I reopened the back

door. "Where is the woman who needs help?"

"We've recently arrived on the island, so..."

What was the problem now? "Out with it."

He cleared his throat. "We had no place to stay, so I constructed a shelter in the woods."

"Blessed—in the dead of winter? Let's go."

The young man hustled, leading me to a stand of trees beyond the hot spring pools. He shifted leaves and fabric, opening the shelter for me. Not as bad as I'd imagined—the improvised tent was snug and his grandmother nestled in Docga-made coverings. I parted the insulating bag from around her head and sighed in relief. Her color was good, skin warm and breathing regular, but she was elderly, probably in her sixties.

"Hello? My name is Eve-*Evangeline*. I'm here to help you."

She didn't respond. A neat bandage covered her neck above her bloodstained collar. "This is the only injury?"

"Yes, a, uh, knife cut."

Those details could wait. I peeled off the bandage. "Your grandmother's name?"

"Graen."

The Aardites' unusual names had ceased to surprise me. The wound ran straight across otherwise unblemished skin. "I never asked yours," I said idly.

"It's Quinn, Madam Evangeline."

No pink-tinged subcutaneous damage surrounded the odd-looking scab. In fact, if I didn't know better... I slid a fingernail under one crusty end, lifted and exposed a wire.

"Why didn't you say she's an electorg?"

"Huh?"

My tight shoulders relaxed. This wasn't the tenuous life of an endangered native person we were dealing with. I slipped a vial from my bag, probed my finger beneath the scab and collected a spark of her power to identify her from the Corps files. "Since she's a 'torg, this changes everything. Circuitry is subcutaneous, so shutting down to prevent further electrical short-out isn't unusual. I suspect a loose or damaged—"

"What are you talking about?" His hostile emotions hit me before I saw his strangely boyish look of confusion and defensiveness.

He didn't know.

I glanced to the scab I'd left mostly in place, now neatly reknitting itself to seal the wound. He hadn't seen either. This had all the signs of a 'torg raising an orphaned Aardite—years ago, judging by Quinn's mature physique—but without explaining how we electorgs were altered. Mothering instincts from organic years didn't just disappear, and though following them served the mission, it was against Docga policy to do more than advise. I wasn't going to be the one to point a finger at her.

I drew a breath. "Let's get her back to—"

"No. You're talking nonsense," grunted Quinn, his narrowed eyes flashing.

I spilled every ounce of innocence and concern I had. It didn't take. His emotions sank from detection again, but his feelings blazed from his irate features.

Please, don't let him resort to violence. Evard and Evangeline didn't know where I'd gone. I emoted apology as I backed from the tented covering. "We can call in...someone, no questions asked. You'll be on your way in no time."

"I'll find other help." Quinn handed me my bag and ushered me to the woods' edge, his lips pressed together above a jutting jaw. With a final glaring nod, he spread his feet and crossed his arms over his broad chest.

His stance conveyed the same vexation as his emotions. Having someone dislike me so strongly was foreign to my harmonizing work on Zeffir. I didn't want discord, especially from the handsome *man* before me. My stomach sank at that thought, and another.

Quinn had aged himself. I doubted he was aware he'd done it.

FIVE

QUINN

I stared at the healer's retreating form, her back as stiff as my own. Madam Evangeline skirted the fields across the hillside, then disappeared over a rise.

An electorg. How could that woman make such an outrageous accusation? "Damn." May as well say it, since no one could hear, particularly Graen. I pivoted and kicked into the leaves—

—and hit a rock. "Damn it *all* to hell."

Tripping forward, I clenched my fists until the throbbing in my toe subsided, and then I hobbled to the shelter and knelt at my grandmother's side. "Graenie? If you have any ideas, I'm happy to hear them."

Her gentle breathing was the only response. We were screwed.

I stared at the scab. Graen's words during our cross-leap, *if I black out*, correlated with the new information—a cut on the neck could cause a 'torg to shut down. She'd *known* she might lose consciousness.

I wiped a hand over my face. *Hold it together, man.* I would view our predicament as Graen always counseled. "Analyze the situation," I muttered.

What exactly had the healer seen to decide Graen was a 'torg? There was no other way. I did my own examination, mimicking Evangeline's actions. Under the scab ran a crimped wire.

"Dam-*nation!*" No wonder Graen always displayed such a composed demeanor: My grandmother was a machine. My failures at keeping a level head made sense—

Hold it. My grandmother? If Graen was electorg, then she was not my ancestor. 'Torgs couldn't have kids. But would a machine have spent weeks healing me, guiding my memory's return, helping me search for my brother?

And what of *our* skills? We shared unique abilities, she'd told me. As did Quil.

If Graen had wires, why did she lambast those bastards mismanaging the Docga mission? Now that I thought about it, she'd shown extensive knowledge of the Biosphere Corps' work, enough to educate me and pick apart their ministers' unacceptable decisions. She—*we* backed the Aardite sentiments the planet was "going to hell in a handbasket" with this unchecked hornwort.

I closed my eyes and held my spinning head. I had to stop this line of thinking or I'd relapse. Until I talked this over with Graen, she was my grandmother. Later, we'd deal with her *status*.

Eyeing the scab, I took a breath and pried it up more. A damaged relay came into view. I tweaked it with my pinkie.

"Quinn?"

I jerked back. "Graen! You're alive. I mean...awake."

Her green eyes were heavily lidded, but her mouth twitched into a smile. "Sounds like I've scared you."

"This was one of our dicier cross-leaps."

"You're okay?"

I knew what she meant. I tapped my temple. "Still all there—or at least what I've gained. Ironic, isn't it? This leap could have been worse than the one that wiped my memories."

"Yes," she said slowly. "About that. I have to tell you...things so you can get me the help I require."

My stomach dropped. "You're a 'torg."

Worry creased her forehead. "We are both electorgs."

A puppet controlled by some alien race? No damn way. Maybe she was, but me...a machine? This was *my* life. I would have known, would have felt the orders, the buzz of electricity, and believe me, if any hint of that had occurred, I'd have done...something. I wouldn't live under the Docga's thumb.

"Quinn, please." Graen pleaded with her eyes. "Trust me."

I swallowed the bile rising in my throat. I had to remain clear-headed while she was delusional, but the most I could manage to humor her was a nod.

"Thank you," she whispered. "You found help to get me repaired?"

"I—I'm analyzing the options."

She smiled. "There are some. Good. Find someone you can trust." The smile faded, and she continued in her typical lecture tone. "I regret I never told you the full story, but the gravity of our situation is real. We're Elite Class electorgs. E-runs, they call us. You may have to go to Dome and find our protect to fully restore my system. Whatever you do, don't let those E-run ministers find you there, or hear about me."

"But why, Graen?"

"We're hiding from *them*. One is rogue, but I don't know which of the three, so can't trust any of them." She sighed. "That's why we're searching for Quil, the only run-mate I *can* trust because he aided our escape. We need him to help straighten out this mess." A tear rolled from the corner of her eye.

I wiped it away. Delusion or not, some of this made sense. "Don't worry, Graenie, I'll find help. If I go for this, uh—protect, you said?—what type of device is it? What does it look like?"

She didn't answer. My touch must have knocked out her circuits again...and poking wouldn't jog her alert again.

SIX

EVE

The thud of booted footfalls echoed through the bookstore, drawing closer to Passages' office-lab. Evard. Perfect timing. I shoved my chair from the computer. After canceling my day's appointments, I'd run "Graen's" speck of energy through our photodiode reader, a device used to read an electorg's frequency and thus learn its ID number, function and assigned Post. Her number wasn't in the PD reader, so I was about to check the Corps' system.

"Good evening, Evangeline," Evard boomed in a cheerful voice, one he shouldn't be using, considering the work the guy had sloughed off. "We didn't know when to expect you."

Wait. Evangeline? I slapped my hand to my face. Jowls. "Oh, dear, I forgot. I'm Eve."

He thumbed up the dimmer switch on our solar-powered lights and peered at me. "You two look amazingly similar at this age. What is it, sixty?"

I didn't bother keeping the sarcasm from my voice. "Thanks. I was aiming for fifty."

"Whatever for? Trying to pull one over on the Zeffirites?"

I shook my head, perched on a counter and focused

on decreasing my age.

My run-mate drew off his fingerless gloves and adjusted the black sweater extending from his coat sleeves. "Our villagers don't have a problem with the visiting 'torgs mixing their ages, like those nymphs on the trade ship."

"True, but our choice to remain stable has been a good one on Zeffir. Better?" I asked of my re-aging.

"A bit high still. You have the appearance of a young helpmate, not a nymph freshly emerged from some dank settlement within the reaches of the woodlands."

I frowned at how accurately Evard hit the mark, in terms I had learned to discern over our decades together. He was right. I hadn't eliminated the few years' difference between a wife and an unmarried young woman in his Tarni world. Dealing with the stranger's—*Quinn's*—arrogance made me want a few years beyond the age of my organic death.

"Hey!" Evard waved his hands. "Don't shoot the messenger. What do I care if you're aging up? 'Bout time, I say. Just don't go menopausal on me."

D'dair. I corralled my grumpy emotes and focused on making amends. "I didn't expect to see you back this early."

"Their ship is leaving soon, so I had to clear out. Had a fabulous time, though, thanks for asking, my...dear."

He was trying, too. "I didn't ask, and I don't want the sordid details, but I'm glad you're in such good humor." No, not humor. I let his feelings simmer through me a moment. "Jovial? Gratified? I ran into—"

"Gratified will do." He grinned and took a seat beside me.

I ignored him. "I ran into a situation this morning and could use your help." I told Evard what I knew of the stranger and the discovery of his electorg companion. "Poor fellow had no idea. But"—I smiled—"her secret presents an *electronic* challenge for you."

"Eh? Tell me more, Evy girl." He flicked his fingers in a coaxing motion.

"Remember the early notice of the new Corps ministers for this term listing five E-runs?"

"Right," Evard snorted. "Imagine if we *had* gotten an E-run quintad."

"I can't find it. Although I pay the least possible attention to headquarters, I saw that announcement, complete with ID numbers. I've searched for those bizarre names—Quality, Quantity or whatever—and can't find them either."

"Well, of course you can't if you don't even know the names to search by. Quantity. Ha. We've not had the formal welcome reception—"

"Which I wouldn't attend anyway."

"—but where's your head been these weeks, my dear girl?"

I glared at him. "You try dealing with moods on a northern latitude island in the dead of winter. Then be told you're interchangeable staff, practically chattel, to be herded to any location. Just because some in-and-out *Q minister* is plopped here for a few years to play god to us doesn't mean I have to bow and scrape." There. That put his teasing in its place. I drew a breath. "I'd like to see that old list, because the PD reader identifies the spark I collected from the grandmother as E-run."

"Surely you...what's the word you use? Ah, this is a jest?"

"No, I don't jest, not about an E-run 'torg on Zeffir."

Evard studied me a moment. "I see you are serious. An E-run, you say? And with a chap who didn't know she was even electorg. Is he one?"

"Can you find that list?" I gestured to the computer.

His eyes widened. "You didn't use that one to search, did you?"

"Er, no, not yet."

He breathed a sigh of relief. "This appears to be a somewhat...*touchy* situation. We'll use this one." He switched on an older unit he constantly tore apart so he could fiddle with the innards. "I have *adjusted* mine to be untraceable when going onto the Docga network."

Was that necessary? "Well, I'm glad to turn this over."

Evard swept his arm to his waist and dipped into a bow. "At your service, my revered run-mate."

I rolled my eyes. "Just get on it. I'll see what's for lunch."

By the time I carried back a tray with a loaf of bread and bowls of carrot-leek soup, Evard was frowning. Not his usual countenance when matching wits with electronics.

"Thought I knew exactly where that old notice would be," he muttered. "Someone's deleted it, and no one has updated the usual contact list. Peculiar, when they manage hundreds of B-runs."

"Which they are clearly happy to do, transfers and all, while ignoring the hornwort growth that will end our reason for being on this planet." I set out the food and served myself while his large fingers tapped away.

"There's this old newscast. It had links...but nothing. Right, I'll try another. Competition is good for something."

A new screen lit up. *"Bloody hyphae!"* Evard's flailing arm barely missed me. "A native news station has both the expected quintad and the actual triad members who arrived and currently serve. No photos, but names and numbers. Now that our Cyrem's using porta, perhaps I should consult his sources more often. What's that ID number?"

I grabbed my notepad and reeled off the string of digits.

Evard rocked the office chair back, a broad grin brightening his face. "Your old girl is Quaene, the *missing* Minister of Development for the Corps."

"Blessed Waters." My hand shook writing her name. "What happened? Why is she roaming the planet?"

"Good questions. Wonder who can answer them? Not her supposed grandson, from what you said."

I snorted. "Quinn was pretty clueless."

"Quinn? His name was Quinn?" Evard darted for the monitor and nearly toppled his chair.

"Did I leave that out?"

"*Grünmann* spare you, *yes*. According to another article, Quinn is the E-run *in charge*." Evard frowned. Our gazes locked. "Uh, that bit about him getting in a snit and—just how much did you upset our *minister*?"

He'd been furious. "Some, but..." I wrapped my arms around my lead-weighted middle. "He didn't act like a minister. Perhaps it's a coincidence."

"Unlikely, since you have a positive ID on her."

And Quaene and Quinn were alliterative names, the same way our triads were identified.

Evard tapped his screen. "Says here, Minister Quinn is the Minister of Facilities and the E-runs' current lead. He's in charge of all Biosphere Corps electorgs, including the two of us."

I sighed. "You don't suppose his presence here is related to the protocol meeting?"

"Bloody good point. Those ministers"—he checked the list again—"Quinn, Quala and Quetta, might have set it up as a front, freeing them to do field checks. Our man Quinn wanders over to Zeffir, one of the women somewhere else. Quaene might have arrived with the others and be functioning behind the scenes. *Grünmann* only knows what goes on in that fortress. And what about the other fellow?" Evard asked. "Quil. If Quaene is here, Quil is probably skulking around G47, too."

I shook my head at his wild speculation. I didn't care where the fifth minister was. As long as he stayed away from Zeffir. "It's far too complicated. I wouldn't know how to begin to discreetly ask, especially when Quinn's not too eager...uh, willing...or even agreeable to meeting with me again."

Evard looked pensive. "With Evangeline, you mean. And *she* is away. We don't want to be viewed as renegade. In fact, if he wishes to maintain a covert identity, I think it wise to humor him for this surprise assessment on our care of the Zeffirites."

"I'm not so sure it's simply a test. I sensed a genuine stress over Quaene's injury. Like he really believes she's his grandmother."

My gaze met Evard's concerned one. This was serious. A failure regarding the native people would lead to a 'torg's deactivation.

"If he returns," I said, "we must be careful what we say. I wish you had found photos. I'd like some proof Quinn is a minister, too."

"*You* could get proof." Evard's brows rose. "At Dome. Say, what if this chap *has* kidnapped a minister? We'd be in worse trouble for not rescuing her."

I groaned. Neither of us needed to revisit this morning's conversation. *I* had to go to headquarters, a safer prospect than confronting Quinn. Squeezing my eyes shut, I tilted back my chair.

My run-mate scooted behind me and massaged my shoulders. Evard never quite understood, though he kindly sympathized with the burden my gift brought me. As liege of an agrarian collective, he'd conducted his trade in Tarne's cities. In contrast, I spent the entirety of my eighteen organic years in a rural British village with only a handful of cottages and a few outlying farms, easily manageable for someone with my gift.

Getting to Dome was another worry. With the restriction on B-run travel, I'd have to entrust myself to Evard's custom-rigged *alternative* exit at Dome—the one that bypassed the facility's monitored Conducer and guarded gate. I let Evard's strong fingers knead the base of my neck another minute before I heaved a sigh. "Fine, I'll check up on Quinn and the whereabouts of the other ministers."

"Attagirl." He patted my shoulder and swung my chair to face his. "You're the 'torg to tickle information out of people. Yet, even you can't very well waltz in, ask to see the ministers and check their ID numbers. So what's your plan?"

Unfortunately, it didn't take long to devise one. I trudged upstairs and dug out my official jumpsuit, the pale green outfit I hadn't worn in years. By the time I changed, Evard had a map for me to review and a few tips for getting around, but I'd have to rely on my wits, and we both knew it.

He accompanied me to our Conducer. "If you run into a problem and can't emote your way out of it, say some villagers had a fight and we need Evangeline. I'll back up the story." He hugged me a last time and stepped aside.

As Quinn had inadvertently discovered, the Post Conducers had concealed activations in lieu of operators—book titles, in our case. A blue volume on the shelf at my elbow listed them, but Evard's shortcut wasn't in it. I walked into the aisle where the Conducer's accelerator plates lay behind a façade of book spines and read the first glowing spine in the sequence.

The hidden plates hummed to life.

I didn't want to think too much about the process of breaking apart into particles and having my pieces accelerated across an ocean and most of a continent. My fraying nerves couldn't take it. Reciting other titles of Evard's illegal code, I advanced along the accelerator with the alternating field of energy flowing over me. The bookcases blurred, and seconds later, I emerged around the corner of a little-used corridor on Dome's lowest level.

A few pats of my middle and thighs assured me I was solid. I blew out my relief and, assuming an air of belonging, I strode toward the kitchen.

SEVEN

EVE

Dome, Biosphere Corps Headquarters

With Evard's headquarters schematic uploaded in my files, I found the kitchen on the main level of Dome easily enough. 'Torgs wearing white aprons over green jumpsuits danced around one another, carrying food, pots and utensils between piled tables. The emotions each staff member gave off in the hot, steamy turbulence had me befuddled in seconds. After a quick assessment of the feelings assaulting me, I shut down my gift.

"Yes?" squeaked a skinny man dressed in a pressed jumpsuit that still looked fresh. "What have you been sent for?"

"I'm transferring. They said to do a stint here until they sort out my new job," I lied, opening my eyes to their widest and looking every direction in confusion, only partially faking.

"I'm sure we can use the extra hand," he said impatiently.

"She can take my place," said a brunette with curly hair who'd set her age a few years older than mine. "I'm tired of ferrying the extra food upstairs. I don't see why *they* can't eat down here."

"We don't make the decisions," retorted the supervisor. "And I'm not sending a new 'torg to serve the invalid and *them*, so get moving." He swiveled to a man entering with empty dishes. "Is that the last of it?"

"Yes, sir, Mr. Wellsey."

"Max!" He pointed at someone else. "Time to serve the coffee."

Beside us, the brunette heaved a sigh—obviously intended to be noticed by her boss—and hefted a tray of covered dishes onto her shoulder.

As she left, Mr. Wellsey's hand circled my upper arm. "Now for you. The simplest task would be—"

"Mr. Wellsey," called a man setting out cups and saucers. "Charlotte forgot the jams."

"And the rolls, sir," added a woman carrying a dessert tray.

"D'dair," Mr. Wellsey muttered under his breath. "I would hate to be there when Minister Quala finds her bread missing."

Quala? Had I heard correctly? "I can take them, sir." I reopened my gift and exuded sincerity and confidence. A good dose of eagerness must have accompanied them. I'd see Quala and possibly the other ministers, or Charlotte might know their locations.

"All right." He shoved a carousel of jam pots into one of my hands, a covered basket into the other and hustled me to the door. "The elevator is down on the right. If it's gone, take the next to Level Five and ask the guard for directions. Don't you go into the invalid's room. Let Charlotte do the serving." With a little push, he sent me on my way.

Half trotting down the hall, I saw the elevator door move. "Charlotte! Wait!"

The door jerked open. The brunette's eyes widened when she saw what I carried. "Oh, bless you. I don't need to be yelled at on top of everything else this horrible day."

I entered and opened myself to reading her emotions. "What's happening?"

"You didn't hear? Minister Quinn called in every lead first thing this morning. Then *I* got called in on my day off."

Quinn. He'd been here before he showed up on Zeffir. What had happened since then that led to Graen's injury and their arrival on our island?

"No notice and two hundred grumpy leads to serve while they wait their turns to report. And no one eats more than a stressed 'torg."

"Are the leads eating with the ministers?" Might Evangeline be up there, with Quala?

The girl rolled her eyes. "Nope. Those two prefer the seclusion of their quarters for breaks between meetings, requiring constant coffee service and now a late lunch."

Good, I wouldn't run into Evangeline, but only two ministers? And who was the invalid she was to serve? "Sorry to hear you've had to work on your day off," I murmured.

She sighed. "Mostly I like my position, you understand. You'll like it, too, if you stay. Kitchen's a real welcoming crew, even Mr. Wellsey, though he doesn't seem it today. He'll stand by you through anything, even the flakiness of the current ministers."

Before I could ask more, the elevator stopped. The door slid open, revealing a guard. He was the first I'd encountered today, but there was no mistaking the black helmet, seamless jacket and trousers that fit the man like a glove. Body armor.

Being from the sixteenth century, I didn't understand how the Docga adapted the polymer to work in combination with our electorg technology, but I had heard the disturbing rumor the formfitting material didn't come off until they took it off—thus the derogatory epithet *Blackguard*. Definitely a position I planned to avoid during my career as an electorg.

Charlotte stepped out smartly and nodded. The guard's face mask was down, but his eyes were visible through slits, the eye slots blinking when he did. He ignored Charlotte and locked me in his sights. I tried to counter the instant suspicion rolling off him with my calming emote: *Just doing my job, following orders, no one to worry about, beneath notice.*

"Freeze." He thrust his stun sword between us.

I froze.

"State your number, position and Post."

Automatically, I opened my mouth to comply.

"Charlie! She's new," said Charlotte, cutting off what would have been a dangerous mistake. "Probably doesn't even know half her reassigned number. For now, she's kitchen and helping me serve the ministers." She jerked her head to me in a *let's go* signal.

I attempted to follow, holding up the meal items I carried and continuing to exude my innocent-lackey demeanor, but the guard's sword still wavered before me.

"Charlie, I swear I'd never get one of my own triad in trouble. Put away the moray and let this poor girl deliver the bread and jam."

Moray? As in eel? I knew firsthand that the broad blades stung, and though that training experience was forty-nine years old, it wasn't one I wanted to repeat. The zealot who'd introduced us to the modern Docga munitions believed in show, not tell, and the fifty thousand volts he'd jolted through my new circuitry had knocked me out. At least my considerate demonstrator hadn't sliced into me with the weapon's osmium alloy blade.

Neither, I hoped, would Charlie.

The guard looked far too long before he lowered the shiny sword. "Go. You're harmless enough. But keep out of her sight. Don't need anything setting her off today."

I hustled after Charlotte down a wide hall, paneled floor to ceiling in gray granite. "Is she that bad?" I asked under my breath, no clue who I asked about.

"Minister Quetta is as considerate as she can be, given her condition. Depression, they say. She lost a loved one during her previous mission and relapsed just before the transport arrived. The Docga will collect her on their next trip in two weeks."

This answer ticked another minister off my list, but Charlotte recited it in such a pat manner that I couldn't help but ask, "Really?"

She side-glanced at me. "Well, I serve her most days, and if you ask me, sometimes I wonder if she isn't drunk."

"Or drugged."

Charlotte frowned.

"Medications can do that," I said. "What are the others like?"

"Minister Quala is formal. Likes everything just so, on schedule, and today it's worse. She's had an edge to her, snappy, more like *him* than I've ever seen her."

Friendship, I sent her way. *Confidants.* "No kidding? So he's—"

"Maybe because of all the comings and goings, but earlier I walked in on her yelling, and her face was beet red." She snorted. "And they worry about *us* bringing in disruptions."

D'dair. Charlotte hadn't noticed I was asking about the man. "What—"

"Shush, now!" She darted her eyes toward the Blackguard posted before a set of polished wooden doors.

"Freeze," he directed from beneath his helmet.

Again, only I heeded the order. The guard strode past Charlotte to block my way with his drawn stun sword, but the feisty serving girl whirled around and snatched at his arm.

"Avery, you leave her alone. She just transferred to kitchen duty and already has been a big help with my delivery, which I bet they've been grousing about."

"That they are." He lowered his sword, shoved up his visor and flashed Charlotte an embarrassed grin before moving aside. "Sorry, miss."

Blessed Waters. This girl was a piece of work when it came to manipulating people. As good as I was, but with no trace of a gift.

Then Avery's feelings drifted by me—oh. He liked, *really* liked Charlotte. The soft smile she sent him confirmed the feeling was mutual, and I knew in an instant they had a long-running, comfortable relationship. Intimate.

Something twitched inside me, and a feeling I kept deeply contained broke its bounds for a moment. I fought to squelch it while Charlotte sauntered past.

Avery opened one of the doors and resumed his position.

I followed Charlotte in, escaping Avery's discomforting amour. A tenor of uneasiness hung like a haze in the stale air of the well-appointed but empty salon.

"Good evening, Ministers. Sorry for the delay, Ministers," Charlotte called and darted across the room, which was decorated in shades of green with clean-lined furnishings. At a table along a wall of windows overlooking a lushly vegetated atrium, she perched her tray and transferred one dinner plate and several small dishes to a waiting bed tray.

Then, with the bed tray in hand, Charlotte pushed

through a half-closed door to my left. I trailed after her, disregarding the earlier warnings not to disrupt the invalid. I'd come this far, and I meant to see Minister Quetta.

A full-figured woman lay in bed, propped by pillows. "Charlotte dear, we know you have nothing to do with the hour. We are simply famished and grateful you have come." The words were measured and refined.

I'd expected a fastidious person to be attached to the voice, but her long dark hair fell limp around a tired expression and lackluster eyes. A moment later, her feelings hit me like a harsh wind.

Fear.

I gasped. Sweat beaded on my brow, and my palms clenched as an invisible strap cinched my lungs. I stumbled out, hit the wall and sagged against it, clutching the jam pots.

"Gracious me," came the woman's murmuring voice through the doorway.

With her issues, she noticed my near faint? I struggled to purge her emotions from my system and listened for warnings that Quetta would report me.

"You look quite peaked, Charlotte. Has Mr. Wellsey been running you overtime? He knows that's against the rules."

"No, ma'am. But today has been busier than most," Charlotte answered matter-of-factly. "I'll get your water."

Charlotte's footsteps neared. I raised my barriers and almost had them in place when a second woman—

this one small and blond—entered from the far side of the salon. A new wave of emotion hit me, just as strong as Quetta's, though not precisely the same. I didn't take the time to decipher it. I closed my eyes and blocked.

Seconds later, the jams were pulled from my hand. "What's with you?" Charlotte whispered.

I thrust the bread basket at her and muttered, "Haven't eaten. Better wait in the hall." Numbly listening to Charlotte cover my exit to the other female minister, I made it through the door and sank down. The wall blocked the worst of the emotes, and my head cleared.

"Uh, are you all right?" Avery asked. "If you're going to be sick, don't do it here." He hoisted me up. "There's a lav—"

Ding!

"Hell." He pivoted toward the elevator.

Now alert, I followed his gaze down the long hallway to where a light blinked above the elevator door. Charlie also watched the yellow flashing as he threw back his shoulders and cocked his arm, ready to salute.

"Was that the—here." Charlotte slammed her serving tray to my chest. "Not a word. Just wait while I finish."

"Ah, hell. Stand over here." Avery spun me by the shoulders to the far side of the hall.

From the doorway, Charlotte put her hand up in the *stay* signal used for training dogs.

What else would I do with a Blackguard glaring at me? So much for not drawing attention to myself.

Ding!

Charlie saluted as the elevator door opened. "Sir."

A brown-haired man exited and returned the greeting, but that's all I could see around the Blackguard. The cadence of the man's deep voice carried, but not his words. I needed to know more. I let down my blockade and opened my senses.

"Don't gawk," Avery hissed.

I straightened.

A second later, the man clapped Charlie on the arm and advanced alone.

I locked my gaze on Avery for clues on how to behave. He'd opened both doors to the salon. Charlotte had distributed the dishes and was filling the water glasses while the man's footsteps drummed closer. Then like a two-moon tide, the waves of emotions swept onto me. Assured. Determined. Controlled.

Not emotions that caused me to falter physically, but... D'dair, that was some take-charge attitude he had. I turned and saw...Quinn. Or an older... Was it Quinn?

Avery saluted. "Sir!"

Staring stupidly, I watched him run his gaze over the guard.

"Excellent form," he said.

His deeper, modulated voice only added to my bewilderment. Quinn hadn't used that tone earlier, and his appreciative words were at odds with his controlling emotions. Was he just returning? And what had he done with Quaene?

Once more, I struggled to calm my system. Thank the Golden Waters the wall held my body upright—and his attention was focused on Avery. He didn't recognize me. Either that, or in this setting, his glance hadn't registered my B-run presence.

The lack of notice allowed my 'torg research function to record the similarities and differences. Quinn's smile took shape easily on his matured features, but— was I correct?—failed to reach his chocolate eyes. He had the same strong nose, more pronounced cheekbones and sharp jawline, visible under a now tightly trimmed beard. He'd had cut his curly hair as well, and with its length off his shoulders, I saw exactly how broadly they spread above the rest of his well-built body.

"An incident occurred early this morning," he said, "and I'm alerting my personal guards before the report goes out. Two rogue electorgs forcibly commandeered the Cavvert city Conducer and disappeared. We're scanning their images for a system match, but in the meantime stay alert for any non-Dome-assigned 'torgs, particularly on these private floors."

"Sir! You can rely on us." Avery's words earned a shining smile from the minister.

I basked with him in the aura of his approval. After all, this handsome man had matters well in hand. Aged up, Quinn *was* a real catch, as I'd thought when first meeting—

A wave of contempt hit me—*his*—coupled with thick, unbridled disgust. And...pride in...his trickery?

Just hold those horses, as we used to say. What had I been thinking? How great he was? Facial expressions, emotions, words—none of them matched up. The puzzle sorted. The minister was a master of superficial charm. This conversation was nothing but empty flattery, a...a... What was that modern word Evard had discovered to describe the dealings of his least favorite traders with his mushroom collective? Spilling—no, spin. Right, a creative way to display the facts. But which parts were the facts and which the spin?

"Which brings us to"—the minister turned on his heel and, in two strides, planted himself before me—"you. I've never seen you serving in our quarters. Avery?" he barked out.

Under his hard gaze, I flinched, the back of my scalp tapping the cold wall. The awkwardly held serving tray separated us. His body was at least twenty pounds more muscular and fifteen years older than the Quinn I'd met on Zeffir. My research function wouldn't quit filing data. Probably to avoid the emotional input I was too horrified to process: Suspicion and mistrust rolled off him, mixed with a good dose of dominance and—I swallowed hard—supremacy.

D'dair.

"Sir," Avery said smartly from a half step off his right shoulder.

Quinn put out his hand without breaking his stare. "Your PD reader identification on this electorg."

Avery fumbled with a compartment on his leather weapon belt, shot a glance to me and extended the inch-wide reader with a shaking hand.

The tray slipped from my grasp, bounced off the

minister's foot and clattered into Avery's legs. He jerked aside, and the PD reader ricocheted across the stone floor.

Charlotte darted from the salon doorway. "I swear, I can't leave you for a moment. Minister Quinn, sir, I'm so sorry, sir. She's transferred, first day in—"

Crunch!

Charlotte spun, lifting her heel from the reader. "What was that?" She picked up the shards of black and silver and held them out. "Oh, sorry. Was this important?"

Several moments of silence ticked by, and then the minister jerked his thumb toward the other guard. "Charlie's, then, to recheck her frequency."

Avery's helmet eyeholes closed. "Sir, a team only receives one PD reader, so he—"

"Clearly doesn't have one," he snapped, his manner superficially within control.

His emotions, however, read unfeeling, ruthless and...

"That will change. What was this inept 'torg's reading?"

And callous.

I held my breath.

"Sir, I can't recall the number, but her function is server assigned to Dome's kitchen."

The minster swung his gaze from the Blackguard, lingered briefly on Charlotte and finally stopped with me. He scrutinized my face, as if searching his data-banks for a match, which surely Quinn remembered from this morning's confrontation. Why the act?

Unless it wasn't one.

I clenched my hands to keep them from twisting together.

"How long have you been in this function?" he rapped out.

"I...I..." *Come on, Eve, hesitation reeks of lying.* I took a breath. "I started today. Sir."

"Return to your Post. I do not wish to see you on these floors or serving me until your training is complete. Do you understand?"

"Y-yes, sir."

He turned on his heel and walked into the salon. Avery closed the doors after the E-run I definitely had not met before—and had no wish to encounter again.

EIGHT

QUINN

Zeffir Island

When night fell on this northerly island's short day, I left Graen in the shelter again. A wind chased me down the hill into town, and not unpleasantly. Its warmth was both extraordinary for this time of year and welcome after cold hours of grappling over Graen's revelations. My footfalls repeated the relentless *'torg, 'torg, 'torg* plaguing me all afternoon.

Was I?

Graen wouldn't lie, but I didn't feel...different. If it were true, then no one from *our people* existed for me— or Graen—to return to. Then what was my life? How could she have tricked—*hell!* The treacherous cycle caught me again. I had no time for anger, bargaining, depression...the stages of grief that had so conveniently popped into my head, as if I'd had to work through them before. Which I probably had, if in fact I was a 'torg.

I'd love to wake up and discover this was all a bad dream, but until I did, one solution to our current troubles bested the others: solicit help from Eve's family.

My plan to remain unobtrusive failed. The bookstore

was closed. The residential windows above the adjacent darkened shops blazed with light, so banging on Passages' door risked attracting attention.

My steps echoed down the deserted street until I rounded the last building. A dirt alley bordered the backyards. I prowled it, steeling my nerves and peering into a few old-fashioned country kitchens where the residents were fixing dinner.

Damn. Graen and I should be sharing a hot meal at *our* home, where the conversation would include her typical query, "*Analysis, Quinn?*"

For a moment, a pang of despair hit me. I pushed aside my misery and fought the urge to tear into the last of our amino acid-rich nutrition blocks. I had to focus on my target and goal. For Graen.

The kitchen windows of Passages were curtained. The blurry shadow moving behind them could be either of the women. I tensed my gut muscles, advanced and tapped upon the glass panel.

The door opened without so much as a check past the curtain, as if nighttime visitors were common. It wasn't either Eve or Evangeline, but the man I'd seen leaving the shop this morning. He still wore the unorthodox orange coat, which from the front looked even more unusual. Its stand-up collar, black cording and offset buttoning gave it a military air.

"Good evening?" His deep, accented voice held the hint of a question, but his gaze was open and welcoming.

"Hello." I cleared my throat. "May I speak with Eve?

Or perhaps her mother?"

His face registered immediate comprehension. "You're the—Quinn?"

When I nodded, he pulled me inside by the elbow.

"Bloody happy you've returned. Any change in...your grandmother's condition?"

Blessed Air—I invoked the local exclamation we'd adopted to fit in—the stranger knew about her? But I didn't know him, so repeated, "May I see the healer, Madam Evangeline?"

"You want Eve." He smiled confidently and smoothed a large hand down his uniform.

Of course. I'd insulted the older woman and now she'd have nothing to do with a rude stranger. I could kick myself. Trying for a contrite manner, I said, "I'd like to apologize and ask her to consider seeing Graen again."

The large man chuckled, but caught himself. "Evangeline hasn't seen her yet, and I sincerely doubt she'll be of much use to your Graen. Evangeline's specialty is animal care. Regardless, she's away, as is Eve now. Don't know when either will return. Sit, please." He waved to a chair. "Let me introduce myself and see if we might devise a plan in their absence."

This affable man had me confused—or was he the muddled one? I knew who had accompanied me this morning. Remaining near the door, I resisted the temptation to cross my arms. I kept my tone light. "I can spare a little time, but then do need to seek help."

"Ah, good man. My name is Evard." He offered his

hand, and I shook it. "I am an electorg with the Docga Biosphere Corps, stationed here with my run-mates Eve and Evangeline. I'm happy to help."

No, they couldn't be. My empty stomach twisted. That pretty young woman had acted nothing like the forbidding, stiff-armored Blackguards we avoided every day. But with this large man—er, electorg—looming so close, I heeded Graen's warnings and held my tongue until I could pull a congenial response into my head.

The silence lengthened uncomfortably.

He cocked his head. "Am I correct in assuming you're familiar with electorgs and our roles with the Biosphere Corps here on G47?"

"Yes," I said, surprised to hear myself speaking. The risk of appearing to be a total idiot must have fueled me. We'd seen the results of the Corps work—livestock and agricultural productivity, modern communications and informatics—but I wasn't sure how these beings functioned using electronic components or...how *I* functioned, dammit.

Evard's gaze held mine in a friendly manner I'd never experienced from a 'torg. Not that my experience was vast—Graen had insisted we keep to ourselves for the past months. But she wasn't here to run interference for me.

This electronic man was waiting, willing to help.

"Some roles. Guards," I ventured in hopes of learning more.

"Eh! Despicable lot." The disgust on his genteel face

seemed honest. "Give some people power and it goes to their heads. Try to steer clear of them myself. Our triad is research and assistance."

"You...*assist*? Who?"

He swept a hand toward the bookstore. "We advise the native Aardites, within their lifestyle, but sometimes must *urge* their ways to better Docga technology and research. A fair amount of counseling is behind every step of every project."

"Yes," I said slowly. "I imagine so. How else would the Corps convince people to return to the Spore Zones?"

Evard laughed. "Once they do, I've heard no complaints. And *I* would. Here on Zeffir, we grow the particular fungus that crews of 'torgs spread as compost across the land to be recovered."

"But those 'torgs—"

"Unaffected." Evard tapped his chest. "A filter installed in their air passages. Part of the electronics. After a fallow period, the fields can be plowed without danger of anyone inhaling the deadly, dust-like seeds. The indigenous mycelium, Misha's Glow Waxy Cap, eats through those tough spiked spore cases better than a mortar and pestle."

"It's red?" I guessed from the name for Aarde's rosy moon.

"More of a pink, actually. Every farmer knows Misha's now, credits it with the food on their tables, their growing businesses and their hope for rebuilding trade. We plan to resettle all but the most thermally active lands of this volcanic planet."

"I hadn't heard of soil treatments, just crews of 'torgs hand-scraping hornwort thallus from the pools." I eyed Evard's formal orange uniform. Difficult to believe we'd overlooked the Post 'torgs if others were like him. I'd thought all research was handled at the headquarters building we avoided. "The Docga oversee you from, uh, Dome, isn't it?"

"The *Docga* don't oversee G47's day-to-day operations. That's left to the Corps ministers working at Dome." Evard's chest swelled and, for some reason unclear to me, he looked pleased at giving this information. "The Docga are space travelers."

They weren't on planet? But they'd spent seventy-some years on research and control of a mysterious coughing disease that had killed almost the entire population? And installed Conducers, elaborate cleansers to isolate the spores and hundreds of electorgs to carry out recovery? Graen wouldn't discuss the Docga themselves, responding only that when I remembered more, she would tell me more.

"The Docga make quarterly checks on their humanitarian missions," Evard said. "Or come when the ministers put in a call—though our satellite is on the blink at the moment."

"It's good of the Docga to become involved after the Dead Air Years, but I'm curious why. The rampant growth of one species of native plant is hardly their fault. What is their connection to this primitive people?"

Evard stroked his goatee. "The favor of a technology exchange long ago, I understand. Plus, the Docga helped set up Aarde's intra-galaxy Aeroport on La'adir, at the city-states' request."

"Aha, I've heard trade was somehow indirectly the cause of the plant growth."

"That was never proven." Evard lifted a finger. "The allegations ran from someone not owning up to a chemical spill, to exposure to foreigners' dust, or that selling Aarde's metals made the planet *too light*. Ridiculous, but people were sure the hornworts going into their sporophyte stage for the first time in recorded history was due to *some* change caused by alien transports."

"So travel was restricted." The reason Graen and I had a deadline to find Quil and leave this planet.

"Not"—Evard rolled his eyes—"that traders were jumping to enter a death trap."

I nodded. "Spore paranoia. Justifiable." Sadly, everyone exposed died, even those who fled the Spore Zones. Medical research revealed the spores not only lodged in the lungs' smaller airways, but also coughing caused the spiked spores to cut the tissue, resulting in internal bleeding and collapse.

I leaned against a counter casually, but alert, because I wanted to gauge Evard's reaction to information that had infuriated Graen. "All this careful restoration, yet I hear tell multiple pools of hornwort thallus are again approaching spore stage. With no action by the ministers."

Evard stared for a second, then slowly nodded.

"Isn't there some fancy equipment these ministers could dig out of storage?" I asked. "With fire proximity suits and jet packs, a crew could enter the hotter zones and knock back the plant by torching it."

Now Evard blinked in surprise. "A valid suggestion, better than some I've heard tossed about."

Graen and I didn't sit around evenings discussing the weather. It was heartening to hear one of our ideas might prove useful. Then my stomach sank at the thought: Would Graen be around to see any plan carried out?

"Unfortunately, the various factions disagree on what should be done. The ministers are standing by some hypothesis the Biological Resources division has cooked up about allowing the hornwort to run the natural course of its carrying capacity."

I'd heard that as well. "The botanists' data show the hornwort is spreading far faster—"

"Than the available nutrients found in those waters can sustain it," Evard finished, the corner of his mouth quirking. "The same line, eh? Well, it's down to two weeks. Then the Docga will be on planet to check on the mission for themselves."

All this so the Docga could mitigate the improbable aeroport pollutants and reciprocate for some long-ago favor? Somehow, these details rang familiar and true, like many of the memories I'd forgotten. What technology did this regressive planet provide the Docga that was worthy of supplying advanced twenty-first-century machinery and running it for decades with free labor?

"As part of the Corps staff," Evard said, "I'm at your service. Perhaps transferring your grandmother here to our Post housing would be a place to start."

The suggestion seemed reasonable. "Once she's here, will Madam Evangeline—"

"Eve will. She's our healer." Evard said this firmly, but looked uncomfortable. He cleared his throat and opened his hands, palms up. "I better apologize on the nym—girl's behalf for the confusion. In an effort to assist you this afternoon, Eve shifted her appearance to give you confidence in her ability to help."

"Shifted her appearance?"

"Right. Eve aged her looks to fifty-ish..."

What? Pain burst at my temple, my mind unable to take in the train of words that ran so contrary to any possible logic.

He clutched my elbow. "Surely you know 'torgs can—here now, have a seat."

I collapsed onto a hard chair. No, it was impossible. Illogical. People didn't just... Well, they weren't people. They were electorgs, something my grandmother—

An image of a much younger Graen winked into my head. She was in her twenties, blond hair hanging loose around a line-free face. It would be normal to have memories of a relative, except as her *grandson*, I shouldn't remember her as young as I did.

I winced and my mind skipped to another memory. Several weeks ago when discussing my particle transference skills, Graen said I'd done decades of research.

I'd jokingly responded that'd make me ancient—like *forty*. She'd smoothly assured me it'd been a slip. She'd meant I'd packed decades' worth into a few years.

Yeah, it *had* been a slip. I *had* done decades of research, proof I was a 'torg, too.

Oh, hell. My head sagged into my hands.

"Quinn?" Evard pressed something into my hand. "Drink this, mate. You need bolstering."

A glass. My fingers curled around the smooth surface, and my arm rose, with help, I think. The burn in my throat halted further thought. A familiar fire hit my gut and then flowed to my toes and fingers. I drew a sharp breath and pinched my watering eyes. As rarely as I had whiskey, it always jarred me the same.

Wood scraped as Evard took a seat. "I've the bottle here if you care for another, but I daresay we better see to fetching your grandmother to the house first, so we can tend to her."

At his words, I slumped lower and rested my forehead on the wooden table, hoping its cool surface might take away my headache. If she couldn't be *tended*? Was there any point in my carrying on...as a 'torg? The damning situation flooded me with an unbearable weight. But if I didn't try, I had no answers. Okay, we would bring Graen here. The healer woman, no, the younger—*damn!*

Having to think like this was at least a distraction. I inhaled and exhaled until I could ask, "How old is she? Is Eve the girl or the older woman?"

Evard laughed. "Quinn, my good man, top rule with

a woman: Never ask her age.”

“Then how do you keep straight who is who if you’re constantly changing?”

“We don’t change all that often. Try to keep the situation stable for the locals, you see? And no matter your run-mates’ appearance, it’s still the same person. Eve at twenty, forty or sixty is still Eve. Just as your grandmother is still the same person she always was, even though you’ve found out some new things about her.”

“Yeah,” I muttered. “Too many new things.” When would she have told me if she hadn’t been injured? When we found Quil? What if we never found Quil? What if Graen never—

I dismissed the cyclic worries. *Find someone you can trust*, she’d said. Yet again the image of Eve with her cute nose and intense gray eyes came to mind. The *girl* who’d gone to great effort to help me, despite my shoving her off. Twice, apparently.

I drew a long breath. She might be less than human, but Eve was persistent in her duties. Perhaps even loyal? I raised my head to study Evard, bizarrely dressed, but a friendly, honorable man who was run-mate to Eve. Triads had some sort of family relationship.

Straightening cleared my head, as did coming to a decision. I could do worse than picking this triad to trust, though for Graen’s sake, I’d better be making the right choice.

I stood and Evard rose. I offered my hand. “If your triad is willing to help us, I would be grateful for the assistance."

"Excellent." He grinned at me, banishing any last doubts I had. "Shall we?" He gestured to the rear door just as footsteps sounded in the store.

A woman called, "Anyone home?"

My gaze met Evard's.

His brow creased. "Evangeline has returned."

NINE

EVE

I'd closed my gift while stacking rack after rack of hot plates from Dome's dishwasher. Alone with the mundane work, I let my mind race over my reads on the ministers.

Minister Quetta's unbridled terror made no sense for a woman supposedly kept secure and quiet. Unless she was a prisoner.

Though I'd shut her out too soon, the petite Quala, whose identity Charlotte had confirmed, had been torn, on the precipice of making a decision, though not quite ready to leap.

In contrast, power rolled off Minister Quinn. Something was terribly wrong with his attitude.

By the Waters, something was wrong in every one of their behaviors, and their dynamics, if I trusted Charlotte's tale of the fight. This, to me, validated the 'torg and Aardite rumors: Something fishy was going on at the highest levels of the Biosphere Corps administration.

With some of our questions answered—including Charlotte's confirmation she'd neither seen nor heard of additional ministers—I completed my shift and escaped Dome, as wary as when I arrived. I didn't trust that *Minister* Quinn, but more important to my triad and me: Could I trust our mysterious stranger claiming the same name?

I emerged between Passages' Conducer stacks in the darkened bookstore. Low voices came from the kitchen. I headed toward my run-mates, though I wished I didn't have to.

"Immediately?" Evard's deep voice boomed behind our kitchen door.

At the edge in his voice, my nerves shot to high alert and I paused at the bottom of the stairs.

"But, Evangeline," Evard continued. "I don't understand. It's ludicrous to halt the Corps projects when native well-being on G47 hinges on electorgs continuing their work."

It sounded like we were shutting down our activities. My belly twisted as a pair of beloved faces flashed behind my closed eyelids. *No, not this soon!* I was counting on the distant transfer date, giving me two months and seventeen days more. Evangeline's faint answer eluded me.

I shuffled closer to the swinging door.

"It must be a mistake."

I froze at the sound of this second male voice. Quinn. Not the harsh, firm voice of the minister I'd met at Dome, but what I'd expect from the concerned man who'd guarded his grandmother. Rich and lyrical. When had it become so confident? Sexy even.

D'dair! Under different circumstances, I might indulge in that thought. But not now.

I leaned to the line of light spilling around the door's edge to listen.

Quinn's next words rang with subtle authority. "Your leader would never—"

"Well, she did," snapped Evangeline. "And I didn't say the projects were being halted. All 'torgs must report in person. Triads together, with Corps equipment for *inventory*."

That didn't sound like my run-mate. Something was amiss—something more than an order to shut down our Post. Her abrupt delivery and higher pitch were even more pronounced in comparison to the careful soothing in Evard's voice. I longed to take a direct reading of Evangeline, but what else might she say without me present?

"Projects will most certainly halt if workers and equipment are absent for any length of time," Evard said. "Come now. Two o'clock Friday afternoon? Four days to gather everything? We all know that's ridiculous."

"I didn't make the order, I'm only following it," Evangeline said. "Some triads got a mere twenty-four hours. The first assessment appointment is eight tomorrow morning. Quinn, if your run-mate can't be revived, she should be transferred to Dome immediately."

"We stay together."

She started to argue. This wasn't the sensitive, caring Evangeline I knew. What had happened at Dome? I pressed shaking fingers to my forehead, sickening fear for her building—

A chair scraped over the floor, and Evard said, "Come on, Quinn. Let's fetch your grandmother. You'll feel better about the situation once she's here and her repairs made."

"The instructions were clear." Sharpness edged Evangeline's voice. Her words were measured. "Every electorg is to return to Dome."

Her cadence mimicked that of the assured Minister Quinn.

What had they *done* to Evangeline?

"Easy," coaxed Evard. "Assisting Quinn is a priority, but that doesn't mean we're ignoring the orders. Plenty of time to help these strangers and to settle our situation here. Eve will return from Sabein's any minute. She'll help you list equipment while the two of us go—"

Stifling an exclamation, I retreated out of earshot. Evard knew I wasn't at Sabein's. He lied to our lead, sweet Evangeline, and that could mean only one thing—he also felt something was wrong.

I spun. Sprinting on the balls of my feet, I rounded a stack and dashed a quarter of the way through the shop as our swinging kitchen door issued its usual piercing squeak. I listened from the shadows between aisles.

Evard's heavy footsteps crossed the back hall, Evangeline's lighter steps echoing after him in a firm stride.

"I don't like it, Evard." Her whisper carried above the sounds of the storage closet being riffled. "How long will this take?"

"Half an hour, I expect," he answered, his tone still consolatory. "Have a bit of patience. No one will fault us for assisting another 'torg." He grunted, and metal *thunked* the floor. "Here. Hold the stretcher."

They returned to the staircase near the kitchen door. "Be careful," Evangeline said. "Return whether he comes with you or not."

That last—so callous, so unlike her. More like an order than a run-mate suggestion.

"Have no fear, my dear nymph. Simple trip. Rest, why don't you?" Evard didn't respond to her challenge. He'd learned his lesson in dealing with challenges long ago, thanks to the duel that killed him.

Then the kitchen door whined open again, and deeper voices murmured before the back door slammed. Evangeline paced the hall, and then her footfalls tapped closer.

I took the chance. Edging toward the main aisle, I extended my hand in the bookcase shadows. My thumb rubbed over my ring. I'd shut out the golden crystal's power at Dome to shield myself from the intense magnification it brought to my gift. Now a flow of goud hydro-vapors stretched my senses.

Evangeline passed by. Assured. Determined. The one in control.

Minister Quinn's emotional signature.

The sickening realization lodged in my throat. The minister at Dome had reprogrammed his lead staff.

I rested my forehead against a shelf and steadied my breathing. When Evard returned, I had to get him alone and tell him. Then I needed a clear, uninterrupted read on the younger Quinn's emotions to determine just who the hell he was and if we could trust him, because we certainly couldn't trust the...impostor.

Antsy as a caught-out child, Evangeline patrolled the shop's perimeter, spinning my emotions with her non-stop movement. I couldn't even pretend to come in by the front door.

Or leave.

I sorely wanted to confer with Sabein. After years of negotiating with the Corps, our Zeffir associate would have an opinion on who to trust, as well as know what this call for an inventory really meant. But Evangeline's constant shoe-tapping held me in place, cupping my crystal to my chest and urging the flush of goud to clear my head for whatever came.

Finally, the back door opened, and Evard's voice boomed their arrival. The men carried the litter in heavy steps to our office-lab. Evangeline paced along-side, again directing Evard. Then he escaped, headed to the kitchen and, I suspected, a round of bolstering.

I eased through the stacks to intercept him. Before I reached the kitchen, Evangeline stormed out of the lab.

The kitchen door whined. Evangeline issued orders in that horrible measured cadence. Footsteps danced around the room, wood scraped, something crashed.

"I don't care what backup plan they gave you," Evard said. "I won't be party to—"

The back door banged open. Then nothing.

No. I sprinted to the kitchen door, cursing its whine

when I peered in. The kitchen was empty. Several chairs were toppled and the back door ajar. But even the crisp winter air didn't disperse the sense of vexation—an emotion quite foreign for us. In my memory, the steadfast Evard had never been so affronted.

Torn between chasing after them and getting help, I ran for Quinn in the lab. A Mylar-wrapped figure lay on the island workspace, Quinn's "grandmother." Where was—

Splayed legs in muddied canvas trousers sprawled on the far side of the island.

"Quinn?" I dropped to a squat beside him.

His beautiful eyes stared blankly from his slack, handsome face with its untidy beard.

I felt for a pulse on his neck. Strong and steady. "Quinn, wake up." Had he fallen and hit his head? No sign of bleeding. My fingers automatically closed his eyes and swept his scalp. At the nape of his neck, I found the small disc.

A Death Disc, it was nicknamed. Quinn was fine. Just shut off.

D'dair. I'd heard rumors of these devices. After fifty years, who wouldn't? Supposedly, only the ministers' bodyguards carried them. The adhesive-backed mechanisms emitted an overriding frequency to interrupt a 'torg's circuitry for as long as it remained affixed. I'd never imagined Evangeline might have one—or more. This must be the backup plan I'd overheard Evard mention.

The back door slammed.

I hoped it was Evard. By the time I got to the main corridor, my stomach dropped at the lighter footfalls. Thought of conflict with Evangeline tore at my heart, but she no longer functioned as herself. She was a danger to the Zeffirites and us. We'd figure out how to help her later. *We had to.*

"Hello?" I called as if just entering the shop.

The kitchen door whined again.

"Eve." Evangeline emerged, one hand in the pocket of her official jumpsuit. "Everything all right at Sabein's?"

"It is." I paused at the stairs. "Where's Evard?" I asked as innocently as I could.

"Gone to get Cyrem."

That could be true. But her demeanor was so non-Evangeline-like, so completely businesslike, that my nerves roiled with déjà vu.

Assured. Determined. Controlled.

"The news from Dome isn't the best." She closed the last few steps, pulling a cupped hand from her pocket and raising it.

I forced my gaze from her hand—and the Death Disc it must contain.

She planned to pull me into a hug, the typical greeting our triad—and most of our close Zeffirite friends—shared. The embrace would be hard to avoid. Blessed Waters, I didn't *want* to avoid it. I wanted everything between us to be right, or at least the way it had been for fifty years. The betrayal pierced my heart. *This isn't Evangeline*, I reminded myself, and when she reached for me, I blocked her.

My boiling emotions flashed her with resistance, and with it, goud shot from my hands and covered Evangeline head to toe. My disbelieving gaze skipped from the yellow mineral swarming her skin to my ring.

"Take this off me." She swiped at the glowing film of liquid crystal. "What are you doing? I have orders."

What *had* I done? I backed away.

"Compliance is mandatory." As Evangeline scraped, the solution shifted and flowed, visibly thickening from liquid to viscous. Her motions slowed, her limbs weighed down. "You didn't meet with the ministers. You don't understand the significance of our mission's next phase on G47."

Those words snapped me from my stupor. I did understand. However, my instincts said these people were up to no good.

"No," I said, speaking more to him than to my runmate. "You need to be stopped."

To both our surprise, the goud sank into her skin. Evangeline collapsed.

Clink! The silver Death Disc hit the floor.

TEN

EVE

I slid back the bolt and squeezed through Passages' front door. The freezing air enveloped me as it had during my search behind our house. I hadn't found Evard. I needed help, for the situation *and* my nerves.

I darted over the cobbles and pressed into the shadows of a crimson door surrounded by a gold-painted doorframe. My fingers traced a familiar path over the frame and found the large iron key. I dropped it. The clunk sounded like the toll of a bell down our deserted street, but no one came running.

With a cry, I fumbled in the dark. My hands shook, my knees wobbled, and if I didn't sit down soon, I would faint. My fingers grazed cold metal. I attempted to fit the key into the lock, but the door swung open.

A strong hand grabbed my shoulder. "Eve! What on Aarde has come over you?"

Sabein. Thank the Waters.

Her hand loosened and slid under my elbow, steadying me. Facial details weren't visible in the darkened shop, but I knew that sturdy touch and, even better, the tenor of this woman's essence.

"I've coated Evangeline in goud," I gasped.

She started, her fingers pinching into me. Crystals at

her neck and upper arm flashed amber, echoing in her eyes before she blinked.

"They've done something to her, to make her obey some order," I blurted. "She's not herself. She knocked out our visitor, chased Evard from the house and turned on me. I don't—"

Sabein put a finger to my lips. "Hush, my friend." The glow in her crystals died and she squeezed my hand. "Nothing has happened to Evangeline's essence that cannot be corrected. Your coating has suspended it, bringing her comfort."

I hiccupped a breath in relief. "Her orders are we're to leav—"

"I'll hear none of this until you're calm." Sabein's arm wound around my waist.

"But Evard! She said he went for Cyrem, but I'm sure she lied."

"Taior will find Evard." Sabein swept me through her tea shop and upstairs to her small sitting room. In a matter of moments, she bundled me in an afghan on the settee, lit an oil lamp and turned up the gas inserts in her fireplace to warm the room.

She left, and the murmur of voices from her bedroom told me why she'd said Taior would go after Evard. I let my head fall back. Sabein's sometimes lover was also her second-in-command. They should both hear the news from Dome. But when the tall, thirtyish Zeffirite passed by the doorway, I didn't stop him. I needed to know Evard was safe.

Sabein returned. "Let me find you a remedy before

the tale of what has you in this state."

I groaned aloud. If only it could be so easy to solve this with a remedy. Sabein's brows rose at my insolence, and though her fair, heart-shaped face registered exasperation, the warmth of her reassurance wafted over me.

"Fine," I said in my meekest manner.

It did nothing to fool her. Sabein's wavy golden hair shook over her shoulders as she turned to poke through the dozens of stoppered glass vials on a wall shelf. She picked out a half dozen, sat in a rocker and held the bottles to the lamplight to examine their labels.

The room grew warmer, but I was concerned for the slender Sabein, who wore nothing but a flannel nightgown. "Your feet are bare."

"Couldn't leave you crying in the street to get socks," she answered absently. "I think this will do." She replaced the extra bottles and plucked an eyedropper from a basket.

"I wasn't crying."

"Yet." Sabein shook the remedy, removed the cork and inserted the dropper's long nose. "My friend, you have to learn to let things go, or your emotions will be the undoing of you."

I knew. Sabein had drilled me in lessons since the day we met and she decided to mentor me with my gift—one that was a blessing and a burden. She drew up the clear liquid, and I breathed a sigh of relief. "This isn't going to be one of those awful-tasting brown ones."

"Do you have bronchitis?"

"Never mind. Just give it to me. But"—I turned my head aside as the dropper came at me—"after you do, please go put on some socks. As indestructible as you think you are, I won't be responsible for you catching a chill."

Sabein laughed, her sapphire eyes twinkling as if I'd made a joke. "I will, but only to silence your nagging. Now open wide."

The remedy was quite palatable, even slightly sweet.

"Let it relax you. Close your eyes. Allow your stone to guide the path for your senses."

Under the soft wrappings of the goat-hair afghan, I brought my hands together and rubbed the golden crystal on my ring. Awareness of it flared to life in my consciousness.

Sabein left again, and when she returned, I didn't dare check to see if her feet were covered. The Zeffirite leader didn't tolerate anyone questioning her authority, and with my news of the ministers, I didn't want to prematurely push her into an edgy frame of mind.

The current ministers weren't in her good graces. Twice in the last month, they'd stood up Sabein and her Alliance group, a coalition of several city-states on Aarde. According to Sabein's few remarks, previous ministers had never snubbed the native leaders in such a manner. Taking into account the Corps switched ministers every five years, this didn't reflect well on the current administration's record.

Seated beside me, she took my cold hands in her

warm ones and rubbed briskly. Despite the quick motion, her placid emotional state soothed my nerves. My crystal responded to her Zeffirite touch, releasing a stronger wash of gold-colored goud than I normally called forth. The hydro-vapors of the crystal compound flowed sedately over me. Would I ever be able to maintain serenity as she did?

Before long, my turmoil settled, and my mentor-turned-friend invited me to tell my worries. I held nothing back and in fact came to realize the ministers had dealt B-runs a greater insult than the pending transfers. They included the B-runs as part of their inventory assessment, cataloging us as equipment. Like we weren't even people.

When I finished, the silence stretched. I floated in our shared equable state.

Finally, Sabein spoke. "No wonder I felt your anxiety from my bedchamber. I'm surprised you didn't rouse half the street dispatching that much alarm, but only Cyrem inquired."

"He probably did it at the behest of the others. Can nothing be private?" I muttered, though I well knew the answer.

"No," Sabein snapped. "You are one of us, and we guard our own. I agree, this inventory is demeaning, on top of untimely with the hornwort issues. The ministers will answer to the Docga. I'd send them a missive myself, if only that blasted communication satellite was repaired." She drew a sharp breath. "Or haven't they told us the truth about that either?"

By the Golden Waters, she had a point. Aside from that, the break in Sabein's composure told me what she didn't—this was dire, grave, urgent. "What will you—"

"I don't know yet," she answered calmly, her equilibrium restored. "We will involve ourselves as we must to maintain our existence here. Do you have a few minutes for me to converse with the others?"

Taior hadn't returned with news of Evard, a worry not even the goud could disperse, so I welcomed her continued company. I snuggled deeper onto the settee in front of the fire, closed my eyes and let tranquility settle over me.

I floated as if in a stream. Snatches of conversation reached me along with internalized directions, turnings and adjustments to the course. Then there were greetings, followed by discussion, which I ignored to sense my new surroundings. The warmth of the breezes. An earthy smell. A dappled light danced on my retinas through closed eyelids. High, sharp calls of birds and other animals sounded in the distance.

I drifted in and out, playing my fingers through air that was nearly as thick as water with its fine droplets of moisture and amazing myself with registering all the tingly parts of my body one at a time.

Tingly.

My eyes flashed open.

The gathered crowd shimmered like bodies consisting of heat waves. They would have been barely discernible even if they had been fully formed, for thick clouds of yellowish mist boiled over the broad pool.

Dense greenery surrounded the clearing, reaching skyward to a height I had never seen. The tops of the trees created an ever-shifting canopy above us.

This wasn't right. Instinctively, I reached for Pier to help me find myself, but he wasn't there. Hadn't been there. He was gone, of course. I'd have to fix this myself. Not impossible, but this was far different than anywhere we'd traveled together.

"Eve. What are you doing here?" Cyrem had my hand.

I glanced down. Our gold-blurred limbs sharpened into focus. The tingling fell from my arm as it solidified.

But the gentleman who used Passages' wireless in the sitting room each day brushed his fingers over my face and closed my eyelids. What one moment ago had been the very real sensations of a populated forest glade fell away, and I plummeted.

Cyrem called to me, but too late. A golden cascade swept me off and threatened to lose me in some unknown eddy. My thrashing lasted minutes, or nanoseconds, then I was plucked from the course.

"Eve, you shouldn't be here." Sabein's gentle reprimand anchored me.

"But I didn't—"

"Hush, it's my fault for forgetting we'd linked. Go back to yourself. Where are you now? Think, my friend."

"On your settee."

"More," she encouraged, her voice low and close to my ear.

"It's dark, except for the fire. I'm holding your cream afghan made from Rosie's fur."

"That's correct." Her crooned words vibrated within me.

"I remember the winter you knitted it sitting in your rocker. It's still so soft. I love stroking it as much as I loved petting Rosie with Tristam and Gwyn when they were small."

"Perfect. Go home."

The tingling coursed through me and then dissipated as I clutched at the hand that wasn't there. I bolted upright on the settee and hugged myself, drawing relief in the firmness of my body.

"May the Waters preserve me," I whispered in thanks. I had sworn I'd never do that again without Pier. Indeed, it had been decades since I'd traveled the Waters, never allowing myself to be carried along when the others went out.

Sabein hadn't gone to talk to the Zeffirites as I'd thought she would. She'd taken the Corps issues straight to the Alliance. From the subliminal tenor trickling through me, they were angry and ready to act, soon.

I was far too aware of their business, something I didn't dare disclose to Quinn—either one of them. What remedy had Sabein given me? I grabbed the bottle she'd set on the table and turned up the lamp's wick. "Sukka" the label read. Why that was...

"Sugar water? For the love of... I did that myself?"

I was going to kill her, if such a thing was possible. I

threw off the afghan and left, not bothering to look for Sabein. Her bed was empty. Probably several others in town also were.

Outside in the night, a light snow fell from an off-shore bank of clouds, which, as always, were trapped around the island by the Bounded Winds circling Zeffir. As I scurried across the street, the amber glow of Roamer setting at the western horizon and Misha's pink orb at the zenith. Within days, they would make their periodic trip together. So despite the ministers' orders, I would still be here for one last—

No, no thoughts of departing. I passed my thumb over my ring crystal. Sabein's belief that I needed nothing in the way of real remedies bolstered me, to use Evard's phrasing. If she had confidence in me, then I must also.

Passages' door opened before I reached it, and Taior ushered me inside. He led me to Evard, on our couch. "I found him by your chicken house, but even when my sons carried him in, he didn't wake. Could something be wrong with his special system?"

"I think I know what the problem is."

"It's not whiskey," said Taior with a slight smile that didn't quite reach the worry in his blue eyes. "I've never known Evard to be put under."

I shook my head. "I can revive him. I've shared another problem with Sabein that I'm sure she'll want to discuss with you."

ELEVEN

EVE

The first thing Evard did upon reactivation was kiss me. "*Grünmann*, Evy. Never in my life have I been so glad to see anyone as I am to see you. We've got to get out of here. Evangeline consumed some hallucinogenic mushroom that not even I dare to guess the origins of, and she's run rampant. If she finds us—"

"Chill, Evard, to use your newfangled words. I've taken care of her."

I bade him to stay on the couch—to postpone *how* I'd taken care of her—and went to get his whiskey. The emotions in the kitchen still swirled with a swampy mix of rankling and desperation.

I helped Evard to sit and poured a shot. He downed it in one gulp and held out the glass for more. I set the bottle beyond his reach and lowered to the seat beside him.

"Bloody hyphae. You're an evil nymph, but I suppose I must resist the temptation, for we have a deadline."

"So I hear." I told him of my eavesdropping.

"I lied to keep Quinn from knowing you'd gone to check up on him and Evangeline from returning to Dome for you. Once she acted unlike Evangeline, I fig-

92

ured keeping you on the track of the truth was even more important."

"I must say, I think it's time you let Sabein train you. Your instincts are becoming strong enough to—"

"Put the idea out of your head." He fingered a loop of silver chain at his collar that held his hidden crystal. "I've grown attached to these Zeffirite customs, but best you and I stick to our work and its current problems. Leave your free-time activities to you and mine to me. I find far more interesting things to do with women than *read* their emotions."

"Fine. Point taken." I relayed what I'd learned at Dome and that Sabein had taken the information to her group. Then I handed Evard the Death Disc I'd removed.

"One-time use, thank the Waters." He lobbed it into a wastebin. "Can't believe she didn't want me taking time to repair the woman's damage. And disabled a fellow 'torg for *interfering*. That's not our Evangeline, obsessed with this *inventory*—a cover for a bloody recall, if you ask me." Evard rubbed his hands around the back of his neck. "Never thought my run-mate would do such a thing to me. Where's Quinn?"

"The lab. She tried it on me also." I held up the disc Evangeline had dropped, its adhesive reattached. Taking a breath, I said, "Perhaps now's a good time to look at what I did to her."

We examined Evangeline's rough coating of minute yellow crystals. Her organic and electorg functions were normal, but we didn't want to disrupt her comatose state until Sabein was free to oversee the goud removal. Evard carried her upstairs to her room, and I tucked her into bed. We locked her in, just in case.

Evard moved Quinn to a second table beside his grandmother, and we wrapped each in a blanket. We stared across their prone forms. As 'torgs, they wouldn't suffer any ill effects from the suspension, and I was actually a little envious of their oblivious state. Evard felt the same, and by mutual agreement, we went upstairs for a few hours of sleep.

In the morning, I came downstairs soon after our cook arrived. We offered Mylta the rest of the day off if she'd fix us cold food for our meals, then took our breakfast in the bookstore's sitting room. Evard had a few questions about my encounter with Dome's callous Quinn, which reminded me of the questionable coincidence of the *rogue* 'torg attack on the Conducer.

Evard stopped with a forkful of potatoes halfway to his mouth. "Up and disappeared, did they?"

I sighed. "I came to the same conclusion."

"*Great Grünmann.* And we just shut down our lead. How does that all look?"

"Bad. Unless our Quinn isn't an impostor, and really is G47's minister."

"It's easy to learn the truth now," Evard said. "We'll get a sample and run his ID through our PD reader while he's out."

"True, Quinn would never know."

Evard lifted a finger. "Keep it between the two of us. There's something off about the fellow. In my dealings with him—carefully handled in case they were testing us—he acted clueless, despite conducting himself like a leader."

"About being a minister?"

"About the entire Corps setup."

"It is strange. His emotions are present when the older woman is concerned, yet if he's not focused on her, he's blank. He may have a gift for concealment."

With a shrug, Evard set aside his plate. "Could be. Perhaps with her reactivated he'll be more willing to confide in us."

He went to the lab. I refilled my coffee and loitered in the front room, straightening and dusting until Cyrem arrived.

The short man, who had a good dose of gray throughout his brown hair, blew through the front door. He wore his usual tweed suit and round wire-rims, the picture of a scholar, down to his leather satchel bulging with papers. He was in fact, Zeffir's academic, the only one. Also one of the few locals to use a porta, for all he didn't trust it to save his files. When we'd set up the Post on isolated Zeffir in the all-but-abandoned village library-combination-bookshop, he'd discovered the wonders of researching wirelessly.

Exploring Aarde's natural history was Cyrem's main interest and his business, run from a shop down the street. He'd curtailed his trips the last month to focus on the hornwort issues, becoming a fixture in our shop to keep the Alliance up to date when the Corps reports turned grim.

He carried his porta now, a pseudo yellow pad with a checklist lighting the screen. He tapped once before sliding the unit into his coat pocket and offering me a hearty good morning.

His cheer grated on my nerves. Two cups of coffee hadn't balanced my lack of sleep. "You look tired," I baited him. "Did your leaders' meeting run long?"

He chuckled, a deep, friendly sound. "And how are you this morning, Eve?"

"Feeling old since I missed my beauty sleep."

"But you don't look a minute over..." Cyrem paused in his pat reply to peer at me.

I stepped back from his scrutiny. With an elder Zeffirite's astute realization that I wanted my emotions left alone, he did the same. Later, I'd have to delete those extra five years everyone seemed willing to comment on.

"I had to see for myself that you'd returned through the Waters without...with no worries."

He meant without Pier. My deceased mate's best friend was a gentleman to the core. "I'm fine," I answered softly. "Thank you."

"Very well, then." He turned to go, but the door opened before he reached it.

Taior entered, dressed for who knew what in a rugged jacket and heavy trousers with many pockets. Gloves stuck out of one, a flashlight from another and a pocketknife hung at his belt. He carried a list, too—on paper.

"Well." I cleared my throat. "Evard and I have urgent work to address today. We're closing the shop."

Cyrem smiled. "She's even put on a bit of age to give us this bad news, eh, Taior?"

The seemingly younger Zeffirite lifted his eyes skyward. "As if that adds leverage."

Cyrem muttered, "It should."

Taior ignored the jibe. "Sabein won't have time for tea today," he said to me, "but she wants to see you first thing tomorrow. Bring Evard with you."

"She's gone back to bed, then?"

"Hardly. Ready, Cyrem?" Putting a hand on the knob, Taior stared down his sunburned nose, relaying that they had work—elsewhere.

I looked from one to the other. Neither had so much as a shadow under his eyes, but they couldn't have gotten much more sleep than I had. "What's going on? You both seem anxious to leave. No petitioning for access to a workstation and printing today?"

"We can't afford more time on research," Cyrem said. "The writing's on the wall."

"What?"

"You've given us enough missing bits to know to secure our livelihood."

Taior opened the door, allowing the cold to wash us. "Cyrem has our refuge preparations to oversee while I direct volunteers and assure the community in Sabein's absence. She would have asked you to assist, but you have visitors to attend to, if the news is correct."

It was, as usual. Sabein, and Taior in her stead, didn't miss a thing on this island. I'd expected the Zeffirites to retreat to their refuge, just not so soon. And Taior had shared their news with me, in his usual short manner, though it technically wasn't my business. Our Post provided assistance, not monitoring of local activities, even if the Corps had hired many Zeffirite farmers for the fungal cultivation.

"Good luck to us both, then." I locked the door behind them and went to the lab to tell Evard that Sabein must be off with her Alliance, hopefully resolving the minister issue for us.

Evard resumed work on Quaene, nodding to the still deactivated Quinn. "The ID matches the listing for Quinn, the Minister of Facilities. Not the lead. The fellow at Dome took some liberties claiming that position. Wonder why the others let him?"

"Quetta is in no condition to challenge him, but that might explain her fear." I took the opportunity to compare our Quinn to Dome's impostor. The differences were few. If he aged up another ten years, would this fit outdoorsman also gain the smooth charm of the silver-tongued leader? Complete with his underlying contempt for his subordinates?

I didn't change my internal attitude when I accessed my aging function, but if this man's gift *was* concealment... No. It couldn't be possible with what I'd detected in him so far. Or did I not *want* to see an unsavory side of this handsome face?

From where he tinkered at Quaene's neck, Evard said, "Is this one a better-looking chap?"

I started and stepped back. Evard was becoming far

too intuitive for my liking. "They could be twins. Or brothers. Sought-after gifts like ours run in families. Maybe the Docga saved both, and the other was jealous of this one's advance to E-run."

"It might be what Quinn's hiding." Evard shrugged.

"Maybe so." My gaze lingered over his face again. "He needs a shave."

"He needs to be reactivated. Go help Mylta, why don't you, and hurry her out of here."

Good thing I did, for our cook had planned on food for three, and we'd soon have five in the household. Fortunately, in addition to a platter of sandwiches, she'd made salads enough for the week—she thought—including double of Evard's favorite, the potato salad. My favorite, chocolate cake, was just coming out of the oven.

We put together a dozen more sandwiches, and by the time I had our cook out the door, Evard had Quinn reactivated and drinking a cup of tea—one he'd *bolstered*, if I knew my run-mate. I took the cup, but Evard snatched it from me and returned it to Quinn. "Don't give me that look, my girl. It's oral lubricant."

I rolled my eyes and rested the back of my hand on Quinn's forehead as if checking his temperature. Opening my gift, I searched. "How are you feeling?"

He covered a yawn. "Like it's the middle of the night and I should head to bed."

An honest response. No hint of a cover-up, deception or *spin*. I lowered my hand but continued to search his emotes. "A deactivation leaves you at the function position in which you stopped. Those hours don't manifest as sleep or refresh your organic system." Quinn frowned at this explanation, so I suggested, "Why don't you sleep for a few hours? We have guest rooms upstairs."

At that, his frown deepened. Did he not trust us? Couldn't say I blamed him there. Or was it distress, agitation or grief over coming to terms with being an electorg? D'dair, why couldn't I get a clear reading on him, as I'd been able to do yesterday?

"I wish to remain until my grandmother wakes. Or, er, revives."

Evard glanced up. "That may be a while. I've replaced the damaged relay with one that should work, but it's not an exact duplicate and doesn't seem to be func—yow!" Evard jerked back from a spray of sparks.

Quinn jumped to his feet, but I reached her first. "Pulse strong. Breathing steady. Evard? You all right?"

"I'm fine, but that was quite a jolt through the old system."

"I'm not sure you should continue," Quinn said. Solicitude and distress emanated from him, pure and honorable.

I had my answer. This Quinn was the minister I preferred to support.

"That makes two of us, my good man," Evard said. "But we don't have any other options if we are to assist you *and* keep your presence beneath the notice of the ministers, as you desire."

They exchanged a look, and I knew. I rounded on

Evard. "You told—"

"Confirmed." He dropped his hands on my shoulders so I could accurately read his feelings. "I confirmed this pair's *E-run* status outranks ours in 'torg hierarchy."

The emphasis told me Evard had said no more. Through the shift in his emotions, I knew he'd had no choice. There'd been a confrontation of sorts, albeit a civil one, resulting in Evard choosing to acquiesce to...Quinn's authority?

"May *the Waters* preserve us," I breathed the words with my own emphasis to signal Evard. Agreeing to allow this unknown man to direct our actions not only undermined Evangeline's position, but also risked our commitment to the Zeffir community. Our native people came first. To strengthen that point, I crossed my arms, placing my ringed finger on top.

"Excuse me?" Quinn had come to stand beside us.

"Give us a minute," Evard said.

Quinn backed away.

Despite my finger tapping, Evard emoted positive feelings for this 'torg. His rising brows sought my agreement. "Reading?" he whispered and, in a few additional words, relayed his opinion that Quinn might address the situation brewing in the Corps, and resolve it. Was I willing to take a chance on this Quinn, the one we knew was a real Corps minister?

My run-mate's independent conclusion matched mine. Thank the Golden Waters. I'd do anything to avoid our ordered trip to Dome, which would certainly

102 | LAUREL WANROW

include an audience with...Impostor Quinn. I groaned. After my infiltration of their quarters, he'd never let me return to Zeffir.

My gaze slid to Quinn, who continued to watch from his grandmother's side while Evard and I engaged in what he must think was a strange sort of interaction. Indeed, as I focused on him, Quinn's emotions flew at me.

Uncertainty. Or was it doubt in our abilities? He didn't know us, so that would make sense. However, his frowning brows and compressed lips confused me.

Surreptitiously, I ran my thumb over my crystal. The emotions sharpened. Quinn was jealous. Of Evard and I? He thought...we had an intimate relationship. That made him jealous? Oh, my. I warmed at the thought of Quinn, handsome Quinn, thinking of me that way—

Oh, no!

My stomach sank. I couldn't deal with this again. It was just too hard. Especially for me. With my gift, a suitor's every shift of emotion, stuttering heartbeat or gut-deep plunge would carry to me, influencing the tenor of my days and sending me soaring with giddy happiness. However, when the relationship broke down, exactly the opposite would occur. Or worse, when Pier had died...then there was nothing. Long, empty days and nights of nothing.

Quite simply, once I allowed a person to become my intimate, there were no defenses, no secrets. Despite what Sabein had said, locking away that part of myself was for the best.

A pinch at my shoulders—Evard's fingers—jerked me back to the present. I dragged my gaze up to his. He made a pointed eye roll in Quinn's direction.

D'dair. Evard had picked up every thought. I frowned at him.

In return, he softened his face and began a silent plea. Personal issues aside, he felt this 'torg might be the answer. Quinn offered more opportunities to take a hand in making our future what we wanted it to be. *Please*, Evard begged me, *take the chance on* this *Quinn*.

Golden Waters, I couldn't argue with that. I nodded.

Evard leaned in and kissed me for the second time in as many days.

Quinn's unbridled envy slammed me.

I grabbed Evard's arm and corralled him a few steps farther from Quinn's emotes, as well as his flaring nostrils and narrowed eyes.

"He's in your hands," I hissed. "You deal with him."

Evard whispered, "He wants you. If the man could figure a way to call me out, he'd be doing it."

My breath sucked in sharply. "If you knew that, then why'd you kiss me? We know it means nothing, but he doesn't."

"Fuel on the fire, babe, fuel on the fire." Evard wriggled from my grip. "So, Quinn? Eve's with us. Time to strategize. Your Graenie is our first priority, since she holds the information we need."

Quinn nodded and made eye contact with Evard as he talked. But he muttered abrupt phrases through a tight jaw, and his fists clenched.

He wasn't taking any of it in. No, instead he was churning over what he'd just seen, what he also desired.

A corresponding pang of longing rose in me. I closed my eyes as the emotion blossomed. The feeling was wholly mine. Only I...couldn't. I just couldn't. I wrestled the feeling away and joined Evard and Quinn, intent on the job I had to do instead. Putting out amiable vibes, I stood closer to Quinn than I would have normally. "Evard? You've forgotten Quinn missed a night of sleep and hasn't eaten. Why don't you go to the kitchen and see what you can find for him?"

Evard inclined his head in a courtly bow and gave me a sympathetic smile. "Certainly, my dear sister. Back in a moment."

Blessed—why did my run-mate now pick up each and every nuance of what I felt? Of what Quinn felt? He acted as if he'd instantly turned on a gift similar to the one I'd been developing for decades with Sabein. Then I remembered Taior's message. *Bring Evard with you.*

"Uh, Evard?" He turned in the doorway. "By chance, have you seen Sabein today?"

He grinned. "As a matter of fact, she did pop by this morning. Said she'd see you tomorrow."

TWELVE

QUINN

Sister? The man kissed his sister like that? Evard had said they were 'torgs. Electorgs were produced—or whatever—in runs and grouped in triads so they could support each other, that was all. Yet, Graen was family. No, we were...

'Torgs. We. Were. 'Torgs. Not the emotionless machines I'd cast these humanoids as. Not preprogrammed, thoughtless, unfeeling—hell, far from that—electronics. I might not have a complete grasp of myself yet, and I was sure my head injury played a role in that area, but clearly I'd been wrong. 'Torgs were not puppets. Thank...whoever.

I drew a breath. Now to claw my way through this mess. The importance of our search for Quil hit home. He wasn't just a missing family member. He connected me to a functioning triad in case something went wrong. Like it had.

"Quinn?" Eve smiled slightly.

Despite how I'd just seen her with her run-mate, I welcomed that smile. I yearned to throw my arm around her as Evard had so casually done and confide in this capable woman. Yet, I didn't have that relationship with her. With anyone, for that matter, with Graen gone.

"You'll feel better after you eat. We're still human, and bodily functions often override our electronic functions. Please let us know if you have any questions or concerns about your new situation. Evard and I are here to help you, to fill in for your missing run-mates."

Seriously? As if she'd read my mind, her words communicated acceptance. Could they mean more? "Thank you," I said, searching her sweet features for a mutual hint of the attraction flooding my body, threatening my normally calm head. Certainly her solicitude indicated a deeper regard. Was it too soon to hope her feelings extended to affection?

Suddenly, she was too close. Physically, she hadn't moved, but I felt her. Intensely. How was I to act around her? Graen had laid down specific rules for interactions with the Aardites. But Eve was not a native, and thus within bounds. Instinctively, I knew the behavior norms a man—a gentleman—followed around women. Yet, within my limited range of memories, I'd never had a chance to practice them. And dammit, I did *not* want to make a mistake.

I spun aside and walked over to check on Graen. I wasn't born yesterday...though it felt like it with everything going on. Graen, Quil, this business with the other E-runs...

"Quinn?" Eve gripped my elbow. "Sit a minute while I see what's keeping Evard."

She scooted the office chair up behind me. But instead of sitting, I clasped her elbow in return and held her gaze. Her eyes seemed a little brighter than when I last looked at them, more golden. Unnaturally so. But I dismissed it when a phrase popped into my head—woman's intuition. That's what she had, along with a healthy dose of confidence.

Well, Graen said to pick someone I could trust. "How long have you been an electorg?" I asked.

"Nearly fifty years."

"Do you remember..."

"My organic years? I do. Not everyone does. Even more rare, I chose to become a 'torg before I died. I—discovered, shall we say?—Docgans stalking my village. They were considering me."

"How?"

She shook her head. "I'd rather not tell the story right now. It's a difficult one."

"Yeah? Well, you'll also have to wait to hear mine. I don't know it." Her look invited me to spill everything. "Graen won't divulge the details, but I lost my memory in a mishap that landed us on Aarde and resulted in the loss of my brother Quil. We've been looking for him for over two months."

She nodded, not seeming surprised at the bizarre tale. "Where?"

"We've covered G47—the three main continents, their major city-states, on down to the smaller towns. Now we're making the rounds of archipelagoes and villages of this size. Everywhere, except Dome."

A grimace flickered across her face at the headquarters' name. "You haven't missed much."

"Graen revived for a minute after you left us in the shelter and said to find help there."

Eve's grip on my forearm tightened. "Your brother? She knows—or thinks he's at Dome?"

I couldn't tear my eyes from hers, for their glow compelled me to confide everything I'd pieced together about our role as Docga consultants. "No. He got away. She said we're E-run electorgs, but hiding from the 'torgs in command. She asked me to go to Dome to get something to repair her, something she called our pro-tect...a device, I guess. Maybe protection device?" I drew in a breath. "Will you go with me to get it?"

Her eyes widened. "Go to... I, uh..." Then, within her, some door closed, shutting me out. "We should consult Evard."

I dropped her arm. Was this an excuse to say no? "Why does Evard get to make the decision?"

Eve blinked at me. "Our lead, Evangeline, is, uh, in-disposed, so of course Evard is before Eve in the triad rotation for lead. A before E, you know."

No, I didn't. "What does the alphabet have to do with who's the next lead?"

"Run-mate names begin with the same letters, then take their order from the subsequent letters in the names. It's the 'torg triad hierarchical system. Surely you E-runs use it as well?"

"Graen said I'm the youngest, so Quil and Quinn do fit what you're describing, but Graen doesn't fit, and without question, our systems align."

Eve ducked her chin to peer at me.

Uh oh. The systems aligning part. The phrase just rolled off my tongue, and I had no explanation for how I knew it, only the evidence, such as Graen's and my ability to mind-link. But—

My clear thinking stuttered. I closed my eyes and waved off Eve's concerned questions. The mind-link was supposedly *our* peoples'—Graen's and mine—skill, as was Lacuna, cross-leaping and other particle work. I'd done them instinctively before my head healed...and as part of that recovery, Graen had me *teach* her so I could spark more memories.

And so I'd given the lessons, mind-linking so she could locate the circuit and visualize the steps I used for cross-leaping. She'd played the stubborn student, insisting on many details, encouraging me to recount my increasing memories. In a week, my research in particle transference had flooded back, but little else.

Graen had refused to let me dwell on why. Nor would I now. That Graen's and my systems aligned...okay, it confirmed we belonged to the same Elite-run group. I opened my eyes to find Eve waiting patiently, her gray eyes not judging. She made it easier than I would have believed possible to smile and tap my temple. "I'm remembering. Please go on."

With only a passing frown, she said, "Graenie—grandmother—is not her name, it's her role on G47. Being a grandmother is a role among the natives, so we correlate with their perception of people in family groups. Like Evard being my brother and Evangeline our mother. There is no shared blood between us, but we are a familial unit. A family."

She said the last slowly, as if making a point. Evard was family. "Huh. I knew that." And I did, now that I thought about it. "Graenie is...was my melding of 'granny' and 'aenie.'" But had the knowledge been in my head these few months, or had it just appeared?

"Aenie? That doesn't fit the name system either, does it?" She looked at me expectantly, but I had no other memories to draw on. Eve sighed. "You should ask her to tell you her name."

"If I ever have the chance to talk to her again."

"You will." Her eyes searched mine, and then she clasped my arm. "If a protection device exists to help her, we'll find it, together. You're not alone, Quinn."

"Right you are, my dear nym—girl." Evard strode in carrying a tray of food and began to sing in his rich baritone voice. "Consider yourself at home. Consider yourself one of the family. We've taken to you, so it's clear we're going to get along. Consider—"

Eve swept by me and slapped a hand over his mouth. "Cut it out. Pay no attention to this cross-wire, Quinn. He just gets weird when he's happy."

"But his wires aren't really crossed?"

Evard escaped her hold and handed me a sandwich. "Not sure, surrounded by water like we are. Awkward for a lifelong forest dweller." He took a bite out of one of the bread triangles.

"No, it's definitely in his organic makeup. Watching old musicals is his passion. Since he's now lead, he'll have to give it up." Eve shook her head in a way I now could tell poked fun at her run-mate.

But Evard brightened. "Say! With Evangeline out, I am, aren't I? What shall I put you minions to doing? I have it. Serve me breakfast in bed."

Eve crossed her arms and gave him a stern look, almost as if she were the one in charge. "Perhaps tomorrow."

"Now don't you go forgetting." He flashed her a grin, finished his sandwich and brushed the crumbs from the front of his uniform. "Right, mates, now what's this about a protection device? Something we should fetch for your grandmother?"

"It's an instrument left at Dome," Eve said. "She's told him it'll revive and heal her."

"A diagnostic scanner?" Evard motioned with his large hands. "Handheld? Bigger?"

I shook my head. "I have no idea."

He considered this for a moment, then shrugged. "We'll get you in for a search."

A flood of gratitude hit my...system.

Our plans unfolded over maps, monitor images and lists Eve made in neat printing. Each detail was examined: what we'd wear, excuses for being there, places to look and instructions for how to return to Zeffir if we were separated.

The completeness of their preparations eased my worries over Graen's warnings. My knotted innards settled back into place, and I found myself smiling at the easy camaraderie the two shared, and opened to me. For the first time, I didn't feel like an outsider on G47.

When Eve disappeared upstairs to find me a Docga jumpsuit, Evard asked if I was all right with her accompanying me. "Eve gets along with people in a special way. Should you encounter any problems, she'll be a better troubleshooter than I. Besides, the girl blends, whereas I tend to stick out."

The burly man had a point. While blond hair tended to be very common on G47, Evard's height and build weren't. A shorter, slender stature had evolved among the native population.

"How tall are you anyway?" I asked.

"Six feet six. Average for Tarne, my world, colonized long ago by Earth explorers."

"You remember it?"

"Very well. Eve remembers hers, too. Earth."

"She told me," I said.

"Not all, I bet. That nymph has a few stories about hiding her inborn gift in a time when women were hanged for witchcraft. We'll have some tales to trade when your grandmother revives."

"Eve has a *gift*?"

He gave a slow nod to my surprise. "Ah. You've forgotten the Docga scour the galaxy for individuals with extraordinary talents and even...paranormal abilities."

I had...but I remembered now. "So you each..."

"*All* 'torgs. Our space-traveling patrons also access time portals, yielding a veritable smorgasbord of expertise. For example, on Tarne, fungi are practically all we grow, so naturally everyone is well versed in mycology. It's in the genes to have heightened olfactory sensitivity. Develop the talent and you rise to the top of the feudal system with skills that, thank the Great *Grünmann*, the Docga sought. Heritage, talent and work."

I nodded, more to myself as a new understanding filtered through me. The "lessons" I'd given Graen in particle transference weren't a skill of our people—they were skills of *mine*. From an advanced society, if I wasn't mistaken.

"On the other hand, my run-mates' gifts are beyond science. Inborn, but transcendent, metaphysical—" He shrugged. "Spooky. Abilities you don't flout, anywhere, anytime. Evangeline, also Earth-born, practically speaks with animals. Evy reads people through their emotions." He gave a sharp nod, eyeing me for understanding. "Every one of us is an open book to the nymph."

As if on cue, she walked in, and I found myself wary. But she showed no signs of elaborating on what she must have overheard. Instead, she held out a pale green jumpsuit.

"We've been issued several over the years and rarely worn them. Luckily, they're unisex. One of Evard's would look ridiculous on you."

I took the suit, but she didn't let go. She looked me over, and I felt suddenly naked under her scrutiny.

"On second thought, may I suggest a shower? Towels, soap and shampoo are in the bath down the hall."

They had a shower in this antiquated town? "I'd love to. Bathtubs seem to be the norm on Aarde. I've preferred to shower at home."

"You have a *home*?" Eve jumped on the word.

I wasn't such an open book after all. "We can't travel continuously."

"Where is it?"

"I can't say." She frowned, and I hastened to add, "Don't be put out—it's that I *can't*, not that I won't. It's hidden, in a complex manner, quite remote. That's the main reason I haven't gone back. No point until I've exhausted every way of reviving my grandmother."

"It's hidden?" asked Evard. "Can you describe it?"

I shook my head. Our home existed securely in a dimension I'd accessed through my particle-transference abilities. I had an inkling the molecular complexity of the concept would appeal to Evard, the technophile, and I wanted to tease him a bit. "Nope. No one can see the outside of it—it's pure interior space, no doors or windows."

He grabbed my shoulder. My nerves went into defense mode. Evard was big, bigger up close. I clenched my fist to stop it from moving upward.

Eve shoved him aside and pulled me against her. "Evard, you're scaring him. Intimidating, threatening...*don't*."

Her reprimand hardly registered, since it wasn't for me. I had the woman pressed to my side. A first in my fractured memory. Everything about her was soft and warm—her arm around my waist, the swell of breast at my ribs, and the curve of hip against mine. Each point of contact was duly noted and registered like a brand upon my brain.

Scents of leather, the musty books and a hint of lilacs wafted to my nostrils. I couldn't say how it happened, but my arm lifted, draped around her shoulders and brought her even closer.

Her gaze snapped to mine. Her lips parted around my name, and at the warmth of her breath, my muscles tightened. "Evard is just excited."

"Just excited!" He tugged at her arm, cutting through my daze.

It was as he'd said earlier. She knew both that I was startled by Evard's gesture and that he meant no harm. Of course, the signs were all there—expressions, intonations, physical cues—but she'd "read" them instantly, eerily so, but not entirely out of the realm of scientific believability.

"Evy, you don't understand. He's living on Edge. This is so much more than exciting. An adventure in the making—"

"No! No discussing it, not now. Quinn, go shower." She rotated neatly from under my arm and shoved the jumpsuit to my chest. Her firm hand directed me to the door while she squabbled with Evard to force him back to work.

I lingered to watch them, reveling in the memory of Eve's softness pressed to me. Eve had hugged me. Never mind that she now focused on her run-mate, holding him by the chin and then the ear, like he was a toddler whose attention she had to refocus from an unattainable toy. I grinned at his predicament.

"Okay, okay," he said to her. "I'll defer discussing Edge, *if* instead he promises to instruct me on cross-leaping. I'm lacking the routing in the internal system and the location of the circuit that handles the function, and then I'm good. Is that a fair deal to all?"

I stared at Evard with new respect. He understood the theory and the technology, possibly better than either Graen or I, the only two I had thought aware of my special methods of travel and hiding. Working with him would be a genuine treat.

He was just slightly off about how I'd created our home. "You know, Evard, our home isn't on Edge." If he'd heard of that concept, he had certainly heard of the one I did use, and I couldn't help bragging. "It's in Lacuna."

"*Lacuna!*" His exhilarated roar followed me as I jogged down the hall to the bathroom.

THIRTEEN

QUINN

Thirty minutes later, I stood between the bookcases in the shop's back corner, listening to Evard review the operation of the unmanned station I'd almost opened.

"Using book titles for coordinate points makes it one of the more difficult to decipher because of the hundreds of options, *unless* you have the guide." He took the Conducer codebook from my hands and slipped the lackluster volume onto a shelf. "Evy says your electronics picked out my alternative access, which I'd thought was well hidden."

His look indicated it was my turn for an explanation—one that would disclose how attuned I was to particles and their movements, including in a particle accelerator. I was coming to know this man, but it'd take a lot more before I trusted him—or anyone—with my process, or my data, including the G47 trajectories I'd collected into a mental manual of sorts.

Footsteps sounded behind us. Good, Eve had arrived just in time to distract—

Blessed Air. Distraction *was* the word for her new appearance. She hadn't just aged into her thirties. Her hair, in a coiffed roll, seemed darker, as did her eyebrows. Makeup highlighted her features, and long silver earrings dangled with glinting gems from her earlobes. Sophisticated despite the utilitarian jumpsuit. I would never approach this woman for a date.

"Eve?" I glanced at Evard, but he was grinning unabashedly at her. "Perhaps your younger, less groomed appearance would better allow us to slip around unnoticed."

Evard laughed. She shot him a look and ran her fingertips over her smooth hair, almost nervously, but her words conveyed no hesitation. "It's the rare person who sees beyond appearances, even among 'torgs. We tend to rely more on the organic side, as the Docga allow us to. I think this look is a good one for today's trip. Right, Evard?"

"Definitely. Anyone who has ever seen you there before won't recall *you*, my girl."

Someone would forget her? I certainly wouldn't have a problem recalling those sweet lips or her soft body.

Evard paced out of the Conducer and crossed his arms. "So, quick trip?"

"My memory is unpredictable, but I'll do my best," I said.

"Lacuna," Eve grumbled. "You had to tell him. You couldn't leave it at Edge." She waved off Evard. "We'll hurry so you can play."

He stomped away, muttering, "*Bloody hyphae.*"

"Sorry," I said, though I didn't see why it mattered. Both involved the breakdown of molecular structure for access. "What does he mean by that phrase?"

"A reference to some invasive Tarni mushroom, which, as I understand, the farmers dread ridding from the soil. Its mycelia are red." She rolled her eyes. "A Tarni liege's nightmare, akin to hell. Ready?"

I cleared my throat. "I need to operate the Conducer."

Her brow quirked over eyes that appeared blue because of the surrounding eye shadow.

Evard stuck his head around a bookcase. "Get on with it, Eve. The man lives in Lacuna, for *Grünmann*'s sake. He understands particle transporters. Activate it, Quinn."

With an exasperated look, she took my hand. I knew it was only so we'd pass through together, but my heart revved up. I glanced at her as we began the walk.

She wore a funny smile, one I couldn't decipher.

I stopped. "Can I ask you something?" She nodded, so I dove into it. "I'm having a difficult time grasping a view of you when I know you're ageless. I mean, do I refer to you as a girl or a woman?"

She eyed me strangely. *Go ahead, Quinn. Insert foot in mouth.* I doubled back. "I made a mistake when we first met. I'm sorry I said you lacked experience."

"Apology accepted. I don't care how you refer to me, so long as you remember I'm not an adolescent. I have experience doing my job and expect equality on this trip."

"You have it." I walked forward. The glowing titles began rising from the bindings. "*The Mirror of Her*

Dreams. Roadmarks." My mind slipped into the sequence as the floor and walls blurred and opened. "*Stranger in a—*"

Her groan broke my concentration. "This isn't the access to the back corridor."

"I'm searching for the title triggers Evard gave me, but others are emerging."

"Ones that shouldn't appear. Evard!"

He checked over the Conducer, starting through it and retreating as we'd done. "Must be something amiss on the other end." He snapped his fingers. "Didn't Evangeline say the recalls were to start today? They must have revised the system somehow."

Eve chewed on her lip, doing serious damage to her lipstick.

I resisted the temptation to rub it smooth with my thumb.

"Will we be able to return?"

Evard shrugged.

This was my territory. "We can." They stared at me. "This is why I want to operate it. Once I use your coordinates in my system, I'll have them memorized. Then, with access to the Conducer energy, that alternate one you—"

"Which may be shut down since it won't open now," Eve said, her voice sounding higher-pitched. "And how do you know so much—"

"He doesn't want to share the details. Not that we'd understand them on the first pass." Evard patted her shoulder. "Don't jump to conclusions, Eve. There's always the transport bay's Conducer. It's used primarily for cargo distribution, but I'm sure it's operational."

Even to my inexperienced eye, she didn't look happy, so I added, "I assure you I can get you back with any Conducer."

Evard bent and fixed her with a firm look. "The three of us could go over this until the cows come home and wouldn't be any closer to knowing the situation at Dome. Go, would you?"

"Fine," she said, a hard edge to her tone. She grasped my hand. "Do it."

Centering my gaze on the length of the aisle, I glanced from side to side. Titles swam into focus. The same first two rose, and I intoned them while others fluctuated and submerged, until one stayed. "*Stranger in a Strange Land.*" We walked the aisle. "*The Fly.*" The last came up. "*Lo!*" Abruptly trees displaced the bookcases, and we shifted locations.

Elbows and the bulk of luggage blocked our way. Some sort of crowd—right, the recalls. I formed into solid flesh sooner than I might have and tightened my grip on Eve's hand, pulling her back from the travelers. She solidified with a gasp, and we jostled to a halt at the end of a line of triads hauling their equipment cases for inventory.

The hum of the Conducer died. We were bunched between the low walls of an outdoor garden, with pink-blooming camellia trees arching over the artfully integrated energy corridor.

"Post you've arrived from?" said a weary man well in

front of us.

The group shuffled forward to the Blackguard stationed at the console with a porta-scan.

"Ferrent," a traveler replied. "Sorry we're late."

Nervousness hit me at seeing the same scenario as in Cavvert.

"D'dair," Eve cursed under her breath. "Evard was right. Come on."

She edged me along, inserting us between two groups. To my surprise, no one protested. Instead of my muscles tensing for a fight, or flight, I felt amenable with Eve's hand on my arm. She helped push one of their cases and offered my services to carry another. The woman relinquished it with a smile, and we joined the company of several triads who announced to the Blackguard they'd come together from Osster.

"Yep, here you are." The guard tapped his device. "Move ahead for ID verification at the entrance gate." He looked up, his gaze sweeping over Eve and me with the strangers, and pointed across an expansive plaza of pink granite beyond which rose the solid gray façade of a castle-like building, complete with faux crenulations. "First lull we've had today, so you should get in fast."

Eve tugged my elbow. We passed by the guard without a second glance. On the plaza among other milling people, we returned the cases and said good-bye to the group. Eve tucked her hand through my arm and pulled me to one of the fountains. The friendship feelings lingered, now striking me as strange. Minutes ago, we hadn't known these people.

I eyed Eve. "That wasn't too complicated. At first, I anticipated trouble."

"Did you?" Her lips twitched into an odd smile. "I didn't."

Yeah, *spooky*, as Evard had said. I'd save my questions for later. I glanced around. Besides the obvious travelers, other 'torgs walked the plaza or reclined in chairs gathered into odd circles of sunlight. I followed the shafts of light up to the expected sky, but found a blue-tinted surface arching overhead. Giant lenses mounted within it tilted to produce the sunbeams.

Dome. Of course. A vaulted synthetic shield encased the Corps headquarters, necessary because the Docga had located the facility in the worst of G47's Spore Zones. Saving the good land for the Aardites was fair, but meant the headquarters wasn't large enough to accommodate the entire Biosphere Corps staff ordered to report in. "How many 'torgs already live and work here, and where do you suppose they're meeting these extras and accounting for their equipment?"

Eve frowned. "I'm making a guess, but about two hundred reside at Dome? I have no idea what happens at these appointments. Maybe we'll learn that."

"Maybe," I muttered. "Maybe firsthand." The limits of my memory loss slammed me. As an Elite Class 'torg, I should know these details. Yet, I was sneaking in without knowing what I was looking for, and putting Eve and Evard at risk.

"Later," Eve murmured absently. She urged me forward, and we sauntered behind the Osster 'torgs around an oval of yellow daylilies. "We can't just reel off our ID numbers and allow the guards to run us through the system. Give me a minute to think while the others check in." Her attention focused on the head of the short line we'd joined.

Shrugging off the twinge of lameness, I studied the sole entrance in the stone structure, a pair of broad doors cracked open wide enough for one person to pass at a time. Two Blackguards manned it, though they seemed more lax than the ones I'd met in Cavvert. The older sat in the guardhouse, his head propped on a hand as he bent over the console. Before the doors, the second guard checked the readout as each 'torg placed a hand on the tabletop scanner.

Eve said, "We'll enter while the younger one's at the scanner. He'll be easier to influence."

"So you think."

Her brows shot up.

"He *looks* younger," I explained. "You warned me about judging 'torgs by age."

She glanced to the guard. "Ah. Well, maturity-wise, he matches his looks, trust me. When I approach him, you dawdle behind," she ordered. "Don't make eye contact, and watch my hand for a signal."

"Hold it," I hissed. "What about the other guard?"

"Not a problem. He's napping." In a complete reversal of her edginess back at the bookshop, she strode forward to wait behind the last Osster 'torg at the scanner. Her hands—which I was supposed to be keeping an eye on—were busy at her belt, and seconds later, her jumpsuit cinched tighter, accenting the curve of her narrow waist. She fiddled at her suit's neckline, then stepped to the table.

But Eve made no move to place her palm on the touch pad. Instead, she engaged the young-looking man in a lively conversation. One finger twirled a dark strand of hair at her cheek, while her other hand rubbed a slow stroke over her hip.

Blessed Air. She was flirting with him.

To my irritation, it seemed to be working. The guard's features relaxed. He leaned against the sunbaked wall and smiled down at her. Eve shimmied closer, and when she half turned to rest her shoulder to his, I saw she'd lowered her jumpsuit zipper. If the swell of her breasts looked that good from my distance, no wonder the guard dipped his face to peer at what must be an incredible view.

I crossed my arms. How long was she going to indulge in this? When would she signal to me? Following *orders*, I watched her hand run the length of his arm, stroking his bicep. My jaw muscles tightened as her luscious curves pressed against his undeserving body.

No, I didn't have to watch *this*. I squeezed my eyes shut and tried to erase the images, but instead, others appeared...*a woman pressed to me. No, to him, while I stood at her bedroom door watching. Hurt. Betrayed...* My eyes flashed open.

Eve's fingers smoothed over his chest and caressed him before they trailed to his neck.

That should be my neck. My chest. I was hot and

bothered by the proximity of her, and yet, she wasn't anywhere near me. She wasn't asking *me* to check out her body and...

But she was. Something in the angle of her head, slightly turned in my direction, told me. Eve was calling to me, urging me, even begging me to come over. I didn't get it—she wanted him *and* me? Together? A threesome? She didn't seem the type, but hey, who was I to question her? I took a step, but stopped when a new movement caught my eye. Her hand—not the one on his shoulder, the nearly hidden one—was frantically motioning toward the gate.

The gate. Oh, yeah.

I upped my pace and strode through the narrow opening. Before I sidled through, I caught sight of the guard's other hand—the one kneading the soft roundness of Eve's rump.

FOURTEEN

EVE

Quinn was not in a good humor when I approached him at Dome's foyer, but neither was I. He'd been so distracted that he nearly missed my signal. It could have ended badly if we'd been caught. But we'd never worked together before, so I had to overlook a beginner's ineptitude and focus on our search for the repair device.

He joined me in a casual stroll among loitering triad groups. We entered a side hallway with the elevator up to the meditronic wing, where I fervently hoped we'd get a clue about this protection device, if not the unit itself.

"I thought we were supposed to be sneaking in," Quinn muttered at my side, still exuding irritability.

I glanced down the empty hall. "We did."

"Are you saying he won't remember that...that encounter?"

Threads of closely controlled jealously poked at me. My senses leaped, but I said, "It was nothing to him." At least my influence was subliminal.

"From what I saw, he enjoyed your attention."

Golden Waters, he had—more thoroughly than I'd intended. But tell Quinn this? No. "Maybe he did. Forget it. Let's focus on the search."

He stopped me. "Then let's look like that's what we're doing." With his determined eyes fixed on my face, Quinn ran my lowered zipper to the top of my jumpsuit, his knuckles brushing like liquid fire up my chest and neck.

My skin hadn't heated like this under the guard's pawing. "Uh, thanks." I swiped a hand across my collar to close the Velcro flap and turned my burning face down the hall. I did not need my body reacting like this. Absolutely did not.

Yet, his emotions chased me, assailed me and, against my better judgment, touched me. Quinn's tension, and attraction, dogged me all the way to the elevator. D'dair. Why now, when I was in *this* unfortunate position—having to keep my gift active to pick up any hint of suspicion? Or worse, any trace of Impostor Quinn, so I could hide. On top of it, I was about to be confined in a tight space with *this* Quinn.

Steeling myself, I punched the elevator button.

"I'm to stay out of sight while you question the med-tech?" Quinn reiterated our plan. "Should I expect a repeat performance of the gate scene?"

How dare he? Staring straight ahead, I paused long enough to ensure my tone stayed neutral. "It depends on who the person is and what will distract him. Or her."

"True, the contact might be a woman."

"Exactly. In that case, I expect you to handle her. Hope you're up to it."

The doors slid open, and we stepped in. The waves of resentment kept coming. Somehow, I made it to the second floor without killing him. When the door opened, I darted through and fled well beyond Quinn's range, not waiting to see who might notice my odd behavior.

Actually, there wasn't anyone—my senses were so ramped up I could tell immediately. But d'dair, I was ticked at my rash reactions. Sucking a breath, I waited for Quinn to catch up.

"You've got to calm down," I said without looking at him.

"Me? I'm not the one blasting out of the damn elevator like an elephant-sized rabbit. They must have heard you on the other side of Dome."

"No." I pinned him with my eyes. "No one was there to hear me. I can tell. But you, Mr. Trouble, are making me fight to get a clear emotional read on the place. Just—"

"Are you saying I'm the cause of your problems? Pardon me, but I haven't done—"

"Look. This is not the place for explanations. Just get over the guard already." I settled my nervous emotions. They were swaying Quinn, too. "He's nothing. What I did with him is nothing. A means to an end. We're in. That's what matters."

Like a fish, he opened and closed his mouth. But even before he acquiesced, the tide turned. The testosterone dispersed, and the barrage of outrage quit. "Fine. We'll discuss it later."

Not likely, but I'd gotten what I wanted. "Thanks," I muttered. "Let's go."

While Quinn waited in the hall, faking an intense study of a snack machine's offerings, I peered through the meditronic wing's glass doors. The receptionist *was* a woman, but I didn't trust Quinn to handle the questioning, which would be like any day of work for me.

She looked up as I entered. "What can I do for you, dear?"

"One of my run-mates is, uh, indisposed." I emoted sympathy and wrung my hands for effect.

Her gentle smile was a relief. "We're seeing a lot of that. Upset stomach or heartburn?" She pivoted to her keyboard, fingers lifted and waiting. "We can prescribe something."

I shook my head and dropped my voice. "This inventory has him—" Acting like a lunatic, what I wanted to convey from my organic experience, seemed too harsh. I grappled for one of Evard's. "Freaking out."

With a slight nod, she started tapping. "Bad case of nerves, hmm? We have openings this afternoon. How soon can he get here?"

"I don't think that's possible." I waved in the general direction of the entrance. "They have the Conducers tied up. I barely got through, and he's—" I sighed deeply. "What with knocking around some equipment we must account for, he's gotten a few abrasions and crimped a wire, we think. He's having periods of blacking out." That description was close to Graen's issues. "One of the 'torgs from the adjacent Post is a technician and can do the repair he'll probably need. Do you have a diagnostic device, er, scanner, I might take back with me?"

This produced a frown. "A scanner?"

"To detect broken wires. Or circuit damage."

"I've never heard of such a thing. Besides, blackouts indicate possible organic damage, a concussion. That's serious. You better take one of the openings. We only have two med-techs now. Reduction to essential personnel, you know."

The Corps' meditronic services had been reduced? "Even with"—I hoped Charlotte's gossip was common knowledge—"the minister as she is?"

The woman snorted. "They seem to think they know more about depression than we do." She tapped her nametag, which identified her as a med-practitioner. "They threw us our orders the day before yours. All procedures suspended, and three corridors of rooms closed down to hold the excess field equipment. With everyone's plans crossed, it's slow. What if I arrange for a med-tech to accompany you back to your Post?"

I bit off my instinctive negative reply. "That would be kind. But I think your first suggestion is the best. We'll get him in here. What time?" I made up a name, collected the reminder card and left.

"No luck." I told Quinn of her lack of recognition of such a device, along with the news of reduced personnel and the closed corridors. "They're using the vacated rooms for the Post equipment storage you wondered about."

"The reduced meditronic staff concerns me more. One would hope the ministers have sent them out to dispatch some hornworts, but I doubt that's the case. Something else is going on."

I couldn't think about that. "She offered to send a med-tech out."

His jaw tightened. "It might come to that. We'll move on to our guess that the device might be particular to the E-run system. Shall we head upstairs?"

I nodded, but my stomach dropped as we returned to the elevator.

After my last trip to Dome, Evard had studied its 3-D schematics and verified the ministers' suite was on the fifth level, high in the central, blocky tower. One smaller level lay above it, providing weight reinforcement for the arching dome. Evard hadn't been able to discern its use, but had found references to the ministers' *floors* in several old newscast articles featuring the construction and interior design. Photos showed a spiral staircase in the fourth-floor atrium that obviously led up. As best we could tell, that staircase was now located within the Biological Resources office, a room connected to the division's lab.

We strolled the atrium's paths, passing a few 'torgs and stopping like any couple to read the labels of the native plant collection assembled by early botanist teams. Alone, we approached a wall of windows separating the heated lab.

I scanned the interior for occupants. No one worked in the well-lit room. The office door lay beyond the table-height vats of steaming water containing the thermophiles, primitive heat-loving plants from the geothermal areas of the planet. The water lapped at rocks, all encrusted with colorful scum, different ones in each glass tub. I'd never realized Aarde's active volcanic regions might be pretty.

"Twelve artificial hot pools," Quinn said from behind me. "They've replicated the temperature gradients to grow every native bacteria, algae and hornwort." He pointed to a vat containing tiny, rock-hugging, crimped-edged leaves.

The plant didn't look at all like Cyrem's photos. "This sample isn't sending up the horn-like spore stalks," I said.

"Oh?" Quinn bent to the door's lock and removed the keypad cover. "There must be a reason," he said and stuck his finger into a mess of wire. A glow lit up his skin.

"What do you think you're doing?" I hissed.

"It was locked. Quiet a sec."

Blessed Waters, he should have been flat on his back, electrocuted. I waited while he closed his eyes and let sparks fly over his skin.

The door slid aside with a whoosh.

"How did—"

He replaced the cover. "You're not the only one with talent." He raised a brow and ushered me inside.

No 'torg, not even an E-run minister, could intuit electronics that way. It would render even the Docga's security vulnerable. Who was this man? Still, I followed him through the vats to the office door, the humid air beading my neck with sweat.

Quinn removed the keypad cover, but hesitated.

"Afraid this one might electrocute you?"

He frowned. "No, I can disperse the charge, but..." He pointed to a tiny metal plate fixed between two wires. "The current will flow through it, but I don't see why someone added more metal, and not even a clean piece at that."

The surface did look tarnished. But Quinn stuck his finger to the wires.

The outer door whooshed opened again. "What are you doing here?" a woman asked, her voice like ice.

I whirled, hoping to block Quinn until he could replace the cover. Her petite figure and flowing blond hair seemed familiar, but her green apron indicated a different position than that of the kitchen 'torgs I'd met.

"You know the policy," the woman said. "No one enters the lab without approval from me. I should call my guards." She held up a communicator and advanced on us.

Small and blond, authoritative manner—and backed up by guards. That she also wore a dark green jumpsuit clicked my memory clicked into place. As Quinn turned beside me, I stammered, "We-we're sorry, Minister Quala."

Quinn froze. Fear rolled off him, and before I could do anything to counter it, her steely blue eyes shifted to him.

Her haughty expression fell into a puzzled frown. A wave of doubt replaced confidence.

"Why are you dressed like that?" she asked Quinn. "Your hair—" She glanced at me. "Is that a wig? I've never seen—" As her mouth gaped, she dropped the communicator and the basket she held, scattering cut plants over her feet and her emotions over me. Her feelings rolled through disbelief and into confusion. "Qu-Quinn?"

Quinn's fear, Quala's insensibility—the emotions caught me between them, becoming mine. My muscles tensed with the urge to run. I pushed my barricades, but they moved too slowly, my thoughts like Zeffir's glaciers. I'd never save us.

Quinn caught my arm and propelled me between two steaming vats. His painful grip cleared my head. My gift snapped closed. He spun away, toward Quala, ducking to the spilled plants. Quinn scooped up the communicator. Metal flashed—he'd snatched a knife from the cuttings.

Quala dove. Quinn dodged her and lurched back to me. "Wait outside for me," he snapped over his shoulder.

His tone sent a shiver down my spine. I wasn't losing sight of him, not with the fear I'd just detected. He was supposed to have hidden from the ministers.

On the other side of him, Quala straightened, horror frozen on her face as her gaze shot from her knife in his hand to the exits. Both lay closer to us, thanks to Quinn's maneuver.

He brandished the blade at Quala. "Down on the floor."

Blessed Waters, he was going to cut her circuit wires—or stab her.

"No, wait," she cried. "I didn't recognize you at first. Just listen. Please. I never would have threatened *you*, Quinn. Not the real you." She lifted her empty hands. "I need your help. G47 needs your help. Please, it's only me."

He stepped toward her. "Now."

She backed to the wall, her gaze flickering to the knife. "Quinn. I don't blame you for doing this. It's your duty. But it's mine, too. Always. I've scrambled to trick him, that fraud pretending to be you."

"Get down *now*," he spat with a wave of the knife. "Hands up, on your head." He sounded harsh, impatient, but when she lowered to sit, he glanced to me, frowning in a different way.

Sweat beaded over his brow. Mine also perspired freely in the heat, but I suspected his discomfort ran deeper—old memories assaulting him.

Quinn kept a hard glare—and the blade—directed at Quala. Seated, with hands clenched into her blond hair, she couldn't harm us.

I didn't trust her, but neither could I let him hurt her.

I removed my barriers and waved off the lingering emotions of minutes ago. Then I steeled myself and crept to Quinn's side. No anger or ill intent crossed to me. Quinn was blank, bless the Waters, so I focused on the woman sitting feet away.

Quala's gaze skimmed over me before saying to Quinn, "Alone, I can only delay him, not stop him."

One emotion lay behind the statement. Fear. I glanced to Quinn's cold eyes, set jaw and glinting knife. I'd feel the same.

Again, he glanced at me. I had no hope of communication with Quinn like Evard and I did. That came with decades of living and working together. I pulled him back two steps—giving Quala space *and* positioning the door closer. "Give her a chance to talk first."

Relief tumbled from Quala, desperation and concern, all in keeping with her gasped, "I need you, and the others. Quil? Quaene? Have you seen them?"

But she felt nothing that led me to trust her.

Quinn didn't respond for a long minute, during which beads of sweat rolled from Quala's brow. Finally, with no emotion, he said, "And if I were to help you?"

Quala released her breath. "We must restore the workforce to us. Or we lose the planet. Even the natives' news reports haven't got the story straight. We have an imminent spore release. Minneri Pools first, then several others within days."

My stomach plummeted. There wasn't worse news on Aarde. Minneri, near Dome, was on the largest land mass surrounded by Bounded Winds—and thus the largest Spore Zone.

"When?" Quinn asked.

"A week, minimum." Her eyes pleaded with him as she wrung her hands above her head. "That fraud 'torg pulled my Bio Resources staff. He's shuffling everyone. Quinn, I need you, you and Quaene. She was with you at Cavvert, right? Help me get 'torgs to destroy the hornworts that are entering their sporophyte stage."

Quinn remained stone-still, the pleasant gurgling of water cycling through the artificial pools the only sound.

Was he purposefully noncommittal, or fighting a flood of memories? I inwardly cringed and readied myself to yank him through the door, hoping we could lose ourselves in the corridor crowds. But I couldn't let go of something she'd said. "If he's a fraud," I asked, "why is he allowing you to still function as a minister?"

Quala looked at me—really looked at me—for the first time. An annoyed expression relayed her opinion of my B-run interruption. "He thinks I'm under his control. I've thwarted his influence on my circuits."

Despite her opinion of me, she'd answered. Yet, dishonesty laced her confidence. Guilt at tricking a captor she had to pretend to like, or a ploy to gain our trust? I wasn't...*buying it*, as Evard would say. "How?" I asked.

"Herbs." She nodded to her spilled greenery. "Plants and their properties are my life's work, skills that brought me to this mission."

"Then why haven't you helped Quetta?" Given my organic years as a healer, I had no doubt a gifted herbalist could contrive a solution.

"Don't think I haven't tried. I can't get a mix to work for her body chemistry. We're all different."

True, so why didn't I trust her? *Because she trusts us,*

with too little information. She was desperate. Desperate people said and did whatever it took to get help. Especially with a knife involved.

Buzzz...buzz...

Quinn jerked. The noise came from her communicator in his hand.

"It's my call from the fraudulent Minister Quinn," Quala said. "Another group has reported to Level Two for their inventory." Creases furrowed her brow with new concern—contrived? "Quinn, I can't afford to blow my cover. You have to let me go. And *you* have to leave before any of the other staff recognize you and ask questions."

She didn't spare a second thought for me, the lowly B-run. D'dair. Why was it always like this? As soon as Quinn got his feet under him, he'd probably be the same way. I pushed the notion aside. Protecting myself here meant staying alert and gathering information. She'd confirmed the other minister was an impostor. And he was on a different level, so we were safe—for now. "How long will the appointment take?" I asked her.

Quala glanced at me, but spoke to Quinn. "Anywhere from fifteen minutes to an hour. It depends on the extent of their project assignments and equipment. Can you exit this facility yourself, get Quaene, return to help me?"

Eagerness flooded from her, and genuine concern. She wanted us to go.

The buzzer sounded again, followed by a man saying, "Quala?"

My stomach sank. She'd told the truth—it was Impostor Quinn.

Quinn caught my eye, brows lifted, but he shifted his look to Quala, asking, "Can I trust you?" He'd figured out how to ask *me* the question.

Quala's emphatic *yes* and wave of sincerity was the answer I needed. We might be able to pull this off. I nodded when Quinn glanced toward me again.

He stepped closer to her. "Don't blow your cover. Or mine. I'd like to think you're telling the truth. If I get out of this facility without security being alerted, I'll think over your request."

"Days," she said. "We have only—"

"Lie down, keeping those hands on your head," Quinn ordered. "Face to the wall. Now, or I go back to the first plan. It's messier, but 'torgs can always be put back together."

She scrambled into position.

I sidled back from her spike of fear, nodding when Quinn looked at me fully and hovering my hand over the door opener.

His eyes widened, and he shook his head.

What? If we weren't leaving, then what were we doing?

"Wait thirty seconds," he said to Quala as he backed from her. He slipped the communicator into the nearest vat with barely a ripple. "Then you may leave."

Quinn swung around and hit the door opener. But we didn't dash through the doorway; he jerked me along the wall and through some sort of curtain I hadn't noticed. It blocked the light, and under the sound of the whooshing door, he hissed, "Don't move. Don't speak. No matter what happens."

Panic rose in me. How could he count on Quala not seeing us? But we huddled in the dark corner, my heartbeats nearly drowning out the sound of the gurgling water.

Not ten seconds passed before she began cursing.

I held my breath, cowering behind Quinn as footsteps crossed the room at a trot and a *whack* resounded. The door whooshed again. She ran out. For a few seconds, the sounds of voices echoed in the atrium, and then the door closed. Silence.

Quinn pulled me with him, somehow turning on the lights, but I was frightened, relieved, confused, so when he said, "Get low," and scuttled to the back of the lab, I followed.

Crouching, he removed the office keypad cover again and stuck his fingers to the sparking wires.

FIFTEEN

QUINN

We jogged up the flight of stairs. Beside me, Eve asked, "How did she miss us?"

Her voice trembled, and I felt like an ass for getting her involved in this mess. Lacuna explanations had to wait. "Later. Just stay together, prepared for..." Damn. Nothing I said would make this better.

She sighed. "Anything."

"We're doing great." I shot her a smile and removed yet another keypad. These ministers were over-secured. Thankfully, their salon on Level Five was deserted, and our quick search turned up empty bedrooms. We avoided the one Eve knew was Quetta's.

I saved the question of how she'd learned this. Again, later would do. We ascended the stairs to Level Six.

At the top, I scanned the office-like hall of closed doors, well lit by a row of skylights. No keypads graced them, and when I grasped the first knob, I remembered why. E-runs used their higher-level frequency for a number of Docga security measures. Graen said I was at the Elite level, but would my frequency match the minister triad?

The doorknob current hummed through me, but

didn't release, for the wave kept circling, searching... I closed my eyes. The string of pulses was very similar to my own—

"Quinn?" Eve asked.

"The rogue must have changed it," I muttered. "This lock releases to a specific E-run frequency."

"Oh. An E-run frequency that's not yours, then."

I sucked a breath. We couldn't come all this way to return empty-handed. I immersed myself in the flow of it, to use my gift to push a change—

The knob clicked in my hand and turned. A storage room lay within, exactly what we were looking for.

Our gazes met. Eve shook her head slightly. "How?"

This I could explain faster. Plus, I now trusted Eve. "I have a gift, too, in analyzing and transferring particles. I directed the flow of electrons to change it. Same thing I do to cross-leap and access Lacuna."

She nodded. "Leave the door open so I can detect anyone coming." We tiptoed through the dust motes hanging among the tables, shelves and file cabinets...and a collection of native clothing and accessories. Eve scanned the rack. "Odd to store clothing here. Where do we start?"

"An electronics repair device won't be paper, so ignore the books and files." That left a mix of Aarde artifacts and a workbench scattered with dismantled parts of Docga electronics. I made a hurried scan but recognized nothing. I started another pass, but Eve stopped me.

"It would be better to check each of the rooms on

this level while we can," she said. "Then if we don't find the device this trip, perhaps on another we'll know where to start."

I agreed. The next shiny doorknob hummed with the same security current and opened at the touch of my hand. We entered a roomy office. Aside from a chair and desk holding a locked computer, the only other piece of furniture was a table filled with rocks. A G47 map with dozens of yellow, red and green numbered dots hung on the adjacent wall.

"Does this mean something to you?" Eve asked.

Clearly, this assortment of fist-sized rock samples must be important. "No." I moved back to the map. "And these numbers are useless without their reference list. I recognize some of the locations, but what do these places have in common? Olannit, green, three. Zeffir, yellow, eighty-five. I need more time to glean their connection."

"Simple. Take a picture of it."

"I don't have a camera."

"Of course you—oh. Uh, I do." She tapped just below one of her beautiful eyes. "B-run function for research."

A camera was part of her built-in electronics. Mine, too, probably, but the reminder that her soft body wasn't entirely human hit me. Of course, the gate guard hadn't minded when he—

"It's all right, Quinn. I often use it for our work. You go open the next door, and I'll copy the map for you."

Yeah, my dwelling on this woman and all her...functions wouldn't complete our search. Yet again,

I compartmentalized my feelings. Along the hall sat two smaller offices that appeared unused and a bedroom with an adjoining bath. Each room was as clean-lined and impersonal as the first office.

The last door opened into a dimly lit and mostly empty room. Two bowls sat inside, food and water. A box of dirt had been placed to one side. The surface of it was disturbed, and the smell made its use obvious. The light of the hall shone almost to a mound in the back corner. It moved.

I pressed Eve aside, pulling the door to protect us.

She blocked it open. "I sense no hostility, aggression or opposition."

The animal got slowly to its feet and stepped from the shadows. Eve's fingers pinched into me, but the pain was nothing against the swirl of confusion surrounding the familiar animal. The big dog had been... I shut my eyes, reaching for the image.

Eve released me. I grappled to dismiss my churning memories, opening my eyes to the unbelievable sight of her stroking the wiry hair of the wolfhound's head and unlatching the chain from his collar.

I rushed after her. "Be careful! We don't know—"

"*I* know. This is—" She eyed me in an odd way, then shook her head. "D'dair," she swore. "He shouldn't be locked in here."

Her tone indicated something was seriously wrong. She ushered the stumbling dog toward the door of his prison. His gait was stiff and awkward, the poor beast, but he came directly to me and pressed his head against my thigh. Familiarity flooded me. Elusive threads of memory wove forward.

"Quinn? Help me rub his legs to get the circulation going. Once we're back, Evangeline will take proper care of this boy."

The barrage of images compromised my concentration. I shook them off and dropped to a squat on the other side of the dog. "Evangeline?" I repeated.

"Right, the Evangeline you met probably didn't seem the type, but that wasn't her true personality. Our Evangeline has a gift with animals. It took her no time at all to correct the husbandry problems on Zeffir."

Zeffir. Where Eve worked. If I kept my focus on her and her conversation, I wouldn't dissolve into my confusing past. "I did notice the agriculture on the island was top-notch."

Eve massaged the dog's thigh. He was leaning into me as much as I was leaning back. He poked his nose to mine, making a soft rumbling sound. The prickly fur, the sloppy tongue, the intelligent eyes staring steadily at me. He seemed so familiar...was he my dog?

"Humph. Why are you getting the thanks when I'm the one doing the work?" Eve grumbled, but she was watching closely. "Here, turn him."

The sturdy canine frame shifted when she pulled him, but the dog danced around until his broad face was in mine again. He whined. Smoothing the gray hairs of his muzzle back to the black ones on the crown of his head, I stared deep into his dark orange eyes. A memory came...

A desperate cross-leap, the dog pushed against me—no, leading me—with someone—was it Graen?—forcing me through the Conducer, but the dog—

Like in my memory, the wolfhound jerked forward, his ears perked. Footsteps sounded. Together, Eve and I tripped to the threshold. I intended to close the door, but the wolfhound slipped through with a growl.

"So much for hiding." I peered around the doorjamb.

The dog cantered to meet the single guard, who dropped bowls similar to the ones at our feet. The man lowered his face guard and reach for his stun sword.

I bolted forward. "No!"

My appearance was enough to make him hesitate. The dog leaped. With well over a hundred pounds of force, those huge paws struck the man's shoulders and down he went. The dog bounded on. At the top of the stairs, he turned to stare, as if summoning us.

We ran. The guard rolled to gain his feet. I shoved him down again and raced past. The wolfhound yipped and descended the stairs. I followed with Eve just paces behind me.

Thud! Someone tripped and fell.

I whirled. Eve sprawled across the tiles, her expression frantic, her limbs twitching. The guard lurched up, shoving the stun sword before him. "Unless you want the same, freeze!"

SIXTEEN

QUINN

The guard stepped over Eve, swung the lit sword and hit her again.

Light flashed, her leg jumped, the jolt stiffened her body...for seconds...long painful seconds. She slumped into unconsciousness.

My jaw dropped. *The son of a—* "She was down! What the hell are you doing?"

"Arms up. Back to the wall. Sit." He waved the sword.

Like hell I would. I plowed straight into *his* arms, knocked *him* against the wall and smashed *him* into a sit, *dammit.* I barely felt the bite of his sword.

The Blackguard yelped—surprised, I guess. What sort of an idiot flies at the Docga's best fighters? I had, and the current stung, but I forced the electrons off.

He shoved me and rose, fighting madly. Burning filled my nostrils. A jolt too strong to disperse blinded me.

Another face, unhelmeted, loomed above me. Who—

The stun sword bit again. I wrenched aside.

A tour—on a spaceship? Laughter with my friends, turning to embarrassment at a dressing down...meetings—

Each jolt of the sword brought another image. I let

them come until I was so confused I batted the guard away. I fell.

A man with a knife, lunging—

I ducked the sword, swung my arm and hit him. My knuckles cramped with pain, but I'd knocked off his helmet. It wasn't the same man, but I hit him again, just like I'd—

Punched my own face again and again.

The guard slumped, feet from Eve. Memory fragments rocketed through me, some clicking into place, some slipping off. But the images were nothing compared to the script in my suddenly revived retina display.

Red3 Alert! Take corrective action.

SEVENTEEN

EVE

I woke with my body tired and worn, as if my systems had experienced an uncontrolled shutdown. It'd been years since I'd let myself go like this—*no!*

It all came rushing back. The trip with Quinn, the guard and the stun sword's biting jolt to my leg.

The sting was gone, but new discomforts replaced it. Hard floor. Cold. Dark.

I must be in Dome's secure section. Jail. I groaned. At least Quinn had gotten away. And the room didn't smell moldy. In fact, it smelled rather crisp, like sparks. Strange.

"Eve?" Callused fingertips brushed my forehead. "Are you awake?"

Quinn. D'dair. "They got you, too?" I croaked. "What about the...wolfhound?"

"He's here."

A cold nose skittered across my cheek and burrowed into my neck. How could anyone hold the gentle—and definitely sentient—Docgan hostage? If I needed another reason to support Quinn in thwarting these impostors, I had it. Not that I could reveal I knew this being's origins, given Quinn's amnesia.

With great effort, I raised my leaden arm to stroke

the wolfhound and ended up hugging his giant head to me. Doggy smelling, he was warm and comforting, but not nearly as much as Quinn's bulk at my side. I wanted to cuddle him, too, but that would complicate everything. Besides, a different feeling emanated from him. My foggy mind couldn't make it out.

I struggled to sit up. "Where are we?"

"After I knocked out the guard—"

"Hold on a second." He'd knocked out a *guard*? Oh, were we ever in trouble. Double for me, if the impostor minister found me in this jail cell. I still had no sense of Quinn's emotions—or a good look at him in the murky darkness. A faint light wavered at the edges of my vision. I blinked, trying to clear my sight and my head. For someone in lockdown, he seemed awfully calm. "We didn't get hauled in?"

"No. From the activity, I'd say we're close to the kitchen."

I sagged back in relief. "In a storeroom?"

Quinn laughed, an odd sound that cut off abruptly. "Uh, no. I had to be sure of safety while you recovered. We're in Lacuna."

I sat up. "Lacuna? That...space?"

"Exactly. The same space between molecules our dissolved particles move through in the Conducer before they're accelerated to transport. It's possible to access the gaps—Lacuna—for a stabilized use."

"*Stabilized*, he says," I muttered to myself, patting my body. I was solid. The wolfhound was solid and, though I didn't dare get personal, so was Quinn.

"You survived it back in the lab," he said. "That was Lacuna, too."

"*This* is how we hid from Quala?" I gasped.

He caught my hands. "Eve, it's okay. We're stable. Only the transitions are hard."

I pulled my fingers loose and hugged myself. "Look, being disintegrated for Conducer transport is one thing, but staying broken up is too much. Evard was the one keen on wandering the dark recesses of Lacuna, not me."

"It doesn't have to be dark." He jiggled the fluctuating wall beside him. A faint glow grew to illuminate a shifting bubble, inside which the three of us were crammed together on something resembling Dome's slate floor. "Is that better? Because you were unconscious, I dimmed it, but the light can be as bright as our surroundings." He scooted back and waved an arm. The taint of burning tickled my nostrils again as the bubble flowed outward. "It didn't matter to me since I see well in the dark."

He could see well in the dark. Right. The man had night vision and hadn't realized he was an electorg. *Duh!* I wanted to snap at him, but didn't, because at this particular moment I was at his mercy. Lacuna. May the Waters preserve me. I sucked in a few breaths and repeated his assurances, hoping the normalcy he felt would rub off on me. "Lacuna. In Dome. In..."

"A side hall with low activity..." Quinn narrowed his eyes and frowned. He pressed his fingertips to his right temple.

His faulty organic system. Splendid. If he became as flustered as I was, we were sunk. On my own, I could deal with my heightened emotions, regulate my gift and keep us out of trouble. But with him in the mix...

A moment later, he got to his feet. "I'll check if it's safe to leave." He seemed to be looking through a brighter area of the bubble surface.

I rose, rubbing my limbs, but when Quinn turned to watch me, I stifled the impulse to make sure I was real. The calmer, different feeling I had detected before flowed from him. His eyes had taken on a sharpness. The set of his shoulders seemed broader. I couldn't put my finger on the change in him, but like the burnt odor, it existed.

"You want to look?" He stepped back.

I took his place at a clear porthole in the murk. Close to us, the hall was empty, but farther down, 'torgs carrying trays emerged from a doorway. "That's the kitchen. I was here a day ago."

"You know our location, then." Quinn's voice resonated right behind me, deeper, steadier than before. His heat poured over me. My thoughts jumped like my heart, and abruptly my body tuned to his. From under the burnt smell of something I should remember but didn't, his musk flowed—the scent of a forest of drying leaves on a fall day—and the unmistakable assurance of a man in charge.

I had my answer. "You remember your past."

"Some. Enough. Are you feeling better?"

"Fine. Let's go. That guard is bound to report us and

the missing wolfhound."

Quinn glanced down. "Getting out of here with him will be tricky. Can you locate that transport bay Conducer Evard told us about?"

My research function brought up the filed schematics. I groaned. "The second Conducer is in a separate complex some distance from here—the Aeroport. It's situated in the center of a triangular cluster of three transport bays."

His jaw stiffened. "Dangerous or not, this option beats the plaza Conducer."

Especially trying to sneak out a wolfhound. "We can access the walkway connecting the facilities on this level. I have the directions loaded."

"Thanks. Stick close. We'll hide if we need to." He clasped the wolfhound's collar with one hand and offered me the other. When I didn't take it, he gestured for me to go first.

I clenched my teeth and grabbed his hand. Leaving rippled my insides like...I didn't want to think about it, and when I released Quinn, I had to put my fingers to the wall while I walked.

The back corridors were clear. We managed three turns before hearing voices at the intersection ahead of us—the entrance to the Aeroport walkway, my internal map showed. I hesitated, and Quinn's hand curled around my arm. The *bing* of an elevator arrival was followed by the whoosh of a door.

"Halt!" a man said, unmistakably a Blackguard.

I froze, just as I had a day ago, and in the next moment, my vision blurred. *What?* I felt floaty, but no sting—

"What are you doing in this elevator?" barked the Blackguard.

Quinn's arm held my shoulders, his mouth to my ear. "Shh, don't let them hear us."

What was happening? I couldn't see, I didn't understand, but Quinn exuded safety, so I pressed myself to him and waited for another jolt to take me into unconsciousness.

"W-we use this shortcut to the k-kitchen," answered a woman, her fear palpable.

"Not anymore. Get out of here."

The unseen man's tone was steel hard, making my stomach sink. But this nastiness wasn't reaching me somehow. I lifted my head—

"But," said a different man, "it's never been a problem before—yowch!"

"Off-limits. Understand?"

Quinn swiped his hand before us. The blurriness resolved.

Blessed Waters, I hadn't been stunned. He'd taken me to Lacuna again. He stared out.

I looked, too.

A couple of kitchen workers trotted by, the man pressing a hand to a black mark on the sleeve of his jumpsuit. Behind them stalked a Blackguard.

Seconds later, he pivoted and disappeared around the corner in the direction we needed to take to the Aeroport, saying, "That clears the elevators for us. Report the walkway as vacant with a functioning lock. Station those guys from the field—" The elevator doors closed on his words.

"We don't have much time." Quinn jerked me forward and around the corner.

My innards screamed along, then slammed into place seconds before we reached a set of double doors. "You...I didn't..." I gulped air.

"You did great. We're almost home-free." He pressed his palm to the keypad. Nothing happened. "It's not on the E frequency?" He tried several times, then removed the cover.

Home-free? I sagged against the wall. He'd dragged me in and out of Lacuna. I couldn't believe I was still in one piece. Unable to even chastise him, I watched while he stuck his fingers into the wires again. And again.

"No metal plate, but it's there, blipping—" He stopped. "*Hell!*" He covered his mouth.

Disbelief. Dismay, then fear rolled off him in quick succession.

I straightened, ready to flee, not sure what to do, but not wanting to move closer to this potpourri of alarm. "Quinn?"

His gaze flicked to mine. It narrowed. His jaw tightened, and abruptly the emotions cut off. He replaced the cover and took my arm. We retraced our steps around the corner, then without warning, the world blurred again.

He steadied me. It took some minutes gasping in that

burnt smell before I felt myself come together. "Don't you dare—"

"Eve. The report's out." He gestured to the wolf-hound.

I snapped my mouth closed. They were looking for us, all three of us.

"I can't risk the Blackguards finding us or hurting you again..."

A thread of fear wafted from him, but he drew a breath and it was gone. He couldn't guarantee anything a Blackguard would do. I rubbed my arms, noticing for the first time the black marks crisscrossing the shoulders and back of his shirt—stunner scorches. The burnt scent. He'd fought off the guard without succumbing.

"Besides, we're stuck. That lock? It changes moment by moment, a computational security that only opens to someone synced with the system."

What did this mean? His emotions were gone, under wraps. "So we hide?"

He shook his head. "We need help, someone on our side. And I *won't* let you get hurt again." His hand brushed my shoulder and his fingers fluttered at my neck.

Oh, Blessed—I should have known this would happen, keeping company with an E-run. I heaved a sigh, a mental one, for a 'torg couldn't move while a minister activated one's keypad. He accessed the files of my electronic components. Sequences of images, procedures, rules and more, shuffled like a deck of playing cards.

Couldn't he have just asked for my help?

Quinn selected a function program, and it fell into my database. Three seconds later, an internal click indicated he'd completed the process.

I gaped at the new notice scrolling across my view.

CLASS 1 BLACKGUARD FUNCTION INITIATED.

Quinn withdrew his warm fingers. I shivered and pivoted. Light from the viewing port lit his hardened features, but they gave no clues as to why he'd done this to me. Another directive did.

MINISTER UNDER STAGE RED3 THREAT. IDENTIFY BODYGUARD.

My lips opened, and I asked the question my new function demanded. "Who is safeguarding you?"

"I don't need anyone keeping me safe. It's your safety that concerns me."

ASSUME PROTECTION. IDENTITY LOCKED.

"You made me your personal bodyguard?" I hissed. "Now look here, Quinn..."

Confusion scrolled through his emotions like the instructions in my Blackguard function sub-vision. "No, I don't need—didn't realize—" He wiped a hand over his face, and then those dark pools of brown locked on my eyes. His stare shook my resolve to put him in his place, to make him return my function to the one the Docga had promised and I had fulfilled productively for fifty years.

Commitment—more like a sense of devotion— coursed from him. Now composed, he said, "This function gives you the skills to protect yourself if attacked, to fight back, to get us out of this facility. You're... I trust you, Eve. And you are going to have to trust me."

I shrieked, "Trust you?"

Quinn covered my mouth. "*Shh.*"

I slapped his hand away. "You don't *trust* me. I only made you *feel* like you do. That gift I have? Being able to 'read' people? That's not exactly what I do. I'm an emotional savant. I pick up on your emotions and sway them with mine." Or be swayed, as his...had been. His emotions cut off. I clutched my belly, regaining balance. "That trust you're touting? I instilled it when your grandmother was injured and I thought she was an Aardite. I did it so you'd let me help her. So you'd *trust* me to help her."

His face was as blank as his emotional readings, but his gaze never left mine.

"I'm not the person you think I am, Quinn. I'm not a good person to be a guard. I'm overstrung by emotions—mine and others. They can override me. A guard needs to be calm and collected in the face of danger. If everyone else is a mess, I will be, too."

Did he know he was a minister of this planet, or not? If he gave me—my function—an order, then I'd have to obey it, whether I wanted to or not. Even if my actions would harm someone. This was wrong, just...wrong.

Quinn didn't speak. I tried again. "My gift? I need it free to assess people, to judge at a moment's notice how they feel, what they might do. You have to believe me, it's better protection than a Blackguard function."

No emotion, no words, just the look on his face. Fi-

nally, he spoke. "You don't have to make a choice between your gift and the guard function. Use both to
protect yourself however you can, to stay safe while we
escape this mess—and beyond. Aarde's situation is deteriorating. The supposed inventory, reductions in
Dome personnel, a disgruntled 'torg compromising the
mission, the pending hornwort spore release. We E-
runs must resume our orders to advise operations on
G47, *threatened* operations."

Advise operations. He hadn't claimed the command
position, yet his voice had that distinctly commanding
tone.

I sucked in a breath. He was in denial, maybe a defense mechanism due to his head injuries. I didn't dare
aggravate his memories, but I couldn't resist telling
him, "You've remembered a lot more than *some*."

* * *

Hours later, I rounded the end of the main corridor into the back halls. With a dagger hidden in my boot, a
weapon belt weighing on my hips and a sword thump-
ing my thigh, I strode along in my new black polymer
armor, ignoring 'torgs who scurried out of my way.

They had no clue who I was beneath the lowered
helmet, nor did they care. I wore the garb of someone
of power. Ironically, my wish had come true—I now
wore a disguise. Impostor Quinn would never recognize me.

I'd have laughed if I weren't so blasted upset. It had

taken incredible control of my every nerve to follow Quinn's *reasonable request*, as he'd labeled it.

The Armory captain himself had conducted the scan, but after he confirmed my function, it was business as usual. The function code reading *Class 1 Blackguard* meant one thing—assignment to a minister. And since Quinn was in fact Minister Quinn, the staff had had no problem with him requisitioning a full outfitting for a new guard. Every Corps electorg acknowledged and accepted my new position. Except me, and I didn't have a say.

Within the interior rooms of the Armory, the staff had acted promptly, though in a bored and impersonal manner. A few questions got me the information that the new ministers—specifically Impostor Quinn—had requisitioned dozens of Blackguards in their short term on planet.

Measuring and fitting for the polymer armor had flown by, as did the thorough scrubbing of every inch of my skin. To my relief, I was deactivated for the final fitting—I did *not* want to think about the interfacing my new "garments" would have with my electronic implants. Or that every surface of my body from my collarbones down to my toes would be a dull, inescapable black. That is, until I was relieved of this function—and I would be relieved of it.

Afterward, a female team member showed me how to operate my second skin. While the full armor was an impenetrable barrier against even osmium alloy metals, its quality could be changed with a thought to rugged clothing, a lightweight jumpsuit and even dissolved into something like an artificial skin for bathing and other bodily functions.

Most interestingly, I no longer needed undergarments. The guard suit was comfortable and supportive, making my figure look far better than it ever had, which was nice, but not as handy for the provocative stunt I'd pulled this afternoon. No zipper.

Their last intrusion had been cutting my long hair to fit under the helmet. A hack job of a jaw-length pageboy was the limit of this department's creativity. My instructor suggested styling at Dome's hair salon, but after hours of being handled like a piece of equipment, I was ready to go home.

Calm yourself, Eve. This isn't the worst that's happened to you in life so far—get over it. I hustled past the kitchen, the aromas making my stomach growl, and down the deserted corridors. I slowed and hugged the wall. This time, I knew it was coming. Just as I reached the corner before the Aeroport walkway, a hand from nowhere clenched my forearm and tugged. A narrow slit widened, like the crack of a door, and I came apart.

I closed my eyes and let it happen—the sensation of being fluid, of floating as if I were traveling the Waters. Except for the anchor of the pinch at my arm, I imagined I would disperse with the slightest current of air and blow away to nothingness.

"Eve! Open your eyes and be *here*."

COMMANDER DIRECTIVE. OBEY.

I followed the function suggestion and opened my

eyes. The borders of the Lacuna wavered, and my stomach flipped.

"Be with us." His urging came from far away. "Touch me. Touch the dog. Bring yourself completely to me."

OBEY.

Yes, I agreed, it would be a good idea. But this was just so hard to believe. I tried, I really did. He shook my arm. His hand skimmed my shoulder and back. The wolfhound rubbed cat-like around my legs. My body— or pieces of it—went back to the hall, but not as myself—I was melting into a puddle.

Twin growls snarled at my ear and waist, both sounding like, "No!" My drifting particles jerked to one piece, one body grabbed from thin air. Squeezed. Clutched. Quinn's hands scrabbled over me, rough and insistent, pressing and pinching.

"Ow! Stop—"

"Blessed Air, Eve!"

Blessed Air. What a thing to say while the smell of his burnt clothing filled my nostrils. But this time I was grateful for it. I clung to him to catch my breath. His urgent handling settled to gentle stroking, and I pressed in, my lungs managing only the shallowest of breaths.

"I thought I'd lost—*shh,*" he hissed in my ear.

With the sharply fearful emotes coming off him, I stiffened. And listened to the distant argument.

Holding my body to his, Quinn hooked a finger to a bright spot on the surface and drew it closer. He peered out over my shoulder, leaving me panting at his temple.

The pressure of his arm squeezing me to his side was

both familiar and unsettling. His solid warmth, the beat of his heart. My traitorous body recalled all the good things about being with a man, the exciting things. A rush of raw feeling slammed me and my innards turned to hot, melted cream.

Clear thinking threatened to shut down. If I didn't do something quick, I'd jeopardize years of nurturing my defenses for the long haul, as well as the lives of many people I dearly loved. I could not be in a relationship right now. Particularly with this man, an E-run minister of the Biosphere Corps. The one who had reassigned my function and reconfigured my life.

Sucking a breath, I hooked my finger in the bubble and shunted it from Quinn's eye to mine. Every muscle in him went rigid, but I didn't care.

Two Blackguards stood in the intersection. They said a few more words, then parted, one going toward the walkway doors and one down the corridor ahead. He disappeared.

"The corridor is clear. Let go of me." The words sounded harsher than I'd meant them to.

"Sorry. You were...slipping away." He released me, but kept one hand manacling my wrist until I removed my helmet and glared him into dropping it.

"Don't you think I know that? It was terrifying. Don't ask me to come into Lacuna again."

"You may not have the choice." Quinn's tone held the same edge as mine.

D'dair. I just wanted out of here. But if I tried to talk now, I would cry, the last thing I wanted to do in front of my new commander.

The wolfhound nudged my hip. I squatted and pet-ted him, feeling around his collar until I found my ring where I'd strung it before leaving. I slid it back on my middle finger, rubbing the crystal furiously beneath my cupped hand. It took a few seconds, but then the hy-dro-vapors flowed through the polymer suit and into me. It still worked, even with all this synthetic crap coating me. Every muscle in my body sagged in relief, and I fell from the squat onto my rump.

Instantly, Quinn clenched my shoulders. "Eve? Are you okay?"

"May the Waters preserve me," I muttered under my breath. Then louder said, "Yes, but I'm ready to go."

EIGHTEEN

QUINN

Eve's glare said it all. She wanted as far away from me as possible. Her temper hadn't cooled, though for a moment there I thought—

Who was I kidding? Making her my guard, I'd severed any chance I had of winning her favor. But what choice did I have? The function would keep her safer than I could, and unless I assumed my responsibilities, neither we nor anyone else on Aarde would be out of harm's way. I had no one else to turn to, no one else to *trust*. I clenched my fists. Duty before self.

Not that my memories of that duty were exactly straight. Some would have been better left uncovered. Still others needed grounding. Like why my overactive intuition told me the sight of this...dog would please Graen.

I studied the wolfhound nosing at Eve while she collected herself and stood. My gaze met his, and my mind stuttered again. I pinched my eyes closed. The effort of trying to remember while we waited for Eve had sapped me.

I hadn't found the device Graen needed, but I had no energy left to search. Had I even heard her correctly? Maybe she hadn't meant "protect," but what else could she have meant? Best to return, regroup and make a new plan. The next attempt would benefit from a bodyguard—or two.

As efficiently as she'd done at the gate, Eve finagled her way into replacing a guard at one end of the Aeroport passageway. I joined her.

"I had to trade to take his tunnel duty, whatever that is," she muttered. She put her palm to the keypad.

The light flashed green, and I reached for the handle.

She blocked me. "There's a reason you have a bodyguard," she said coolly. "Let me perform my function."

Good point. I had to get used to using the protection, which was saving our asses. I followed her with... Calling this animal a dog didn't feel right.

When Eve checked inside the door at the far end of the walkway, her body stiffened. She closed it to a finger gap. "It opens into one of the bays. There's a transport ship between us and the Conducer, with three 'torgs working in the open hold at the back. They can see this door."

Was it unusual to have a ship here? What size was it? What were they doing? My mind reeled with questions, but again I had no background on Dome to answer them.

"Stacks of boxes line the bay to the right," Eve continued. "You should be able to duck along behind them to reach the far door."

"Good. Talk to them and get them facing the other direction so they don't have a chance to see me. Get a photo of what they're doing. Hold the door and I'll enter as low as I can. Four seconds." I squatted and wrapped my arm around the wolfhound.

To her credit, Eve did as she was told. I rolled over the threshold into Lacuna, and the wolfhound tumbled with me in silence, if not gracefully. We lay in our awkward heap, and I waited for a yell. When only the thud of Eve's retreating boots sounded, I scrambled up and polished a viewing port.

Before my eyes sat a U-97 interplanetary transport, the latest in—*damn!* I recognized the Universal vessel. I drew a sharp breath. I didn't have the time, but still I stared at the craft I'd toured. And recommended for use here, probably. Midsize with powerful antimatter engines designed for heavy loads in the ample hold with shifting or releasable ballast for increased maneuverability. She was a beauty, especially with Eve standing beside her chatting her heart out. Above the craft, arched beams supported the ceiling and ran to the floor to shape what must be an...an *octagonal* transport bay. An image formed in my mind's eye, forcing a confirming glance to the craft-sized exterior door. I'd been here.

Pain spiked through me. I winced. The first visit had been...agony.

The wolfhound nosed me, and I shook off the memory. I had to get moving.

As she'd said, boxes towered not ten feet to the right. I steeled myself and peeled out of Lacuna in a low crouch. The wolfhound beat me to the first stack, and we snuck from pallet to pallet positioned near the hold.

I paused at the final pile. Ahead, carts of nylon-netted panels and quilted packing blankets gave less cover, but they were better than nothing. Under the give and take of the echoing conversation, the dog led the way, and I followed until we'd rounded the bay's perimeter to the nose of the ship. Giving a glance over my shoulder to make sure the bulk of the triangular craft hid us, I darted for the doors and stepped us into Lacuna.

I took a minute to reconnoiter. This wasn't a random assortment of supplies or a leftover shipment stored in this bay. Neatly prepared for export, each cart tag and box had the same code scrawled across it: G2W-A.

Eve arrived and opened the door.

"What did you find out?" I asked as we advanced into the Conducer corridor.

"They're reconfiguring the last of the three transports for a Saturday departure. Those heavy boxes fit across the bottoms of stalls that will be rigged with five levels of net hammocks."

The Conducer's energy flowed over me. With one hand, I got a firm grip on the wolfhound and took Eve's hand in my other, but before I connected us to my cross-leap, I had to know. "What's the cargo?"

"They don't know, and they don't care. They've been promised a two-week vacation as soon as the ships depart."

NINETEEN

EVE

Zeffir Island

The familiar fragrance of our books hit me as soon as we crossed. Home. I was so happy to be home, I felt like hugging someone. But not Quinn, the turncoat. I stormed off in search of Evard, leaving Quinn and the wolfhound to follow or not.

We found my run-mate in the kitchen. If Evard and I had been alone, I would have thrown myself at his very willing chest and bawled. But we weren't, and before he'd put any thought into sizing up the situation, Evard opened his mouth.

"*Great Grünmann*, Evy! I imagine you had to disguise yourself, but did you have to pick that morbid outfit? Or should I ask who died and gave you a leg up the caste ladder?"

That killed my hugging urge. I stuck my thumb in Quinn's direction and shoved past Evard to the refrigerator. Ignoring the platter of sandwiches, I helped myself to a wedge of chocolate cake.

Quinn said, "Eve becoming a guard made it easier to leave."

Evard reached over me, grabbed the sandwich platter, selected one and pushed the dish toward Quinn. "Playing as a guard, what we called a *weardian*, helped you?"

Quinn darted a look to me. I bit off another hunk of cake.

"No one crosses a Blackguard," Quinn said. "She cleared the way to the Aeroport Conducer for our return with the...dog."

"Dog?" Evard looked around.

"Yeah, the—what happened to him, Eve?"

Clearly, Quinn could tell something was different about the animal. But like the scenario in which he believed he was advising operations—not a minister—this memory thread hadn't fallen into place. I didn't dare push it. "I guess he stayed in the shop."

Meanwhile, Evard finally caught up with my mood. He brought me a glass of milk and vibes of consolation. "Lighten up, Evy. It makes sense for you to masquerade as a *weardian*."

I sipped the milk. "Except it's not a masquerade. He expects me to protect him."

Evard peered down at Quinn. "Do you really?"

"Yes." He scowled over the sandwich, looking every bit the high-and-mighty Elite-run. "I downloaded the data functions. She's fully trained. If the need arises, Eve will perform as a Class 1 Blackguard, a bodyguard."

Evard gave me a questioning look.

I slapped my calf. "Dagger." Tapped a fingernail to each compartment of my belt. "Cuffs, a second stun gun disguised as a Docga phone, paralyzing-dart shooter, utility knife, empty—I'm supposed to get a Class 1 communicator from my..." *Minister.* I slid a disparaging glance at Quinn, who was suddenly busy stuffing his face. "Not only did they issue the equipment, I had a practice session for each to confirm my Class 1 data downloads, and passed the proficiency testing." I lifted the stun sword. "Want me to show you?"

Evard grinned at me. "One lone guard, a slip of a girl—"

"I am *not* a girl."

"Okay. One solitary woodland *weardian* does not an army make." He frowned, and shifted a glare to Quinn. "But who will protect your lovely grandmother?"

Quinn lifted a brow. "You volunteering?"

I nearly choked on my milk.

With a glare to me, Quinn faced Evard. "She's in danger. They directed the leads to bring us in, or they'll come get us. Dome is crawling with guards, and I still don't have the device to repair her. She's a sitting duck without help."

"I suppose—"

"Thanks." Quinn slapped a hand to my run-mate's shoulder, and he froze.

I grinned the entire half minute it took him to complete his little finger staccato on the keys. Then Evard came alert. "Welcome to the club," I said, my tone very close to a simper.

He shook his head, his tone as forlorn as his face. "*Grünmann!* Service to a granny."

That's right, *she* was. "I want to trade," I blurted out.

"Let me have her, and you take—"

Evard's head snapped up. "No way. I've spent hours working on that woman—"

"My point exactly. She's a woman. I'm a woman. Personal guards should be of—"

"Stop arguing." Quinn stepped between us, the look on his features fierce. We stammered into silence. "Thank you. Eve, download those photos and then find the wolfhound. Evard, get to Dome. Report to the Armory for a suit and weapons."

Evard's blue eyes popped. "No! My hair—"

"It'll grow back," Quinn said.

The burly man's jaw dropped. Horror rolled off him. "Gr-gr..."

Quinn didn't seem to notice. "Go, before any higher-ups realize there are a few too many new Class 1 Blackguards."

Evard couldn't form a word. I'd never seen my run-mate speechless. The loss of his beautiful blond hair would put him in a foul mood for months. *Months.* I had to intervene, not only for Evard's mental health, but my own.

I patted my run-mate's arm and murmured, "Let me." In fact, I relished the opportunity to assist the run-mate who'd stood by me over the years, especially since I'd appear to be doing it for *my minister.* In the face of Quinn's plans for me, nurturing my relationship with him was paramount. Being a Blackguard wouldn't kill me, but if Quinn discovered some of the things I'd done in my fifty years on Zeffir, he might permanently disable me.

Quinn didn't move willingly when I urged him through the swinging door into the hall. His body was rigid, his mouth tight, and his eyes had taken on a flinty edge I hesitated to test.

"We need Evard in this function. Don't argue with me."

I leaned in close and whispered, "I'm not." Gathering every agreeable, sympathetic and harmonious emotion I had, I pushed them onto him. I didn't have time for subtle.

Quinn's brow smoothed, and his jaw loosened a bit under my barrage.

Time to make my move. "I agree we need Evard as Graen's guard, but you have to insert an exception to the standard suit."

He firmed up his resolve.

D'dair, it wasn't working. I had to go all the way. I rested my hand on his shoulder and paused for my sway to sink in. "Quinn?" He warmed to me, but only slightly. "Evard prizes his hair. We can't do anything to alienate him. You want every person working with you to cooperate, don't you?"

"Of course."

The words agreed, but he fought me. He wanted to...keep the control? No. He wanted to be strong. No. Mature in his decision-making. That worked for me.

I said, "Can I tell you a little something about Evard?"

Quinn nodded stiffly, his hard gaze fixed on mine.

I stepped closer. "Evard's cooperation relies on his mood, and his mood is affected by how he views himself. Unfortunately, how good he thinks he looks on a given day determines how happy Evard will be."

"He'll get used to the look, and it won't matter."

He said the words, but he didn't believe them. I shook my head. "'Fraid not. That hair means the galaxy to him."

Quinn didn't answer. I stroked my fingers over his shoulder. His tight, muscular shoulder. His deep-brown eyes stared beyond me. His emotions weren't flowing— oh. The *minister* was accessing another part of his brain to deal with this. His left side. Excellent. With a logic override, we'd be able to work together.

Confusion washed back at me, and Quinn frowned. "You haven't complained about your haircut. Your hair was just as long and pretty as Evard's."

He'd noticed? In that moment, my heart fluttered happily. I squelched the feeling. I couldn't revel in the personal attention, even as tightly woven as our paths were becoming. Instead, I squeezed his shoulder with cooperation running through my fingers. "I'm not as invested in my looks as Evard is. Please, Quinn? Could you do this for him?"

"This isn't logical. There is no good reason I should make this exception. But..."

I held my breath. His emotions shifted to match mine.

"I'll rely on your assessment. I can key in the requirement 'blend with local population.' Evard's suit will be matched to his typical garb, the hair left to his discretion and the helmet adjusted to fit."

For what seemed like the hundredth time today, I sighed in relief. "Thanks."

"Thank you as well. It's important for us all to cooperate—"

I smiled, a ridiculous happiness blossoming with his words of agreement.

"—and after this talk, I feel better about working together. We'll make a good team."

Yes, a team. Close, bonding. Considering what we'd shared over the last twenty-four hours, we had a definite affinity... My body flushed. My head muddled. *Blessed Waters.* The swirl of attraction bouncing between us were entirely different than the base-level physical reaction I'd had in Lacuna with him.

I had to get away.

"Uh, yes, I think so, too." I stepped beyond our effusion and edged away. His proximity had caused it. That was all. "Shall I go find the wolfhound while you talk to Evard?" Before he could respond, I strode off through the bookshop.

TWENTY

QUINN

Compared to women, men were easier to please. Evard proved no exception when I relayed the outfit change Eve had suggested. The man had a fastidious quirk I just didn't get. He claimed it was due to living with women.

I didn't need to understand Evard. He would be Graen's problem—when she woke up. I rubbed my weary head. For all I'd done and learned today, I still didn't have Graen healed. I'd see Evard off, have a look at the photos of the hold of the U-97 transport and come up with a new plan to search for the device she needed. If I didn't fall asleep first.

I gave Evard a brief summary of our trip, including Quala's claim the hornworts were to release spores sooner than expected, and then accompanied him to the Conducer.

"You have my most heartfelt thanks, Quinn," he said. "I'll search the lab results when I return, which reminds me." From an inner pocket of his jacket, he extracted a porta-scan. "Dome issued a planet-wide special report. You should see it."

Special report? My mind flipped through the possible euphemisms and landed on *warning*. We stopped

177

between the bookcases. "When was it released?"

"A half hour after you left."

"Then this report has nothing to do with our activities in the ministers' suite," I said, mostly to myself, as he tapped the screen several times then held it out.

"No, and I've kept a watch for additional reports, in case you two..." He smiled. "I seriously doubt they'll issue a report on a breach of the Elites' inner security."

"Only if we'd been apprehended." I peered at the frozen image on the screen and, in a wave of déjà vu, tapped the symbol of an arrow, thankful my knowledge of the device's operations returned. I didn't want to admit my equipment blank-outs to this technophile.

"This special report just in." The suited newscaster held out a porta himself while maintaining eye contact with the camera. "Authorities have confirmed the misuse of a Docga Conducer Monday morning in Cavvert. The incident involved two individuals, a young man of approximately twenty-five years of age and an elderly woman, likely in her sixties. When questioned by a city guard, the woman attempted to answer, but the male punched the guard—"

"I did not!"

"—and ran, forcing the woman to go with him. The man gained access to the Conducer and managed to escape, damaging the unit in the process and preventing pursuit."

"Huh, convenient explan—what's this?" A new image filled the screen. Mine.

The newscaster said, "This picture was taken during

the getaway."

Yeah, that was Cavvert's limestone station, and that was my face, but the expression was too harsh. I hadn't lashed out in anger, only fear. "My face has been dubbed in."

"And a fine likeness it is of you."

"Too fine," I muttered as my face grew to fill the screen. The unruly hair could certainly be mine, but the fuller beard was one I'd never managed to grow.

"Docga authorities are asking for cooperation of the native and electorg populations in finding this dangerous criminal. Do not approach the man. He has proven to be violent and unpredictable and is believed to be holding the woman hostage. Report your tips to..."

He rattled off a link, and the segment ended. I handed Evard the porta. "I wonder how they changed the expression on my face?"

"Er..." Evard shot me a strange look and then poked the screen. "Another shorter clip appeared at the start of the evening news."

The scene was a busy hallway. Electorgs in their trademark green jumpsuits flooded from a door, followed by a Blackguard and then a brown-haired man flanked by two more guards.

"Minister? Minister Quinn?" called an unseen reporter. The image jerked as a black-clad arm swept across the view, and it appeared the group would continue on until the reporter said, "A word about Cavvert's Conducer vandal and how much the man looks like you."

The minister jolted to a halt and swung to the camera, his face filling the screen.

It was me. "What the hell?" I jabbed my finger at the virtual buttons along the edge of the picture and froze it. The minister was me. Or what I would look like in ten years—rather, aged up.

Evard cleared his throat. "She did, er, tell you?"

I jerked my gaze from the sophisticated image of myself in a neat, dark green minister's suit to his intent stare. "Tell me what?"

He pointed lamely to the screen.

She? Did he mean Eve? "She told you?"

"Well..." Evard looked distinctly uncomfortable, the first I'd seen him this way. "He's a dead ringer for you."

"How dare she keep this from me? She's my *body-guard*—"

"That's a very recent development. Knowing Eve, there must be a reason. Ask her."

"Yeah, let's do that." With him following, I marched to the rear of the bookstore where Eve had gone to look for...*the dog,* damn my memory.

"Evy," Evard boomed, and she emerged from the lab holding a few papers. "Quinn here wants to ask you about Impostor Quinn."

I held out the porta bearing my...his image. "Quala said this man was pretending to be me, but not that we're goddamn clones. Apparently, you knew."

She threw a worried look at Evard, who shrugged. Her gaze flicked from the image to me in a pleading manner, while her hands rolled the papers to a tight cylinder. "Please don't be upset that I kept the information from you. I met him on my first reconnaissance trip. When I returned, Evangeline deactivated you, and then I deactivated her. Evard and I had to decide whether to trust her, those ministers or you. On top of the bizarre orders coming down from Dome, your system seemed questionable, your memory unreliable..."

She looked at Evard in that private, longtime-run-mate manner they used. "We chose you. I went with you to Dome and... Here we are." She bit her lip. "We haven't had time to stop and talk about everything you probably should know."

Evard inclined his head to me. "Does this change things?"

It took me just a moment to decide. "Oddly, no. I still want to work with you two."

"We'll guard you wholeheartedly," he said, and Eve nodded. "You have our word, regardless of what other issues arise."

"You saw enough of him to trust me instead?" I said to Eve.

"Yes, I more than *saw*—I used the savant gift I told you about. His emotions are quite un-electorg-like."

I wanted to take her word, but feelings were gut reactions, not methodically researched conclusions. To place that much faith in what came down to an organic response was illogical, unlike the careful analysis had served me well during our weeks in hiding.

Logic. It's your strength, Quinn, Graen always said. Of course, when I accessed that part of myself, I functioned...differently. As a machine.

"Quinn?" The papers crinkled in Eve's hands. "I can explain, if you give me a chance."

"Go ahead."

"Impostor Quinn views himself as superior to everyone else. Worse than just the E-run versus B-run thing all 'torgs feel. He doesn't believe anyone rates as highly as he does. He has sweet-talked his guards into believing they're on the right side of things, but I sensed that underneath it's a game to him."

"A charismatic?"

"Not quite that influential." She arched an eyebrow. "Not like me, if that's what you're thinking. He just has a way with spin, as Evard calls it."

"Ah, got it." I was relieved this impostor couldn't do anything like Eve's mysterious gift. He was hot air. Easily popped. But even better, my bodyguard used reason to justify her *feelings*.

And she clearly didn't think highly of the man who looked like me.

"There's more. I not only saw enough of him to draw these conclusions, he saw enough of me." She told me what else had happened on her first trip to Dome.

That's why she'd changed her appearance today. She'd been willing to take me to their quarters despite a minister's directive that would have gotten her hauled off and thrown in confinement. "Regrettably, right now he holds all the power. Until I get Graen functioning, I'm not sure what we can do to counter him."

Evard nodded. "I'll have the Blackguard accoutrements to assist."

"First, let's see the rest of this." I punched the back-up arrow on the porta and held it out so the three of us could watch.

Once more the reporter said, "A word about Cav-vert's Conducer vandal and how much the man looks like you."

I studied my older self as he glared into the camera.

"Unfortunate coincidence. Or is it?" I, uh, *he* said. "I don't know what this man hopes to gain by shutting down one of the continent's most popular tourist at-tractions, but add kidnapping and impersonating a Bio-sphere Corps minister to his charges and I'm forced to scour G47 for him to protect us all, native and elec-torg." My look-alike pivoted on his heel. His guards closed around him, and they stalked off.

"*I* shut it down? He'd commandeered the entire sys-tem before we arrived that morning. What does *he* hope to gain by that accusation?"

"He's effectively made you public enemy number one." Evard cleared his throat. "To send you into hiding or jail. Either will keep you out of his way."

I frowned at what sounded correct to my tired brain and handed him the porta-scan. "It's his face, too.

"He doesn't plan to stick around."

"How did you arrive at that conclusion?"

"Eve and I couldn't find a single bloody photo of the man a day ago. No wonder they 'never got around' to rescheduling the Greeting Reception. If he's kept his face—all their faces—secret since their arrival, don't

you think allowing himself to be seen on public broadcast is suspicious? He's decided to 'out' himself. And
why not if he's about to leave?"

I stared at the man making more logical conclusions
than I was. "Saturday, the transport mechanics said."

Eve gasped. "But he's only just had his power threatened with your appearance. What was his plan for
Aarde?"

Evard snorted. "What was his plan for all of us?"

Three transports leaving. The holds reconfigured
with stalls for boxes and hammocks above. My racing
mind slammed to a halt with a gut-wrenching realization: on old-time sailing ships, hammocks provided
beds in tight quarters. Could this modern design accommodate hundreds of electorgs? "He might manage
it if he's charismatic enough to convince 'torgs to accept the cramped quarters," I thought aloud. "But
would many willingly agree—*hell!*"

"The impostor minister doesn't need our agreement
if he *deactivates* us," Evard snarled through Eve's broken cry. For a moment, the horrific word echoed along
the hallway. The air about us grew cold with desolation,
a sick sense of doomed loneliness falling—

Evard jerked back, hands held high as if warding off
an attack. "*Grünmann*, Evy, stop!" He swatted the air—
and Eve's bad feelings—from the space among us. "It
hasn't happened. It won't."

"Why would he do this to volunteers?" she whispered.

"Agreed. Being a political hostage wasn't in my second life's contract." The big man sighed and gingerly pulled my armor-coated guard into his arms. "Or a slave," he muttered.

No. Never. Time to muster what resources we had. I mentally shifted to developing a course of action. Still, my gut churned as my gaze met Eve's, her face pale above the black suit. "I need those photos of the transport hold."

Her gaze dropped to the crumpled papers she held in her trembling hands.

TWENTY-ONE

QUINN

While Eve went to reprint the photos, I walked Evard to the Conducer again. The normally upbeat man was decidedly down. As an E, I should have had some positive words for him, but right now the best I had to offer was, "I'll do all in my power to stop the transport."

"I believe you will try, but it's a handful of us against..." He nodded glumly. "Say, on a more positive note, while you were gone I worked up a way to access any room at Dome. You can return to search for the protection device with no risk of capture."

I stopped him. "How's that again?"

"I plotted Dome's coordinates in four dimensions to derive specific landing points within the structure, enabling us to bypass the standard routes. Since you can go into Lacuna, I figured this would be a piece of cake."

I could go back to the office suite? Or the transport bay? "You're serious?"

"I am. I just need the access point in our circuitry to test it."

The man was a self-motivated planner—perfect for Graen. "Great news, Evard." Should I postpone his trip to get armored? But once Evard had the circuit location, the two of us would want to test it, and without him prepared to defend us...

"We have to wait. If caught, your scan would show functions beyond research, leading to questions why. Besides, until both Graen and I can make the trip, the risk isn't worthwhile."

"Then we'll give this a go after I'm outfitted?"

"Absolutely. Be careful and hurry back." I shook his hand.

"I will." He stepped into the Conducer. "At least I'm not on the impostor's radar."

Impostor Quinn, as they called him. His broadcast image came back to me. The older man was good-looking. I ran a hand over my scruffy beard. Perhaps if I shaved, Eve—

"Evard?" He turned back. "Is Eve..."

"Angry about being made a guard? The girl will come around. Have no worries about her loyalty to the Docga mission."

"No, I...that's good, but not what I meant. I wanted to ask, is she attached to anyone here?"

His burst of laughter startled me. "My man, Eve is *attached* to everyone on Zeffir. But if you mean does she have a lover, no, she doesn't. I wish you well in that court. You'll need it."

Still laughing, Evard gave a two-finger salute, strode through the shelves uttering titles in quick succession and disappeared.

You'll need it didn't sound too promising. And what about my phrasing of the question was so comical?

I threaded my way through the stacks to the lab where Eve looked up guiltily from a stack of photos. She grabbed a last one from the printer and came to meet me, extending the transport hold photos.

"Thanks." I sorted through them, hardly focusing on the metal configurations. I was torn by the gulf widening between us. I wanted to fix it, but my gaze fell on the empty table where Graen had been.

"She's upstairs," Eve said. "Evard moved her to one of the guest rooms. I'll show you." She led the way up the central staircase.

The house was abnormally quiet. I found myself clenching the photos and holding my breath as we walked along the upper hall. If I could link with Graen again, maybe I'd gain another clue to the protection device. With all I'd discovered today, I needed her calming reassurance we could handle what we had to.

Something hit the floor with a *thunk* from behind an ajar door. In a flash, Eve pulled her stun sword and bounded forward, but before she reached it, a black, wiry-haired head poked through the opening.

Eve released her breath. "This is where you'd taken yourself." She reholstered the short sword.

He rumbled deep in his throat, the sound peculiarly like an answer, but my heart stopped at the familiar call of "Quinn?" I beat Eve to the door and found Graen propped with pillows in the center of a double bed.

She recognized me. Until now, I hadn't realized my biggest fear had been that both of us would lose our memories and be...lost. She smiled and held out her arms to me, her green eyes bright, though tired. The warmth of her hug enveloped me, and I allowed relief to join it.

"You're better. Graen, you have no idea how glad I am to see you functioning again."

"Functioning? I see you believe me now." She chuckled, and I joined her.

Believed her? Hell, I'd used my *function*, in ways I'd not imagined a day ago. I backed carefully from our embrace and looked around for Eve, but she'd closed the door behind me. The wolfhound paced around the bed. On the opposite side, he leaped up and lay down, fixing his gaze on me. I gestured to him.

"My spoils from our trip to Dome. Perhaps you can enlighten me on why I remember—hey." Above the collar of Graen's rumpled blouse, the scar on her neck had disappeared. "Evard fixed your wound? I can't believe he didn't tell me."

"Evard?" She looked from me to the wolfhound. "No, you're responsible, Quinn. Finding and rescuing PT on your first visit to Dome shows me you've stepped up to the job despite what must have been a startling discovery. PT replaced the damaged components and resealed the epidural layers." She stroked her neck. "Good as new, don't you think?"

"Who is PT?"

The wolfhound rumbled deep in his throat. Graen looked at him as if listening. The rumbling did have the cadence of vocalizations. I *had* heard this before... But it'd been...words.

Blessed Air. I pressed my fingers to my forehead as aspects of this creature popped into place. The Docga were...dogs. Well, not *dogs*. They were creatures who presented themselves as dogs to ease our humanoid sensibilities.

I sank onto the bed, unable to take my eyes off the Docga pro-tech. "I can't understand him, but I remember. You sent me for our *pro-tech*, not a protection device. A *proficient technician*, a specialist in the medical and electronic needs of the new E-IV system."

She squeezed my hand. "Yes, that's correct. PT has trained beyond the med-tech level. I'm thrilled with the changes, but I've had to keep a tight rein on my comments with your lapse."

She expounded on the upgrades of our newly installed system—enhanced healing, additional functions, RAM—and my head jiggled together other fragments. I'd agreed to the conversion as part of my Corps assignment to the G47 mission, back during R&R—a month-long break all 'torgs had between missions. Between debriefings and psych testing, I'd soaked up some rays, roared about in an aerocar, hooked up with—

Oh, damn. There had been a woman. I shelved that for later musing—alone. My gaze met Graen's. "Our conversion and R&R happened where?"

"Reboot. A Docga facility leased on W234, locally called Schiftan."

No wonder I had *forgotten* the name.

She smiled. "This is the first significant upgrade in

the Elite class in its hundred-and-eighty-four-year history. Let's hope the B-run upgrade doesn't take as long to implement—oh, dear." She patted my arm.

I clamped my gaping jaws shut. "How long...have 'torgs been around?"

"The Docga developed the technology nearly three centuries ago and spent decades perfecting the prototypes that combined the humanoid organic system with their advanced electronic components. I believe the first volunteers were battle casualties, so damaged that they had no hope in their times. But, Quinn, really, this isn't the time to go into that history. Let's stick with the E-IV change and us. The Docga conducted trials, of course, but any new system can have its problems. As a precaution, the PT specialist joined our quintad for our time on G47."

"Quintad?"

"That hasn't come back?" She frowned. "I've never wanted to push your memory return—never had a reason to, without success in finding Quil, but..."

I waved her silent. "Now we no longer have the luxury of waiting for my amnesia to fix itself. I'll let you know if I need a break." The words were bold, but inside I steeled myself. "In fact, please start with your actual name."

She smiled the kind, understanding smile I'd come to love. "Quaene. You're welcome to continue using Graen, if you prefer."

I shook my head. "I've adjusted enough in the last two days to stand on my own feet without a grandmother's assistance. I think I can manage an adult name as well."

"Excellent," she said, but her eyes watered.

Lacking anything handier, I offered her the corner of the sheet.

She dabbed at one eye. "Thank you. So, there are—were—five of us. Myself, Quala, Quetta, Quil and you, Quinn."

I sucked a breath at the names I'd heard at Dome, but since I wasn't looking Quala in the face, my mind wasn't straining to remember. "I met Quala today."

Graen, er, Quaene's eyes grew round, and the Docgan rumbled throatily beside her.

"Sorry, I no longer understand him." I touched my head.

PT made another vocalization, and she nodded. "Something may have gone wrong with the interface of the new system. He'd noticed behavior changes in you and both the other women during the trip here and re-grets that he put off running diagnostics. But Quala let you leave without raising an alarm, so perhaps she's not involved."

"She claimed she's taking herbs to avoid his...influence, I think was her word. She also said Im-postor Quinn has stymied her on the hornwort treat-ment. She seemed frustrated."

Quaene nodded. "This sounds like Quala from the R&R, immersed in her botany."

"I don't remember anything of her." I rubbed my temples. "But PT detected no E-IV problems in you or

Quil, who I gather is not technically my brother."

PT rumbled, this sound harsher than the last.

Quaene's reaction of exasperation confused me. "No, not in us, and as PT bluntly said, it would have been an improvement in Quil's case."

Now it was my turn for surprise. "The guy we've spent weeks tracking down is—"

"Difficult to work with, to say the least—or he was during our short time together. His last mission termination was delayed by weeks. It meant Quil dragged in the day before the conversion, his humor worsened by seeing you with... You two did not get along."

She backpedaled, but I got a memory flash indicating it had to do with the woman I'd remembered. "Still, with his complaints, you've sought him?"

"Actually, his moodiness led to my trust in him. The short version is *he* suggested leaving the others, but we were separated, as I've told you." Her finger tap to her temple signaled she felt the story was more than my damaged memories could handle.

I'd let her keep her reasons to herself, same as I held back on a few of my fragments. I told her about meeting the Zeffir Post triad, and the Corps-wide inventory that Evard maintained was a recall. Then I described the Dome visit, including the guard shocking some memories and my 'torg functions into operation, my acquisition of bodyguards and my discovery that this rogue 'torg looked like me.

Impostor Quinn's looks surprised Quaene, but of course she'd had no more access to the ministers than the B-runs. "I've suspected he's a disgruntled former G47 minister."

PT rumbled, and Quaene translated. "His question is, how did this 'torg adopt your looks? Did you have a twin, or siblings?"

I laughed, though it wasn't funny. "As our tri—quintad lead, you'd probably know better than I would at this point."

She nodded sadly. "Aside from how he's done it, what could have gone so wrong during his term to make the 'torg return and sabotage the hornwort-monitoring program?" She told PT what our travels and the news had revealed of the growing hornwort threat.

"Why, though?" she asked, not the first time I'd heard the question. "The biologist triads should have adjusted their activities. Some new nutrient has to be fueling the plant's growth, yet they don't undertake the simplest procedures to ensure safety..."

Her anger mounted with the tirade, and suddenly I got it. "That's why you were so furious, why your anger at the admin 'torgs and their Blackguard staff spilled into me. They were failing *our* mission, and your hands were tied."

She huffed out a breath. "Was it that strong?" She composed herself and apologized. "I feel horrible for the Aardites. Until we retake our positions, I can't get to the resources to figure it out."

"Perhaps Evard will turn up something when he looks into the lab." I told her about the hornworts lacking sporophytes in the Atrium and then picked up the photos I'd abandoned on the nightstand. "Eve and I stumbled across evidence of a substantial export—a theft—in the Aeroport. Here are the images Eve got. Aside from the boxed cargo—"

"Boxes?" Quaene lunged upright in bed, her gaze sharpening. "Like those in the Cavvert station?"

I slapped my forehead. "Exactly like them. And obviously as heavy, since that portion of the shipment is designated for the floor."

"What resource would be particular to Cavvert?"

"Not just Cavvert. Conducers can transport cargo from anywhere on the planet, right to the three bays. I'm sorry we didn't check the other two. I'm sure pallets lined them as well, but frankly, the boxed mystery cargo doesn't concern me the way these do." I pointed to Eve's clear image of a rack, its support bars and hooks. "These structures are designed to hang hammocks seven deep. Given the electorg recall, I suspect the *resource* theft also involves kidnapping 'torgs."

She gasped and promptly shook her head. "Then why a massive recall? They can't squeeze six hundred and fifty-some 'torgs into this space—"

"Deactivated? Wrapped and stacked like goods? Using the pictured worker for scale, I calculate three to a hammock. At seven hammocks per stall, ten stalls per transport and with three transports, that yields space for six hundred and thirty. A very cramped, inhumane space, but nonetheless, they'd fit. And think how efficient it is to take them all at once."

Her eyes narrowed. "I'm afraid it can't be that simple. The Docga Empire is strong. No foreign republic would be foolish enough to harm the Docga's people."

"No?" I murmured at her patent denial. "I'm sorry, but all evidence points to it."

"Was there anything else you observed in the ministers' quarters?"

"Just what I told you. Nothing stood out other than the rack of native clothing and the map—oh. You should see the map." I stood up. "I'll get that copy from Eve."

PT nosed Quaene's arm and gave a brief rumble.

"Something to eat also, if you will, Quinn. He's reminding me I'll need sustenance before a nap. After that, he wants a more thorough check of my system. We've made good progress here. Together with the bodyguards you've acquired, we'll ensure the safety of the 'torgs under our command."

"C-command," I choked out.

TWENTY-TWO

QUINN

How stupid to miss the logical conclusion of many clues. I was in fact Minister of Facilities. *I* was a relatively new E-run, and a trainee in my position, something not announced outside of the quintad. Apparently, Impostor Quinn had claimed he was the replacement lead, and the others must have had to agree to the charade.

Our actual lead was Quaene, Minister of Development. The mission's other operations were divided out to Quala, Minister of Biological Resources; Quetta, Minister of Electorg Resources; and Quil, Minister of Technology, a specialist returning to overhaul the systems he'd installed seventy-some years ago.

Now that I fully understood, acknowledging and accepting my position with Quaene was logical. We had to act, with or without our run-mates, to maintain the security of electorgs on G47. The planet's recovery and the Aardites' well-being depended it, but just as important, the electorgs depended on it. On me. I had responsibility for six hundred and fifty lives, including that of the woman silently trailing me to the kitchen.

Eve helped prepare food and hot tea and then followed when I carried dinner upstairs. She opened the bedroom door, but kept her arm extended across my path. "Do you want this now?" She held out the roll of paper. "The map from the impostor's office?"

Oh, damn. I'd forgotten. I did my best to smile. "I appreciate everything you are doing for us. Thank you." I lifted an elbow, and she slid the paper roll under it, but didn't let go.

Her eyes searched mine. Their soft gray had warmed with a hint of gold. "You mean that, don't you?"

I blinked. Why would she think otherwise? "I do."

She nodded and let go of the paper. "You're welcome." She closed the door behind me, and her footsteps retreated across the hall.

After Quaene and I ate, I unrolled the map, and we spent several minutes studying the excellent copy Eve had—I did *not* want to think of her this way—produced. We had been to many of the map's marked towns and cities, including Cavvert, labeled green, five. "What do the numbers and colors mean?" I asked. "Do you detect any commonalities?"

"Traditionally, green indicates all clear and red, stop."

"Yellow would be caution? As in our current location?" I pointed to Zeffir.

"Perhaps they have studied these communities, set up programs for them or infiltrated them using the native costumes you discovered. Of the marked locales I recall, there is no correlation in size or level of native development with the numbers. But I'm having difficulty thinking today."

"Of course. We've talked far too long. While you nap, I'll prepare a spreadsheet of these locations and their numbers. Perhaps with them in numerical order—"

PT rumbled sharply. Quaene started to interpret, but I stood. "I get that. I'm going."

The wolfhound uttered another long string of throaty sounds. Quaene licked her lips. "When he finishes my work, he'll address your memory functions. However..."

"Don't get my hopes up?"

Her forehead creased into fine lines of worry. "You sustained molecular trauma during our cross-leap escape—being jerked around while dissolved. PT hasn't had experience in that area, but he suspects organic damage."

"Because my memories have continued to return on their own?"

"Yes. Every occurrence of recall is positive, and your electronics should be fine since you've had no problem mind-linking." She cast a look at the pro-tech and raised a finger. "One more important item to discuss. The E-IV system upgrade includes a new fail-safe, one done via mind-linked frequencies. The additional safety measure requires three Elite-runs to administer an override signal that will disable another E-run. That's why we've searched for Quil, a third E-run, to mind-link with us."

Ah, in the previous system a single E could shut down a B-run, but not an E.

"After PT runs your diagnostics, he'll reacquaint us with the fail-safe procedure. Then the two of us can link with Quala at Dome." The moment she said that, her jaw tightened.

It was a sign I recognized. "You're not sure we can trust her?"

"Are you? You said your focus was on escaping her. I hardly knew her, whereas Quetta and I worked together several times over the decades before we were reunited with this quintad, so of course I trust her before new run-mates. During our week on the transport to G47, one after another we, and the crew, got a stomach bug. You were in the sick bay after the stabbing, and decided to remain with PT to avoid your cabin mate, Quil."

"The *stabbing*?"

She rolled her eyes. "I'm failing at keeping the details out now. It happened our last day at Reboot. Do you want to—"

"No." My typical recall pain sparked at her reference. "Unless it relates to this?"

She shook her head. "Quala retreated to her beloved plant projects and took over your duties when PT insisted your contributions be limited to staff roundtables. I was grateful for her efficient assistance, but later realized we never got to know the solitary woman. Nor Quil, who spent every free minute at his workstation, fixated on rechecking 'the integrity of his systems.' He never showed the inclination to be a go-getter."

"Huh? You said the guy was slated to overhaul G47's computer systems."

"I didn't say he couldn't do it, just that I had to prod the 'torg. Look, under normal circumstances I wouldn't discuss my personnel management issues, but we have some tough decisions to make regarding 'torgs I know little about."

PT thumped his chin on the bed, and she nodded to him absently. "For days after our escape, I wished I had dear old Quetta to help me. But wishing was pointless, and I had you."

I snorted. "Me, a damaged, half-functioning—"

"Intelligent. Resourceful. Innovative. A collaborator in our time of need. A *friend*."

Tears filled her eyes. They threatened to fill mine. "I... Thank you."

"Thank you. We'll do this, Quinn. We have—when is this triad's inventory appointment?"

"Friday at two in the afternoon."

"We have two days to solidify our plans before Dome notices this Post's electorgs are missing. It gives them time to acclimate to their new functions and complete a few training exercises under PT's direction. And Lacuna training under yours. Please bring our bodyguards up to date on everything we've discussed."

I returned the dinner things to the kitchen and put them away with Eve silently helping. Until I started washing the dishes.

A chair scraped behind me. She fell into it and commenced an irritated tapping on the table. Finally, she sighed. "I'm doing my best not to pry, but there's too much at stake. We're either in this together or not."

She didn't need to tell me. I was now fully aware of my function and mission. Painfully so. The impostor's imposed schedule left no time for me to adjust to my new situation, though my sub-vision directives were speeding my recall. In spite of the weeks of hints Quaene had fed me—our discussions of Docga policy and role-playing *what if you could decide?* on each search trip—something in my damaged brain had kept the truth from sliding into place. Even of a stabbing I had no memory of. I suspected it, the cross-leap mishap and our loss of command were all connected, but the memories jumbled in terrifying images from my shock-therapy encounter with the guard.

I was too scattered to analyze the theory and too worn to continue. Shaking the water from my hands and drying them on a towel, I delayed turning until I made sure my visage had remained at its thirty-year maturity. Eve's gaze met mine, concern in her gray eyes and tight features. Relief flooded me. I wasn't burdening her, so much as sharing as a partner might—

What am I thinking? Protecting me was her function now. I sank into another chair and told Eve what I'd just learned.

"Since you and Quaene are E-IV run-mates," Eve said, "what special roles have the Docga assigned you?"

I saw through her ploy immediately. Eve, in her gentle way, was easing the conversation in case my memory hadn't retrieved this fact. "Ministers overseeing G47."

Her audible sigh confirmed she'd known.

Made my life easier. "A quintad. Unfortunately, there are three ministers residing at Dome. Quil isn't one of them, or a danger. Quaene saw him leave before we did. Quinn is obviously an impostor, but the others..." I shrugged. "We need to find out who we can trust before those transports remove all six hundred-some deactivated electorgs from G47."

"You don't have proof," she whispered.

"There is enough circumstantial evidence to draw the conclusion," I countered. "And we'll be returning to verify." Evard had smoothed that opportunity with his plotting work-up of Dome's coordinates, but I wouldn't get into an explanation. Not now. "Frankly, this day has been more than I anticipated. I need time to recharge." I frowned. Where had that phrasing come from? "I'm tired. Is there a room I can use?"

Eve led the way upstairs and opened a door down from Quaene's. "Consider this room yours. The bath is through that door." She pointed to the far corner beyond the room's twin beds.

I stepped inside. It looked more inviting than the table I'd been laid out on. My lovely sub-vision system messages scrolled protocol about bodyguards bunking with ministers when danger levels pass certain... We'd surpassed every risk marker. I stared at the second twin bed. My body flushed, my *feelings* clamored, my aging slip—*no!*

Before learning of my command, I would have given

in to my desire and plotted a move. Now, I couldn't act humanoid. I steeled my willpower. My electronic functioning clicked into place. Suddenly, the need to sleep became my foremost concern. When I lay down, I would be out, protected by my guard, whose respect I wouldn't jeopardize by losing my professional persona. I gestured for Eve to enter our room so I could close the door.

Her eyes grew wide, and her lips moved in what could only be "No."

"At Red3 Alert, the bodyguard remains with the minister," I repeated from my too-sophisticated E-IV system, which also relayed the directive from her internal database.

But Eve backed up.

My system flashed.

BLATANT DISREGARD OF FUNCTION DIRECTIVE.

Damned warnings. Yet, I shouldn't override the function, not with my determined look-alike searching me. "Eve, you need to—"

"My room is across the hall." She stepped in that direction. "Call and I'll hear you. Uh, Minister Quinn."

Minister Quinn? We were taking things to that level on top of this hassle? Great. "Just Quinn."

RECOMMEND CORRECTIVE ACTION.

"You do understand that's the problem? My system dictates the guard—you—remain with the E-IV—me—whenever the risk level exceeds Yellow3." I reached to redirect her.

She leaped aside, and my fingers closed on air.

IF CORRECTIVE ACTION IS NOT—

With a groan, I pressed my fingertips to my aching temples and searched for the connection...and found a way to silence the internal calls, but not the lettering in my sub-vision. "Damned messages." I looked up at Eve.

The surprise on her face was genuine. Why? Similar mental stimuli must be assaulting her.

She cleared her throat. "We're quite safe here, on Zeffir."

I was *not* taking a chance. I stepped forward. "Given the situation at Dome, the security function of your Class 1 guard system dictates regular checks with mine." I advanced another step. "It's protocol."

Eve backed up. "Protocol can be altered."

Like the deviation with Evard's hair? No, this was different. She shouldn't even be able to consider re-fusal. Hell, what if she ignored a command I gave to keep her safe? My surprise gave way to determination. "Your guard functioning is amiss somehow. Let me fix it."

"There's nothing to fix." Slipping past me, Eve sprinted down the stairs.

DISCIPLINARY ACTION WARRANTED.

Cursed messages.

BODYGUARD AT LIMIT OF SECURE RANGE.

With lights flashing in my retina display, I jumped into action.

I tailed her through the store, out the front door and into the night. Up the cobbled main street we ham-mered. She darted down a side street. I followed. She cut through the dirt yard of a stable, bolted over a gate and fled through a field along a thread of smooth dirt. I pounded behind her.

Strings of new—or latent, perhaps suppressed?—information came to me. Eve was using the enhanced speed of a Class 1 Blackguard. If I wanted to catch her—

E-IV FUNCTION DESIRED? ACTIVATION PROCE-DURES.

A demo clip appeared. I slowed and jabbed at the spot on my outer thigh. Eve looked over her shoulder, saw my action and burst into the fastest gait available in her system, ten miles per hour.

Seventeen seconds later, I snaked an arm around her waist and jogged her to a stop against my chest. "Zero to twenty-five in fifteen seconds," I panted. "Duration, four and a half minutes, but adequate. To outrun an enemy. Or catch my prey."

"Damn your E-run-only features," she muttered with a glare, but then her yellow-tinted eyes froze in place.

I tapped my fingers across her keypad rapidly, then slowed as every diagnostic returned a normal result. Normal, except for a hum I detected in the overall system. Or rather, her body.

The air was frigid, and both of us were sweating, yet I had to get to the bottom of this. I released her from the suspension, but not my hold. I rested my fingertips on her warm neck and melded my gift into the strange harmonic waves coursing through her. "No system malfunction. Interference of some kind, a wavelength—"

Eve moved her hands together. The waves cut off.

"Why—what did you do?" I snatched up her hands and inspected them. She still wore the golden-colored crystal I'd seen on her left middle finger. "This ring. It's affecting your systems."

Her eyes widened. "No, it's not. You said yourself there's no malfunction."

"Take it off." I pulled at it.

Eve wrenched away. In a flash, her dagger pressed lethally to a pale throat. Hers. "The ring stays. Or I go."

ALERT! BODYGUARD THREATENING—

I dismissed the message. Blessed Air. She'd kill herself over a piece of jewelry? Maybe this emotional woman hadn't been a good choice. She acted as determined as I'd felt a minute ago. Now... I held up my hands and backed away. "Eve. Let's be reasonable. Please put down the knife. Talk to me."

"Not till you promise"—her breath rasped sharply—"to leave my ring alone. I won't allow it to interfere again."

Won't allow it to interfere. What in the galaxy did that mean?

She swallowed. Hard. A drop of blood welled around the dagger's edge. It trailed an ugly dark line across her pale skin and disappeared onto her polymer shirt. "I give you my word. You are going to have to trust me."

Trust! What the hell—

DEACTIVATE ERRANT BODYGUARD.

No, dammit.

I froze, afraid of setting her off, but inside I fumed.

Why did the issue of trust come up with every woman I interacted with? An explosion of pain lit my vision. *Damn. What thought caused that?* I squeezed my eyes shut, stopped thinking, stopped the hurt... I took a slow, deep breath... And returned to the present and logical analysis.

Careful now. Eve held the blade to her carotid artery, one of the few cuts that would kill a 'torg. I thought I trusted her. I'd put my life in her hands, after all. She'd stood by me. Odds were her reliability would continue. Evard, her run-mate, presented as honorable. Quaene had commended my choice. Logic said Eve would make a good guard.

But logic leaked away as another trickle of blood joined the first. *No.* How could she do this? What in my life would I kill myself over? Nothing. Right now, nothing was as important as having Eve by my side, to protect...no, just to be by my side. I couldn't lose her. Anything I had possibly done before paled in comparison to this one decision.

"Keep the ring. I won't touch it again. I promise."

Way too slowly, she lowered the dagger. Wiped the blade on her thigh. Slipped it back in her boot sheath. Without so much as a glance in my direction, she marched toward the village.

BODYGUARD AT LIMIT OF SECURE RANGE.

Permission granted to go. "What..." I took another deep breath. "What the hell was that about?"

Uncompromising devotion to a rock? Did she realize the power she gave me in placing so much value on an object? On the flip side, would the crystal endanger our plans? And how did such a...*thing* work with our electronic systems?

Clearly, Eve was no ordinary electorg. She possessed a power that rivaled my superior system and allowed her to override her prescribed function, one that should be under my control. More important, she had aligned herself with me.

And I...had reciprocated. I jerked into motion and followed, admiring this lovely, strong woman more than I'd thought possible.

TWENTY-THREE

EVE

Bang. Bang. Bang.

The pounding on Passages' front door diverted my path from the kitchen and my morning coffee. Quinn had gotten up as I left *our* room and wouldn't be far behind, so I should send this person on his way. I couldn't see anyone today. Not when I had an Elite-run minister to *guard*. One who felt his needs outweighed mine. Or my villagers'. If this were a serious concern, I'd send the Zeffirite on to...Taior?

To avoid scaring anyone, I tucked my helmet out of sight and peeked around the shade.

Crap. With all this, I'd actually forgotten my standing appointment. I let the shade fall and bent my head to the doorframe. Why couldn't she have sent a note?

Footsteps sounded behind me. Evard and...

MINISTER RETURNED TO SECURE RANGE.

Bang... I jerked my head from the jarring wood.

"Who is it?" Evard asked.

Behind him, Quinn stood closer than my function liked. What if it had been a stranger, or a contingent of Impostor Quinn's guards? I frowned at him, but answered, "Tristam."

Evard reached past me and undid the lock. "No getting around it."

"I suppose not." I opened the door.

"'Bout time, you layabouts." He leaned in and kissed me on the cheek. "Granny sent me to fetch you. The tea's been steeping for half—" He stepped back, ran his gaze over my fully armored suit and laughed. "What's this getup? Off to wrestle spiny gophers on the mainland?"

"Trist?" I had to get rid of him. "This isn't a good day. Please tell your grandmother—"

"Oh, pardon me. I see you have company."

He knew we had *company*. Everyone in town knew.

And to confirm his status, Quinn skirted Evard and stepped over the threshold first, casting Tristam a stony look. Like he was coming to *my* defense.

"Aunt Eve." Tristam crossed his arms. "You know she won't be kept waiting a moment longer, and I'm sure observing the locals is part of his assignment as well." He looked at Quinn. "Have you had your breakfast? My grandmother makes excellent coffee cake."

Quinn shot me a speculative look. "I'd love some."

"Good. Coming, Evard?"

"Of course." Evard edged me out and closed the door. He and Tristam shook hands in greeting and hustled across the street swirling with snow.

Quinn put his hand to the small of my back and nudged me forward. "Can't wait to hear the explanation on this one, *Aunt Eve*."

Tristam must have said it. I hadn't even noticed. Great, it'd be hard to ignore this squalling cat. I brushed off his hand and followed the others into Sabein's busy tea shop. The *minister* had no right to touch me. But after last night's confrontation, I had to finesse handling this flat-out irritating, annoying—I shot a glare to Quinn and received such a sharp look in return that I stomped ahead to the back hall. D'dair. These emotions might not even be mine.

I allowed the ambience of Sabein's back parlor to envelop me the moment the door closed. The room full of overstuffed furniture and china knickknacks was familiar and comfortable. As Tristam promised, a cake along with the tea and coffee service sat on the low table centered before the fire. A settee and four upholstered chairs encircled it, ready for an intimate conversation. Or more likely an interrogation. But our hostess was absent.

The sooner I had my coffee the better. I perched on the settee and poured for everyone. Perhaps I could relax for a few minutes and forget what I'd become, what guarding this E-run might bring. Nonetheless, he couldn't blame me for whatever happened in this room. I'd tried to avoid it, but since he'd agreed to the meeting, he could navigate it.

Though, honestly, we couldn't dodge Sabein. After decades, my daily updates to the Zeffirite leader on Corps activities had become as much social habit as Docga policy. They'd started as a way for our triad to integrate into a community torn apart by Aarde's deaths and laden with survivor's guilt since they were untouched themselves. It had taken me years of mediation and harmonizing to ease attitudes. I'd considered it a mark of success when Zeffir joined the Alliance.

With my new function as a minister's bodyguard, my loyalties felt divided. I handed Quinn a cup and saucer, mindful of my obligation to inform him of Sabein's premier position in the community.

"Thank you," he said politely and plunked onto the settee, closer than necessary, but good for a private word.

I leaned in. He did the same, and his thigh pressed to mine. Our gazes locked. He'd matured to the age of the handsome Impostor Quinn and exuded the same self-assurance. Entangled with his fading irritation lay tendrils of protection—ironic, since he'd made me the guard—and attraction. Deeply possessive attraction. My heart raced.

I straightened with a start and picked up my cup and saucer. They clattered. I raised the cup and willed the drink to calm me. I had to keep myself safe. I shuttered my gift against this man's messages, which were more enlightening than Quinn intended and far more appealing than the impostor's. D'dair. *This* did not matter, because I was not going to enter a relationship with either one of them. This Quinn was our solution, and I needed to remember it. If he and Quaene pulled together a plan, we stood a chance of thwarting the mass abduction. Did I dare believe I wouldn't be forced to leave Zeffir?

I ventured another look. Quinn was shooting a speculative frown at Tristam. Fortunately, Trist was offering around generous wedges of coffee cake and intent on hearing Evard's opinion of a design he'd drawn on a scrap of parchment.

For a minute, we each forked bites of the moist, sugary treat. Eating limited talk on both sides, but if Tristam's *granny* didn't show soon, the conversation would resume, and if I knew Tristam, he would answer any question. If Quinn chose to ask one.

Then Sabein breezed through the door, her silky gold hair swinging about her shoulders and her tropical-print muumuu skimming her figure like a sheath. "A glorious morning, every... every..." She stuttered to a halt, staring at me. Her expression went deeper than contemplative when it darted to Quinn. She muttered, "I'll get my scissors," and left.

Why did I think seeing him surprised her? I checked Quinn's reaction. Same damned look as many a male visitor to Zeffir—slack-jawed awe. Thank the Waters I'd shut down my detectors.

Sabein was beautiful. Perfect in every way. Youthful. Blond. Heart-shaped face. Blue eyes. Full lips. Musical voice. Slender, but rounded enough in all the right places.

Of course, most Zeffirites were youthful, blond and blue-eyed. Sabein just combined the other attributes in the neatest package of them all. Being mousy in hair and eye color and unexceptional in figure and features, I'd been envious when I first met her. Sabein allowed that to last for all of a week before she showed me what really mattered.

Evard snickered and snapped his fingers in Quinn's face. "Taken."

Quinn jerked. He shot an embarrassed glance to me before attending to Evard.

I had to stop him. "Evard, don't—"

"What?" Quinn interrupted.

"I said she's taken," Evard went on. "Many times over. You could spend decades on this island and still not qualify. Ask me, I know. My advice is move on. Right now."

Quinn cleared his throat. "Don't know what you're talking about."

Evard ignored him. "Besides, if ever there was a woman on a mission, it's Sabein, leader of Zeffir. A mission no ordinary man could ever hope to sway her from."

As if Quinn, the E-IV, was an ordinary man? Ha, that was good. My gaze caught his for a moment. Quinn resumed drinking his coffee. I glared at Evard, hoping he'd notice and shut up. Telling Quinn that Sabein held the island's principal position saved me the trouble, but his hint about the Zeffirites' history landed too close to the truth—information we'd promised them we wouldn't share.

"Scissors?" asked Tristam, going back to Sabein's words before she left the room. "Aunt Eve, what's that about?"

Sighing, I ran my fingers through my cropped hair. "This, I bet." I set aside my plate and fetched a wooden stool from the corner. I had taken a seat on it when Sabein returned, bearing the scissors and more. I secured a cape around my neck while she wet my hair with a comb dunked in a glass of water.

"So?" Sabein started combing and snipping. "Evangeline's status? The second trip to Dome?"

That's why Evard and I were here. To report what had occurred. Purportedly. Sabein probably had the basic information and was seeking our reactions before plotting her next step. Enough had occurred that she hadn't spared Quinn a second look or thought of introductions.

Quinn, however, knew he'd never met her. Still peeved at his reaction to her, I offered the briefest version. "Sabein, I don't think you've met our guest, Quinn. Quinn, this is our friend and head of the island community, Sabein."

Sabein set down the scissors and took Quinn's hand in both of hers. "Make yourself comfortable in our town. We're happy to have you and your grandmother with us during her convalescence." She smiled. "However, I have a few stipulations."

Blessed Waters, what was she about?

"My charge on Zeffir is to ensure our people are not disturbed, or risk losing their lives," she said firmly, and Quinn nodded. "You may go about your business, which now seems to include Eve. But I will not have her essence disrupted either."

"No, of course not," he said. "I'll make sure she's safe."

I snorted, then faked a cough. What else would a

man say when under the gaze of so lovely a woman? Or should I say spell? What had happened to the strong-willed man who'd altered my functions? And chased me into the night? Though still annoyed at him for this rude change in my life, I was disappointed in Quinn.

Sabein lifted a ringed hand to pat his cheek. "Good answer, young man." Returning to my hair, she began lifting and clipping the back portion.

Quinn cleared his throat. "Surely you've heard I'm electorg and ageless. Hardly a young man."

"From my perspective, you are."

What? My gaze met Evard's, his face as astonished as mine must be. Sabein was all but telling Quinn the very secret the Zeffir community held dear. I held my breath, waiting to see if he'd stop to analyze her words.

"I'm not any younger than you are." Quinn pressed his lips together.

Oh, no, that bloody chip still sat on his shoulder. But, Golden Waters, I found myself pleased to hear the challenge in his voice.

This time, Sabein paused and stared at him. Evard laughed aloud, but Trist managed to hold a steady straight face. A true Zeffirite. Ah, I was proud of him. But I was also close enough to Sabein to detect her disappointment in Quinn. She was assessing him...to help? To receive her backing? Which one, I wasn't sure.

Giving a graceful shrug of one shoulder, she broke the gaze first. "Trust me."

"Instead of my eyes?"

"Exactly." Sabein went back to cutting my hair.

"Eve? Tell me about your trip to Dome with your inquisitive guest."

I did. To my surprise, Quinn didn't interrupt. I'd have thought he wouldn't want his affairs shared. Evard picked up with his journey to the Armory, including his side excursion for a trim with his favorite stylist to get the news.

"Marj said the day was hugely chaotic," he said. "First thing in the morning, the Post 'torgs started arriving, stressed and complaining over the rush, especially when forced to wait in the corridors. After a while, some returned to their Posts, for other equipment or such, and when the ministers discovered it, the place went up in a bloody uproar."

Sabein paused. "The ministers are sequestering the field 'torgs?"

Evard shot a glance at Quinn, who shrugged. "Appears so. Quinn believes they may be deactivating them to—"

"Ouch," I yelped.

Sabein released my hair. "You are joking," she said quietly.

Evard shook his head and continued with the evidence I refused to believe.

Slowly, Sabein resumed cutting my hair, but her motions were jerky. When Evard finished, she murmured, "I understand the need for bodyguards now. How do you like your new position with our other visitor?"

"I'm pleased with the functions, and Quaene is pleased with me. Transferred my fealty from Quinn to her immediately. I like the woman and think we'll have a jolly time together."

I groaned. *Jolly time together* was Evard's euphemism for getting in bed with a woman.

Sabein chose that moment to take my chin in her hand and survey my face. Lips pursed, she gave me a stern look and then covered it by parting my hair. Her message was clear—I was not to interfere with anything Evard chose to do.

Fine. I didn't know Quaene. She wasn't a part of our community, so I wasn't under any obligation to promote her harmony on Zeffir. One less person's emotions to worry about.

Sabein removed my cape and pointed me to a chair in front of the fire. Then she crooked her finger at Quinn. "Next."

It wasn't a question, and Quinn knew it. He rose, took my place, and she began wetting and combing through his mass of curly hair.

"So, Minister Quinn? What next?"

"Just Quinn, please. I have been...discussing plans with Quaene."

"Surely you can come up with a better answer than that."

Evard, Trist and I sat back to watch the master at work. Sabein cut Quinn's hair, asked questions, and he answered. Her technique wasn't anything a stranger would recognize. Quinn certainly didn't. He probably thought—if he gave any thought at all to his actions—he just wanted to please the beautiful Sabein.

Indeed, that might have been the case, if Sabein hadn't been wearing all of her jewelry. Her Zeffirite crystal jewelry. Earrings sparkled with crystals from a quarter of an inch to an inch long, as did necklaces draped high and low. Five of her ten fingers bore rings. But most impressive of all was the cuff she wore around her left upper arm. A three-inch-long, inch-wide, deep-gold crystal sat affixed to the metal. I'd learned a mere twenty years ago that this crystal was the largest in the community. Sabein never took it off.

Quinn didn't stand a chance at concealing information Sabein wanted. He confirmed their rank, a little background and that he and Quaene must resume their command of G47.

"We'll make our move Friday. Two days to prepare. My pro-tech will review my system while our bodyguards complete defensive exercises, then I'll train them in Lacuna for added security. Afterwards, we'll take another furtive trip to Dome to learn the exact status of the recalled 'torgs."

Evard and I shot looks to Quinn and then each other. "Bloody fantastic," Evard breathed, but I hushed him. I had to hear the next phase of their plans. Things were moving fast, much faster than he'd let on last night.

Quinn said, "Quaene wishes to continue the search for our run-mate, Quil. We *know* he isn't an impostor because he aided our escape. A handful of places remain unchecked so far. Sabein, you're an Aardite. If we give you a list of cities, can you suggest the most likely location?"

What? Had I heard correctly? Quinn asked Sabein's opinion?

"Why don't you tell me more about this man so I can come up with contacts?"

"Quaene is the person to give you those details. I have no memory of him."

"Is Zeffir a place you searched for him before?"

"No, I'd remember it. I have no memory problem with the weeks I've been on Aarde. I even recognize the crystals in your jewelry. They match the one Eve has."

"All our residents have them. Goudrogen crystals form alongside the rock underlying Zeffir." She shifted in her snipping and stepped around to look him in the face, a courtesy I knew had more to do with what she was detecting than their discussion. "My people and I will be happy to assist you."

"Thank you. Where do your residents find these rocks with the crystals?"

My—and everyone else's—gaze riveted on Quinn. *Two* questions? This was highly unusual when Sabein conducted one of her crystal-influenced interviews. But it didn't seem to faze her. She laughed lightly. Musically. "You don't. They find you."

"The crystals do seek people, I see. Or more properly, I feel."

As the fire snapped in the grate, Sabein lowered her scissors and comb. Evard and Tristam sported open mouths. Strangers never showed an awareness of the Zeffir goud. They couldn't, not until the Waters accepted them, and as I understood, that only happened when Aarde's two moons were in conjunction.

On the stool, Quinn smiled pleasantly. "The energy of your crystals seems to have a particular fondness for entering my system and trying to sway me into being an agreeable sort of guy. Please don't, Sabein. I'll tell you what you need to know. When I'm ready."

How could he feel the crystals if he hadn't been to the hot springs? I couldn't very well ask the question aloud, but surely Sabein would know. She was smiling, but tightly.

Quinn ran a hand over the crown of his head and raked up the layered waves of brown curls. "This is nice. Much neater than my previous style."

"Let me finish up." Sabein adjusted his shoulders to face forward and with undue concentration trimmed the few odd ends she'd missed. "You're sure you haven't been to Zeffir before?"

"I haven't. I'd tell you if I had. In fact, how about an information trade?" Quinn said. "Why does Tristam call Eve his aunt?'

Tristam grinned. "She was my father's—"

"Close family friend." My words rushed over his. "Look, Quinn, I—you and I can discuss Docga policy in private. These people don't need to be involved."

"Oh, but we are involved." Sabein tilted Quinn's chin to meet her gaze. "Eve is family, and we'll continue to take care of her." She began combing his beard and clipped the tight curls to a tidy quarter-inch length over the square line of his jaw. When she finished and removed the cape, the man standing before us was a duplicate of Dome's Impostor Quinn.

My stomach lurched. Sabein may not have known of his acceptance, or its *extent*, but her Alliance must be working overtime at gathering Corps information. We'd been in this parlor long enough. I rose and gestured Quinn to the door.

He thanked Sabein, adding they'd get back to her with the possible locations for seeking Quil. At the door, he said to me, "Weren't you supposed to meet with Tristam's grandmother?"

The others started laughing. "We've talked enough." I shooed him into the hall.

But I didn't get the door closed before Sabein called, "Tell him, my friend. Trade him for E-IV information for the Alliance's help. This man needs to know what we Zeffirites stand to lose."

I met her gaze. Clearly, her Alliance contacts felt the information I'd brought back was every bit as bad as we did. She wanted to establish a relationship with *these* ministers.

Quinn had stopped.

There was no avoiding him. "Sabein is Tristam's grandmother."

TWENTY-FOUR

QUINN

E ve waited, her gray eyes expectant. Breakfast chatter and the ring of china filtered from the shop into the dim hall. The morning's activities continued around me, around us, in a space that suddenly felt so similar to Lacuna.

Sabein is Tristam's grandmother.

Logic stuttered when I considered Eve's words. My mind skipped, unable to link the connections. These locals' relationships were less important than the help they could provide to our mission. With our spare resources, Quaene would be pleased I'd connected with the native leader, though she would expect a report on our benefactress.

I snuck another look. The gorgeous blond looked about twenty-five. And so did her supposed grandson. I hadn't scrutinized my competition in that same way, but he was as good-looking. Certainly, they were related. But two generations apart?

Pivoting, I swept a glance over the shop patrons. Any of the half-dozen blonds—*young* blonds—sipping their hot drinks could be related to Sabein.

The waitress noticed us, her eyes lighting up when she saw Eve. Another blond twenty-something, dressed in the town's old-world garb of a homespun skirt and blouse. Tray held high, she wove between the round tables to a booth.

I nudged Eve. "Who is she?"

Eve shot me a quick side-glance. "Sabein's grand-daughter, Gwyn."

"How old is she?"

"Twenty-eight."

"And Tristam?"

"Twenty-nine."

"Their ages seem high. What about their parents?"

Eve crossed her arms tight to her chest. "Their mother appears to be young as well. Their father is dead."

She must have known him. "Sorry," I murmured. "Just trying to sort if anyone here is old enough to die."

Eve laughed, but the sound was short and harsh. "Indeed, they may be."

What foolishness had blurted from me to get that reaction? May be? Funny way to phrase it, instead of *are...* Rounding to Eve, I hissed, *"Blessed Air.* These people never age?"

She sighed. "Correct. Although on Zeffir we say, 'Blessed Waters.'" She lifted her hand bearing the crystal. "Immortality comes via the island's thermal waters."

This was huge. No one on this island aged. They did elsewhere on Aarde, but we hadn't been *everywhere.* Were the Docga aware of it? Would these people influence our planetary mission? Sabein's last comment resounded in my head. *This man needs to know what we Zeffirites stand to lose.*

Were *they* our real mission?

Eve touched my arm. "Quinn? You all right?"

The concern lacing her features certainly made me feel all right. Immortal natives. At least, some of them. What a perfect place for Docga electorgs to assist a native population, one behind the modern universe in so many ways, but offering so much in others. Command of this planet would have very unique rewards.

And I had been chosen for that role. If I could only *remember* it.

The waitress—Gwyn—bounded over and threw her arms around my bodyguard, saving me from having to voice my concern.

They hugged. Kissed.

With her blond ponytail swinging in time to her giggles, Gwyn inspected Eve's black uniform. "It becomes you! And your hair—the wedge cut is so cute." She fingered the longer side strands of Eve's more stylish haircut. "I predict within days you'll have every man on the island at your feet. Now, introduce me."

Eve opened her mouth, but the door jingled, and a man called, "Gwyn?"

Throwing Eve a sly grin, Gwyn sashayed to the counter. "Right here, Cyrem. Your lunch is ready."

Cyrem was the man from Passages with the porta. The gray-haired man, one of the few old men I'd seen. *Older*, I corrected myself. What had happened to his youthful looks?

Gwyn handed him a basket bundled with a cloth. "Did the elders decide what to do?"

"We're opening the refuge now. I've made one reconnaissance to check its status and set an easy travel route," he said. "The place is in sore need of a cleaning, but we've got volunteers to do it. They're gathering supplies, and I'll guide them for the first trip."

He passed the basket to the boy who'd accompanied him, blond of course. His blue eyes sparkled eagerly. He peeked beneath the basket covering.

Cyrem hefted the giant thermos Gwyn gave him. "Taior's crew is on track to activate our perimeter security. Now it's a matter of aligning the crystals to cast the shield."

I turned to Eve and gestured to her ring. "Are they talking about the same crystals?"

She nodded. "Sabein already had her doubts about working with Dome's administration, so with the 'torg workforce recalled on top of the hornworts about to erupt, the Zeffirites must have decided to close the island."

"The entire island? How will crystals do that? Harmonic vibrations?"

She shrugged. "I've heard they set up a successful blockade during the Dead Air Years. The local Bounded Winds protect Zeffir from any spore contamination, but that makes it attractive to outsiders. The limited resources here can't support more people, so they seal the perimeter."

"Which wouldn't need to happen if the hornworts

didn't reach that sporophyte stage."

Eve murmured some agreement that was drowned out by Gwyn's cry of dismay. "There's so much to do. How will I ever—ah!" Her finger flew up. "Perry." She darted to catch the boy juggling the basket and the door latch.

I took Eve's elbow and steered her out behind them.

Cyrem was halfway down their street, following Gwyn and the boy to the last shop. I read the hanging sign, "Guided Tours, Cyrem, Proprietor."

"Most people call it Cyrem's Tours," Eve said. "He arranges trips."

"Today, to their sanctuary. How will the Zeffirites transport months of supplies there?"

She gave me a funny look and started across the street.

I caught her arm. "Sabein said to tell me."

"Not that," she muttered.

Damn, the woman wasn't making this easy. Clearly, Eve was still mad. On impulse, I squeezed her shoulder and guided her down the street for a private talk. "This guard function is only for as long as I need you. I promise. Afterwards, I'll revert you to your original function, and they'll remove the armor. Now ask me something in our information trade."

Her pace didn't falter, her gaze stayed distant. "Do you..." She licked her lips.

I waited. And said a silent thanks few people were on the street.

Her gaze didn't waver from where the sea met the

sky. "If I perform well in this function for you, would you allow me to return to Zeffir? Instead of being transferred, I mean."

Eve sought to remain on this isolated refrigerator? Having seen the rest of G47, I knew this Post had to be at the bottom of the request list, despite its brilliant agricultural progress. "You like it here that much?"

One nod.

"Eve, I don't know what is in my power to grant, but if you help me resume my command, I will do everything I can to place you here."

"Thank you."

She didn't say more than that. Nor did she alter her physical bearing. However, something between us changed. Nothing I could put my finger on, but I felt like pulling her into my arms.

Instead, I walked on, Eve at my side. I allowed myself to enjoy her company for a few minutes, right down the cobbled street to the dock bordering the open water. A sharp gust blew away my warm, muddled emotions and brought back cold logic.

I couldn't indulge in thoughts of Eve, not now. My future, at least the near future, was laid out for me. I should be gathering information on this second walk around town, or returning for my diagnostic check from PT.

Out of habit, I scanned the dock. The trade ship was long gone, and the fishing boats had sailed for the day, leaving one boat that looked more like a yacht. Two pieces of information clicked. Hunching my body against the wind, I asked Eve, "What's so strange about water travel that you couldn't say so?"

Her look bordered on stunned. She swallowed visibly. "How..."

"Cyrem coordinates tours, and that vessel's a few steps up from a fishing boat." I jerked my chin to the fancy boat with the row of windows at the waterline. "Is that guy his cruise captain?"

She gasped at the figure emerging from the cabin. "D'dair, he's the last person I want to see now. Let's go home." She yanked me around and ducked behind my body.

Blessed Air, there was nothing I would like more than to go home with her. The woman was fairly cuddled into me. I put my arm around her shoulders and inhaled her lilac scent. Exquisite femininity. I cast a glance back to the boat and the lanky, dark-haired man who'd stepped onto the deck with a sandwich. He didn't seem to have noticed us.

When we turned the corner, she relaxed and leaned away from me. I dropped my arm. Our gazes met, and I lifted a brow in question. "Let me guess. The cruises are a cover for running drugs you grow covertly in the Docga-supplied greenhouses?"

She smiled at my joke. "No one runs cruises. Pen is a local fisherman, even though he does have the fanciest boat in port." She cleared her throat. "Thanks for leaving. He's tried every which way to approach Evangeline, but since 'torgs aren't allowed to mix romantically with natives, she avoids him. Though he's a bit of a pushover, it's just easier if he doesn't see me."

We retraced our walk, passing many Zeffirites carrying baskets—stocking supplies for the imminent departure. I'd relay this to Quaene as well, before my diagnostics with PT, which could mean hours of deactivation. I didn't want Eve seeing me in that vulnerable state.

Ridiculously, I missed her warmth at my side, though I hardly knew the girl. Woman. I snuck a look at my guard, who'd requested to remain on this cold, windy outpost where people had a choice between dying or living beyond their years.

The loose ends in her disclosure bugged me. At the door to the bookstore, I stopped her. "Okay, I've got the Zeffirites' reason for wanting to protect their island and its precious resource. But what connection to these people has made you want to stay here?"

All expression slipped from her face. Eve clasped her hands over her crystal ring, closed her eyes briefly and then nodded. "You're not someone I care to lie to. I—"

The door burst open. "Evy?" Evard grabbed her arm and pulled her in, and I followed close behind. "Glad you're back. Evangeline is awake."

TWENTY-FIVE

QUINN

Eve yanked free of Evard. In a one-eighty whirl, she flew to my side, her back pressed to my chest, every muscle tensed and her short sword aloft. "Tell me," she barked.

"Whoa," I breathed at her rapid response, but neither of them noticed me.

"It's not like that." He waved the sword down. "Had the same reaction myself, and PT nearly took my throat."

"PT?" I said. "My pro-tech is defending a rogue B-run?"

"Right, your pro-tech. I knew he'd finished with Quaene, but I never suspected he'd be interested in Evangeline. Or do anything to her. Then she appeared in the kitchen with the wolfhound at her side, returned to our old Evangeline, quiet and withdrawn."

Footsteps sounded in the main aisle, and the older woman crept into sight. Though still wearing the official jumpsuit and her graying hair pulled into a bun, nothing remained of the stern, frowning demeanor on Evangeline's sun-bronzed face. Her clear gray eyes darted, hardly daring to meet anyone's gaze. One tanned hand clenched nervously. The other clutched the wiry hair of the Docgan at her side.

"Uh, hello, Eve." She stopped a good distance from us and held her empty hands aloft. "I can't explain my actions when I returned from Dome. I gather I wasn't myself. I'm sorry. And, Quinn, I'm sorry I attacked you."

Okay... This woman sounded and acted reasonable, with no trace of the authoritative tone or demanding orders of the triad leader who'd accosted me two nights ago.

Before me, Eve shifted, her stance, her weapon and her attitude creating a formidable barricade none dared defy. "Tell me what happened at Dome."

"A Blackguard escorted me to a meeting room for a short film. At the end, he patted my shoulder. PT says he overrode my functions. My memory bank is blank until I was seated in the dining room. Once I finished eating, I realized how important I was to the ministers. How much they were relying on me to carry out these orders."

"To the point of turning on your triad?" Eve's voice broke, the sword faltered.

I felt her draw a breath, steel her position. Clearly, my bodyguard had reservations about accosting her run-mate—a meek soul, if I'd ever seen one.

"Forgive and forget, I always say," Evard started, but Eve waved the sword.

"I need to know where she stands," she whispered. "So do you. We have a new function. One Evangeline doesn't share."

Evangeline blanched. PT growled. Eve's body pressed me back as she readied to spring, the stun sword pointed to the wolfhound's neck.

Eve would do this—for me—but I couldn't let her. I slid my hand over her trembling shoulder and squeezed. "Let Evangeline answer."

The Docgan rumbled a throaty string of sounds and Evangeline wrinkled her nose. "PT says my actions resulted from a form of electronic brainwashing. It sounds odd, but I felt like I'd be elevated to their class upon completion of my tasks. I'd be one of them. I desired that beyond anything. PT says he removed the influence. You don't need to worry about my dedication to our Post and triad."

PT says. Evangeline kept using the same phrase. I was about to question her when Evard said, "She's repeating exactly what he said."

Simultaneously, Evangeline and I swung around to gape at him. Eve did not.

Evard grinned. "How do you like that, Evangeline? You're no longer the only one who can communicate with animals. At least this one. Quaene linked me to her Docga language access. Said it'd be useful. Let's move on, my fair nym—ladies. Er, and gentleman. Sorry, Quinn. Fifty years in a house with women."

"And he still calls us girls," muttered Eve.

"Well, stop squabbling like one," Evard snapped. "She said she's sorry. Had no control over it. Listen to the Docgan, and get along. First thing, Evangeline is loopy from the additional goud. The best PT could do was to liquefy it and force it onto her crystal. We decided you best try to take it off, Eve. Then, it's to bed for her. PT is ready to initiate your repairs, Quinn, and has downloaded a series of practice maneuvers for you and I, Eve. *Verstanden*, everyone?"

Uh, right. If Quaene had linked with Evard to the point of allowing him access to PT, then countering him would be like defying my grandmother's—my quintad leader's wishes.

Eve glanced at him, then to me. The message was clear. She'd stand by my decision. Blessed Air—or Waters—selecting her had been an excellent decision. I nodded.

She slid the stun sword into its belt loop. After a moment's hesitation, the women hugged each other, Eve apologizing and Evangeline generously saying Eve knew best.

The wolfhound sat back on his haunches with another rumble. Evangeline smiled at him, the fond expression transforming her face. "He's curious to see you control the goud, Eve."

"He's in for the same treat I am," she said. "Because all I can do is ask. The goud decides for itself who it goes to."

Evangeline brought out a silver chain upon which hung a yellow crystal the size of my forefinger.

Eve whistled. "If I released that much goud, I'm surprised my own didn't shrink more." She raised her hand to show her ring with its comparatively smaller crystal.

Abruptly, a humming flowed outward from the crystals, filling the air. The frequency of the vibration increased as the women brought them closer. I could see the change. The crystalline structure was dismantling, the latticework melting from the mineral.

PT whimpered and shook his head, causing Evangeline to jerk around. "Oh, no, it's hurting him. Hurry." She shoved her crystal to Eve's.

A light flashed, and the air shook.

From a great distance, I heard Eve cry, "What are you doing?" while a buzz zinged me head to toe. It was exhilarating. I'd never felt anything so good. Eve's face loomed above mine through a yellow fog, and I extended to connect to her through the symmetrical cubic structure.

"No! Not again," she cried. "Not to Quinn." *Whump!* She slapped my chest, calling, "Here!" The mineral flowed out like a stream of water. A glow entered Eve's hand, illuminating her ring, then fading.

My sensations ended, leaving my body...normal. I frowned at her. "Why'd you do that?"

Her eyes sparked with a yellow fury. "You fell into a goud transfer, coating yourself. I pulled it off before it went into you. You would have been crystallized—as Evangeline was—if it had entered your body."

"Evy, chill." Evard hovered between us. "You got it off in time. He's fine. Right, Quinn?"

"Yes, how do you feel?" She stroked my cheek, her hand still humming. "I don't detect the element in your system, but the amount I saw..."

It had gone in. It had gone in so easily and blended with my system so readily...my particle talent. It allowed the goud to interface with me, probably much easier than with others. Yet, the way Eve eyed me, agreeing I was fine avoided more conflict.

Much to my regret, Eve dropped her hand and backed up.

"PT says it might not be the same for Quinn," Evangeline said, "being a newer generation of electorg. He's never had the opportunity to test goudrogen and would be interested in—"

"No." Eve crossed her arms, dismissing the suggestion.

They inspected their crystals. Evangeline's had shrunk by two-thirds. If Eve's had grown, it wasn't that noticeable. They didn't seem concerned.

I had to know, though. "Where is the extra goud?"

Eve looked sheepish. "Uh—"

"Gone, right, Evy?" Evard patted her shoulder. "You saw how readily it flows. Even in the crystal form, the element constantly rearranges its lattice structure. Repeatedly taking the Waters allows the element deeper into the cells, until a user can direct the atoms—in liquid or vapor. They go, dispersed among the more in-tune Zeffirites."

He shot me a smile, as if that mini-lecture answered the question. It did, it just didn't clarify which one she'd done.

"Eve, why don't you help Evangeline upstairs?" Evard said, cutting off any other questions.

Eve put her arm around Evangeline, and with a short rumble to us, the wolfhound paced at her other side. I started to follow, but Evard beckoned to me. "PT says he'll meet you upstairs. Can I have a word first?"

Once the women reached the stairs, he said, "Just giving Eve a bit of space. Emotions and all. She probably told you by now, being your guard." At my nod, he smiled. "Believe me, no one on this island needs fun in her life more than that girl. You saw her just now, uptight about the least little thing."

"Protection function of the Class 1 Blackguard. It's to be expected. But thanks for the heads-up on giving her time to regroup." I turned.

His raised hand halted me. "Eve's warming up to you. What's your plan?"

"Plan?"

"For courting her."

This was awkward, made more so because the conversation had just moved beyond my memory's experience. Not Evard's, obviously. Perhaps I could pick up some pointers. Did guys do this? I cursed my memory.

Evard didn't wait for me to decide. "You want her, don't you?"

I did. And while I didn't want Evard to think I was the complete failure I appeared to be, he'd probably understand. "You know I just found out I'm an electorg. Did Eve mention I have memory loss? So I'm functioning with deficiencies in both arenas."

Crossing his arms, Evard tried to stifle it, but the laugh burst out. "Sorry, man. The irony is hitting me. E-runs are usually the more experienced B-runs, elevated after proving their superior functioning. You lost a hell of a lot, hundreds of years, if I'm not mistaken. Well, if you're back to the basics, allow me to assist you."

From a pocket, he offered me a black leather-bound book, the palm-sized volume I'd seen him hand Eve back when—had it been only two mornings ago? "Everything you need to know about being an electorg."

I flipped open the cover. It wasn't a notebook, but a micro-com. The screen lit up with a table of contents for *The Electorg Handbook.*

Evard's long finger directed me past *Conduct*, *Policy*, *Review* and *Uniform*, to the last entry, *Questions*. "Use the stylus to write in any question you may have. About any function, electorg or organic. Even those of an emotional or physical nature, if you get my drift."

I did. I pocketed the handbook for later study. "Nice. Thanks, Evard. What about Zeffir information? Eve has merely touched on what Sabein allowed her to reveal— that they don't age. If you don't mind, could you explain how the society is structured, how they halt their—"

"No can do." His head shook adamantly. "Eve is your go-to girl for everything Zeffir. Just suffice to say Zeffir is its own little world. When folks live centuries with the same community, they make their own rules. During our tenure, our triad has followed them, as directed by the Docga mission statement. Sometimes I wonder if those old boys knew. The rules will change when we leave the island. Dome policy is different, and you and

Eve will have to work it out between the two of you. If there is a two of you. Work on making that happen first."

He thought Eve would accompany me to my minister's position. Evard didn't know of her desire to stay on Zeffir—or my promise.

"One last word of advice, Quinn? Presenting yourself as a twenty-five-year-old Aardite traveling with his grandmother was a gem of a disguise. It kept you safe, but the gig's over. May I recommend aging up another five years and locking it in place? You'll fit in better with what 'torgs expect in a leader, especially when compared to that impostor."

His words poked at my memory, a scene of someone else I knew who'd used a disguise to hide. Not 'torg aging, some different—pain flickered at my temple. I shrugged it off and focused on Evard's suggestion of aging. "But how do I lock it?"

He tapped the handbook.

TWENTY-SIX

EVE

"**S**abein believes you can help Aarde," I told Quinn and Quaene as soon as I sank onto a chair in her bedroom. I'd decided both ministers needed to hear why I wanted to return to this island, to keep trust on all sides, or that promise of a permanent Post on Zeffir was gone.

But that didn't make the tale any easier, especially with the freshly groomed and mature-looking Quinn watching me expectantly from his seat on the bed beside the more youthful-looking Quaene. But the excess of goud running through my body helped calm me.

"Zeffir is not unique in using the crystals for immortality," I said. "Other secretive goud-using enclaves reside across the planet at hot spring locations where goudrogen channels from underground. After the Dead Air Years, a handful of these peoples bonded to protect their members and thermal resources. The Alliance has offered their assistance to support your mission to regain your command."

Quaene rubbed her forehead. "I acknowledge every Aarde native has a stake in our success. We'll accept their help to find Quil, but I won't allow Aardites to accompany us into a confrontation. Preserving their lives is our mission."

It was, as I well knew.

"The crystals, you say?" She gestured to my ring. "Why do you, an immortal electorg, wear one?"

"Simply because I've been accepted into the enclave community. Yet, in my case, being accepted means more than it does for my run-mates." I took a breath. "I'd like to share that story."

Quinn darted a sharp look at me, and I felt the edge of his tension immediately. So did Quaene. She put her hand on his forearm. Thank the Waters I'd included this woman who was so obviously prepared to run G47's mission.

"Thirty-two years ago, I became romantically involved with a Zeffirite. Pier had been living off the island, in a wilderness area through which a drift of hornwort spore passed. He suffered minor lung scarring and returned. The goud couldn't save him, only extend his life. We were together eight years before he died."

Quinn's features turned stony, but his clear wave of pain left my stomach unsettled.

Quaene nodded and once again answered in her level voice. "Eve, dear, I know this violates policy, but I'm sure we can work something—"

"I'm not finished." I sucked a breath. "I bore two children with Pier."

"Impossible." The word burst from Quinn in a low and rough voice I hardly recognized. His narrowed eyes brimmed with disbelief. I caught the wisp of his emotion and then nothing. Like when he'd confronted Quala, Quinn had gone to his analytical side, hard and silent.

Yet, his and Quaene's gazes fixed on me.

Three beats of silence passed before Quaene said, "The Docga sterility implants leave a 'torg unable to reproduce, part of the agreement to our electronic life."

"Apparently, a 'torg accepted by the Waters, in combination with"—I had to say it—"mating with a goud user, can result in fertility."

Each looked uncomfortable, and when they said nothing, I added, "Tristam and Gwyn are grown. They're Zeffirites, of course."

The quiet in the room stretched to a minute. Again, Quaene broke it. "Well. That does make the situation more...complicated."

"No wonder you requested to return to Zeffir," Quinn said in a flat voice. Even his face gave no hint of emotion as he stared past me.

"You wish to remain with your family. Understandable." Quaene's green-eyed gaze flitted to Quinn.

Relief surged through my veins. Another woman— she understood.

Then, to my dismay, she frowned when her gaze returned to me. "However, a review may be needed, once our mission is complete. I hope you're not asking to be relieved of your guard duties in the meantime? I'm not sure we can spare you."

"I'm not requesting a change in function."

"Quinn? You do want Eve to remain your guard?"

He refocused long enough to glance at me before nodding to Quaene.

I rubbed my arms, suddenly cold.

Tap, tap, tap. The door opened, and Evard leaned in. "PT is anxious to start on Quinn. He doesn't know what he'll find, and we have a schedule to keep."

"Yes, our schedule." Quaene rose and offered me her hand. "Eve, thank you for your honesty. I appreciate having someone with your skills on our team and look forward to working with you. If you need anything to make your job with us run more smoothly, let me know."

An E-run who viewed B-runs as valuable members, to the point of thinking of us as a "team" after I'd dropped my news? Sincerity underlay her words. She exuded authority in a quiet competence I liked much better than Impostor Quinn's approach. Evard hadn't been wrong to suggest we take a chance on them, but our decision had changed everything—from our work to our allegiances.

I shook Quaene's hand with new respect.

She looked expectantly at Quinn, and he gestured me ahead of him to the door.

My stomach clenched. What did he wish to tell me privately?

On the threshold, his gaze barely met mine. He offered his hand, accompanied by a gruff "Thanks."

It wasn't an encouraging response, but better than the one I'd expected. Then a feeling floated from him as our hands parted. The brown of his eyes deepened, and his gaze flitted to my lips. The space between us filled with his urge to touch them, kiss them, to kiss...me.

His mesmerizing attraction pulled me closer, closer... Then cut off like a bucket of cold water. His sudden fear swamped me—he might never get a chance to kiss anyone if he didn't wake from the death-like deactivation.

Quinn stepped back. "Go practice the guard maneuvers PT has assigned you. Evard? You, too. Out." He steered me over the threshold and closed the door behind us.

With a hint of a laugh, Evard said, "What almost happened there, Evy?"

I threw a glare at him and spun, nearly running into Evangeline, dressed in the old sweater and trousers she wore to make animal calls. She caught me and glared at Evard herself.

He put up his hands. "Come on. Anyone with a gram of crystal on him got word you revealed your breach of Docga policy and child-bearing, but that was an odd sort of reaction Quinn—"

"Be nice," Evangeline admonished him. "Eve's upset, so much even I can tell."

Her arm circled my waist, a hug I would have very much appreciated if Evard's words hadn't sunk in. "What do you mean, *anyone with a gram of crystal*?"

He gestured to the stairs down to the bookstore. We stepped forward. A group of Zeffirites had gathered in Passages' back hall, including Mylta, Cyrem and Taior. The bell on the front door rang as it opened, and Tristam ran down the center aisle.

"Is everything all right?"

Gwyn broke from Cyrem's side, hugged her brother, and they came up the stairs.

I frowned at Evard.

"What?" he shot back. "I didn't tell. When you told Quinn and Quaene, your goud broadcast the news of a possible threat like a Docga special report."

"What was I supposed to do? I couldn't keep that from him and expect the minister to trust me with his life." Especially after he'd promised to post me back on Zeffir.

Gwyn wrapped her arms around me. "Was he angry? When you told him about us?"

I sighed into her blond hair and kissed her forehead. "I don't think so." Tristam hugged me, too, but before everyone ascended to where the E-runs might hear them, I called down, "Quinn still wants me as his guard, and he's promised if he successfully takes back his command, I can return to Zeffir."

"Fantastic," Gwyn squealed above the group's relieved well-wishes.

Evard clapped me on the shoulder and boomed, "Right-o! 'Bout time we got to that assigned guard practice then."

Like a child headed for his toy room, my run-mate told the others to pass the news and herded me to the lawn of our backyard. Darting his hand *through* the midthigh length of his camouflaged armor, Evard whipped out his hidden short sword and swung it.

In a split second, my sword blocked the flat of his blade bound for my neck. "Evard! What the bloody hell do you think you're doing?"

Donning our helmets, Evard and I circled, making a series of feints and parries, before we backed off and came at each other again. Our slicing blades clashed in ringing waves as we fought. It was easy, taking out my fears and frustrations on a 'torg I couldn't possibly hurt. We darted around the yard, springing from behind the shed or chicken coop for an edge of surprise.

Then, with deactivated weapons, we ran several adventurous Zeffirites through a few trials. Despite my smaller physique, I evaded the rugged outdoorsmen as if they moved through water, pinning them easily. I was quicker, stronger and better *trained*.

Yet, throughout the practice, the function reminders—

CONTACT WITH YOUR MINISTER ABSENT FOR ONE HOUR, TWO MINUTES.

—haunted me. What if Quinn came out of his repairs not remembering? Or remembering too much and his attitude regarding the use of B-runs altered? Would he keep his promise to post me permanently at Zeffir? Would he...would he still be interested in me?

When we entered the kitchen, Evangeline was pulling on her boots while listening to a farmer's tale of a goat birthing gone wrong.

I sighed and lifted her woolen cape and hat from the peg. The kidding season would have Evangeline out all hours, arriving with the vet or without him, because many farmers believed a calm delivery translated to a healthier kid and a better milk yield. She'd return from these handholding sessions half frozen and afterward catch cold. She never said no, or even questioned the request.

Though, when she accepted her cape, uncharacteristic creases crossed her brow, and her gaze met mine. "Are you free?" she asked.

Though confused, I nodded.

"I think you best come, too." Then she left with Neil, the farmer, on her heels.

"It's Amber, the silvery one," Mylta said, and solved the mystery of why Evangeline needed me.

I got my cloak and followed at a slower pace, putting away my personal worries and preparing my emotions to work with a distraught mother, for certainly that would describe Suzy—Neil's mate—if Amber was in trouble.

When this couple hadn't been chosen to bear a child during the last fertility period, Suzy had taken on the bottle-feeding of a frail doe triplet. For weeks, she carried Amber everywhere, doting on her. Now Suzy lay in the straw, hugging Amber's head as bleating and crying filled the birthing stall.

At the struggling goat's tail end, the vet and his boy had stripped their shirts and massaged an ointment over their hands while watching Evangeline try to insert herself under Suzy's arms.

"Don't blame yourself, please," Evangeline said to Suzy. "Stubborn Amber has learned all sorts of tricks in nine years. She knew you didn't want her to breed her this year. You put her in a sturdy enclosure, watched all the signs, everything you could do to prevent a clever goat from having her way with the buck. But Amber wanted one more kid, and she thought you'd understand."

Suzy cried all the more.

Maybe Suzy did understand, in theory, but not when her substitute child's life was the trade-off. Yet, up until this last sentence, Evangeline had done a reasonable job of placating the distressed human. She'd do an even better job with the goat, if she could focus on the animal. I bent and placed a hand on Suzy's shoulder.

Evangeline shot me a look of relief. "Here's Eve. Go to her while I comfort Amber. She's torn, seeing you like this, you know. She wants us to be happy for her. She's excited to see this one." Evangeline dropped her voice. "Please? Hold yourself together for Amber. We'll do our best, I promise, Suzy."

I helped the young woman up and guided her to the stall doorway, the farthest she'd go. Evangeline's words had done part of my job, and Suzy willingly leaned into me and accepted my consolatory emotes while watching my run-mate murmur to the now-quiet Amber.

The vet nodded his approval and gestured to his son. When the boy eased his smaller hand into Amber's swollen rear, I turned away.

"There, there," Evangeline crooned.

I held to Suzy and, in a way, shared her distress. How could I have threatened my run-mate? My function had directed every step, compelling me to obey...until I'd stopped it. Thank the Waters I had. If I'd done anything to her, I wouldn't have been able to live with myself.

In her pure-hearted manner, Evangeline kept up an encouraging patter to the goat and relayed instructions from the vet. Within minutes, they had the misaligned foot redirected and a wet and bloody kid lay in the straw.

Evangeline and I walked back to the house together.

"Thank you for coming," she said. "I guess after years of seeing Suzy with Amber, I should have suspected she'd be difficult. She loves that goat like nothing I've seen."

I glanced at Evangeline, holding her cape tightly to her middle, a perplexed frown on her face. "To Suzy, Amber is the child they didn't have the last fertility period."

"Really?"

"Really. Suzy cannot imagine being without a child to raise. Even a disobedient substitute like Amber."

"So if Amber died," she said slowly, "Suzy would grieve as if she'd been human."

"Exactly."

Evangeline shook her head. "But she's not. I love animals, but I know they aren't the same as people. Amber wanted that rut. Nothing was going to prevent her. Animals have shorter, simpler lives. Their needs are innate, and no amount of love from Suzy is going to change Amber's inborn urges."

I touched her arm. "I think it would help if you explained that to Suzy, with Neil there."

She rubbed her brow. "At the adjustment center, they taught me to access my files for instruction on how to deal with unfamiliar situations. But even after fifty years, I struggle to understand people and their motivations."

It tore me up to watch this sweet and sensitive woman grapple with the mysteries of humanity, which came so easily to me. I helped when I could, but somehow, smart as Evangeline was, she never caught on. I smiled to ease her worry. "Even after fifty years, no one could prepare you for every bizarreness people get into their heads."

She smiled back at me. "I'll just have to keep at it, starting with using your wonderful explanation. Thank you for coming along."

Mylta had the kettle on in the kitchen, but I heard heavy footfalls overhead so went through to the shop—

Contact with your minister absent for one hour, fifty-four minutes.

Evard strode down the stairs, shaking his head. He whispered, "It's bad."

TWENTY-SEVEN

EVE

From within my crashing emotions, I croaked, "Quinn's system is beyond repair?"

Evard's brow furrowed. "PT can't restore the memories, which is one blow, but worse, his frequency is no longer his quintad's. PT tries resetting it, but it flips off to something else."

My emotions careened between despair and sympathy at the same time I was realizing we now had to find two run-mates to mind-link with Quaene in order to be able to enact the fail-safe.

"Quaene's trying to rally, but the loss is a blow to her as well. She wants your reads on Quala. I'm off to check on Sabein's search for Quil." Evard gestured me to the stairs. "We need to train in Lacuna techniques this afternoon, so go get your lad back on track."

"He's not my *lad*. Why would you call a Corps minister that?"

The answer was apparent as soon as I walked into our room. A young—eighteen, twenty?—Quinn lay on the far bed, his upset emotions tumbling all over the place. He was reading an Electorg Handbook. A good sign—

"I haven't called for you. Please leave."

Of all the—d'dair. I hadn't had to deal with a teenager's attitude in a decade. I sidled up to him, exuding positive vibes. "Quinn, I can help you."

"I didn't realize you'd become a Docga programmer in the last few hours," he hissed.

"You possess other skills to assist—"

"Those skills pale compared to having the *right* frequency to shut down that damned rogue. Quaene relied on me to participate. I've failed her. Leave. That's an order."

It was, and I obeyed to avoid the inevitable fight should he discover I was allowing my goud to override his directive. Between Quaene's Lacuna lessons, I tried again. My efforts to sway him were like salmon fighting to swim upstream, almost as if the man—for he'd aged up again over the course of the afternoon—wanted to wallow in his self-perceived failure. He left my chest tight as I fought his swamping hopelessness.

Finally, Evard quit the Lacuna training—which wasn't proving easy—and came to my rescue. While Quaene went to meet with Sabein, my run-mate roused Quinn for a walk.

I reheated Mylta's curried goat and vegetables and set the low table in front of the fire—the same as I'd done for Pier and me. Before long, the men returned, with Evard bearing a bottle of whiskey. Amber liquid glazed the bottom of Quinn's glass. He looked dazed, not at all the confident man of the day before, or even the confused one who'd stumbled into Passages. Except he *was* stumbling.

254 | LAUREL WANROW

"Evard, where have you been?"

"Never fear, my dear girl. We only made it as far as Taior's. Good ol' *weardian* invited us in. Figured Quinn was due a status check."

"Splendid," I muttered. Quinn might be so liquored up I wouldn't be able to find out what made him think he couldn't fulfill his duty to Aarde despite his lack of memories. If he didn't resume responsibility for Aarde, I'd lose everything.

Evard lifted his shoulders in a much-exaggerated shrug. "It's how guys handle stuff."

"Status check?" Quinn said. "I'd say more of a sergeant's grilling. The few old farts on your island are grumpy."

"Grumpy?" Evard widened his eyes in mock horror. "How can you hold that against a man who's given us his best bottle? I think you need more time on Zeffir to straighten out your priorities. I know just the thing—"

"So do I. Dinner." Taking Quinn's glass, I pointed to the couch and served him a plate of food while he slumped. Evard hovered. I snatched the bottle from him—I might change my mind about needing it—and jerked my head toward the stairs, where Quaene had headed not long ago. "Good night, Evard."

He frowned. "Now, Evy, you have to understand that was a loan. Taior expects—"

"I wouldn't do anything to make Taior unhappy. Or you. Sweet dreams."

"Oh." His face brightened and Evard shot a look upward. "Right-o. Sweet dreams. Good night, Evy. Hang in there, Quinn."

They saluted each other. I ignored them and slathered a piece of bread with goat cheese to appear to be joining Quinn as he ate. I hesitated over which seat to take. Evard had done a pretty good job of peeling away the worst of Quinn's negative emotions. But could I sit beside him? Should I sit beside him? The closer our proximity, the more likely I would influence him with my emotions. Had I promised not to? No, only not to use my ring.

Quinn decided for me. "You gonna stand there and lecture me like Taior did?"

I dropped onto the couch beside him. "Did it work?"

"You tell me, lady savant."

An invitation. I took a bite of my bread and opened my gift. His emotions didn't take much effort to detect, but what he emitted was elusive. Drunk, Quinn was all over the place. His feelings flowed loose and fragmented. Some upset, some cavalier. Anger. Loss. An underlying current of desperation.

I picked the loss. "So what if PT says you haven't retained your original frequency? You're still functioning as an E, and that's what counts. Why not focus on your half-full glass?"

He didn't answer.

"You still have Quala, and Quil can take your place if Sabein comes through in her search. We'll all go to Dome, get Quala, and then they can—" He wasn't listening. I put down my plate and laid a hand on his arm. "Quinn, you're still an active quintad member."

"Yeah? How, with no mind-link?" He grabbed the bottle I'd left on the coffee table, sloshed whiskey into his glass and swallowed half of it.

His emotions flared. New waves blossomed outward. Closing my eyes, I settled back and let them overtake me, trying to get a better handle on him. The depth of his feelings amazed me. The sadness of his loss covered something... Jealousy. Same as when I'd touched the gate guard at Dome—but Golden Waters—that'd been nothing compared to how he felt about Quil taking his place.

"Finding Quil won't change how Quaene relates to you, even if you can't link. Your relationship may alter with Quaene as her mentoring role diminishes and you regard each other as equals, but she'll still feel close to you."

"Not as close as she does to Evard."

Oops, I'd guessed wrong. This jealousy wasn't about Quil. "That's different and you know it. You're a quintad, you're family—a relationship you'll always have. Evard may be out the door tomorrow."

"I doubt it. He never leaves her side. She asks his opinion. He jokes with her. She stares at him. They're..." Quinn held up crossed fingers.

"You picked him for her guard. Didn't you think of how closely they'd work together?"

He ate a few forkfuls of his curry before answering. "Sort of. But does he have to be touching her all the time?"

For the love of—

"This morning, you touched me. A lot."

"That's different," he muttered and drained the whiskey glass. Suddenly, the tenor of his emotions softened. He focused on me.

Why had I brought the conversation to us? "Let's skip Evard and Quaene for a bit. Tell me about your functioning. I won't pretend I'll understand the technology of how it's different, so tell me when it changed? Why did it change?"

Quinn pushed the dishes aside and, in the cleared space, carefully poured another glass of whiskey. He didn't pick it up, just stared at it. His stupor lasted so long I thought I'd have to do something I'd regret—like spill Taior's best Aardness Gold malt on our wool rug.

"I think," he said, "it happened when that guard on Level Six stunned me."

If that was the case, then he'd lost part of himself because of me. My stomach sank and I closed my eyes to shut out the ramifications of his selfless act. We might lose the planet, the lives of every Aardite. I drew a breath. We'd find some other way to save them. We had to.

I had to keep Quinn on track. "I never did thank you for rescuing me. Not properly. You came back for me after you'd escaped the guard. You didn't have to."

"Aw, Eve." Quinn slumped against the couch and turned to me. "I couldn't leave you."

His slurred words sounded sweet. And something more. Something I wasn't sure I was ready for. I inched back. Yet, I wanted to know. "But I'm B-run. Dispensable. Why didn't you leave me instead of confronting the guard?"

Quinn heaved a sigh and snuggled closer. "After the first jolt, I wanted him to do it again. Because I remembered something. Some*one*. I let him stun me, pretending I was going down but fighting it, 'cause each time the current jolted me, the images got stronger. Clearer. Even let the guard do a couple of extra buzzes just to make sure."

"Make sure of what?"

"That I'd never forget my mistake. Seeing that face from my past assures me I won't."

Abruptly, deep waves of desperation poured from him, bringing tears to my eyes. I struggled to keep my composure. I had to level him out, so I flooded him with a calming emote.

Quinn yawned in response. "Evard's kissing her, you know. Doing more than kissing, too." He nodded sagely.

Bad choice to relax a drunk. If I didn't soon find out about the person he'd recalled, I wouldn't. I seized his shoulders and stuck my face right into his. "The person—that face you saw when the guard shocked you? Who was it?"

He groaned. "Ugh. I don't wanna think about him. Drinking is helping me forget." He shifted until his head rested on my shoulder.

"True, but I need you to remember one time, just long enough to tell me, Quinn. Then you can forget about it."

He nodded ever so slightly as he stared at me. "Don't remember having liquor before." Another nod affirmed this. "Or kisses. Think I could have some?"

"Kisses?"

"Yeah." His lips closed in on mine. "Kisses. Yours."

Blessed—what to do? I thought fast. "For a trade."

Quinn dipped his head in agreement. "Okay." His breath warmed my skin. Then his lips warmed mine. They were soft and tentative, glazed with the slight molasses smoke of good whiskey and a bite of the curry. And Quinn.

My tongue flicked forward, searching for the elusive flavor beneath the drink. Manliness, of a new variety. One better than I had imagined possible.

Quinn broke away first. "That was a good kiss. I think... I think I've done that before."

"I'm sure you have," I murmured. My hand steadied itself on his shoulder and pulled ever so slightly, even though it shouldn't. If only I had a little longer to test his flavor, maybe I would be satisfied. Then I could ignore Quinn and everything about the man that threatened to bring me trouble.

"I like trading with you, my Eve. I like everything about you. Are you making me feel this way?"

No, and I very easily could. As she lay dying, my widowed mother pressed upon me the need to find a man, one able to keep food on the table. All of sixteen, I focused my growing—but raw—gift on the farrier's son. We snuck up to his father's hayloft, and while he was obviously satisfied, I was bound by guilt for my trickery. After my mother died, I dropped him and earned my livelihood apprenticing to the village healer-midwife, working my garden to put food on the table and selling the rest to make ends meet in those lean times before The Great Pestilence swept through our village.

That first awful relationship contrasted sharply with the open one I'd shared with Pier, my Zeffirite mate. Here, I could be myself, unafraid of my delicate gift. Our love had built slowly from friendship to tenderness. In his quiet way, Pier taught me the wonders of using Aarde's crystals. In return, I gave him new reasons to live the special life he'd once given up. But reclaiming the goud had come too late for Pier.

Quinn wouldn't remember how we'd gotten to this point when the liquor wore off. But I would. "No. You're doing it all yourself."

His lips met mine, and parted. Gone were the distracting whiskey and curry. Stronger now was the woodsy man. Golden Waters, his taste made me swim. I submerged until he pulled me up with a happy laugh. "That's good. I like feeling this way."

My thoughts swirled, desire with danger. "Me, too."

"Really? It's a good trade for you?"

Oops, I'd forgotten. My finger on his lips stopped another submersion. "Trade first. Tell me about the person you remembered."

Quinn leaned away, squeezing his eyes shut and pinching the bridge of his nose. "I met him at R&R. The guy wanted to be a pilot, so I invited him onto our transport for a tour. No harm done, really. He never messed with the equipment. No breach of security..." He shook his head and muttered, "No reason for Quil to get pissed off."

Quil? Quinn was getting sidetracked. "This would-be pilot is who you remembered?" I asked.

Quinn blinked. His gaze returned to me, then narrowed. "My friend wouldn't knife me. Wouldn't. Someone did...another time I can't quite remember. Missed my heart by thiiis much." He parted his finger and thumb a sliver. "Nearly killed me." His face scrunched in disgust. "Too trusting, Quil told me in the sick bay."

A sheen of sweat glistened on Quinn's forehead. I wanted to reassure him, but so far I was able to follow most of the story and didn't want to throw him off by interrupting.

"Quil was right, but he argued, all the time. Quaene wanted us to make up, but he opened a Conducer. I followed him in. To bring him back. I could have done it, if someone hadn't stopped me." Quinn rubbed his temple. "He looked like me, me holding a knife. *Another damn knife.* I punched it away, then he caught me—or pieces of me. It hurt to reverse my leap. Just when I couldn't do it anymore, PT returned. I escaped."

Quinn heaved a sigh and straightened in his seat, reached forward, and neatly picked up the glass of whiskey. He downed the liquid in one long draught and set the glass on the table with a clunk. "There. I did it. With this drink and a little luck, I can forget the worst mistake I ever made—trusting a stranger. Got stabbed, my identity stolen and lost my memory." He poured another drink.

Trust—well, that explained a lot. We had more in common than I'd thought. This breakthrough accounted for some of Quinn's memory loss—who wouldn't try to forget seeing your mirror image come at you with a knife? Surly that had been Impostor Quinn in the Conducer. The pilot was also a clear memory for Quinn, leaving only the person who first attacked with the knife. My reasoning said this was also Impostor Quinn, but did Quinn agree? "Did you discover who attacked you first?"

His face crumpled for a second before he shook his head. "It's right there, behind another wall." He swallowed the next whiskey and peered at me. "Fair trade?"

"More than fair," I agreed. "But where was that knifer—"

He grasped my shoulders. His whiskey-glazed lips found mine. My heart leaped in anticipation of tasting his special flavor, of being tenderly swamped with affection. But this kiss was neither soft nor tentative. He crushed me—his lips, hands and body hard and demanding.

It hurt—not physically, but the sheer passion enveloping us. A searing fire ripped over my skin, catching and igniting every nerve. As the flames traveled my length, waves of longing engulfed my mind.

Being kissed by Quinn was nothing like being kissed by Pier. My heart pounded. My loins heated. My head reeled. With desire. With...complications. Quinn emoted a fervent ardor, but mixed with twinges of pain, anger and desolation.

I pulled back. "I—I can't."

Quinn dropped his hands from me. He slumped into the couch, raking his fingers through his hair, his face a mix of confusion and worry that I longed to kiss away. Desire rolled over my heated body, and I reached for him—

What am I doing?

Emotion—*our* emotions—lay thick over the couch. I stood up and paced out of the cloud, fighting my urges and cursing my stupid gift for getting me into this state that was destined only to hurt me. I shut it down, half wishing I could be more like Evard.

Quinn rose, and concern furrowed his brow as he halted feet from me and studied the floor. "Sorry. I should never have done that," he mumbled.

I couldn't explain. "Accepted. So, uh..." The remnants of the meal lay on the table, but wasting food was better than another emotional plunge. I would *not* suggest going to bed. I just had to get him upstairs and retreat to my room, since he'd released me from my guard duties earlier. I walked to the back hall, and he followed until I mounted the first few steps.

"Come on." I wrapped an arm around his waist and tugged him off the railing. He draped his arm across my shoulders, and we climbed the stairs.

"Thanks," he murmured at my ear, the smell of whiskey strong. "You aren't as beautiful as Sabein.

You're different."

D'dair. Did he have to remind me I didn't begin to compare to her? Didn't what we'd shared mean anything to him? Fine. Quinn would be a risky addition to my life. I'd be better off without him.

After a few steps, he stopped. "That wasn't a good way to say I like you better, was it?"

A complete lecture formed at the tip of my tongue, but I said, "No."

"Forgive me?"

"Sure. I understand." I stepped up and so did he.

"I'm glad. You're the best, Eve. I mean that. I'll learn how to talk to women again, and then you'll like me more."

I should leave him thinking he was the problem. But some part of me didn't want to undercut this passionate man. "The way you talk to me isn't the issue."

"I've seen the way you soften a little, then I say something that must be wrong and you cringe. You toughen up."

I stopped at his door. "Maybe that look isn't about you. Maybe it's because I have to be tough for other reasons." I steered him into the room. "We'll talk in the morning."

Quinn pivoted. "Eve? We're not sleeping together. I'm with it enough to remember that. Good, because the last—" He winced and raised a hand to his head.

I steadied him, and he straightened.

"Something went very wrong. It's not safe for me without you. I need my guard in my room."

TWENTY-EIGHT

QUINN

Bong! Bong! My head rang...rang... *Bong!*

I rolled and reached for my pillow. Before I could smash it atop my head and stop the insistent gong, rustling cloth stopped me cold. Someone was in my room. I fisted my hand. No sneak attacker was going to knock me senseless again.

Bong! Instead, he walked away. Opened a door. Water began to run. A shower? The familiar sound dismissed my nightmare.

Bong! That was a real bell. I wasn't in some bar, but in the bedroom Eve and I shared. I sat up in the dark. Holding my head, I stumbled to the bathroom. She hadn't put on the light, so I flipped it. "Why's the bell—"

"Ahh!"

Black. Her naked body was black from the polymer coating. But definitely naked. She'd dissolved her armor. My eyes flew over the figure I'd longed to see, to touch, to hold. Shapely legs. Beautifully taut skin. Softly rounded breasts, perked—

She whipped a towel over her body.

I dragged my gaze to her face.

Flushed face. Angry face. You-are-so-screwed face.

Eve's eyes flashed gold through narrowed slits. Her thinned lips parted the least amount possible. "*What* do you think you're doing?"

I swallowed. "Sorry, I didn't think—can't think right now."

"Obviously." She snapped off the light. "Get out. In a minute, the shower will be yours, and then we go."

"Go where?" I managed to ask as she shoved me out. "What's that ringing bell for?"

"It's the call to the Waters, up at the hot springs." The door slammed.

During the wait, I dredged up enough of the previous night's events to know I'd better keep my mouth shut. As ordered, I hustled through a warm rinse and donned the soft, woolen robe Eve left me. What a fool I'd been with my clumsy attempts to woo her last night. At least I hadn't embarrassed myself further than a kiss—unless my falling directly into bed insulted her.

Stone-faced, she opened our door and strode into the hall.

Blessed Air, my mind should be on regaining control of the planet, but my pounding head directed every thought back to Eve. *My* Eve. How could I regain the ground I'd lost with her?

No chance now. I followed her. Quaene, Evangeline and Evard were standing in the hallway. Their gazes shifted from Eve's departing back to me.

Damn. I could've used a little privacy.

Quaene gave me her usual morning greeting of a quick hug. "You've heard we're invited? Evard tells me the bell signals the Zeffirites to a healing spring that rises every month or so when the moons converge. I gather it's regarded as something of a religious ceremony." She leaned close. "With Sabein's gracious commitment of her people's time to help our search, we should accept the invitation for a few hours."

I found nothing to argue there, especially if these *Waters* would help my aching head.

Looking far better than I felt, my drinking buddy Evard gestured to the stairs. "When in Zeffir, do as the Zeffirites. Electorg Handbook."

"Everyone goes?"

"They do. Every man, woman and child."

"Evard, that's not exactly true," Evangeline ventured softly. "Some do refuse the call."

But today I didn't believe anyone had. The street teemed with bodies, all dressed in long robes. Curiosity—plus the weapon belts hanging on both Eve's and Evard's hips—put security from my mind. Eve resumed her position at my side, and our group melded into the moving crowd.

An eerie quiet surrounded the walkers. Even the few children stumbling in their parents' grasp were robed and serious as we proceeded up the moonlit street. The change hit me—no wind. Not only did the cloud-free sky reveal Misha and Roamer together at the zenith, but also the lack of a breeze left the air unseasonably warm.

I leaned to Eve's ear. "I thought this isle was permanently windy."

Behind me, Sabein's soft voice answered. "During

268 | LAUREL WANROW

the conjunction of our moons, the Bounded Winds spiral farther offshore. The settling calm prompts your spirit to remain in your core. Only then are you truly present in your body, open and receptive."

"Receptive to what?"

She smiled and skirted ahead to join Taior. I would have hurried to catch her, but Eve caught my arm.

"Can I ask Sabein about her search for Quil?" I whispered.

She pursed her lips and shook her head before staring into the distance. I'd never make progress with Eve if she wouldn't talk to me. Perhaps spending more time restudying relationships in the little black handbook Evard had lent me would help.

At the edge of town, we entered a floating, wispy fog. It didn't obscure the surrounding fields, but I couldn't make out the hills above us, the plateau where I'd sheltered Quaene. The fog thickened among the rocky outcroppings, causing the climbing path to all but disappear. Evard grasped Quaene's arm to guide her, and a moment later Eve slipped a hand into the crook of my elbow.

My headache dissolved with the smell of lilac from her hair as we jostled together over the twisting path. The warmth of her body sent a wave of longing through me. It didn't matter where we headed at this unreal hour. It didn't matter that this show of caring came from her function directives to keep me from harm. And maybe it didn't matter if my Eve wouldn't talk to me. I still wanted her.

Groups of townspeople split off, hopping over full, running streams and skirting the various pools. Water filled them to the brim, unlike the first morning I'd passed this area. Nor had the water surface steamed when I drank from it.

"How did the water turn *hot* today?" I asked Eve.

"The moon conjunction also creates a strong tidal pull on water from deep in Aarde. The Waters rising to Zeffir come from directly over volcanic mantle plumes."

She kept me following Evard, who followed Evangeline and PT. A few turnings led us to a pool. Someone was swimming, but through the mist I couldn't discern their identity, let alone see to the far perimeter. Evangeline picked her way around the edge ahead of us. She dropped her robe on a boulder and entered the water, her pale skin luminescent in the moonlight.

A sharp elbow jabbed my side. "Avert your eyes," Eve hissed.

Yeah, I knew it wasn't polite to stare. But it was hard not to. I couldn't remember seeing a woman naked, but before dawn today I'd seen two.

Eve poked me away from where the swimmer—a woman—and Evangeline exchanged greetings. Evard and Quaene had disappeared into the fog by the time Eve said, "Here."

She set her weapon belt aside and placed her dagger on a stone at the edge before shooting me a frown. I averted my eyes as she disrobed and stepped into the water. I dropped my robe next to hers and dipped in a foot. The water was hot, not unbearably so, but it felt odd. My molecules tingled. I hesitated, crouched on the side with one leg immersed.

Fingers clenched my wrist and yanked. I plunged and dunked completely before my feet found the bottom. I rose, sputtering.

Eve settled onto an underwater rock at my side, a curve tilting her luscious lips. "Nothing will happen to your family jewels. It's entirely safe."

My... "What happened to the 'avert your eyes' rule?" My glare did nothing to change her smug expression.

"I'm your guard. My eyes are to be on you at all times."

"Was that payback for my bursting into the bathroom?"

She shrugged so just a slight swell of her breasts emerged from the surface, then leaned her head into a natural depression in the rock, closed her eyes and reclined. Her black toes bobbed in the water, but a shimmering glare prevented me from seeing below the surface.

Of all the luck, I had the worst. "You're going to sleep? Here?"

"Aren't you tired?"

"Yeah, but—"

"Then lie back and give yourself up to the Waters. It makes the morning pass faster."

Morning? I sank down on a rock ledge beside her. "Surely we aren't spending that much time here?"

"We are," said another woman. Sabein strolled

through the water, naked except for the wide silver band high on her arm. Its enormous crystal glowed in the rising steam, yielding me a glimpse of her golden hair, beautiful face and small, pert breasts. I snapped my gaze up as she said, "I think from the migration of the goud, the time promises to be productive for you."

Despite my overstimulated senses, I tried for logical thought. What could she be talking about?

The question must have shown on my face, for Sabein laughed and nodded at my chest. Tearing my gaze from her, I nearly choked on my breath. Yellow slime coated me. It flowed in waves that solidified into lumps, dissolved and moved on. I raised a hand to scrape it off, but Eve grabbed my arm.

"It's all right, Quinn," she murmured. Sabein joined her, and both women half-rose, studying the pulsating ooze.

I closed my eyes before they got me in trouble, but first noticed that Eve's ring also glowed. Its image registered on my retina while she stroked my arm. Her featherlight touch soothed me. Under other circumstances, I would have stroked her in return, and not just her arm.

With that thought, the feel of the slime intensified. It crept over me, ebbing and flowing in the manner of a short, repetitive wave. This wasn't just strange—it was creepy. Obviously, the bathers were expected to tolerate this part of their hot-spring ritual. I stiffened and waited for the sensation to settle. My angst gave way to a feeling of compliance.

"Eve," Sabein chastised her. "Quinn must choose his own path."

My eyes flashed open. Eve started to protest, but stopped. The compliant feeling dissipated—Eve's doing. How dare she think to use her gift on me? At my glare, she also released my arm and sank back, but Sabein loomed into my face, her gaze fixed oddly off to the left of mine.

Between my crawling skin and their intense scrutiny, I'd had it. Yet, I couldn't insult the Zeffirite leader who had promised to help my quintad. Instead, I sent my glare—with a plea for help—to my bodyguard.

She shrugged—apologetically?—and linked an arm through Sabein's, pulling her back. "The only way to stop it is to leave the Waters," Eve said to me. "Go, if you wish, but may I stay?"

"Of course. I'll..." What would I do around the pool edges for hours?

Sabein crossed her arms over her breasts and sank into the water. "You'll be safe without your guard if you stay among the rocks here at the top. Refreshments are just beyond that group of boulders." Her chin jutted to the area.

Both women turned their backs, giving me the opportunity to scramble out. The slime sloughed off, glazing the water for a second before melting away. I was left clean and flushed with heat as I rewrapped in my robe. While I picked my way around the rim of the pool, Eve and Sabein whispered. About me, I was sure. I didn't care. I just wanted to get away, and the fog helped me separate myself from the weird water.

Not only had the Zeffirites set out breakfast, but they'd also brought reclining chairs. A few were even occupied. So I wasn't the only one avoiding the slimy water. To one side, a man bent behind a table, unpacking display cases of some sort. After accepting an egg sandwich, I wandered over to peer at his wares. The cases contained empty jewelry settings. One of rings, one of arm bands, one of earrings.

"Morning, Quinn," said a familiar voice, and Tristam straightened.

Tristam, Sabein's grandson and Eve's son. Did he know I knew all that? As soon as the thought formed, he smiled. That smile—or something—told me he did.

He held out a black case. "Here's the one you want."

Feeling more than awkward, I accepted the box of silver rings. "Good morning. You're a jeweler?"

"Apprenticed to one. Frater"—he nodded to a man sleeping in a nearby chair—"isn't ready to let the business go. Though, after twelve years, he'll skip the early shift. See something you like?"

Well, if he was willing to avoid that other conversation, so was I. I inspected the case's contents using the light of a lantern on the table. The velvet-lined case held split-back rings, each with empty prongs waiting for gems. Various swirling designs covered the solid bands, and fancy lace-like metalwork made up others. I wondered vaguely if Eve would like any of them before handing back the case. "Nice, but I don't need a ring."

"No, you don't. These are ear cuffs. The opening in

the back allows you to slide the piece to the same point the crystal selected." He pointed to a spot on the outer rim of his own ear.

"Well, thanks, but I've never been one for jewelry, so I think I'll pass."

Tristam chortled. "You don't feel it, do you? That's often the case when one decides immediately. Just a sec." He unwrapped a lady's hand mirror and offered it with a flourish. "Allow me to be the first to congratulate you on your acceptance by the Waters of Zeffir."

Rather than be rude, I took the mirror and looked at myself. A crystal glowed at my left ear. "What the heck?"

"Shall I mount it for you? They don't get much bigger than this on your first few visits. If it does, I can adjust the setting."

The crystal was...beautiful. I nodded.

"You have to remove it, you know. No one else can."

Watching my hand in the mirror, I pinched the crystal between two fingers. The inch-long, pencil-thin rod glowed warmly. The ends tapered to matching points, the color between them a dark amber, deeper in color than Eve's crystal. The beauty of it was compelling, its symmetrical planes perfect, its faces patterned with regular growth striations. I shifted to viewing the internal cubic structure, accessing my special sense of individual atoms. A unique fluidity melded them... Hmm, this would take some study, a deeper reach with my gift—

"Uh, Quinn? Do you need help? Shall I fetch Aunt

Eve?"

"Huh? No." I cleared my throat. "Can I see the case again?" I picked through the cuffs while Tristam set up his portable workstation. "Does Aarde boast other precious metals besides the silver?"

"It's not silver. Evard mentioned you have memory loss, so I suppose you don't know much about your assigned planet. We're rather famous for our abundance of osmium."

Osmium. The name tickled at the edges of my memory. "It's the same metal used for weapons, correct?"

"The very one. It's strong and sharp when in an alloy."

I remembered now. The Docga were one of the few empires to use the rare element, giving us superior weaponry. With it, the Docga had convinced every galaxy government to allow less-advanced planetary systems to remain self-ruling. Could this planet's metal be the Docga's reason for assisting this otherwise unnotable planet?

If they didn't know of the goud, that was.

One of the cuffs featured a swirl design that reminded me of embossed book bindings—and the scent of leather in Eve's bookshop. I handed it to Tristam, along with my crystal.

"Nice choice." He sat on a stool and locked the cuff into a padded vise. "Osmium veins run throughout Aarde's substrate, so the planet has dozens of mines. Or did. Many shut down decades ago. With our decrease in population, Aarde doesn't need additional metal. We simply reuse what we already have." He set my crystal among the cuff's prongs and began to fit them to grip its flat sides. "When I first came to apprentice with Frater, he took me around to the largest mines on the La'adir continent and enlisted a couple of the old-timers to instruct me in taking samples and smelting the raw ore."

Ore. Rock. There was a connection here. My mind just needed a bit more information. "You don't happen to have any of the metal in rock form, do you?"

He laughed. "Just have a look around. Osmium underlies all of Zeffir."

Sabein had said that about a rock, the one with the crystals. "The goud comes from osmium, then?" I asked, though clearly my crystal hadn't.

"Not quite. Goudrogen has properties unlike other elements. It remains liquid until the thermal waters carry it from deep in Aarde's core, which is also where osmium originates. So the two are always found together." He rose and dug in his crates. "We keep a sample for the kids. Ah, here we go." He handed me a rough hunk of gray rock jutting with metallic rectangles. "A piece of Cavvert's finest."

"Cavvert? The spa resort also has a mine?" I flipped the heavy ore to and fro, making the light glint off it. I'd never seen a rock like it, yet—

"That's what I've been telling you." Tristam sat at the vise again. "Aarde's thermal waters flow only at osmium outcrops, and the Cavvert mine follows the purest osmium vein found on the planet. Mind you, you won't find these"—he tapped one of several yellow crystals on his bracelet—"outside of their goud enclave, but at least one Cavvert merchant peddles Aarde's other beautiful minerals to rock collectors."

Rock collect—*damn*. Impostor Quinn's rock collection hadn't been a bunch of pretty crystals, but ore, the same stuff I held in my hand. The map I'd never gotten back to deciphering—it had to be of the mine locations, the number-color combinations some sort of rating system. Cavvert had been green-five. I whacked my head—*of course*. Those boxes at that Conducer station and in the transport bay had been heavy. It all fell into place. Impostor Quinn was stealing the planet's rare osmium.

With a sinking stomach, the reason came to me.

Weapons.

* * *

When I returned to the pool, Sabein wasn't in sight and Eve slept with her head supported on the rock edge. I'd wake her soon, but before I did, I wanted to follow Tristam's suggestion of anchoring my crystal to me by spending a few minutes with it in the water. I slipped in, pushed off the rocks and glided forward. Fine ripples flowed before me, barely tossing the tendrils of mist, thin now in the predawn light. I rolled to my left, and with the cuff submerged in the amber Waters, I sidestroked across the pool.

Staying in the water was no problem, even pleasant. As Tristam promised, the goud no longer fought for placement upon my body, since I'd chosen my crystal.

While I swam, the solution to a number of my worries sharpened into focus.

These *gut feelings*—though I hated the term—excited me. Nurturing the crystal would not only nurture my relationship with Eve, but also create bonds with the Zeffirites. They would be tenacious allies in overthrowing the rogue robbing their planet. The more I dwelt on the thought, the stronger it grew. In fact—now the idea became more fact than feeling—*I* would be stronger as a result of accepting my crystal and its intricate connections.

By the time I reached the rock edge at the far side, I also knew our search for Quil was resolving. How wasn't clear, as if the outcome was under someone else's control, not mine...but of course, Sabein had taken charge of the hunt.

With my concerns shed, my return swim felt more meditative, as if I was carried along in a current where I wasn't asked to do anything in particular, just be there. Be a part of my surroundings, enjoy them and the people who shared them with me. With a sense of peace, I completed my swim. The rising sun crested the eastern hills and I blinked into its sudden brightness.

The mist had dissipated from the low rock nestling the pool, leaving a view down the valley. Fields, houses and fishing boats lay distant and dreamlike under the pink haze stretching to the clouds on the ocean horizon.

"Mmm. Beautiful," Eve said.

I turned. She sat close by, wrapped in her robe. The sight of her, damp and rosy-cheeked from the water and the sun, made my heart leap. "It is," I agreed. "You've chosen the best pool."

"It's Sabein's, the one our triad always uses." Eve got to her feet and picked up my robe. "I think she first issued the invitation so she could keep an eye on us. But now, we're friends." She smiled. "Are you ready to go?"

I stood in the waist-high water. She opened my robe and held it for me. Not wanting to appear prudish, I climbed out and slipped my arms into the sleeves. I tied my sash and lifted my gaze to find hers fixed on my left ear. I self-consciously fingered the crystal. It hummed slightly at my touch, and a wave of energy coursed through my body, a more controlled version of what had happened when I'd been drawn into Eve and Evangeline's goud transfer.

Like with my gift for breaking apart, I recognized the molecular-level effects of the substance. I didn't understand it, and I probably couldn't control it, but in this case I didn't question the safety of nudging the phenomenon with my mind. It leaped to action. My body sang with exhilaration. It sang to Eve.

Our gazes met. The crystal gave me the confidence I lacked, even after reading Evard's little black handbook. I closed the space between us and brushed my fingers up her arm.

The hum heightened. Eve didn't move. I did.

Embracing her gently, I nuzzled my left cheek to hers. A ripple of energy flushed from my crystal, asking her permission.

There was no answer. Then I felt, rather than heard, a small whimper.

"Yes?" I asked.

Her body shuddered against mine, and as I pressed closer, my crystal rang in my ear. Its vibrations directed my hand down her side, under her robe to the source of her goud's call. I ran my thumb over a hard lump, creating a pleasant trill that echoed through her to me.

"Your second crystal," I murmured. "It's singing."

"What?" Her voice rasped, and she gazed at me through heavily lidded eyes.

"Here. Look." Pulling slightly apart, we peered to the right side of her belly. A small crystal, the size and color of mine, glowed a deep amber against her black armor.

Eve slowly shook her head, as if clearing it. Then she slid her palm between our chests and pressed, the metal band of her crystal ring cool on my skin. I loosened my hold, but froze when a telling ripple whirled from her hand. She wanted this. Totally, completely, with her entire being.

Yet she said, "Quinn, I can't."

I tensed, my fingers flexing on her arms. "You mean it?"

A wall went up and cut off her goud. Quick as a heartbeat, my goud searched to break through the shield, but I didn't have her experience to carry through. Instead, I gathered her close and bent my head to hers, willing her to stay. She sagged into me as if her knees had given way, her heart pounding against my chest.

The handbook said a rapid heartbeat was a sign of attraction. That and... I tipped up her chin and turned us so the sun fell on her soft features. There—her cheeks had reddened, flushed. I stroked my fingers over her hot flesh. She gasped, another sign. The flashing eyes... I wasn't sure what they signaled.

She whispered, "Quinn?"

"Yes?"

"If you don't let me go, I will knee your very available groin."

The words replayed in my mind before they registered. Logic overrode emotion, and self-preservation kicked in as my threatened parts recoiled. But I knew she'd made the threat to cover something. Okay, I'd let her. I lifted my hands and stepped back.

Eve adjusted her robe, avoiding my gaze.

I pivoted before she saw my smile and walked to the edge of our grotto to wait for her. She was fighting her attraction to me, I was sure. The knowledge sent my body humming in delirium. The crystals relayed her true emotions. Eve wanted me. I wanted her. Soon, I'd discover the reason she kept raising a shield of toughness and break it down. But for now—

My thoughts froze. A robed couple stood outside the entrance to our pool. The man's arms wrapped around a blond woman while they shared a passionate kiss, their hips tight, her fingers tunneling through his gray hair.

Behind me, Eve muttered, "D'dair," and tugged at my arm.

The couple broke apart, and the woman squealed in delight. "Eve! We've been waiting for you." Gwyn— Eve's daughter—bounded forward.

As the man's gaze met mine, I recognized the other half of her *we*. Cyrem. The older man was Gwyn's lover?

He smiled broadly at us. "Morning, Eve. Quinn."

Gwyn grabbed Eve from my side. For a second, they glowed as they touched. "You'll never believe it!" Her rush of words was barely audible. I stepped closer, straining to hear. "A new one came. I didn't feel it, and look where it is." She parted her robe, and there on her belly, slightly to the right at her hipbone, sat a crystal.

"Same place as yours, Eve," I said without thinking.

Gwyn's eyes widened. "Where?" Her hand flew to Eve's armored middle, visible under her parted robe.

The amber-colored crystal was no longer there.

If looks could kill, I'd be dead. Eve's stony glare left no doubt that this was the last piece of information she wanted spread around.

Unfortunately, Gwyn persisted. "Is it true? Show me."

Eve opened a pouch on the weapon belt that once more rode her hips and extracted the crystal. She didn't get it much beyond the cover flap when the stone flew from her fingers, slammed her right hip and attached itself to her rock-hard suit. Before our eyes, the crystal sank into the material, until only an inch-long angled edge showed.

At Eve's groan, Gwyn laughed. "Oh, you've got it bad."

Cyrem's lips formed an O, and the look he slid me was startled and speculative.

"I can't wait," bubbled the radiant Gwyn. "We've both been called to bear next year."

With that, I got it. Babies—these crystals were about babies. Gwyn's face shone. Clouds shadowed Eve's. I didn't want to think about what was on mine.

Cyrem and I exchanged glances. We spoke at once.

"Gwyn, we need to find Perry."

"Time to go, Eve."

We separated them. I don't know what Cyrem did, but I kept my mouth shut. We left, taking the path through the boulders, skipping over rivulets of golden water and winding by dozens of pools, some occupied, some not. When we were about to emerge from the rocks to a grassy area, I knew I had to say something to fix this situation. I caught Eve's wrist and slowed her before we merged with the many townspeople gathering there.

"Sorry I spilled the beans, as Quaene says."

She released her breath, but didn't answer, didn't even look at me.

I took my hand off her as a precaution. "Come on, give me a break. I'm clueless about what these things mean. I won't tell anyone else. Besides, I have another matter needing our attention. Tristam—"

"Finally," boomed Evard. The big man strode forward, hand-in-hand with Quaene.

Even with my crystal giving me a steadier outlook, I wasn't sure how I felt about that kind of closeness with my ever-more-youthful *grandmother*. Her face had smoothed, her hair turned even blonder—late thirties? But she hugged me and settled my qualms about our connection.

"I wanted to fetch you," Evard said, "but Quaene insisted we remain in this area."

She held me at arm's length, studying the crystal at my ear. "Do you feel differently after taking these Waters?"

"A bit," I admitted. "I think we have new allies."

"And our issues will resolve with their help," she said, like it was fact. "Funny way to make a decision, but..." She shrugged and gestured to her foot. A bracelet on her ankle sported two small crystals. "They indicate we should remain around here."

"Has Evangeline gone ahead?" Eve asked.

"*Nei*. She's waiting with PT." Evard pointed beyond the shifting Zeffirites. "And now you're here. We could head home for lunch."

I didn't know what that meant to Quaene's crystals, but she linked an arm through mine, and we followed Evard while Eve came behind us. Many of the Zeffirites waited on low rocks in the grassy area, including Evangeline. PT lay by her side, watching people emerge from the many trails exiting the pools.

As we drew closer, the Docgan stood. His ears perked, and his tail wagged. Ahead of us, Evard went directly to greet them, but Quaene halted me while a group coming from an adjoining path crossed ours.

Everyone walked by, except for one straggler carrying a cuff set with two small crystals. The man passed, and I felt a burst of recognition from the goud zinging between Quaene and me.

Her hand shot out and she grabbed the dark-haired stranger's sleeve.

"Quil!"

TWENTY-NINE

QUINN

Quil's face ignited my memories, one after another. *He blocked the transport corridor, blocked me, my guests, his narrow chest draped with the straps of several cases, his delicate fingers closed on another two. His harsh accusations of endangering his precious electronics stung, instantly alienating us...*

The unwelcome news at a staff roundtable that I was assigned a project with that rude squirrel of a geek, the look in his small, dark eyes no more pleased than my own... Then he asked intelligent questions no one ever had, and I realized what we could do together...

I had to break off the talk. I had to see a woman... He wasn't pleased. And after, he'd been at the bar. A drink, or three, an apology smoothed it over. Talking, talking, until...

Quil held me, my chest throbbing with pain, my world shrieking...

His anger, so furious. Quaene running after him, his black hair flipping with the shake of his head, his back dissolving in the Conducer...leaving us, leaving me facing the pain—

"Quinn?" Fingers pinched into my arm, and I startled out of the visions, my gaze careening off Eve's con-

286

cerned face to Quil's shocked one. "You know Pen?" she whispered.

"Deserter," I hissed before realizing I'd spoken aloud.

Those dark eyes narrowed. The thin mouth I'd just remembered twisted into a snarl. "Better a deserter than dancing attendance to your womanizing whims, postponing the precious work the Docga are chomping to acquire. I understand you've promoted yourself from particle analyst to lead of G47's Corps, a position at which you are woefully inadequate since you clearly ignored the data reports in time to knock back a simple plant that's stagnated here for seventy-some years."

Hell, he was just as volatile now as he'd been at our first meeting. I stepped forward. "You can't blame me for that faulty analysis. I wasn't even there to—"

"Well, you sure as hell can't blame the system I designed." His jaw jutted defiantly. "I'm sick of you putting our mission at risk."

"He's done no such thing." Quaene shoved her way between us, rougher than I'd seen my grand—*her* act in the time we'd been together. Apparently, the same was true for Quil. He jerked back and would have stormed off if Evard hadn't bounded into his path.

Quil's hands flew behind his back. "Don't you dare—"

His fingers, I remembered, he was neurotically protective of his fingers. If he wasn't able to use a keyboard, and he might as well die, he'd told me.

"I'm not doing a thing, Pen, my good man."

Pen, the same name Eve had called Quil.

Evard said, "But you need to listen to your lead. Simple Docga policy." He gestured to Quaene, who thanked him with a nod.

Quil eyed the hulking Tarni much the same way I first had. He turned back to us. A few Zeffirites skittered through the area, giving our group a wide berth. Evangeline and PT came forward.

The Docgan rumbled.

Quil muttered, "Can't say I share the sentiment." His gaze lingered on Evangeline's face. He said a soft, "Good day," before darting a wary look to Eve, standing at my shoulder.

His eyes widened.

I glanced at her. She'd dropped her robe and stood fully armored, her hand on the short sword. Good, that might make the bastard think—

"So he's added you to his team of fancy Blackguards?" Quil's hard gaze fell on me. "Not once in my eight stints of command have I requisitioned a single guard for a humanitarian mission. What are you playing at?"

"I might ask you the same thing," Quaene said, "but let's get something straight first. Have you seen an image of the Minister Quinn currently overseeing our G47 operations?"

Quil opened his mouth, but Quaene cut him off. "Until recently, you *hadn't*. Though he goes by the same name and looks like him, the minister at Dome has never been our Quinn. That rogue 'torg stowed away on our transport, which I pieced together only after learning he is a near copycat of Quinn. He tried passing for Quinn and failed enough that he raised PT's suspicions. PT thought the cause was E-IV conversion issues, so he watched Quinn 24/7, which prevented the impostor from making a move on Quinn."

She had his attention. Mine, too, since the tale connected bits of my memories.

"When the impostor couldn't get Quinn alone, he made a desperate attempt to kill him after we landed, seconds after you left through the Conducer. His attack pulled Quinn from a cross-leap and damaged his memories, but we escaped." She drew a breath. "Do you see? Your grievances aren't with this man."

Anger dissipating, Quil darted speculative looks between Quaene and me.

Why had she waited to tell me? *Oh, hell.* I'd flipped out yesterday, then tied one on.

Quaene's manner relaxed as she saw Quil's understanding. "We need your help. The situation on Aarde is dire."

He snorted. "Just because I'm in hiding, don't think I stopped getting news. I've been holding my breath—almost literally—that the Docga's quarterly inspection transport arrives before the hornwort spores so I can get the hell off this deathtrap."

With more sarcasm than I should use, I said, "*You* won't be the one to die."

"*You* have no proof of that."

Quaene gave a cry of exasperation. "Can we drop the

taunts? Start fresh?"

"Start fresh?" Quil sneered. "With this—"

"Are you kidding?" I barked back. "If you'd stuck around and helped, we could have fought that impostor upon arrival. Our workforce wouldn't be scrambling to cut back killing spores, on top of 'torgs facing deactivation and kidnapping."

Quil tensed, his features shifting as he processed the bomb I'd purposefully dropped.

"It's true," Evangeline whispered, and we jerked to face her, a timid figure clenching PT's fur for support. "He has the transports ready. Our recall is tomorrow, Blackguard-enforced if we delay by so much as an hour."

While she outlined the proof, he listened politely, unlike his reaction to the rest of us. Afterward, it was easier to have the necessary conversation about the 'torg recall, what we knew of Quetta and Quala, the potential use of the fail-safe to take control, as well as the demoralizing loss of my frequency.

From under long black bangs, he eyed me.

I caught Quaene's look, but I already knew what I had to do. We needed him. Aarde needed him. I drew a breath, aware of a faint hum at my ear. "I'm sorry there have been misunderstandings and ill feelings. You won't see any resistance from me as we move forward." I stuck out my hand. "I'd be grateful if you'd join us."

He dropped his gaze and shuffled forward to offer a brief, limp grip. "Your hostility is—was understandable. I probably deserved it, but I'm seeing the planet through new eyes since I arrived on Zeffir, thanks to living with the natives instead of apart from them." He stared at the crystals in his hand, then shoved the cuff onto his arm, under his robe. "What's the plan?"

Eve promptly invited him to Passages. He threw her a look of surprise, followed by a pathetic puppy-dog look to Evangeline. At her nod, he scurried to her side for the walk downhill, passing Quaene with a last caveat. "But I'm warning you, aggression isn't my thing."

He could have fooled me.

THIRTY

EVE

Furious. Irritated. Apprehensive.

Quaene, Quinn and Quil.

Naturally, *Pen*, the *fisherman*, felt trapped by his discovery. In his defense, the welcome hadn't gone smoothly. Clearly, the E-IVs weren't the team they were supposed to be, but they'd rebounded, thanks to Quaene and, to my surprise, Evangeline. After taking the daring step of speaking up to assist, she assumed her usual quiet demeanor under her admirer's watchful eye.

I rose and cleared a few dishes, hovering near the lanky Quil while the others finished.

"Damned awful way to end a session at the Waters," he mumbled after refusing seconds, amusing Evard with his ridiculous attempts to gain Evangeline's attention. Even with his identity revealed, he was the same man I'd steered away from my run-mate, a woman his *type*, but who hadn't a clue what to do about him. Because the Zeffirites and the Waters accepted Quil, I'd never guessed he was a 'torg, but it made sense now. He'd adhered to Docga policy, not showing any interest in the native women who approached him.

At least the fisherman's presence gave me something to think about other than Quinn.

I'd let things go too far at the pool. If his question about the second crystal hadn't interrupted my total immersion in our combined lust, a minute later I'd have been lying with him between my legs. I had to keep my distance.

I crossed our kitchen to put on the kettle and gather cups for tea. Seconds later, Quaene joined me. I sensed her request before she said in an undertone, "What's your take on Quil?"

"He feels uneasy. Wishes he was elsewhere." *With Evangeline.* I didn't add that as I handed her a paper bag and shuffled a glass dish between us. "Would you refill the sugar bowl, please?" I said louder and then dropped my voice. "You knew him well? Before?"

"No. Less than two weeks."

That's all the time they'd had together before launching a long-term, interplanetary mission? "Oh?" I set a tray on the counter.

"The Docga trust their matches. Usually excellent, but this time—" Seething frustration burst through her stoic exterior. "I'd heard of him. He's an often-requested computer expert who's shunted from mission to mission for short-term assignments. You may have guessed from his manner why. No people skills. Please do what you can to smooth the situation between him and Quinn, before I kill them both."

She set the filled sugar bowl on my tray and picked up the cream pitcher.

I took it from her and nodded to the table. "Tell him

your plans," I muttered.

She retook her seat. I skirted to the refrigerator to get the milk *and* feel out Quinn. He'd lost his amorous emotions. In fact, Quinn's logical leader demeanor had kicked in the moment we'd run into Quil.

I was the one who couldn't move on.

Quaene finished relaying the still incomplete scheme. "It'll be tricky getting the impostor under wraps and securing enough control of the B-runs to move adequate workers to halt the onset of the horn-wort sporophyte stage. I hope we can find the data to develop a triage for which pools to address first."

"It'll be a snap to access it in the mainframe." Quil dismissed the technology search they'd worried over with a few explanations beyond my scope of under-standing. "What were the Docga thinking to create a 'torg from a man who would relegate people to the lev-el of possessions to be stolen?"

The kettle whistle blew. I grabbed it and poured the hot water into a teapot to steep.

"Electorgs aren't the only planet resource he's got on his shopping list," Quinn said. "He values what's in those boxes, and I discovered a lead on the contents of the Cavvert ones while talking with Tristam." His gaze darted to me as he touched his ear cuff. "He showed me a sample of the raw ore of osmium, a rare metal that's common on Aarde. I believe it matches the rocks we discovered in the minister's office. Putting together Tristam's information with the map and the weight of the boxes, I suspect Impostor Quinn is mining the metal ore for weapon production."

"No," Evangeline cried. "The Aardites have so little to use in interplanetary trade. This loss would tip the balance, making them always beholden to some other empire."

"I hate to pour oil on the fire," Quil said, "but if they're stealing metal for weapons, then absconding with the electorgs may be a way to create a conscripted army."

"*Great Grünmann*," Evard snarled, and Evangeline's worried gaze met mine.

Quaene motioned for silence, then asked Quinn, "Do you have a plan for verifying this?"

"Go to Cavvert, of course. To the mine."

"Why?" Quil asked. "Just open a box in the transporter room."

"Guarded," Quinn said.

"Then access a system that's not guarded, at least not from me. Computer files."

"I could be to Cavvert and back by the time you break the codes."

Evangeline nudged me. "Time to work," she murmured.

Without touching them, my best efforts weren't taking. I darted for their plates, brushing shoulders. Each settled back in his chair. The effect was minor, but something.

"Gentlemen." Quaene rose and fixed each with a look that should have sent them cowering, yet they barely concealed their competitive ire. "I can't have discord between run-mates. Quil, don't get us wrong, Quinn and I are glad to have you back on board, but there is a certain...annoyance at your disappearance. The three of us ought to pull aside for a period of reacquaintance, but the clock is ticking for G47, *obliging* us to suspend personal feelings."

She waited until each man cleared his expression, and nodded. "Thank you. Hacking into Impostor Quinn's data has to be done, for many reasons. I trust that Quil, Minister of Technology, can do it."

"Thank you for the reminder," Quinn said evenly.

"I admit that my search may not be as fast as Quinn's trip if he can still perform his particle transference," Quil said. "But I'm sure the industrious impostor has left some juicy tidbits."

Evangeline poured tea, and I served it. Evard offered his services in his less-than-conventional search methods, including Cyrem's sources.

The techie exchange bolstered Quil's confidence. "Let's get this fail-safe test over and done. I certainly haven't done anything so inept as to change my frequency"—he didn't bother disguising a smug look—"but I admit I only paid half a mind to that E-IV lesson. Never thought any of us would have reason to shut down a fellow E. Where's that circuit again?"

PT commenced with another of his lengthy rumbles. Quil got his answer, then he and Quaene rose and clasped hands. PT stood between them, his eyes closed and head cocked.

A minute passed, and Quaene blew out her breath.

"Thank you." They dropped hands.

The Docgan yipped and growled.

Quaene rolled her eyes. "Point made." They clasped hands again.

I looked at Evangeline.

"Their mind-link access is slow. Practice will improve it. When they've got Quala combined, their joint flow of energy will help her access her circuit. Shutting down the impostor then requires just a touch, a finger anywhere on him for a split second to interrupt his frequency."

It sounded too simple to be possible, but of course the three E's must act in accordance. After another dozen trials, they reached their circuits to PT's satisfaction. The sense of relief in the room was apparent.

Evard threw his arm around Quaene for an unminister-like hug when she finished. "You're positive it'll do the trick?"

"It will," Quil said. "Now that we have the fail-safe settled, I assume I'm back in the quintad's good graces?"

PT growled. The rumble extended with Quil shifting uncomfortably until Evard broke in, a false cheer in his voice. "Buck up, Quil. Perhaps if you resolve this impostor business in some stellar manner, they won't deactivate you for desertion."

Quil dropped his gaze. "I understand it was wrong. But it wouldn't have helped to stay only to be trapped." When the silence lengthened, he said, "Fine, I admit I was selfish, looking after my own ass."

The words matched the simple pragmatic outlook typical of many Zeffirites. What had Quil's organic life been? Hold it—I knew Quil. So did Evard and Evangeline. Not well, but at least better than Quaene and Quinn. And the man we knew was a poltroon, to use an Earth-century term. An utter coward. But did that describe *Quil*, the E-IV Minister of Technology?

As if in answer to my question, he said, "Never was much of the outdoorsy type, but here... I downloaded the watercraft function as a scheme for hiding, but the sea has gotten a hold of me. I'm coming to like the whole nature thing. When it's not trying to kill us." He gave a wry smile. "Time away from electronics has changed me. I'll do my duty and help pull the mission back on course."

"Thank you," Quaene said, and Quinn echoed her a second later.

Quil got to his feet. "I'll pop down to my ship and get the porta I've programmed to accelerate searches. Evard, can I use your office connection?"

"Excellent idea! I'll boot up while you're gone." Evard rose and held the kitchen door.

"Thanks." Quil turned to me. "Eve? Would you show me out?"

I tried not to show my surprise. Because of my constant presence when he wanted to be alone with Evangeline, *Pen* and I had never been overly friendly. But when Evard lifted his chin in agreement, I said, "Of course," and led the way.

Before I could slide back the lock, Quil said, "Since

I'm exposed, we can be honest with each other, can't we, Eve?" A tenor of determination emanated from the man.

"Certainly," I said with more assurance than I felt.

"I respect your close relationship with Evangeline, but now that you know I'm like you, would you cut me some slack? Let me get to know the woman. I promise you I'll make her happy. Happier than she is now."

D'dair. If I hadn't known things about Evangeline that made her unable to be with any man, this would be a nice request. "I want to see Evangeline content, but it's up to her to decide—"

"You interfere." He jabbed a finger at me. "I don't know exactly what you do with the goudrogen—or whatever—but it no longer matters. Just stop."

Standing my ground, I crossed my arms. "You've lived among us for a few months. Aren't you familiar with my role in this society?"

Quil clenched his fists. "I'm all too familiar with it. But we're not talking about smoothing over differences between the natives. Evangeline and I don't even know each other well enough to have differences. And we're not Zeffirites," he retorted, an escalating edge to his voice.

"You were when it was convenient," I snapped back, my temper rising with his.

"And you weren't?" His nostrils flared, his body trembled. "That's over and done. Leave us alone to interact like mature 'torgs. In fact"—he looked me over, head to foot—"as a minister, I should have a personal guard myself. Evangeline would be perfect."

Anger spilled from him and rebounded within me. "No!"

Quil crossed his arms over his chest. "Give me one good reason why not."

"The stress of guarding would kill my baby sister, or plunge her innocent mind—" I slapped a hand over my mouth.

Blessed Waters, what had I said?

Gasps sounded, hurt flooded my body. From within, from him and others. I closed my eyes and shoved the emotions away, but they kept coming. Not just mine and Quil's, but also the reactions of the others who had sidled from the kitchen when they heard our argument.

"Sister?" Quinn said from close behind me.

Quaene whispered. "How old was she?"

"Five." I opened my eyes and met Quil's stare. It was on the tip of my tongue to ask if that was reason enough for him, but the anger had drained from him.

He shook his head in clear disbelief. "Innocent."

The word was more acknowledgment than question. I was about to nod when his gaze veered...to Evangeline.

She'd heard, too? No! The Docga had warned if Evangeline ever did learn the truth, her body might reject the electronics.

Wide-eyed, she took a step back, then another, then turned and ran down the long aisle. Her footsteps pounded on the stairs. I moved to follow her, but Evard stopped me.

"Give her a few minutes."

He was right. I had to calm myself first. He pulled me into a sympathetic hug.

"I blew it," I mumbled. "I was so immersed in analyzing his every emotion, drawing them in, that I didn't realize his feelings had overtaken me. Evangeline. She...her body and function integrations could—" *Fail.* I couldn't bring myself to say it.

He lifted my chin. "Perhaps the time has come for her to know."

Quaene said, "The Docga would never—"

"Oh, yes, they would." A distressed sound broke from me, half laugh, half sob. "If they want you badly enough, they'll do whatever you ask."

After a moment, she squeezed my arm. "I can see why they would. But... The poor girl."

"Quaene," Quinn said roughly. "Don't make Eve feel any worse than she already does."

I wiped the corner of my eye. "Obviously, I owe Evangeline the story. Minister Quil, does my word that she's far too emotionally sensitive answer your question? A guard's obligation to fight and injure or, worse yet, kill someone in your defense would break the fragile hold she has on her maturity."

He raised a hand. "Say no more. I understand. I—" He shook his head, his gaze falling to the floor. A heavy weight of guilt wafted from him.

"You had no way of knowing. Don't blame yourself."

He glanced up, his lips bent in a rueful smile. "Easy for you to say. I feel like a louse." His gaze flitted to

302 | LAUREL WANROW

Quaene. "Under the circumstances, I hope you don't mind if I take a bit longer to collect that porta."

She nodded, and he left, with Evard following to calm the Zeffirites arriving due to my distress.

As soon as the door closed, Quinn threw up his hands. "It's all coming back. That man is next to impossible to work with."

"I know he's high-strung," Quaene said. "We'll just have to make accommodations. I think Eve can adjust her talent now that she knows the situation. Right, Eve?"

"What?" Quinn said brusquely. "You saw how he went out of his way to confront someone he just agreed to work with. I don't trust him not to hamper her guard duties."

"We have to work with him, Quinn. You have to trust him, or..." Quaene tilted her head and gave Quinn a narrow-eyed look.

He glared back. "I don't think—" He shot a look to me, and practically in unison they said, "Excuse us."

Quinn gestured Quaene ahead and then followed her brisk strides up the stairs where the door to her room slammed closed.

Thank the Waters I had shut down. I had no idea what their problem was, nor did I have the energy to find out. I had to see to Evangeline—to my little sister.

THIRTY-ONE

EVE

Evangeline called, "Come in," on my first knock. She shifted on the bed to sit against the headboard, a pillow clenched to her chest.

I winced at her puffy eyes and red nose. "I thought you might like some tea." I nodded to the tray I held. "While I explain how terribly sorry I am."

"Why did the Docga take me at five when the minimum age is eighteen?" she asked.

"Because I asked them to. I—I loved you too much to let go."

"Loved me?" Her question came on a hiccupping laugh, but she squared her shoulders. "We're friends, but I never got a hint you were...you are..."

If it was hard for me, it was harder for her. I sighed. "Your older sister and...after Mother died, I practically took her place." The shock of the news was obviously still raw, but she seemed ready for me to tell her more. "Can we sit?" I gestured to the settee before her fireplace.

PT took a spot on the rug while I poured and we settled onto the couch together. I drank my tea and stalled. She held her cup, her face shifting through emotions as she stared into space.

"How could you..." She drew a breath and faced me. "I've been...not exactly unhappy. There are the animals, but..."

I leaned back so I didn't have to see her accusing eyes. "For the Docga to agree to save you, I had to let go of our previous relationship. It doesn't mean I stopped loving you."

"So you asked them to bring me?"

"You were all I had left. Father died soon after your birth, Mother when you were three, leaving just the two of us. Then the sickness hit our village, and the losses were much worse. Everyone died. Or was about to. Even Emma, my healer mentor who had been like a mother to me, died. The Great Pestilence took every last person in our village. Through meticulous hygiene, I'd managed to keep it from us. Then you caught it. I couldn't stand the thought of my—" I gulped in air to keep going. "My precious baby, the last of my family, being gone."

Her fingers brushed, and then squeezed, my arm. "Tell me. Tell me the whole story."

I slipped my hand over hers and squeezed back. "I've missed you." Then we were hugging each other with no barriers, no guilt, and it felt like not a day had passed.

"There isn't much to tell," I said when I could. "We came from a village in central England. The disease, the plague, progressed from the cities to us. Carried, they tell me now, by fleas on rats. When things got bad, several of the young men went for help. They never returned.

"Three dogs arrived. The big fellows circled the village in the most terrifying way, watching us from afar, like vultures waiting to pounce, the people said. I knew this wasn't their intent, and I told the animals they were making it worse for us. They all left but one."

"You told—no. You sent out your emotions to *animals*? You've never done that here."

I shrugged. "Mother taught us to keep our gifts secret. We'd have been hanged for witchcraft. I used it, though, to become one of the healers. I sort of graduated to mediating for the community, though in those times, the men handled the village affairs, so my counsel went through the women who came to me for advice and then passed it to their men."

"And the dog?"

I smiled. Of course she would be most interested in the tale of the mysterious dog.

"One night, while leaving another household in which everyone had died, I caught sight of him watching from the garden. I emptied the larder and set it out, calling to him to take what he needed to survive in our harsh world. To my surprise, the dog expressed his gratitude directly into my mind. Then, as if it were nothing unusual, he selected a shoulder of beef and accompanied me home. On a whim, I invited the dog inside. He accepted. Over the next few days, he was a supportive companion. For both me and you."

Evangeline smiled. "I wish I could remember."

"I do, too. I felt more comfortable leaving you with

Shadow, as you called him. He was content to wait. For me. I had been singled out for my skills. Because I could understand him, he asked if I was willing to go on to another life, to help others. For always, he told me. I thought the dog was some form of angel sent to watch over you so I could help people."

She looked at me, wide-eyed, and giggled.

My breath caught. Before all this, we'd giggled together over stories I'd told, a way to dismiss my fears. I swallowed and continued. "His offer sounded like heaven to me. But it would only be heaven if we stayed together. They said you were too young, so I said no.

"Then my worst nightmare happened: You fell ill. I stayed by your side, neglecting the handful of people left, because I believed they were too far gone, and if I tried my hardest, I could give you the will to make it through this with me."

"But you gave me too much of yourself, didn't you, Eve?"

Tears stung, and I blinked them back. "I did. I caught the plague. I was sick and heartsick over failing you, but our angel insisted I listen to him. After his time with us, Shadow saw your young gift's potential and understood our bond. He had approached his Docga superiors on our behalf. They would consider you and let us remain together if I agreed to two requirements. One was you had to age. The procedure to save you—what I learned later was the electronic implants—worked only on adults." I stopped to catch my breath and wiped at my cheeks.

Evangeline handed me a handkerchief, and after I'd dried my eyes, she slipped her hand in mine. "What else did you promise?"

I sighed. "After you became this young woman, I would only be allowed to remember our history if I didn't reveal it. The med-techs could age you, but we risked your body rejecting the implants if you learned you'd been only five. They hadn't done the procedure on so young an individual, so couldn't say when the danger would end, if ever. I was so afraid you might die, I promised them—and myself—never to tell."

A growl erupted from PT.

I'd forgotten he was there. Evangeline said, "He says the danger is obviously over. The Docga will understand you acted to protect me. He'll make sure of it. Please continue the story."

"The conditions were difficult to agree to," I said. "Shadow explained the Docga would treasure our commitment and return the favor with many lifetimes of happiness in productive work with others." I closed my eyes. "You were so ill, dying before my very eyes, and nothing I did made a difference. I saw no other choice. I agreed.

"I curled up beside you and gave in, happy I'd done what I could for you despite the changes it meant. When I woke to the dog nosing me, I found you dead. He said he had to remove you to his ship to start their lifesaving work. He put his head on yours, and you turned a golden yellow before you both melted away. I thought I'd had a nightmare and looked around the house for you before I finally cried myself to exhaustion and fell sleep."

Evangeline leaned forward and glared at PT. "Why didn't he take us together?" The Docgan rumbled in his throat and looked at me. "Because the Docga time travel, they knew when each of us would die. But they do not change fate, so by their rules had to wait," she translated.

"Which I guess I did. I vaguely remember Shadow returning, and I asked for you, but the next time I woke was at an adjustment center. They thought I'd have difficulty with your aging, but I surprised them. I was just so grateful you were alive, I didn't care that you didn't appear to be my little sister anymore. We were placed with another—Evard—for the skills needed at this Post and set with frequencies and names for our new triad."

Evangeline was silent for some time before she asked, "What was my real name?"

"I don't remember," I whispered. "I wish I could tell you, but they erased it."

PT gave another low rumble that caused Evangeline to sigh. I squeezed her hand clasping mine. "What is it?"

"He says once communications are restored, he'll contact his superiors. The electorg update team he serves on may be able to help me."

Oh? What kind of help? The Docgan lowered his head to his paws, and Evangeline settled against my side. This wasn't the time to ask.

THIRTY-TWO

QUINN

I waited until the bedroom door shut and then rounded on Quaene. "Why do you continue to badger me about trusting people? Didn't I do well selecting this triad to guard us? Navigating Dome? Soliciting native assistance?" I waved my hands like a hyper teen. "I'm taking on more, remembering more and following every guideline you instilled in me. At what point will you consider me your equal and capable of decision-making?"

Her hand flew up, palm out. She didn't have to say a thing. I clenched my runaway jaws and whirled to the window to collect myself, staring over the rooftops lit by the late morning sun.

Quaene allowed me several minutes and then gently said, "You're upset about the threat to Eve, as well as the news about her run-mate. I am, too, but I'm not personally involved. I can distance myself. Let me handle Quil's treatment of Eve. I can do it with a—"

"Clear head," I snarled and immediately regretted my tone. "Damn. Sorry. This is all coming out wrong." I drew a deep breath before turning around. "You're right, of course. I can't make a logical decision concerning that woman."

"You can. Just not after hearing something as complicated as another secret this 'torg has kept. Those past events aside, she's been nothing but honest. And that makes all the difference in where we go from here. You said you'd keep her as your guard. Do you still feel the same?"

"I did. I will. The Docga are responsible for Evangeline's presence here, not Eve."

"Excellent. Next problem: Quil. Aside from his poor people skills, he has talents we need. Just as Eve does. He's shaken your trust, but he's all we've got."

Because I'd screwed my frequency. I raked a hand over my head. "I know it. Except he's such a pain in the ass." I blew out my breath. "I'll do it. For you, and for Eve, and for this planet. At least Quala is on board to help."

Quaene sighed. "I spoke with Eve, and though she's not a mind reader, what she discerned of Quala's intent is interesting: Under her requests for help, Quala felt more fear of you than anything else."

"I wasn't in a position to be nice."

"Yet, she kept asking you to return. Eve said Quala's urgency centered on the hornwort spore release and stopping it, which didn't surprise me coming from a woman who spent every spare minute with the cargo plants."

"So her love for Aarde's plants surpasses my scariness. That *is* why she was appointed Minister of Biological Resources."

"According to Sabein, the division has continued

their monitoring. The follow-up for removing the plants fell under the impostor's direction. So no faults with Quala doing her job, which I cannot say about Quil. He's done *nothing*." Her low voice rasped with disappointment.

I rubbed my racing head. "What can you tell me of his time with you—us?"

She looked pensive. "How much have you remembered about the R&R on W234?"

No way around it. I repeated what I'd told Eve while drunk and my newest flashes involving Quil. "Though I have no face, name or clear recognition, a woman was part of my stay there. Do you remember her, or other events?"

Quaene settled onto the end of the bed and took a breath, as if willing calm upon herself. Eve would be of help here, but she must be with Evangeline by now. I pulled up the chair and steeled myself for another rush of memories.

"She was Myriah Feldfine, a liaison appointed by the local government to work with Reboot. Quil brought that you knew her to my attention. He ran into the two of you and the pilot trainee—who was her brother Javion—on our transport. As Minister of Technology, Quil took a firm stand on security, particularly when it involved his equipment. Since she had Schiftani clearances, I asked Quil to drop it so we wouldn't insult our host government."

Myriah. The fleeting memories of her were painful, so I pushed them off in favor of the brother. Javion. An easygoing, sandy-haired man matching her in looks...I thought. We'd taken out an aerocar together. It'd been fun to fly again, though nothing like piloting the spaceships we both loved. I'd brought them aboard the transport at Myriah's request—a quite persuasive one, which brought a flush to me now. Our tour ended with Quil's rude accusations.

I hadn't seen Javion again. Our E-IV conversions took place the next day. I'd been happy—unlike yesterday—because the deactivation would get Quil off my back. Afterward, the team's initial roundtable had gone about as well as today's meeting, until the talk came around to projects. The tech guy came alive. We'd been paired to convert my wealth of particle-transference information into a usable computer language. No one understood it in the format I did, but then he outlined the concept and needs perfectly. The possibilities of working with him excited me. We would have continued the conversation, initiated the work even, but before we left for G47, I had mere hours to...

To say good-bye to Myriah. Again, stabs of pain stopped me from a full recollection. It must not have gone well. I tried skipping to the next event, and the pain worsened. I lifted my gaze and met Quaene's.

She continued with the story. They'd guessed I'd gone to see Myriah my last night in port. Quil and Quala went for drinks. I came in and proceeded to get sloshed. Quala left with a fellow she'd met over the R&R, but Quil stayed. He considered it his duty to see me back, but when I used the restroom, I didn't return.

Yells from the kitchen staff drew him and the other patrons—to me, bleeding from a knife wound to the chest.

"It just missed your heart," Quaene whispered. "The pro-techs put you back together overnight. Security agreed with Quil that your fraternization had set fire to some local tempers. You were possibly at risk until they found the culprit, so we put you in the sick bay with PT in attendance and left on schedule the next morning.

"*You*—or rather, Impostor Quinn acting in your stead—quarreled with Quil and added more misery to the stomach bug laying out half of us. Our arrival looked bleak. When we landed, both Quetta and Quala were bedridden, so I took the opportunity to pull you two aside. To keep our conversation private while the crew unloaded, we ducked into the Conducer room. I had you in agreement, or at least chagrinned enough to present a good front, until PT found us.

"The Docgan was distressed. He'd already confided what he thought were conversion-acceptance problems in the quintad, but now that we'd arrived and were free of the confinement with the crew, he wanted to report that he suspected this stomach bug had been drug-induced.

"A stabbing at what should have been a secure Docga facility, and now drugging. The two had to be linked, but how? I was beside myself, but worse, Quil leaped to one of his rash decisions, arguing to sequester the crew—and us. We tried talking him down, but he activated the Conducer, saying he was resigning from *this stinking mix.* When I reminded him the Docga couldn't approve his transfer for three months, he said, 'Exactly. See you then.'

"At the very moment Quil headed into the Conducer, a crewman burst in. He yelled for you, but we ignored him—PT, you and I were arguing a blue streak with Quil all the way down the accelerator corridor. You were on my heels, then you weren't. You know the rest. PT stopped your attacker, but we lost the Docgan while you and I escaped."

For a few minutes, I absorbed more of my forgotten story. Quaene darted anxious looks at me, probably trying to determine if she'd gone too far. Finally, I shrugged. "Sounds good."

She laughed. "Are you kidding me?"

"What else can I say? A fair bit of it sounds familiar, and the rest I can see, like long ago memories. It's easier to swallow than my organic past, which I glean, from a few trickling memories, occurred centuries ahead of—or somehow parallel to—now." I rubbed my forehead. "I'll petition the Docga for my complete dossier after we regain headquarters." I flashed her a smile in hopes of reassuring her. "So, we have business to attend to. Hopefully with Quil when he gets to a better mood."

"*If* he gets to a better mood."

I cleared my throat. "This conversation veered more to me than Quil."

She flipped her palms up. "Interactions with him centered around complaints about the rest of the team, mainly you, even though he was drilled in social behavior at his last—" She slapped a hand over her mouth, her eyes growing wide. "I did not say that." She swallowed. "His programming skills are phenomenal, and he's coming around to relating to others' needs, if begrudgingly. I witnessed his efforts with your project."

Best not to comment on the personnel issues with Quil. After my poor greeting earlier—and our apparent history—I'd come across only as stirring up trouble. "We'll make it work."

"Thank you. I should check what Eve detected in him before the outburst."

"Yes," I murmured. I should do my own checking with Eve.

"Still going to the Cavvert mine? With Eve?"

"Have to. I also have to hope she isn't too down. We don't have much time to give her *space*, as Evard recommends."

"Fix things between you two before you go." Quaene gave me a no-nonsense look and rose from the bed. "Let's see Evard, then, to determine how much more time she needs." But at the door, she paused and put a hand on my arm. "I never answered your initial question. I'm happy with your progress toward resuming your minister's role." She smiled. "You're still a trainee—with only two terms as an E-run completed—so please be patient."

Two terms, with a minimum of three required as a B-run—*hell*. I was two hundred and fifty? *At least.*

THIRTY-THREE

QUINN

While Quaene went to learn if Quil had returned, I waited outside Evangeline's door. It wasn't long before Eve emerged, alone. Perfect. Now to keep from screwing up. "How is she?"

Eve was careful to avert her gaze from mine as we walked downstairs. "As well as can be expected. PT is running a diagnostic check. She'll be out for a few hours."

Running diagnostics seemed a little excessive, but what did I know? "You raised her?"

"I wanted to. We only had two years after our mother died, so..." She tried for a wry smile, but it didn't reach her eyes.

I returned it with a grimace. "I could say I'm sorry, but I'm not. You're here. I'm glad for that. Things will work—" Ah, hell. They'd better work.

She understood, I guess. With a shrug, she stepped off the last stair and crossed to the nearest bookcase and adjusted a few volumes.

"Look, I'm sorry Quil goaded you. I should have interrupted before he could—"

"That's not your fault. Nor your responsibility." She leaned back and folded her arms.

Well, if she wanted our relationship that way. "Also, telling Gwyn of your second crystal acquisition is weighing on my conscience. I'm sorry."

Heaving a sigh, she whispered, "She would have known by sundown anyway, so I'm being ridiculous. Immature. Self-centered..."

Her voice dropped lower, and I had to prop myself close to hear. She didn't seem to mind. I, however, found her proximity distracting, her lilac scent alluring.

"Any discussion with Gwyn is done until the trip to Dome is over. I made her promise."

I filled a moment nodding. I had no time to resolve this awkwardness delicately, dammit. She'd been easy to talk to before I'd screwed up, so I just asked, "You're going to bear a child?"

She shook her head vehemently. "I've only been called—for when the fertility period begins in a few months."

"Fertility period?"

"The Waters determine the fertility for each goud-using enclave's population. It lasts roughly a year, and no one conceives during the intervening ten years. But the crystal is like a suggestion. Not a sign I *will* have a child."

"Gwyn doesn't seem to look at it that way."

"Gwyn is young and loves babies."

"Cyrem also?"

Eve's eyes met mine, but only to roll. "He treats her well."

A deep chuckle echoed through the bookcases, and

Evard crossed our aisle. "I'd say their relationship is beyond *well*. They have the hots for each other. Cyrem positively dotes on her, and their lad Perry as well."

"Evard, please!"

"*Grünmann*, you're so bloody biased, Eve. Get over it already and let the girl enjoy her lover, regardless of the future. You'd do well to take the same advice." Evard cast a meaningful look back and forth between the two of us. "Quil is back and already hitting firewalls. I'm off for some goodies to pacify him." He strode toward the kitchen.

Eve covered her face, pinching her fingers to the bridge of her nose.

We were so close already, her mix of lilac and leather assaulting my senses. Damn the consequences. I pulled her into my arms.

She stiffened, her armor solidifying instantly. The rock-hard polymer barred my fingers from her softness, but I decided not to let go. Until she told me to. Or slammed me...somewhere.

Humming overtook my body, the goud I had no control over. Unlike earlier, hers didn't answer. In harmony with my crystal's vibrations, I stroked her rigid back, then found her neck, exposed above the suit. Her skin felt every bit as nice as I had imagined. My fingertips trailed up her silkiness, traced her jaw and lingered, breath held, circling her cheek. "It's going to be all right," I whispered.

No response. But no pushing away either.

"I like you, Eve. I wish you'd let me show you."

Her gaze briefly met mine. "It's just too complicated."

"Does it have to be? This goud makes communications easy. Can you let yours out?"

"It's not a good idea." Her words were stilted, but a tremor ran through her.

What a stubborn woman she was, holding back like this. Besides tomorrow's trip to Dome to confront the false minister, the fact I was an E-run and she was a B-run and that she had violated one of the Docga policies I'd soon be enforcing, what was standing in our way?

Who was I kidding? She was right—it was too complicated.

If you thought about it much. Or at all.

Well, at least I could do one thing for her. "Evangeline is safe. I won't allow her function to be altered."

In a flash, amber fluid swamped me. It flushed my body, hot and heavy, vibrating at a frequency that blocked every word coming from her barely moving lips. But the gist of her meaning ran through my golden crystal: She was stunned, elated, terrified, grateful. Very grateful.

Eve kissed me. Her passion flowed through the goud, transforming me into a mass of loosely held particles. Every microsecond her lips pressed on mine, the physical sensation branded itself onto some section of my brain.

Hard. Deep. Urgent.

As fast as a hiccup, the kiss was over. Goud drained out of me, leaving me weak at the knees, completely empty and clinging to her. Embarrassing, since she was trying to edge away.

Tear tracks marked her checks.

I adjusted my hold to her shoulders, surprised to find her armor had morphed to plain material. "Don't tell me I've gotten too carried away again."

She shook her head and mumbled, "No. I wanted to thank you, but should have found a more appropriate way to do it."

"Hey, it was appropriate enough for me." She didn't laugh, so I stroked her arms. "But why is my promise making you block the goud and cry? Isn't there any-thing positive you can find in this?"

She gave a small shrug. "I'm happy you haven't deac-tivated me and sent me back to Dome."

I rolled my eyes. "Not a chance. I want you with me." My head was clearing, and I moved my thoughts to what I should be doing—planning the mine inspec-tion. "I *need* you with me. I'm sorry it has to be these circumstances. The Cavvert trip will be complex, be-cause once we arrive through their Conducer, you'll have to fight Blackguards." I squeezed my eyes shut, searching for a solution. I wanted to take care of this woman, but we had a job to do. How could I satisfy both?

She touched my arm, hesitantly, then stroked my shoulder. I pulled her to me, crushing her soft body to mine. Drawing in her scent, I sought her lips and tasted her sweetness. Her hand slipped to my rear.

"Sweet air," I rasped. "Do you..." I bit off the request.

That was my body talking. A gulp of air helped, until she shifted her hips against mine. Heat. Pressure. Agony. Fireworks shot through my head as my body sought hers, fitting her hips closer, a groan rumbling in my throat.

Eve wrenched her lips from mine. "Quinn... No...sorry...not..."

No? I separated us a few inches, my breathing matching her heaving chest. What was she saying? She'd ignited my body with hers. Twice. If she didn't want this, then why reach for me? This wasn't logical. I would never understand women.

"We can't start this," she panted. "You have a job to do. One that's more complicated than we thought, if your guess about the mining is correct."

The osmium mines. Where this luscious body would be guarding me. My mind flashed to another guard—the one at Dome's gate—and the way his hand had moved exactly as mine did now, kneading the sleek curves of Eve's rear.

"D'dair." My hand flew from her ass. I pushed her away enough to stare into her flushed face. She'd set her mind back to business while I'd continued groping her like an amorous schoolboy. She winced, and I realized she'd felt my thought loud and clear. I forced my emotions into line.

"If you want to avoid the guards at the Cavvert station, there's another way to travel to the mines," she said. "Cyrem can take us."

* * *

While Eve went down the street to Cyrem's shop to set up the trip, a stream of cursing befitting the wharfs drew me to Quil. But I encountered Quaene coming out of the office, Evard behind her and closing the door.

"Not as simple as he'd thought?" I muttered.

"Hardly," said Quaene. "Nor does he want an audience. We've been dismissed, so we'll accompany you to the mine. Evard?" They returned with me to the bookshop's sitting area.

He offered me a porta. "We should also check on the hornworts at Cavvert. A lab is set up there, like those hornwort tanks in Dome's Atrium you asked me to check on. The biologists installed a dozen of them fifty years ago to test growth conditions in the various waters. They were looking for conditions giving optimal growth, the fastest advance to the sporophyte stage. And the converse, what inhibited it."

I studied the report on the screen, but it was easier to ask. "Their findings?"

"Mostly dead ends, scenarios applicable to any plant, nothing specific to this native hornwort. Because the Dead Air originated at Minneri Pools near the Aeroport, one interesting theory was foreign minerals got into the water from a transport. The Bounded Winds trap and cycle anything within their region, so it'd eventually end up in the hot-spring pools. But even after the Docga sealed the Aeroport bays, installed the filtration systems and cut off trade in the Minneri region, nothing changed. Research never tied the outbreak to introduced substances or, for that matter, anything."

Nothing that warranted closing down a century of trade.

I blew out my breath in frustration. "So even after fifty years of study, this latest surge in growth is still a scientific mystery."

"Bingo," Evard said and pressed his lips tight.

"And recent studies show?"

He tapped the screen. "All samples are growing, but to varying degrees. The one you saw at Dome is relatively stable, but I learned why when I delved deeper. They haven't changed out the water in over a month."

I groaned. "Either because of the shortage of staff, or a way to hide the severity of the problem in the most visible lab. Quala told us Minneri was within a week of releasing spores. The other bad ones are..." I scanned down the new chart.

He pointed. "Half are growing wildly, a quarter moderately and a few—like Dome—very little. Cavvert is another of those stable ones. The lab is in the abandoned mine. Maybe we can pick up a clue."

"Unlikely," said Eve from behind us, "but we can try."

Quaene took her hand. "You've talked to Evangeline? How is she?"

Eve filled them in, and Evard hugged her, murmuring the type of kind words I wished I had in my repertoire. But I hadn't done *too* badly, and now my head had moved on to the analysis of our next steps, and for all our sakes, it ought to stay there.

Quaene waited until it was appropriate and said, "If it's not too much to ask, could we have your findings on Quil's emotional status?"

"Ever-changing, but that's not necessarily a negative, since now he's focused on doing his job. He's a very 'in the moment' personality."

Quaene's features set into a sage look. Eve's scrutiny must correlate with other personnel knowledge. "What happens when the going gets tough?"

"I've had more than a few interactions with Pen, the fisherman from Zeffir." Eve's brow wrinkled. "That man is a coward. He hasn't stood up to anyone on the island. Not that Zeffirites are mean-spirited, but there is always a jockeying for position in the fishing areas, at the sales stalls and when the trade ships arrive. Pen consistently hangs back."

"That may have been part of his method to hide," I said.

"Agreed, though anytime Evangeline asked me to intervene, he never questioned me. With or without using my gift." She gestured toward the front door. "Today his determination set me back. He showed a backbone when the right incentive—Evangeline—was at stake, similar to how he's picked himself up by the bootstraps to acquire the correct hornwort data you'll need."

Quaene's gaze met mine.

I shrugged. There was nothing else to do. "Let's just hope his 'in the moment' kicks to *determined* when our team leaves for Dome. Are we set with Cyrem?"

"He needs a few minutes," Eve said.

"Perfect, because so do we." Quaene turned to Quinn. "While you were down yesterday, I gave these two and Quil the circuit location and trained them in cross-leaping with the Passages Conducer. Those exercises went well, but not the Lacuna ones. Everyone had trouble separating particles to enter. Perhaps you can take a few minutes to explain it better than I have."

Evard barely restrained his enthusiasm. "Please?"

I looked at Eve.

She shook her head. "She had me try it. I'm no good with electronics."

"Neither is Quaene."

Evard snorted, and Quaene gave me a sheepish smile. "Actually, I am. I've had a few centuries to study many modern technologies, but I always come back to leading or training. I love working with people more than machines."

"Good story, but let's save it," Evard said. "Once I'm in the space, I'm good. It's just making the...what? Slice?"

We did the practice, but Evard still couldn't find the *slice* every time.

"Practice," Quaene said. "It took me a week. We'll just have to stick close."

Evard grinned. "Not a problem."

THIRTY-FOUR

EVE

Quinn and Quaene studied a map in Cyrem's tour shop's front room, while Cyrem and Evard divvied up equipment we might need. I hugged my helmet to my chest, keeping my back to the wall so my jelly-like knees wouldn't land me on the floor.

I shouldn't be so undone. Evangeline was now safe. My future was secure as long as I protected Quinn—a role I accepted as willingly as I guarded my children. My body had all but convinced me to surrender to Quinn's warmth and tenderness. I'd been a hairsbreadth from leading him to my bed.

But now, I had to face a more immediate nightmare: changing forms of matter. I'd never gotten used to the travel every other Zeffirite took for granted.

Cyrem cleared his throat. "I've asked the small goud community who use the thermal Waters in the area of the Cavvert mine to allow our entrance, but I haven't heard back. They aren't members of our Alliance, so I cannot guarantee the reception."

"Yet, on Zeffir everyone seemed so welcoming when I arrived," Quinn said.

Cyrem chuckled. "And why wouldn't we be? Better to openly talk to you..."

"To learn what I wanted. How stupid I must have appeared."

He gave a dismissive wave. "We had a reason for the precaution. Sabein said to tell you. Quinn *has* visited Zeffir before."

"No, we—oh." Quinn rubbed his short beard. "*Impostor* Quinn did."

He nodded. "Our Alliance alerted us to a traveler using different costumes and identities, and until Sabein had a good look at your essence, we thought he'd returned in another disguise."

"Disguises—of course, that rack of native clothing in his storeroom. When was this?"

"Seven, eight weeks ago. He said he was a rock collector, but his attitude didn't ring true. So though we were accommodating in showing him around, he didn't find what he was looking for."

Quinn shook his head. "Osmium—he marked Zeffir as yellow on his map. I won't ask how you hid acres of rocky outcroppings and hot-spring pools." He filled Cyrem and me in on checking the hornwort lab.

Cyrem knew of it from his hornwort research. "It's located downstream from this goud enclave, in one of the caverns. I'd forgotten how close it all is. Their hot spring flows underground, long ago creating the caverns the mining operation used to access the osmium veins." He looked around the table. "I wonder if the impostor disturbed the enclave with his mining? Perhaps they've barricaded their Waters, or they'll approach with hostility like during the Dead Air Years."

His gaze shifted to Evard. "Having you along reassures me."

What he didn't say was I would be of no help if we were confronted en route. But Quinn had other concerns besides my lack of enthusiasm for goud travel, so I led the way to the next room where a six-foot-wide, shallow pool of amber-colored water flashed ripples of light over the empty walls, making the space appear to be underwater.

Cyrem gave me a smile, overconfident as usual, and provided directions. Minutes later, we dropped into the swirling water, submerged and allowed the goud to permeate us. We began to breathe underwater, and neither beginner seemed taken aback. But then Evard was capable of providing Quaene plenty of comfort. Cyrem ushered us deeper and selected a passage. We shot forward.

Quinn muttered a curse and seized me.

I'd been held before within the goud's changeable liquid molecules. Pier had come to insist on it, and I'd never minded my mate's more intimate version of goud travel. But today, my goud connection had issues, even without Quinn's stranglehold.

"Loosen up so I can breathe."

He relaxed. "Sorry. This is the weirdest damn cross-leap I've ever been in. I thought you were dissolving, but it's the current." He played his fingers in the slipstream. "And the composition...we're combined with goud, aren't we?"

Cyrem chuckled. The sound came to us as wavering

tones reverberating in the moving bubble of fluid that contained our liquid vapors. "It's hydro-vapors, rather than the subatomic breakdown in a Conducer journey. We think of it as evaporative propulsion. Our travel is not as your people know it."

"Neither is it my system of cross-leaping. It's open, the destination determined by the user. Is this a wormhole?"

"Not really. The passages are direct, but not instant, and the network uses different forms of goud matter. Users flow through the system by their own direction, or they might be led by a guide who's ferreted out an interesting route." Cyrem's voice rang with pleasure at the chance to discuss his business. "You're familiar with how habitable planets have natural cyclic systems, such as water, air and nitrogen? Aarde has another: the element goudrogen."

He droned on. Although it had been decades since I'd traveled—except for my accidental trip a few days ago—I felt confident I could drop into the semiconscious, meditative goud state most Zeffirites accessed while taking the Waters. Today, it was just a little harder with a new man holding me.

I forced myself to stop thinking of the physical man and listen to his spirit mingling with mine. Our goud-laced molecules hummed in a lulling pattern. I'd known we would harmonize as soon as we'd entered the hot-spring Waters together. It had taken all my self-control to remove my hand from him and let him leave as Sabein had recommended.

330 | LAUREL WANROW

She'd been right, of course. The crystal forming on him had immediately called to me, just as it did now. And when a crystal did that, there was usually only one way to satisfy it.

Zeffirites were happy to comply. D'dair, they had encouraged our triad to join them. Evard wisely chose to follow Docga policy and sought other 'torgs. Evangeline, on the other hand, never expressed sexual urges, perhaps because of her missed development.

My own reserve had melted upon meeting Pier. Our attraction had seemed so powerful, but it didn't compare to the forces at work between Quinn and me.

Cyrem's discourse continued. "Goudrogen is present in solid, liquid and gas. But only when in the solid form of a crystal is it pure. Otherwise, it combines with the natural elements. Because the goud has amalgamated with our bodies, most systems are available for our use, but not all are direct or fluid. Therefore, most of us choose to use the hydro-cycle."

I groaned. No one else seemed to mind the lecture—certainly not Evard and Quaene, isolated in a bubble trailing ours—but I didn't need to hear the impossible technicalities while my particles raced through subterranean passages. "Please, Cyrem. Not now."

A gentle ripple passed over my vapors, and Quinn's voice echoed the pattern. "Relax, Eve. I'm not questioning it, only seeking to understand."

Something—his thumb?—rubbed a gentle circle at my lower back, followed by the sensation of his strong arms tightening around my shoulders. Cyrem couldn't see us. There was no *see* where we were. But he knew.

"My nerves are shot," I said. "Cyrem's lectures on their travel methods get too creepy for me. If you want to discuss it, then let me slide into unconsciousness. You'll be safe with him." *Safer even, here.*

"Anchor yourself to him," Cyrem said. "We can talk, he'll enjoy the trip without worry and I'll rouse you when we arrive on the La'adir continent in thirty minutes."

Quinn's vapors wavered around me. "You'd be unconscious? How will I know you're still moving along with us?"

I cut off Cyrem's chuckle with a wave of my hand. "You'll feel me with you."

"Good idea." The pressure of Quinn's molecules increased against mine. "I don't want to lose you," he whispered.

Cyrem's suggestion held nothing out of the ordinary—for a Zeffirite. But for Quinn and me... *Anchoring* would lay open everything I felt for this man. I spent a moment enjoying his caresses and found myself snuggling closer. As the minutes passed without a way, or a desire, to separate, I finally had to face it. I wanted *this*. I wanted Quinn.

Why fight what the goud sought to bring together?

I sank farther into Quinn's embrace and directly *into* him, merging our molecules.

He shuddered around me.

Cyrem removed his sense of us, the goud equivalent of averting his gaze.

Indeed, Quinn's vapor sizzled and leaped, for parts of us brushed and overlapped in a most intimate way. Then, as we zipped through the golden Waters, I attached my molecules to his basal essence. He adjusted slightly, redefined his molecules and flowed them to fill each infinitesimal gap between us.

I stifled a sigh at how good it felt to be enveloped by this man. I half wished I'd saved this Zeffirite version of togetherness for a private setting. But there was no such thing on Zeffir, as I well knew. Now Quinn did, too.

* * *

"Eve? Wake up," Cyrem said. "We've arrived outside Cavvert's mine."

My eyes sprang open. We stood ankle-deep in a pond below a rocky cliff. But instead of Quinn, Cyrem steadied me. I shook myself alert, but he didn't release his hold over my crystal ring. I looked at him crossly. He had my goud under his control and was decreasing its vibrations. As an elder in our enclave, he had the right, but he hadn't done this to me before. Quite the contrary, most Zeffirites advocated enhancing the use of the compound.

He moved my hand to my weapon belt and nudged the pouch containing the fertility crystal. "Settle it," he whispered. "Or he won't be able to get his mind off mating with you."

Heat rushed to my face. At least the others had their

attention on checking the way beyond the jutting rock face. I willed the goud to bend to my command and felt it comply. The crystal at my hip ceased humming.

Cyrem released my hand and patted my shoulder. "Excellent. But you better do something about that soon."

I glared at him. "Soon doesn't fit the schedule."

"Don't make it so complicated, then."

"You've been listening where you shouldn't."

He shrugged. "Maybe. But the poor man is miserable. Come now, we best get this done." He joined the other men at the corner of the limestone cliff, and I followed, fighting the urge to bang my head against the rocks.

Cyrem's greeting to the local goud users reverberated through my crystal. No response came. He half dissolved in the stream for another attempt.

"That call should have brought someone running, even if our arrival in their passage didn't," he said. He left to scout ahead—the Zeffirite could vaporize in a second and escape harm. In the meantime, Quaene assured me she had no ill effects. I didn't dare ask Quinn how he felt.

Cyrem returned. "No sign of the goud users here. I'm afraid they've been run off—or worse."

Quaene's face hardened. "That's unforgivable. We'll find out what happened, and if he did kill them, he'll stand trial."

Cyrem nodded. "I spotted one guard at the entrance. I could slip us through unnoticed in the stream, but it would be better to disable him and open the gate in case we need it later."

Quinn looked at Evard and me. "This is your function's territory. Suggest methods to disable a guard."

"I, uh..." My brain responded, processing the request like flipping cards in a file.

Evard answered first. "The two of us should be able to *overpower* any class Blackguard, but they—we—can only be disabled by a minister."

Quaene shook her head. "Too risky right now at the start. We don't want him sending out an alert before we even get in, so it's got to be quick."

I opened a compartment on my belt. "How about a Death Disc?" I held up the coin-like device and explained how I'd pilfered it from Evangeline.

"Evy should approach this guard under cover of her armor," Evard said. "Better chance for her to get closer than I would in my mingling garb." He gestured to his coral surcoat.

Quinn nodded. "Show her the guard, Cyrem."

Cyrem flowed me forward and solidified my matter with his behind a large boulder. My nerves jangled as I took a breath, lowered my visor and peered from our hiding place. Twenty paces ahead, slouched against a barred entrance tunneled into the hillside, was the Blackguard.

I waited until he looked at a hole he was toeing in the dirt before I emerged. I'd advanced within yards before he noticed me.

"Time already?"

"I'll take over." I pointed to the hole, and when he followed my gesture, I slapped my hand—holding the disc—to his nape. He collapsed into a heap at my feet, the sun glinting off the shiny metal stuck below his helmet.

I released my breath, but didn't give in to the urge to sag as the others joined me.

"Excellent," Quaene breathed. "I doubt he alerted anyone."

Quinn pointed me to the gate lock and bent to grab the man's feet while Evard hoisted his shoulders. They carried him into the shrubbery and tossed his weapons farther off.

The lock cycle took longer than the Dome ones, but opened. We entered the cave and adjusted the gate panels to their closed appearance before following the stream meandering across the dirt floor. Ahead, plank decking ran down the tunnel.

Cyrem walked up the ramp, darting a flashlight over muddy wheel tracks. "Odd. I don't remember this structure."

Quinn whispered, "Perfect for wheeling out heavy ore."

No dust hung in the air, no equipment sat ready for use, and no chunks of rock littered the passage. This mine appeared strangely clean given all the rock they must be hauling out of it.

No one missed the signs something was amiss. However, only Evard and I had alerts scrolling through our functioning.

Take precautionary measures.
Analysis Inconclusive.

Quinn waved Cyrem to turn off his light, then asked, "You've had good access to the goud. Will that continue inside?"

"It should." He nodded at the wide but shallow water below the decking. "It's the one from the local hot spring. The Waters run side-by-side with the main osmium vein, so we just need to reach it from any side tunnels we may enter. What did you want to do?"

"Explore as far as we can, as fast as we can, and leave when we have to, if you can get us out of here via the goud."

"Individuals must be willing to dissolve with me."

"I'm fine," Quaene said, but Evard and Cyrem weren't looking at her.

"Not Eve's strong suit," Evard said.

Drawing my sword, I lowered my visor. "I'm sure I'll want to leave with the rest of you."

Quinn laid a hand on my arm, but I shrugged him off and took the lead, pointing Cyrem behind me. Evard, in his camouflaged armor, took the rear.

I could see clearly into the rough passageway, but with a greenish cast. Blessed Waters, why hadn't I remembered my Blackguard night vision earlier? Why hadn't Evard thought of it? We were too green at this, despite our practice.

We moved from dim light to darkness as if the slightest sound would set off a bomb. The tunnel ended suddenly in a T intersection. Evard advanced and, with a nod, indicated he'd go left. He melted into the darkness.

I settled my nerves and eased to the right. I needed to utilize *all* the guard function's resources: the practiced moves, the second stun gun, enhanced hearing—

The tunnel was too quiet. I paused and waited.

A *rasp* sounded as a figure separated itself from the wall.

I dropped to a crouch, scuttled a few yards and dove, hitting him low and hard.

"Who the hell—ahh!"

The guard stumbled. I pivoted and grabbed an arm, shoving as I pounced on top, and pressed my knee to his kidneys while twisting his wrist up between his shoulder blades. My gaze darted up and down the tunnel. Evard was returning in a stealth trot. From the direction the guard had come, another gate barricaded the way. There was no sound, save my prisoner's ragged gasps and my quick intakes of breath.

Evard reached me. "Where are your cuffs?"

Cuffs, right. We secured the guard and left him snarling epithets into the dirt floor. I stood and picked up my fallen sword, trying to hide the shaking of my hand.

"Clear," Evard called to the others, and they advanced.

Quinn pulled me into a hug. "You did great."

I shoved him off. "Fine for you to say! You're not the one propelled into fighting because of your function."

"Your functioning is fast, automatic. Your practice paid off for your first offensive maneuver. You'll see when—if we encounter others, your class status will take them all."

"How can you be so positive they aren't at my class?" I demanded, the stress making my voice high and sharp. "This one seemed pretty competent to me."

"Classes, I can check." Quinn's fingers probed at the edge of the man's helmet, fluttered and paused. "Hmm."

I played my light over his belt and weaponry, duplicates of mine. My intuition ratcheted up a notch. Then the trussed-up Blackguard sagged into the floor, totally relaxed. Deactivated.

Quinn rose, and his gaze flicked between us. "Apparently, he's one of my men. Also a Class 1 Blackguard."

THIRTY-FIVE

QUINN

I sent Eve to open the gate. Evard verified the tunnel behind us showed no signs of use, then he and Eve took their positions again.

Beyond the interior gate, the boardwalk and stream disappeared. We bore farther and farther to the right on a dirt floor scored with tire tracks. No more guards or gates barred our passage. At a Y intersection, we halted, and Eve and Evard scouted.

Without the stream, I scanned the walls for rectangular crystals like I'd seen on Tristam's rock. I found them in both tunnels, so asked Cyrem, "Any guesses which passage to take?"

"Goud is stronger to the right. The main caverns are probably behind this wall of rock."

Evard returned. "The boardwalk ends ahead at a manmade door. Let's wait for Evy."

In minutes she was back, reporting only a few scuffed footprints, and let Evard lead us to the right. The door he'd found was shaped to tightly fit a natural opening. Five flatbed carts lined the corridor beyond it.

We'd found their cache. Again, we decided Eve in her recognizable black armor should enter first to throw off anyone who might be inside. Evard accessed the sequence and stood to the side, out of view, and Eve positioned herself before the entrance.

When I pulled the solid metal back to shield my ass, I ground my teeth over the protocols that put Eve at risk again. This was the way our roles had to be. *For now.*

Light flooded into the tunnel, an eerie yellow light. I held my breath as Eve advanced and disappeared.

Evard rounded through the doorway. Behind me, Cyrem hissed a curse.

I startled, and Quaene clutched my arm. Although no one had given the all-clear signal, I peered around the door.

Before me lay a natural cavern as large as a sports field. The stream bisected the center, and from it, a system of rubber hoses fed water to waist-high shallow glass vats on frame legs, each topped by an artificial light. So we'd found the Corps lab. The cavern must have been sealed to prevent contamination. My gaze darted around. As Evard's report had indicated, there wasn't a flat thallus of green hornwort in the stream.

Far from the central research apparatus, Eve and Evard circled the perimeter of the room, systematically inspecting areas behind the stone columns that stretched from floor to ceiling. Those and several jumbles of rocks at Evard's far end could be possible hiding places, but they moved fast in their function. They'd cover it in less than five minutes or so.

There was no danger of unseen attack across this vast space. I squeezed Quaene's hand. "Let's see the hornworts before we continue on." We crossed to the first vat.

Quaene gasped, and my heart missed a beat.

A dozen golden crystals lay in the water, each six inches long and an inch in diameter.

"Blessed Waters," I hissed.

She held a hand over her mouth. "No, this can't be...it..."

Cyrem joined us. "The cavern is empty. You can speak aloud." He cast a worried look at the surrounding equipment. "Your hypothesis about the impostor mining osmium is slightly off. It's the goud he's after."

"You're sure?" Quaene asked.

His deep voice rumbled into a chuckle, albeit a nervous one. "Positive. The presence of goud is so strong in this space, it took me just seconds to blend with it and search the cavern."

"The lab has been converted to an evaporation chamber," I said. "No doubt they've done the same to other field labs."

Cyrem raked a hand through his hair. "Every vat contains the same rich solution. These people have some ramped-up system for crystallizing goudrogen, but more significantly, for removing it from Aarde's natural cycling. It's not like the planet makes more of an element. Once it's gone, it's gone. It'll change the mineral composition of the water and air cycles, affecting what's available to plants, animals—"

"This is the change in nutrients." I smacked my forehead. "The presence of goudrogen inhibits hornwort growth."

"*That's* why the Corps' efforts to remove plants are making no difference," Quaene said.

Color drained from Cyrem's face. "Taior and I would never have figured it out without this missing piece. We'll never thwart it without goud." His gaze shot to the crystal ring on his finger. "And without our crystals..."

His face twisted from panicked to horrified.

Impostor Quinn was stealing an element far more important than osmium. *Damn.*

Quaene gripped Cyrem's arm. "We'll stop this. You have the entire authority of my position at your disposal."

"Our positions," I added. "We'll do everything possible to help you recover your natural resource. Your...lives."

Cyrem lifted his hand bearing a stubby crystal bigger than Eve's. It flashed, and his gaze transferred to my left ear. My crystal hummed and warmed, and I swear I detected a wink of light at the edge of my sight.

Quaene shifted. Her ankle bracelet must be giving a similar signal.

"I wasn't convinced, but now I am." Cyrem looked between us. "You're well chosen." He hugged Quaene, then clapped my back and shook my hand. "Thank you both. I must alert Sabein so she can contact the leaders of our enclaves on the other continents. *All* of them." He closed his eyes briefly. "Some of our people won't approve of going beyond the Alliance with this."

"What choice do you have?" I gestured to the room. "The local goud users must be dead, murdered, for others to devise a theft of this magnitude."

Eve was finishing her rounds and approaching the door we'd entered by. She hadn't been close to the vats...she didn't know. "Quaene? We should tell Evard and Eve and leave."

She nodded, and I went to intercept Eve. She was headed to a closet we'd missed just inside the entrance. With her short sword at the ready, she opened the broad door. Nothing moved inside. The lights came on automatically, revealing a space lined with shelves beyond Eve's shoulder. Most were empty, except for the nearest, which held boxes, some open—

Eve shrieked.

I jogged up as she stumbled back from the boxes half filled with amber crystals, her eyes wide. I steadied her, yet she tore from my hold and stepped gingerly back into the room.

"This is what they're stealing." Her voice trembled. "The lives of my babies. My family. My friends. I can't believe..."

The awfulness of it streamed off of her, threatening my concentration.

"Blessed Waters," Eve breathed, then stomped her foot. "They can't do this!" She reached for a crystal, but I grabbed her hand.

"We'll stop them." I dragged her out, saying some inane thing about where Impostor Quinn might find a crystal. The open air dispersed her alarm. Then something else changed around us, and my nerves prickled beneath my skin. I glanced to the others. Why, I'm not sure, for there'd been no sound.

A startled expression lit Cyrem's face. He called to Quaene—on her way to get Evard in the far corner—and motioned to the door, then dropped his hand into a vat and disappeared—dissolved, rather—into the goud-rich water.

Clearly, we needed to hide. I hugged Eve to me.

"What's wrong?" she asked.

"Someone is coming. Cyrem hid. Quaene is running for Evard. We'll go into Lacuna."

THIRTY-SIX

EVE

I balked, and pieces of myself slipped off even as Quinn clutched me. With a moan of fear, I closed my eyes to this horrible place.

The cavern was a morgue. Every person I knew and loved—Gwyn and Tristam, Cyrem and Perry, Sabein and Taior, every last Zeffirite—everyone was laid out in those glass coffins, left to have their bodies sucked dry of their life-giving element before it was boxed up and shipped to some unknown, foreign planet. They'd bury it there, in some other civilization that wasn't Aarde, where goud wouldn't work and the effort would be for naught. And once the goud was stolen, the planet, too, was as good as buried, leaving me alone after it died, helpless to stop them—or me—from slipping off—

"Eve." Quinn's insistent voice reined me in. "Stay with me."

I shuddered. Strong, muscular arms wrapped my torso, securing portions of it and then my entire chest to his stable body. His fingers spread to stroke the length of my back, shoulder to hip, with a firm, steady pressure.

My fears of dissolving into space disappeared. The fresh scent of rain from his breaking apart to enter Lacuna surrounded me, completing my comfort. It'd held me secure before and would hold me secure now. Behind my shuttered eyelids, I solidified in Quinn's warm grasp.

"I have you. You're safe," he crooned, his touch leaving no doubt I'd reformed my body. "Blessed Waters," he breathed softly. His hands fell away. "Sorry." He drew a deep breath. "I am *so* sorry, and I'll—we'll do everything we can to stop this theft."

I mumbled something. I knew he would. He wouldn't let us down. I had to stop my emotions from spinning downward...

His hands on me were a comfort when my world was falling around me. I fumbled in the shadows, found a hand and brought it back to my hip. "No need—" My words caught in my throat. "No need to apologize. Please hold me. I need...I like it."

"I thought after the pool—"

"When I want you to stop, I'll tell you." I clung to him, drawing deep breaths of his rainy woodland scent.

The low rumble vibrating through his chest was halfway between a laugh and a growl. "I trust you will."

I smiled despite myself, and the dreadful hopelessness of this theft lessened a bit. I lifted my head from his shoulder. "I'm glad we're in this together."

He smiled back, then his gaze flicked down to my lips. His arms tightened around me.

I leaned in. So did he, and our lips met, this time softly, tentatively. The kiss was fleeting, but deeply reassuring, and I sighed in his hold, wishing it could last.

The steady beat of Quinn's heart grew louder, and with a start, I realized the sound came from around us. We parted. His pinching hold on my elbow confirmed his wariness.

He raised a hand to the blurry wall, started rubbing and then stopped. Our gazes met. "That doesn't sound good. I hope Quaene got to Evard. Eve?"

I drew out my short sword. "I'm ready."

"I know. I—be careful, okay?"

Shouts rang out beyond our barrier, and a moment later, a wave-breaking crash jostled my body.

THIRTY-SEVEN

QUINN

Instead of light, an inky darkness filled my Lacuna port. I rubbed harder, but nothing cleared it. What was wrong? Then the black shifted, and I knew. A Blackguard stood right outside.

My grip tightened on Eve, which I fervently hoped she'd translate into a call for silence. She did and brought the sword up in front of us. We held our breaths.

The guard moved. Beyond him, five—no, six—other guards ran among the vats before heading out of my viewing sight. I polished another section of wall. Four guards searched a spot beyond the vats.

I nudged Eve. "Quaene and Evard must be there somewhere, spotted before she stepped them into Lacuna."

Muffled shouts echoed across the cavern. Several guards ran toward Evard, who had just emerged—

Damn!

Eve gasped.

Though he was fending off the first two, he was outnumbered. I activated my physical E-IV system and tensed to leave—no, I should stay put—*oh, hell!* We'd never made a contingency plan for one of us failing to get into Lacuna. "Look, you stay—"

Eve grabbed my arm. "Wait." She pointed. "Cyrem."

Mist rolled thick and yellow into a dense cloud above the vats. Cyrem flowed—there was no other way to put it—between them, the fog spreading in his wake.

Our guard darted forward. "Stop him!" The shriek was unmistakably female.

Cyrem swiped up crystals and ran. The leader swore furiously, and the other guards swarmed after Cyrem, leaving only one to grapple with Evard.

I braced a hand on the Lacuna wall, ready to break it open. My other hand clasped Eve's, both of us clammy.

Surrounded, Cyrem jumped into the stream. Around him, a hissing fountain of water spouted to the ceiling, rising like one of Aarde's geysers.

The guards jerked back in confusion, and the yellow fog engulfed them.

"Now," Eve said.

I burst from Lacuna. We raced across the room, circling the shrouded vats, but the fog kept expanding. I couldn't see a thing in the murk and plowed headlong into a guard.

Eve's hold kept me upright, but the Blackguard leader gasped and fell. Her helmet dislodged, and blond hair tumbled out.

A flash of memory hit me. Did I know this woman?

"Run." Eve jerked us around the fallen leader, kicking her dropped sword.

The woman cursed and yelled, "Over here!"

"Halt!" a male guard cried.

Heart racing, I sped forward and ran into Eve, who'd stopped to avoid a shadow before us. She wrenched me aside, but a stunner's sting bit my ass.

Eve yelped as the current buzzed through us and let go. Another hand grabbed my shoulder. I pivoted and swung my fist into the guard's helmet. Pain shot up my arm. He staggered back, grunted and lurched at me again.

An orange figure rammed him sideways, and Evard careened off with the guard through the yellow haze. A bigger guard tumbled Eve across the stream. They rolled and fell apart, losing their helmets but regaining their feet. They went at each other, swinging swords. I scooped up Eve's helmet and, heedless of the clanging metal, ran toward the half-visible fight.

A third black figure emerged from the fog. I veered after him, jumping the golden water. He was faster, his glowing sword lifted to strike Eve when I smashed her abandoned helmet into his head. He lurched. I leaped to reach his keypad. His weapon thudded to the floor. He followed.

"Take *that!*" Evard's voice came from nearby, loud and triumphant. Swords rang, from Eve's fight on one side of me, Evard's on the other.

"Ahh," Eve cried.

I scooped up the helmet and swung to see her stumbling beneath the guard's raised arm. "Stop!"

The Blackguard hesitated, his gaze riveted on me. "Minister Quinn? Why the hell is your guard attacking me? Uh, sir?"

Beyond the guard, Quaene emerged, a finger unnecessarily at her lips, and I realized the cavern had gone quiet. The other fight had finished. Was Evard...alive? Quaene edged that way.

The guard noticed, either from her movement or my eyes tracking her. He swiveled, and Quaene disappeared.

"Stand aside," I called, but Eve had already sprung. The guard spun back, and their swords clanged. Flecks of blood spattered from her flying hair, but she still fought.

"Stop!"

Again, the man paused at my order, leaving Eve swaying, blood flowing down her face.

Another figure emerged from the fog—the female Blackguard, her blond hair sticking from beneath her helmet. "That's not the minister, you idiot," she snapped. "Get him!"

He jerked toward me, and she lunged at Eve, raising her arm, a dagger tight in her fist.

"No!"

My cry echoed. Quaene darted from nowhere and slammed into them at the same time an orange figure leaped the stream. Evard catapulted onto the guard rushing me. I hurtled aside.

Eve, Quaene and the woman fell. Out of the tangle, one black arm rose—

My breath caught. I lunged.

—and the Blackguard drove the dagger down.

Quaene screamed.

THIRTY-EIGHT

QUINN

"**N**o!" I leaped forward, my heart pounding in my ears.

The jumble of bodies parted. Eve threw herself into the female guard, knocking her off Quaene. The guard rolled, then righted. She veered from Eve and saw me coming.

Our gazes met. Under the helmet slits, hers hardened. I faltered.

She sprang forward, screaming, "Guards," and lifting a bloody dagger.

Eve scrabbled for her lost sword and swung as she rose—but Evard plowed past, manacling the wrist with the dagger, flinging the small woman clear of me.

"Drop it!" he roared, his eyes wide and wild. When she didn't, his stun sword connected to her neck and held, sparks arcing over her body until the hand fell limp, and she collapsed.

Another guard ran up and whacked Evard, sending more sparks flying. He turned with a growl and attacked the man.

"Quinn." Eve grabbed my arm and gasped, "Quaene."

We pivoted to Quaene. Blood soaked her chest, her clothes, the ground...

"No," Eve cried, her hands skimming Quaene, checking, then landing on her neck.

I slapped my palm to the center of her chest, where red liquid still pooled. I could stop this. I would stop this. We'd get her back. PT would fix her, like he'd fixed the slice on her neck, the place where Eve's fingers pressed now, looking for...looking for...

Eve whispered, "She's gone."

My ears roared, nothing making sense until Eve shoved her face in mine.

"Cyrem needs help. Please, Quinn!"

We stumbled up and away from Quaene. Evard was fighting two guards again—and beyond them, the leader he'd stunned had rolled over, about to rise. I hesitated, yet he managed to force one guard into her, sending both down. We ran for Cyrem, sitting atop another guard, barely pinning him to the ground. I released my fury in a punch, followed by deactivating the man.

Cyrem gasped, "Into the stream!"

The golden water ran only feet away. My gaze met Eve's, then shot back to Quaene, who lay several yards in the other direction.

Eve yanked me toward my run-mate, sword raised. I ducked for Quaene.

Evard saw us. "Go," he shouted and, in a fearless lunge, crashed into the remaining guard. He toppled the others.

We ran headlong into the stream with Cyrem. Evard splashed into the water just behind. His gaze met mine. I shook my head and relinquished Quaene to his arms.

We dissolved. Goud filled the space between us, but not my inner emptiness.

THIRTY-NINE

QUINN

Zeffir Island

Zeffirites met us en route, the goud transmitting our desperate loss of Quaene. A band of townsfolk traveled on to the cavern, and when we arrived back at Cyrem's Tours, others had flooded the shop. Strangers who seemed to know us took charge, leaving me to be guided back to Passages behind the man carrying Eve, who pressed a cloth to her head. Evard wouldn't hand over Quaene's body, nor did I wish him to.

"PT," Evard bellowed the moment we entered the shop, and people dispersed to find the Docgan and whatever else was needed for the makeshift exam in the shop's aisle.

I couldn't watch, but I had to watch. I knelt by her head and stroked the blond hair around her ash-white face while layers of red-soaked cloth peeled up at the gesture of PT's nose. Then skin began to fold aside. I looked away.

The exercise was futile. I'd seen the amount of blood pumped from her heart. Death had followed before we'd reached her. I bent my forehead to hers.

The trip back had been enough time for me to analyze the attack. The female guard leader stabbed Quae-ne in exactly the same manner my attacker had tried to at Reboot. Impostor Quinn had an accomplice. I had two people to find. And stop.

I kissed Quaene's cheek. "I am so sorry. I will do my best to make you proud."

When I lifted my head, my gaze found Evard, re-spectfully standing back on her other side. I rose. "Please. Have a private moment."

"I've said my good-byes," he said hoarsely. "Now I'm kicking myself for leaving that nasty piece of demon. I will find her and make someone pay."

I eyed him. "We will. After talking to Quil."

We found him on the fringe of the commotion, near the back hall.

He frowned at us. "What is happening here? I've broken into the mainframe. The bastards changed the coding and reconfigured part of the system. When we get operations back, that unit up on Level Six will need to be secured. Meanwhile, I'm working to avoid detec-tion, a job that's easier without distractions." He shot a glare at the Zeffirites.

"We were attacked," I said. "Quaene died."

"Eh? 'Torgs don't..." His dark eyes narrowed and darted from me to Evard. "You're serious."

"I only wish I weren't." I gave a run-down of our discovery of the crystals, the possible connection with the hornworts and the attack.

Fists clenching and unclenching, Quil listened with his thin lips pressed together.

When I finished, the silence in the back hall lengthened. "So... You're next in command."

Quil stepped back. "Me? No." His hands flew up. "I-I have work to do. Getting that hornwort data." He spun on his heel and marched to the office.

I glanced at Evard, who lifted his hands, palms up.

I trotted after Quil. "I can't—the Docga won't like—"

"It's all yours." He closed the door.

But I don't remember, I wanted to tell him. *You do.* Quaene did. She knew the best course of action. She was our lead.

Evard joined me. "Give the man some space. He'll work through it."

Quil might cope, but I wasn't sure I would. I rubbed my forehead.

"Are you ready to go back and get the demon?"

Hell. Evard might not cope either. His eyes, jaws and shoulders held a positively hard set. One I hadn't seen before. *He's ready for a suicide mission.*

I resisted moving my hands in a slow-down motion and searched my brain for something... *Analysis, Quinn?* The memory of her calming advice sobered me. For Quaene, I couldn't let Evard do this.

"I need to review the plans *Quaene* made."

Evard nodded. "She wanted us to keep Sabein informed. Cyrem said he'd tell her."

"But we should confirm. And get a report from those who went to the cavern. They may have her already."

He frowned. "Or the Blackguards will have returned to Dome."

That would be certain suicide. "They might have, but then every guard will know. For Quaene's sake, we must move carefully." I had to tell him my guess. "It's *possible* that guard who...attacked Quaene was at Re-boot." I told him about my stabbing.

Evard's brows rose. "That's a stretch, since you don't recall your attacker, but neither do we have stabbings, let alone in the same quintad. That reeks of suspicious to me. You're going to tell Quil?"

"I have to. And take his gloating." I relaxed with Evard sounding more reasonable. "I also need to check if he realizes the other labs may have met the same fate, which means the latest data he's ferreting out may not be reliable." Both were touchy conversations I didn't want to have. "Quaene wanted proof of the deactivations. Eve will need repair..."

Light footsteps sounded down the hall, and Mylta hesitated a distance from us. "They're ready to move her to the chapel. Until things are decided."

"Of course..." Evard looked at me.

None of us knew how to handle death. Once the Docga arrived, we'd learn what *we* did. Until then, Quaene would approve of doing this in the native manner. I nodded. "I'd like to check on Eve. Will you do that follow-up with the Zeffirites and report back?"

To my relief, he agreed.

Upstairs, Eve's door was ajar in the quiet hall, allowing PT's rumbling growls and a woman's soft answers to reach me. I didn't feel right walking in, so knocked.

Evangeline answered. "He hasn't started yet, so

you're just in time." She waved me to the rustic-styled four-poster bed. Eve smiled halfheartedly up at me, and PT rose from a crouch beside her, his same position from minutes ago.

My stomach lurched at the gash amid Eve's blood-matted hair, though no one else in the room seemed upset. I focused on the thick snowflakes falling outside the window to settle myself. The Docgan leaped lightly down. He paused and gave a rumble, then paced out.

"He's upset." Evangeline translated while putting a pillow behind Eve so she could sit up. "He can't re-member anything like this ever happening. He said, ''Torgs or not, make them pay.'" She adjusted Eve's quilt, before she gathered up first aid supplies and left.

We were alone. I laced our fingers, so relieved I still could. "How are you doing?"

"Better. PT blocked the pain so Evangeline could clean my wound. Only subcutaneous, he said, but will make the repairs so I'm a hundred percent ready again to guard you."

Ah, hell. There was no good response to that.

A tear rolled down her cheek. "Quinn, I'm sorry about Quaene. It's terrible for everyone, but especially for you. And Evard, though in different ways."

Very different, but oddly I felt even more bonded to the man who'd stolen my grandmother away. "Thank you. We're..." I didn't want to tell her our plans, and the secret spurred some guilt.

That feeling caused her to narrow her eyes. "There's no reason for any of us to feel guilty. Each of us did what we could."

"Yes, we did," I murmured. How did I put up goud barriers like she'd done to me? I better make this a short visit, which PT's clicking toenails suggested he'd prefer. "Good advice, thank you. I'll tell Evard, too."

"Quinn? I'm..." She fisted her hands in the lapels of my field jacket.

"Tell me."

"I'm afraid for you," she whispered. "Impostor Quinn is fiercely determined to have his way. You being the rightful minister means nothing to this man. He'll kill you, like he killed Quaene."

Her intuitive warning concurred with my analysis. "I agree. Anyone who acquires crystals such as these would have incredible power. To fail after he'd gotten this far... He won't fail."

Eve loosened her grip and patted my chest. "I have no right to tell you what to do."

I brushed back the fine hair at her temple. "Wrong, it's entirely appropriate. But I need to go. PT is waiting to make your repairs."

"Thanks." She smiled at me.

Her scent filled my nostrils, though maybe it had never left. If I gave in to my urge to kiss her, I'd never leave. I held myself steady and settled for telling her, "I'll check in after."

She tugged me closer and brushed her lips to mine.

* * *

Silence—spiked by a muffled curse from the office—accompanied my descent to the bookshop. Evard waited at the bottom of the stairs in a formal military stance, obviously a remnant of his days as a Tarni liege.

"The cavern is empty. They've sealed it off. Sabein left to relay the Cavvert situation to the Alliance and other goud communities who will listen. They'll compile statuses across the planet and get back with you on the help they need and can offer."

"Excellent. Better than we can do at this point to safeguard the element sustaining life here on Aarde."

He produced his porta, queued up to Dome's coordinates. "Quaene wanted proof of the deactivations. The 'torgs reported to the Level Two Assembly Hall. My schematics show it backs to the meditronic wing Evy says they've closed. A freight elevator is located nearby, which exits directly across from the Aeroport passageway on Level One. Shall we land directly and have a look?"

A trip together would test Evard's coordinates workup before leaving tomorrow...and save both of us from being alone with our grief. Convenient, but only if it didn't degenerate into the hasty revenge Evard wanted. "I have reservations."

His brow lifted.

"I must stop the rogue 'torgs behind this. That's what *Quaene* wanted."

"Agreed."

"*All* of them. What if we see that female guard at Dome? What do you want to do?"

Evard's eyes narrowed. "Besides carve *her* up?" He huffed out a breath. "For Quaene, I will wait for the

Docga's proper sentence—deactivation. Otherwise, if I take out a 'torg, I'll face the same." He sighed. "PT best get Evy functional, because I'll need calming vibes if my path crosses that demon's."

I clasped his shoulder for a second, pain rocking me, too. "You know what's a worse fear? Eve will kill me if you die, or have to be deactivated."

That brought a quirk to his lips. "Perish the thought I'd make Evy unhappy." Evard rolled his eyes. "*Grünmann*. You have my promise."

We entered the shop's Conducer. "Take the lead," I said with more bravado than I felt.

"At least I can do the cross-leap. The Lacuna..."

"You need more practice. I'll handle that part."

He checked the coordinates and tucked the porta into his pocket.

"Save those to your internal system, so you can use them later."

"Quaene—" He swallowed. "During our lesson, Quil and I set up files with a handful of coordinates from across Aarde, in case we have to run from Dome. Yet, she also said we must access a Conducer's energy to use them."

"Exactly."

"Hmm." He scratched his goatee. "We need an alternative source. Preferably portable."

FORTY

QUINN

Dome

Evard and I materialized in the corridor near the rear door of the meditronic wing and stepped into Lacuna. The space was close and dark.

"It wasn't this confining before," Evard muttered at my side.

I swung my arm to widen it. "You're more on edge. We both are." I thinned a viewing port. He made another on the opposite side, and we peered up and down the corridor. "Keep a hand on me, so we can break apart at a microsecond's warning. Ready?"

He wiped his hands down his coat and nodded. "*Bloody hyphae.*"

We raced to the meditronic door, but as I reached for the keypad cover, I heard voices inside. I jerked back, carrying us into Lacuna as the door swung open.

Our particles shifted, someone moved through us— no, *something*. It took too long to be a body. I tightened my hold on Evard's arm and waited it out. Afterward, I pivoted and polished a viewing port. "Blackguards pushing a flat cart with blankets."

Evard released his breath. "There may be others inside."

Was the risk worth the verification?

He dipped his head. "I'm game."

"Quick look, then."

I jammed the barrier up to the keypad and worked on it through a slit. When the latch clicked open, we opened the door, and I walked us into another Lacuna inside.

"*Bloody—*"

I'd seen, too. Bodies filled the corridor. Worse, the 'torgs were jammed like logs against each other in rows, with tags slapped to the bottom of their shoes. My heart began a fast, heavy hammering I was sure anyone could hear. I didn't need to see more, but still polished a port.

"No bloody way," he muttered.

"Laid out, like in a morgue. Let's get out of here."

We pivoted. My hand broke the barrier for the doorknob when the faint opening *click* reached my ears. I stumbled back into Evard, returning to Lacuna. "Someone's here," I hissed.

The new people entered.

"You don't understand," a woman said. "I let that stupid guard report it like those 'torgs were ultrafast and disappearing into the fog. But they weren't. It's that future method you told me Quinn can do, the leap."

I'd heard her yelling enough to recognize the voice— the female guard. My gaze met Evard's, his face storming with the same realization. He darted to the viewing port. I didn't need his snarled, "It's her," to know. I grabbed his arm. "Don't. Not yet. We must learn what they're doing, to help us—for when we can act. All of us, *for Quaene*."

"Cross-leap?" The deep masculine voice echoed down the corridor. "No, that's a transporter technique."

Evard relaxed back, and I poked my nose to the port.

Only the back of her blond head was visible. "I'm not wrong. They're using it, bouncing around—"

"Don't worry about it, love," said the man, sounding vaguely familiar. "We're days from finishing here. Just get another dozen guards and clear out the place. I'll put extra security on the transports."

"It's you," Evard whispered. "Impostor Quinn's voice is a dead ringer for yours."

I polished yet another port in his direction... Yes, he looked just like me. My head raced. She sounded familiar, too, as were her actions, gathering her hair and twisting it.

"We're steps from passing this off, right, my beautiful Vice Premier?" Impostor Quinn said.

She snorted. "You've got me counting on it. Schiftan's open election is yours, *Premier*. If we succeed here. What happens if they stop us?"

"Don't think about them. They aren't using the mineral. *We* will. Voters will love it. Voters will love *us*."

Eve's summation was correct—this selfish attitude wasn't one the Docga would accept in an electorg.

The Blackguard paused in fastening a hairclip, striking a chord in me. "Your reputation is on the line with this one. If you fail—"

"Put your qualms to rest. I'm the E-run no one questions." He slid a hand around her, jostling so close I saw the rise and fall of his chest. "This blip with the original ministers resurfacing doesn't change a thing. It's six months till the election, so we market the hell out of our forever-life vitamin supplement, build it—"

"Oh, shut up already." She embraced him, inches from my side. I stared over her shoulder, into *my* face, watching myself—*him*—loom forward. As if I was viewing a mirror, his fierce, possessive lips met hers. I squeezed my eyes shut, and a memory flashed—

The yank on my arm consolidated its molecules and forced me to partially materialize, my own angry features snarling above me. I stuttered at the bizarre sight. That was me. No, he was apart, acting independently of me—

"Quinn, no," Quaene yelled from inside the cross-leap. "You can't—"

I jerked toward her, back into the leap. My loose particles scattered and strained toward my run-mate, but my arm stayed solid. Warnings erupted in my mind. I had to free my arm, but I couldn't dissolve it while my attacker held it fast. I formed up my other arm and swung—

My fist clenched, and I rocked forward.

Evard clamped a hand on my shoulder. "No. *For Quaene,* remember? You can't."

Right, I couldn't. She'd worked so hard to save me...

I snapped back into the harrowing memory, hitting him again and again, while being pulled in two directions—

I heated in the pressure of holding myself together. My electronics sizzled under my skin, and lights ruptured, throbbing through my head. PT burst from behind me. A hundred pounds of hair and snarling teeth plowed into my look-alike. The Docgan ordered, "Run!" and bit him. His grip slipped, and my burning molecules raced like they were magnetized through the cross-leap.

"Quinn? Steady."

Yeah, steady. Against our Lacuna, the impostors kissed, and more. He caressed her bare breast, fondling her inches from my own sweaty fist.

"Enough to get going on, love?" murmured Impostor Quinn. He set her back, right into us. "Finish your work. Afterward, I'll indulge you." A second later, the helmet came at us, and we froze as my look-alike set it over her head.

She whirled away. "You ass, I don't know why I put up with you," she huffed from what now seemed like a great distance. She paused at the door and groped along her side.

He laughed. "Because you want that Vice Premier job I've promised you. You can't tell me it won't be worth it."

She snorted, but didn't look up from something she was doing with her suit. A faint rasping sounded, familiar...

Blessed Waters. A zipper. The guard suit she wore *was a costume.*

FORTY-ONE

QUINN

Zeffir Island

Once we returned, Evard left to tell Quil we'd verified the deactivations, and discovered this *Blackguard* murderess could be any of the six hundred-some
'torgs on Aarde. I'd meet them after I checked on Eve. I
hoped we could pull together a plan for this ever-
deteriorating situation.

In the upper hall, I ran into Tristam exiting her
room. "She's still out. A quarter hour more, Evangeline
said, but she's completely...healed. That, er, fellow is
running diagnostics." He shook his head. "More information than I needed to know. I'm sorry for your loss.
From what I hear, Quaene was a sensitive leader. Aardites would have enjoyed a term working with her."

I murmured my thanks and had turned toward the
stairs again when a gentle waft of goud followed. Nothing pushy, just a reassurance.

"Had something I wanted to check," Tristam said.
"Do you plan to stay at Passages? Or take another house
on Zeffir?"

My muscles tensed. What was behind his question?
Quaene's suggestion to trust people echoed through my

mind. Tristam's manner hid nothing. *Careful, Quinn, or you're going to screw it up.*

I didn't want to anger Eve's son, possibly transferring a dislike of me through the community, revoking my opportunity to return. Did I want to return? I hadn't thought of it until now, but I certainly didn't want to close that door.

Okay, that was way too analytical. I really didn't want Eve pissed at me. Honesty had to be the best way to answer his questions. "Regaining our command is my sole focus. We've got to return the crystals to the Waters to abate the hornwort growth."

He cocked his head, indicating I should continue.

I felt like a kid being interrogated. "Eve will continue to guard me. I can't predict what will happen, or where I'll end up when it's over, but as soon as we resolve the situation, I'll reward Eve's loyalty and allow her to return to Zeffir."

Tristam shifted from foot to foot. "Correct me if I'm wrong," he said softly, "but I didn't think your *relationship* with Eve was strictly about service, loyalty and rewards."

I swallowed. This infernal water made these people too intuitive. Why did my little dip into honesty have to turn into a dive? "It's not."

"So?"

"Blessed Waters—I *like* her. Would you give a man a break?"

"Still, you haven't told me your intentions."

"My *intentions*? Why are you grilling me?"

"As Eve's only remaining male relative, it's my right." His voice held an edge now. "Don't get me wrong. You didn't leave her at Dome, or injured back in the mine, when you could have, and for that we're all grateful. But on Zeffir, this is how things are done. Check your handbook. Electorgs must assimilate into the local culture, unless it contradicts Docga policy."

I found myself leaning forward and stopped. I didn't want to be an ass about this. "This isn't a single female relative we're discussing. It's your mother. She deserves your protection, true, but also your respect. And no matter how casual Zeffirites are about their intimate relations, I would never broach that conversation with a woman's offspring."

His features hardened. "Then let me tell you something about *my mother.* I watched Eve's heart break when she had to stand aside and let others raise her children. At the time I didn't understand why this loving person we grew up calling our aunt spent so much time with us, but didn't live with us. Every night after visiting, she'd go home, sad and lonely. Gwyn and I begged Dad to ask her to stay, to move into our house, or at least live there part time like our friends' parents did. But he refused.

"Dad died when I was six, Gwyn five. Eve was devastated. She stopped seeing us, until Granny made her. Everything changed when she admitted she was our mother, but she couldn't act it because of the Docga policy. After that, the three of us had a secret to share. It bonded us."

Tristam crossed his arms, punctuating his point: Eve was part of their crowd. I was an outsider.

"I won't see her go through that again. The next man she has, whether it's you or someone else, is going to be a permanent member of the Zeffirite community."

"Eve isn't a Zeffirite," I said stubbornly. "She's an electorg."

"It's possible to be both. Do you think your acquisition of a crystal on your first visit to the Waters was just a lucky happenstance?"

I didn't want to think it was, but had no idea.

"It's not. You've been called. Invited."

Did he mean that? My hopes rose.

"In the same way Eve has been invited to bear another child."

I swallowed. "Gwyn told you?"

"She didn't have to. After you left, the messages started circulating and the people who need to know, do know. That's so the women are supported. In the next few months, as the fertile water period approaches, Eve will either accept or refuse. Mates will be drawn to her to help her make the decision. All Zeffirites undergo the process simultaneously." He grinned. "There's lots of sex. It's kind of fun."

I couldn't look at him, so started down the steps. He followed through the now deserted shop. Emptiness washed through me. I promptly shoved it off. I had a job to do, one I shouldn't allow Tristam's curiosity to interrupt. I opened the front door. "Thanks for the advice."

FORTY-TWO

QUINN

Not finding Evard or Quil in the office, I collected some food from the kitchen and was halfway to the sitting room when the floor upstairs creaked. A click of canine toenails and voices on the stairs reached me, so I backtracked.

"I feel fine, really," said Eve.

"PT said you would," Evangeline answered softly, holding to Eve's arm while they descended. "But please let me."

PT passed me with a snort and stalked down the central aisle.

"Hey. What's this?" I would have taken Eve's other arm if my hands weren't holding a sandwich platter and plates. "Up already?"

Near the sitting area, PT rumbled loudly, then turned his back and dropped to the rug before the fire.

Evangeline laughed. "He said, 'It's not like she's a fragile human.' He's miffed we don't have more faith in his abilities."

"Oh, I do," Eve murmured. "The blinding ache above my right ear is gone."

Yes, the gash was healed. Even the hair that had been damaged matched in length.

She met my searching look. "Good as new. Ready to do it all again at Dome."

Uh, right. I'd be damned if I'd lose the other woman I...cared for. We were going into our next trip overprepared and armed—every last one of us. Hell, I'd even include a few Zeffirites, since Quaene was no longer here to say no. But as soon as I had the thought, I dashed it. I couldn't put them at risk either...unless other efforts failed.

The front door opened and slammed shut. "Quinn?"

Evard. I leaned into the aisle.

He caught sight of me and pounded forward, waving a sheaf of paper in one hand, a porta in the other. "Quil's gone. I've been to his boat, stopped anyone who's still in town, sent word to the refuge, scanned the Waters—had someone *else* scan them for me *again*—"

"Hold it. He's...gone?"

"Gone. Not on Zeffir."

Then I noticed the metal piece Evard held with the porta—Quil's cuff sporting two goudrogen crystals. The room canted. He had left...again. Deserted us. Deserted me.

The others were talking, but I couldn't hear. I carefully set down the dishes without missing the table, straightened, turned and walked out the front door. I ran through the deserted streets, going faster up into the hills, past the fields, the woods, the springs and on. I ran until my function reminders flashed red and my lungs wouldn't draw breath, and then I slowed, and slowed, and stumbled and fell into the snow and lay there.

My body hadn't felt this bad chasing Eve up here the night she put a dagger to her throat. She would have died. As Quaene had. My dagger sheath pressed against my calf, so easy to reach... Going on now was impossible. I had just Eve and Evard. I couldn't lead them—I'd only end up killing them. Better to—no, it wasn't, but my other options...

I rolled to my back and sucked in the frigid air, my fingers clenching and releasing as my head swam with snatches of ideas that were nothing, but the rhythm of my fists kept them coming. No stars were visible, dammit—just ugly yellow cloud cover looking like dog-pissed snow. It hung low, stiflingly so. I closed my eyes. My heartbeats steadied, and my breathing returned. A light humming flowed through me.

The crystal. What good would that do now?

The hum accelerated, and it glowed, blindingly.

I yanked at the cuff on my ear. I didn't want this, not now. I couldn't get the damned thing off at first, then finally I did and cocked my arm to throw it, but the glow in my fist was warm on this bitter night.

I dropped my arm. With the cursed thing a distance from my head, I let the blessed blackness overtake me.

Greetings called out to me, surrounded me and swirled me to a cavern. My chilled body warmed. Woven rugs lined the floor, others hung to divide the space, space filled with people and warmth and love. Shelves of baskets held everything needed to settle here and stay.

But I wasn't to stay. The murmurs said this place only connected me. Lines of light flowed among us, crossing and reaching. Steady, strong ties to Eve and Evard and others wavered in and out of sight. Some strands went...elsewhere. I should follow them. Especially bright ones were pointed out to me. I traced one...far off, on the move. Another...to a mind previously cloudy but clearing. My efforts met with approval. Yes, this was the one, the one to connect...

I woke in the snow, shivering—no, tingling. Disappointment washed over me. It'd been a dream. The connection to someone who could help me wasn't real, so I was still in the same hellhole of a mess. I had no one. No one on my frequency, no one in my quintad, no one on my team—

That wasn't true. And I knew it. I just didn't want to know it right now.

"Damnation!"

The echoes of my scream died, and I sat up, my body warm despite lying in a two-foot drift.

"Feeling better?"

I swung around. "Damn," I hissed at Sabein. "You scared the hell out of me."

"You've scared *the hell* out of Eve, and many others."

She sat on a rock a few feet away, the yellow clouds casting her in the same light.

I wiped my brow. My hand glowed. When I opened it, the tiny amber crystal pulsed. So did Sabein's crystals, sending ghostly rays outward, eerily like the strands from my dream. I swallowed. "Were you..." I couldn't admit I was seeing things, not to another leader. Or anyone.

I dropped my gaze to my crystal, every inch of me trembling now. The vibrations jostled my gift open, and I stared into its cubic structure, going deep, trying to see what was there. But I couldn't reach it...not yet, something told me. The latticework reformed. *How*—I raised my head, but Sabein shook her head.

"I can't explain how it works. I can't explain why you were chosen. I can't explain how—or if—you're going to succeed. But I'm asking you to carefully consider the responsibility you've been given. Our Waters are our past, present and future."

Me? Take the responsibility, alone? Impossible.

Her brow creased. "We need your help. Desperately."

I...couldn't. The four of us from the quintad might have had a chance, or Quaene—with her centuries of experience. But to expect me to handle the responsibility on meager months of training.

The crystal in my fist hummed, and Sabein sighed. "Quaene can't respond that way anymore. She's gone, but present, her essence with us, among the Waters. Just as others are. Everyone chosen remains with the Waters."

The chosen. *Like Eve.* My crystal pulsed. *Like me.* My...essence was bound into this element with theirs. And the rogues were stealing it. My piece I could live without. Perhaps it would atone for the mistakes I was sure my brain fought to keep hidden.

But *Eve*.

Again, I stared past the amber light, surrounded this time by an outer layer of lacy webbing leading off in strands to the people I must connect with. "I won't let them—"

Sabein was gone. I sat alone in the Zeffir hills. But my warmly glowing crystal said I wasn't.

FORTY-THREE

EVE

I choked back a sob when Quinn walked into the shop, barely stopping from throwing myself at him. He lifted his arms, and then I did, too. "I started to come for you," I whispered into his neck, "but the goud indicated I should leave you alone. Are you all right?"

He breathed deeply. "I will be."

I picked up on feelings of amazement and confusion underlying a wash of pure need, but they cut off, and he pulled away. "Where are the others?"

I had to smile. Quinn was a master of compartmentalizing. "Evard took Taior a hornwort report Quil left for the Alliance. He said to tell you it's a summary with the bottom line being we should do our own inspections. The Zeffirites are better set up for that than we are, so Evard is arranging it. Then, unless you have other plans, he'll practice his Lacuna for tomorrow."

Quinn's face didn't change its set look. "That...sounds fine."

"Evangeline has gone to bed, but left you a note." I pulled it from my pocket.

"Minister Quinn..." he read and stopped.

"What's wrong?"

"Two days ago, the title sounded wrong, but now..."

He shook his head. "She says, 'I won't be much use to you in combat. I respectfully ask to be excused from accompanying you.' I agree, but I don't want her left here alone."

My heart swelled. "She won't be. Sabein has offered her sanctuary with the Zeffirites in the mountain refuge. If you approve, she'll accept and join them tomorrow."

He borrowed a pencil and wrote *Request granted*, and signed his name.

I put the note on the end table we used for messages at the edge of the sitting area, beside the cuff Quil had left. Quinn saw it, but the scowl I expected didn't come.

"Leaving his crystals pretty much washes his hands of Aarde, doesn't it?"

"I'm not so sure," I said. "He completed the reports. That's something."

Quinn raised a brow. "True." He paced idly along the shop's darkened aisle, something I'd done many times myself.

His crystal glowed at his ear, and seconds later, he raised a hand to it. I didn't dare interrupt whatever consolation he might be getting, so I moved off to dampen the fire.

"There'll be a way," he murmured when his pacing brought him back to me. He gave me a slight smile, then shepherded me upstairs, past his assigned room to mine, and opened the door.

"I should be guarding you." I gestured across the hall. "Though we closed the Conducer."

"The *island* is now secured, so I think I'll be all right." He wrapped an arm around my shoulders and guided me inside. "And you look exhausted."

I was—or had been. I turned into his touch, reveling in its solicitude, tenderness...even the possessiveness. My arms wound around his waist, and he drew me close.

I kissed him. I couldn't help myself. He kissed me back, warm but restrained. I devoured him. With Quinn I could remember what it was like to love and be loved. Even if I had only this one night before everything changed—before Quinn took command of this planet, and I went back to being a law-breaking B-run—I was going to take it. Or worse, if things took a poor turn at Dome—

May the Golden Waters preserve me, *that's* why Evard told me he had no regrets about being with Quaene. *I* might not have another chance.

My hands roamed. Quinn's clothes were in the way. I wanted to feel him, to press his skin to mine, to melt away my armor as my heart already had.

Quinn bit off a groan and dropped his hands. "I'll leave so you can sleep."

"No." I skirted him, closed the door and leaned against it. "I want you here. We might not have another..." I stumbled over the words I didn't want to think about.

"Eve?" He walked toward me, but when I didn't move, he stopped. "Is that a good enough reason?"

Desire and unbridled hope wafted between us. Why

did he ask when his emotions said this was what he wanted? All I had to do was lift my hand, to touch him, to close the distance—

"I'm not saying it isn't," he whispered. "We could take this opportunity."

I wanted this opportunity, and yet... Tomorrow, it would be over. He wouldn't be here, and I would be alone and nursing painful emotions. Compared to his problems, my issues seemed too lame to say aloud. I licked my lips. "It's just...there's so much happening. I wish the Docga had programmed me to time travel like they do. I'd drift us back a decade to the quiet years when Tristam and Gwyn were on their own and no one had considered transfers."

"I can't grant that wish." He gave me a sad smile, reached across the inches of divide and gathered me to his warm chest. Instantly, my body molded to his, my center heating with need. "Perhaps Lacuna would do for your escape. No one can reach us there."

My fingers curled into his flannel shirt, and I hiccupped out an attempt at a laugh. "Right. Lacuna. That'll solve all our problems." But even as I joked, I knew I couldn't let go of him. A push set him in motion. I steered us toward my bed. The light dimmed. I startled aside and bumped a flexible wall.

"What—" I drew a sharp breath. "Lacuna?"

"Okay?" he murmured from behind, stroking my arms in a soothing rhythm. "You moved over right with me."

"I...*Blessed Waters.*"

His shoulder massage and ear nibbles became an embrace, and featherlight kisses brought back the lovely melting in my body. His belly caresses edged lower, bumping my heavy weapon belt with each searing stroke.

My fingers flew to the buckle to rid myself of it, but I paused. "Lacuna is sealed?"

"Better than a lock. But remember, loud sounds carry."

I undid the belt, dropped it and dissolved my armor to nothing.

Quinn's fingers froze on my bare skin. For several long moments, he remained that way, then he pulled me to him, his solid chest hot against my bare back. He nuzzled his crystal along my cheek, and its vibrations reached me. I shivered at his intent.

"Eve, I don't have a memory of doing this before. I want to, but I don't know how I'll be for you. I'd hate to disappoint you in my excitement."

"That's..." My voice cracked. I cleared my throat. "I'll be fine."

"Fine isn't good enough," he whispered hoarsely. "You better bring your armor up again."

Blessed Waters. I felt like smacking my head. Or his. I pivoted in his embrace, and he dropped his arms. I tugged the shirt from his trousers and skimmed my fingers around his lean waist. I found his mouth and nipped at his lower lip. A wave of trembling overtook him, but otherwise he didn't respond.

"Quinn? I'm as excited to do this as you are."

"You are?"

"Can you lose the clothes?"

The shirt flew over his head. The boots held up the trousers a little longer. He fell across the bed to remove them. I sank beside him, eager to see the fine form he'd unwittingly shown me at the springs. Quinn hooked his thumbs in his waistband, lowered it enough to expose his abdomen and stopped. "I shouldn't take advantage of you. It's unseemly for a minister to... I don't *expect* this relationship with my guard."

I groaned. His desire was flooding me, heightening my own. Yet the man persisted in worrying over the details. I pressed my lips to his and darted my tongue to taste him. In moments, his tongue met mine. His wholly carnal urges swamped me, and my head clouded. I gasped, "Quinn, I want you. You want me. I can tell. Take off the bloody trousers."

"You can—my emotions? But that's..." His glazed eyes searched my face, then dropped to my breasts. They perked as if he'd touched them. But he hadn't. He wasn't. And I wanted him moving.

My fingers slid to his waistband. He hadn't quite gotten out that request—if it was one—so I sent out my emotions on a wave of defiance. His hips shifted and wiggled free.

"Excellent," I breathed.

I urged him again with my gift. His hand skimmed my hip, lightly at first and then drew us together. His head dipped, and his lips closed over my breast in a kiss that escalated to exactly what my body cried for. A moan escaped me. He hesitated, and I stroked my fingers through his hair, directing him back with a murmured, "I like it."

Our hips met in earnest, and I nuzzled his left ear. His crystal hummed. The goud washed forth. His emotions were with me, if not fully in agreement. Thoughts of him had totally undone me. In my fervor, I couldn't stop myself. I had to have him.

I moved astride his hips in hopes he'd forget his frustratingly honorable intentions.

Quinn's head fell back, his eyes closed.

This slow tease was good, so good, and I wanted it all. With his fingers kneading into me, pulling me, I could have it... I leaned to his ear. "More," I coaxed with words and emotions.

Quinn stilled. Then with a cry of anguish, he pushed my hips away and shoved me off him, desire turning to rage in a heartbeat.

"Ohh!" I toppled onto the mattress in a tangle of limbs. Afraid, I scrambled free—and hit the Lacuna wall. He slammed into me, crushing my body to the barrier. We hung for a split second, then fell.

"Oof!" The air rushed out of me as we hit the floor.

He pinned me, his breath hot on my face, his eyes narrowed and glinting with an anger I felt to my very core. "What the hell?" he panted, and a minute passed, his ragged puffs slowing to a heated, rhythmic press on my shivering body. "How dare you sway me with your emotions?"

Cutting words, but still, real desire edged his wrath,

all of it wrapped in the woodsy scent I craved. I closed my eyes against the sensations, but it didn't matter. I couldn't close myself. I still wanted him, badly. My distressed arousal escaped with an embarrassing cry that I bit short. "It's torture to be swamped by your passion and not be physical."

"Was that physical enough for you?

"Blessed...*yes*," I hissed. "You're smashing me."

"What?" Propping himself on an elbow, he inspected my chest. "Nothing broken that I can see." An odd look passed over his face. He bent and kissed the hollow between my breasts.

I held my breath and tried to ignore my ramping need.

With a groan, Quinn dropped close to my ear.

I was just going to have to get over it. I wasn't having him. But he wasn't moving his body from mine, so finally—before my hips took matters upon themselves—I meekly asked, "Can you get off me?"

He started to rise, but stopped, scanning my face. His lips found mine.

The soft press turned demanding, leaving me gasping when he wrenched away.

"Sorry about shoving you," he said huskily.

My eyes flashed open, meeting his narrowed gaze. "Sorry about swaying you."

"You willing to start over? No influence?"

My body flushed. "Are you kidding?"

His breath caught. "No, I'm insane. If the Docga haul me off for a trial and deactivation, would Cyrem hide me in the Waters' passages?"

"I suppose mating with a known violator won't look good alongside a rogue commandeering your position."

"Uh, no. However..." He shrugged, and somehow our lips reconnected.

FORTY-FOUR

We twisted, and in a series of movements that blurred in my mind, Eve arched into me, her mewls growing louder. In her lips, I found the same sweet taste from when she'd had me under her emotional thumb. She couldn't change that. By the way she wiggled beneath me, Eve was ready. Tucking into her would be easy.

Instead, I slid a hand between us.

She whimpered, but she brushed my hand away. "Quinn?"

"Yes, my Eve?"

"Mate with me. Properly."

I sucked a breath. "I want to. But I think you're expecting other things to go along with the sex. Like me sticking around."

"No, I don't expect that at all. Matings are fluid on Zeffir. Partners come and go."

Eve said the words, but did she mean them? I didn't think so. And still she tugged at my hips, shifting my balance into her.

I rose to a kneeling position, causing her to frown, but I had to make sure she understood. "I wish I was free to make a commitment to you. While I can't physically commit to you, in my heart, I'm yours. I don't know what'll happen at Dome—"

"Are we going to mate or not?" she snapped.

The words were like a slap. "Do you have to call it that?" I shot back.

"Mating?" She bit her lip and averted her gaze. "That's what it is."

That's what it *could* be, a physical act. But not to me. And definitely not to this emotional woman. "It sounds so cold. I don't feel cold about any bit of you, Eve." Skimming my hand up her body, I cupped the back of her neck and worked a thumb over her tight jaw. "You claim my passion tortures you, yet I detect no emotion from you. Is this just a mating? Something you could do with any Zeffirite?"

A startled look passed through the depths of her eyes before she squeezed them shut. "No, it's not that way at all. Th-there have been no other men since Pier. I—" Her voice broke.

I dropped my forehead to hers and though it was killing me, said, "We don't have to do this. It doesn't change how I feel about you."

It seemed forever before she moved. Her lips met mine, moving gently at first, but seconds later, firmer, more demanding. Her hands alternately gripped and stroked me, creating more urgency than her earlier sway. I couldn't stand waiting for her full involvement any longer. With a curse, I clutched her softness to my hard body and felt her give, physically and emotionally.

Warm, loving feelings flooded me, including desire.

For me, only me. But alongside them came an edge of fear. Fear of where these feelings might lead.

My guess was correct—she wasn't just mating. Being with me meant something special to her. My heart swelled with feeling. With...love. Pulling back, I cupped her face in my hands. She glowed yellow. "Ah, my Eve, don't worry. You're safe with me."

"I know." Her lips flickered into a luminescent smile that quivered in a hum. "You haven't let me down yet, Quinn."

I wasn't going to in this either. I kissed her, murmuring, "That's it. Stay with me." Excitement churned in me. She arched, and I slid farther into her warmth.

Eve moaned and writhed beneath me, her glow brightening, the vibrations blending to a song.

Was I hurting her? I was clueless. No memories came to rescue me. But Eve did. She lifted her hips and scooped my body tight to hers, plunging me deeper.

Holy hell! This was what the handbook meant by *pleasurable*? It was beyond that simple word. I groaned as her goud flashed in harmony with her cries, fully capturing me.

She froze, her fingers biting into me, her moan grinding out long and low. The vibrations in her penetrated to my very core, flooded me with delight, begged me to join her. I lost myself in the rhythm and exploded, my groan taking up where hers left off.

At last, I was done in. I floated, renewed. Strangely light and buzzy. My eyelids cracked open to check on Eve and then widened in horror.

I wasn't with Eve anymore. I wasn't even on Zeffir. Somehow, I alone had dissolved and cross-leaped home, to the house in Lacuna that Quaene and I shared halfway around the planet.

D'dair! Eve's going to kill me.

Where had I gotten the energy to leap—*no way!* Sex couldn't generate this type of power. It had to be the goud. Those vibrations it'd made must have activated...what? Which circuit? Evard would be thrilled.

I materialized to access the Conducer we'd rigged, and the cold of our unused house hit me everywhere. Flinching, I dashed for my room and clothes.

What Eve and I had created together had been breathtaking. I'd never find another woman like her, and now I'd essentially run out on her. What a bumbling mess I'd made of things—well, not everything. I'd satisfied her. That had to mean something, if the handbook was accurate.

With Passages' Conducer locked down, I landed in the familiar woods near the pools. Fog filled the space among the tree trunks. Instead of darkness, eerie yellow clouds boiled in the sky. I kicked through the mist glazing the hillsides, realizing the wet on my cheeks wasn't the rolling fog. Enormous snowflakes pelted me. Fog and snow at once—what kind of weather was this?

The streets were empty, the houses dark as I ran on my toes to maintain the quiet. In the bookstore, I took the stairs two at a time and burst into her room. "Eve?" She wasn't on the bed. She hadn't been in the hall. She—

"Remember something?" Eve asked from the bathroom door. She stood with her arms crossed over her fully armored chest.

I seized her shoulders. "I'm sorry. I don't know what to say. Some new interaction between my electronics and the crystal caused me to cross-leap. Next time I'll be more careful."

Her brows rose.

What had I said? I'd apologized. "How can I make this up to you?"

Still, she stared at me. Blankly. Finally, she licked her lips. "Next time..."

Oh. What a dolt I was, assuming there'd be a next time. I eased my hands from her body.

"Next time," she continued in complete deadpan, "you figure out a way to take me with you."

FORTY-FIVE

EVE

In the morning, Quinn dressed in a dark green jumpsuit Evard had filched, looking just like Impostor Quinn. We embraced a last time and clung a few moments more to everything good that had happened.

"It'll work," I murmured in his ear. "You have to believe."

He held me at arm's length for a quick check of his goud and mine. "I do. Thank you for letting the emotional confidence be mine."

Hand in hand we left my room. Like me, he wanted to continue our contact—and any sense of normalcy—as long as possible. We accepted plates of the eggs and bacon Evard had cooked, but no one sat. The atmosphere wasn't just due to me. The nervous energy was growing. After a few bites, I set my plate aside.

"I'm counting on Quetta being lucid enough to help," Quinn said out of the blue.

I hated to put down any idea, however doubtful, and was too jumpy to inquire delicately from where this one had sprung.

"Separate the rogue from his bodyguards and he'll be easy to restrain," Evard said. "Then we'll ferret out the others who assisted him. Should be a snap now." He stepped neatly to one side and disappeared.

When he reappeared, Quinn thumped him enthusiastically. "What fell into place?"

"PT came across my practice and offered to upgrade my circuit with Quaene's E-IV issue. It has a new tweak adapted to support your particle work, which they are anxious to put to use. I am carrying her into battle with us," Evard said solemnly.

They played out a few hiding scenarios, eventually mentioning we'd be cross-leaping directly into the ministers' quarters to find Quala.

Sucking a breath that did little to calm my nerves, I asked, "And if she's not there?"

"We'll find her," Quinn said. "Worst-case scenario, we hide in Lacuna until we can access the mainframe, secure it and contact the Docga. PT will remain here so any of us can get to him for repairs." He opened the swinging door. "Let's go."

My knees felt like jelly for the walk to the Conducer corridor. Then Quinn said, "Evard, would you like to take us over?"

"Bloody generous of you," he said, his voice practically a trumpet blast.

Bloody generous, indeed. My stomach lurched at the thought of an amateur leading my particles in a trajectory cross-leap. While Evard confirmed the links to Quinn's satisfaction, I leaned into the bookcases and held my middle. *I am a guard. A Blackguard puts duty first.*

Everything was going awry. Quaene dying when

'torgs weren't supposed to. Quil shirking his duty. Me letting Quinn get so close that when he left I'd be bereft. Finding Quala alone—and before Impostor Quinn could stop us—would be a miracle. My head jumbled with imagined surprises and what-ifs. *No. I can't think about them.* I had to perform my function. I would face down Impostor Quinn—

A wave of light-headedness hit me.

I took deep, steadying breaths, but tears sprang to my eyes, and my blurry vision swam with dots. I set my helmet on a shelf so I could use both hands to hold more securely to the bookcase. This time, I wouldn't be helpless or alone. This time, I had the skills of a Blackguard, and Evard, to assist me. We would take back Dome, and Quinn would release me to return to Zeffir. Evangeline would come to accept what I'd done. Sabein would heal her soul. She'd soothe me as well, help me forget this rough patch—

Evard announced he was ready. The book bindings flickered with glowing letters, waiting for our intent.

I stood to go. The strength went out of my limbs, and darkness swallowed me.

FORTY-SIX

QUINN

"**B**lessed *Waters!* Eve? What's wrong?" I cradled her limp body in my arms, my breathing suspended as I checked for hers.

"The girl's fainted," Evard said over my shoulder. "Don't worry. Let's get her to the sofa in the sitting area."

I scooped her against my chest and followed him. "She fainted. For no reason." I laid her on the couch.

He started rubbing her shoulders. "*Nei*, she's seen plenty of action the last twenty-four hours. Surprised she hasn't gone under before this."

I wiped my face to clear my vision. "Eve was right. She's not cut out to be a guard. I can't do this to her. She's too fragile."

"Eh," Evard said, "this is *normal*. For her. Emotional overriding. She'll come 'round in a few minutes. I don't know what Sabein usually does for her that works better, but I give her a shoulder massage. The emotional tension melts out of her, and she moves on."

Fine for him to say, but the frantic lurching of my heart continued. How could I put this woman in danger? I'd never forgive myself if anything happened to Eve. Not after losing Quaene. What if her malady came

395

forth at the wrong time and put the team in jeopardy?

Should I trust her to perform her function? I didn't have much time. I paced a tight circle. We needed her and her gift of reading people on this mission, especially to outwit my opponent. He'd already proven himself a master of disguise in more than clothing, but obviously he scared her, too. And when scared, Eve—

"I'm going to leave her here. Too much risk in a confrontation."

Evard started. "I don't think—"

"My decision. You'll guard me. In fact, I should appear to be without a guard. You can stay hidden in Lacuna. After what happened in the cavern, they'll recognize your orange surcoat, but alone, I might get away with passing for Impostor Quinn again. If you keep to Lacuna—which they now know we can do—we keep some element of surprise. Then if we need you to return for PT, or Zeffirite reinforcements, you can."

"Or for Eve."

I eyed him. "Only if the situation is desperate."

"Sure, sure. Let me leave word for Taior to fetch her help." He strode out the front door.

Damn. This mission might have us walking into the cage and closing the door ourselves.

What we needed was another trick up our sleeves, especially if I was leaving Eve behind.

I cast one last look at her. Her crystal flashed yellow, and I felt its vibration course through me.

Vibration. Energy. Power.

Only a few minutes passed before Evard returned,

but my mind had raced to solve our problem.

"Evard? I have another idea I'd like to show you."

FORTY-SEVEN

EVE

*E*ve, *I swear on the great warm pool beyond the grave, if it's the last thing I do, I will cure you of these tides of emotion that carry you away.*

Sabein! I sobbed into her shoulder, not caring what she thought of my weakness this time. *The worst has happened. Quaene has died. Quil deserted us. We're left with too few E-runs to enact the fail-safe!* My voice rose to a high-pitched hysteria. *We're headed into disaster with nothing to combat Impostor Quinn. We'll be deactivated like the rest, and it's my fault.*

Stop it! Stop it right this instant. You are not responsible for every 'torg on Aarde. Are you in a condition to help them? If not, are you available to help us?

I hesitated.

Eve, I'm in a bit of a hurry here, so make your decision.

I lifted my head. A mistake. The illusion of Sabein being with me slammed back to reality. I was in Passages, on the couch.

Beside me, Gwyn said, "Quinn left orders you were to stay with us."

My minister had made the decision for me. The burden was out of my hands.

"Taior realized later," my daughter said, "no one told

Quinn the Alliance started the crystal recovery in Cavvert. They sealed off the mines and are dispersing the
stones to the worst hornwort pools on Quil's reports to
see if it'll impede the growth. Zeffirites are funneling
back to assist. I was en route, so came here immediately. When I couldn't wake you, I sought Sabein."

"Not Cyrem's reports?" I asked.

Gwyn smiled. "They're locked in his porta, which
Taior can't use—"

"Or won't. Stubborn man."

"—and Cyrem is the best able to travel, so he's out
checking on various enclaves, several of which have
already joined the Alliance efforts. Taior thought Quil's
paper reports replicated the priority list close enough."

At least the disappearing bastard had done something to help. He couldn't be that uncaring of Aarde.
But he'd left Quinn alone to try... Tears sprang to my
eyes, and Gwyn wrapped her arms around me. Her
sympathy washed me, but beneath was a stronger urgency to act. I latched on to that feeling and reached for
Sabein.

I'm waiting, Eve.

Where do you need me?

*Transporting crystals from Cavvert. Taior's crew is suf-
ficient to secure our Waters.*

Splendid. Just the place I wanted to go back to.

The depth of the snow on the street had doubled
when Gwyn and I joined a dozen other Zeffirites hurry-
ing to Cyrem's Tours. A few older teens were among
them.

"Who is watching Perry?" I asked Gwyn.

"No one. He's operating the pool," she said proudly. "He's stepped in for Cyrem."

My grandson, taking on responsibility... More tears welled in my eyes. "What a grown young man he's becoming."

"Exactly." Gwyn patted her abdomen. "Time for another baby." Her chin lifted defiantly, as it had since she was younger than Perry. "And Cyrem agrees."

I was sure he did. "But Perry can't be the last in town. Taior knows to look out for him?"

"Of course, I do," Taior said from behind us. "But Eve, I'm surprised to see you still here." Taior pulled us aside before Cyrem's doorstep.

"I, uh..." I couldn't even say it. I didn't have to. He knew my fears in an instant.

The Zeffirite elder smiled and patted my hand. "You are welcome to come with us. We want you all as a part of our community. There's been no talk of restitution for this slip in security of our resources, but certainly the Docga will not deny our request that your triad be permanently appointed with us to help us restore our equanimity."

"You really think it could happen?"

"Sabein usually has the last word with the Docga. Has for centuries."

"But she's never mentioned, or offered..."

Taior gave a one-shoulder shrug. "You never needed her intervention before."

Incredible. My dream was coming true. I could live

in the community with my children, in an endless life-time of peaceful happiness. But my momentary bliss plunged with a thought of Quinn. I'd lose him if I stayed.

What was I thinking? I'd never really had Quinn. Be-sides, he'd left me. *He left you because he had to consider the others, the mission, his duty.*

All true. I was a danger to his plans. I gripped my sinking middle. "I accept your offer."

Gwyn squealed and hugged me.

"Pending approval of the Docga, of course."

"Excellent." Taior beamed.

"Let's go, Eve. Sabein's waiting in Cavvert." Gwyn tugged me toward Cyrem's shop.

It's the right thing to do. But somehow I didn't be-lieve the words that left me feeling lost and alone.

* * *

The return traverse to Cavvert seemed briefer to my healed head. I steeled myself and emerged with Gwyn in an improvised pool in the stream. The cavern bustled with people this time, and the goud-laden air fairly pulsed with their determination—one bearing an en-tirely different emphasis than Minister Quinn's atti-tude. Still, after yesterday's tragedy, the trip wore on my nerves, not made any easier by the constant re-minders of my function.

CONTACT WITH YOUR MINISTER ABSENT FOR THIRTY MINUTES.

As if I could stop thinking about *my minister*.

Gwyn and I crossed the cavern, each carrying baskets, and joined the queue to another damned portion of stream designated as the exit. We stepped forward foot by foot. However, when I tried to focus on the goud redistribution, my head returned to my absent commander.

All right. I had to admit I had feelings for him. Strong feelings. Along with his attractive looks, he had an honest character, loyalty and a sensitive kindness that made me sigh. Most important, we'd connected emotionally in what could have been simply a mating. He'd made sure of it the first time, and again, following his unintended cross-leap. I'd been confused, and furious, when he disappeared, but after he'd promised to analyze the interface—as he put it—between relationships, electronics, goud and particle transference, my anger had melted away. I just wanted to be with him.

CONTACT WITH YOUR MINISTER ABSENT FOR THIRTY-SIX MINUTES.

I rolled my eyes at the function message. My goud was every bit as alert as my electronics. Its eddying wouldn't be ignored, and as the turbulence increased, I knew something was wrong. I should have gone to Dome.

Our turn arrived. Gwyn motioned me ahead, so I stepped into the yellow water.

"First trip to redistribute crystals, right?" said a man with a clipboard. "Who are you?"

I gave him my name and origin as Zeffir while a

helper loaded my basket with crystals.

"How about we send you to Marra for your first jaunt? Quick trip north to a temperate spring. A local will meet you to accept the delivery."

But as soon as I dissolved, the goud made it clear I wouldn't be going to Marra. I ceased fighting it. Within minutes, Perry helped me from Cyrem's shop pool.

"Aunt Eve? You're going the wrong way."

I flashed him a smile and handed him my basket. "I don't think so. Send word to your mother that I will be joining Quinn at Dome."

FORTY-EIGHT

QUINN

Dome

Evard's accurate coordinates landed us at the top of the stairs above the lab at Dome, and he opened Lacuna for us.

"Excellent work. Try activating a goud-powered return."

Evard gripped his crystal, and pulsating yellow goud coated his hand. His body quaked and dissolved, disappearing for a few seconds before he materialized, grinning broadly. "Better than I ever imagined."

My crystal hummed with the extra Zeffirite goud Evard had called to support us. I tried it as well. While apart, I again saw the thick strands from last night, one leading through the door. I looked from it to Evard. No, I wouldn't confide new guesses at this late point. "Great. This door opens to a sitting room we think is Quala's because it's filled with plants and accesses the Biological Resources office below. Think you can sneak through behind me?"

"I'll do my best."

I left him in Lacuna. After listening at the door, I unlocked and cracked it. On the couch bookended by lush ferns lay a small blond woman also dressed in the dark green jumpsuit.

Her eyes flashed open. Quala gasped, but quickly recovered and waved me in, dropping an ice pack as she sat up.

Opening the door as far as I reasonably could, I entered and left it ajar.

"Of course, I've been expecting you." She looked at the door. "Are you alone?"

Goud hummed through me, prompting an answer. "Expecting Quil." No backpedaling now. "Soon."

She rose, rolling her shoulders, gaze on the door. "Then you found him. Good. And...Quaene?"

I nodded. Why not? Let her think we had a team. It'd give her confidence.

"I do hope you shared how impossible it was for Quetta and I to correct this situation. You can't blame us for not taking action."

"We don't. But to be frank, Quil isn't himself either. That's why I came ahead." Blessed Waters, I was on a roll. I had her complete attention now, and I had better make use of it. I gestured to the door leading to the salon and stepped toward it. "Is anyone likely to interrupt?"

"Not without knocking. But what do you mean? Is there a problem?"

Hell, yes, there's a problem. "He's not in the best shape to do the fail-safe. Can Quetta join us instead?"

At that, she hustled to my side, her back to the landing and Evard. She was short and thin, but looked very sure of her ability to block me. My words had done the job. Now the trick was to keep my gaze on her face.

"You may not remember how she spun into a depression before we landed here. Not even the med-techs can stabilize her. It's a struggle for me to keep my own thoughts, even with my herbal treatments. We can't count on Quetta."

At that, my humming crystal screeched. My gaze unfocused, like when breaking apart, and I found the strands. Neither went to Quala.

A bad feeling came over me.

"How long will the others be?" she asked.

"I asked them to give me a few minutes."

She darted an anxious glance to the door, and I couldn't help following her gaze.

Only the landing was visible. Evard must be in.

"We arrived together." I told her what I wished were true. "They're in the atrium."

Her breath released.

I wouldn't have noticed if I hadn't been so close and spent so much of the last few days paying attention to Eve and her reactions. Relief. But was it because help had arrived, or due to another reason?

"I'll get coffee for us, then when the others arrive, we can get together a plan before going to the upstairs office where Minister Quinn is working." With a smile, she gestured to the couch. "Take a moment to catch your breath."

Her information was complete and assuring. Too complete and assuring. This wasn't at all the impression

I'd had of the woman before. But then, I'd been dazed.

She left, and the moment the door closed, Evard flashed into sight. "What do you think?" he whispered and strode to a spot near the door and slipped back into Lacuna.

I moved to stand next to him. "Friendly, reassuring. Like a trap."

Evard popped his head out. "I wish Eve was here to read this lady."

Hadn't the same thought run through my head? As well as a wave of guilt. "Listen, this sounds a little...different, but I'm getting something like a message from my crystal."

"Go on."

"It, er, *thinks* Quetta is a better bet."

He nodded. "Whether Quala is with us or against us no longer makes a difference. She knows you're here and thinks the others are, too."

"Let's go for Quetta, then."

The salon was empty, the doors leading to the hall closed. We crossed the room to the only door on the far side, the one Eve said was Quetta's room. I unfocused to peer through the goud again. The strand led through the door. I opened it.

An older woman with long dark hair sank back into her pillows, her face going grim when she spotted me.

I caught her attitude. Though she also wore the minister's jumpsuit, me wearing one was a mistake in this case, since she clearly hated Impostor Quinn.

Then her gaze shifted, and she frowned. "Who are

you?"

Evard pushed past me and into the room. "My name is Evard, my good woman. Is it possible you're Minister Quetta, who I've heard of from Quaene?"

Her eyes widened, but with a glance to me, she closed her mouth.

I had to make this clear, and quickly. "I'm not the Quinn who's been at Dome. I'm the Quinn that left with Quaene and Quil."

"He is," Evard said, "As much as they look the same, I can vouch for him."

Her gaze darted between the two of us, then stayed on me. Within seconds, she relaxed. "You look like him, but act nothing of the sort he is. Where is Quaene?"

Evard met my gaze. We couldn't ruin this with that news. "Waiting. There's not much time. How up to performing a fail-safe are you?" If she could, then I would insist we go ahead when Quala came back.

"My head has cleared after my serving girl insisted I eat only what she's brought me the last few days. My electronics are intact, but I'll need help walking." She sat up and swung her legs off the bed. "I haven't had much practice after weeks in bed."

Damn, she'd be no good in a confrontation. But we helped her stand, a robust woman nearly Evard's height.

The outer door opened. My gaze shot to Evard.

"Pardon me," he said to Quetta and moved behind her.

I put my arm around the sturdy woman's waist. My crystal hummed, practically rendering me deaf. "Quetta?" I whispered. "We need to keep quiet about Evard. He's going to hide, until we know it's safe."

"Safe?" A snort burst from her. "There's no such thing here. But I trust you more than them. Lead on."

We walked out of her room, and Quetta seemed to sag in my hold, though she didn't lean her weight on me. Just as I realized her weakness was an act, Quala emerged from her rooms.

Her frown flicked between the bent head of Quetta and my face. It changed to a glare. "I told you she's too fragile to help."

Quetta gave a little moan.

Hell, what was going on? "She can try." I tugged her forward, but the larger woman stood her ground, and as Quala crossed the salon, Quetta stiffened.

Every nerve in my body shot to alert.

"Let me take her back to her room." Quala brushed me aside.

Quetta turned, as if to go with her, then swung and punched the small woman in the gut.

Quala's breath exploded out, and she fell to the floor.

As if nothing had happened, Quetta said, "Let's go." She took my arm and toddled toward the doors.

We'd never make it anywhere. "Will you hide with me?" I whispered.

"Yes."

Quala gasped behind us, finally drew breath and

squawked, "Guards!"

The outer doors flew open, and a Blackguard rushed in. His helmet turned as his gaze darted around the room, and he hesitated.

Quetta didn't. "Let us pass," she ordered him.

The guard looked at me, as if for confirmation. I nodded, and we continued to the door.

"Grab him," Quala gulped. "Guard, get in here!"

Footsteps pounded down the hall.

Reinforcements wouldn't be good. I sidestepped into Lacuna, carrying Quetta with me. Evard dashed into sight as we disappeared. The guard turned to him. I spied my chance.

"Stay still and you won't be seen," I told Quetta and leaped out. Evard disappeared, and the guard flipped to me. His sword shot out. I wrenched sideways, but the blade slashed across—

Evard yanked me into his Lacuna. Seconds later, a burn erupted on my chest.

"Sorry, best I could do at the angle, but—I say! You took one." Evard prodded the slice in my shirt while I assessed the scene outside our barrier.

Our attacking guard searched for us, while another helped Quala bat at the space where I'd left Quetta.

"Flesh wound," Evard said. "Doesn't look too bad. Hmm, except at this end." He rummaged in a pocket, produced a patch of second skin and secured it over my wound.

"Thanks. That'll hold me. But this has gone to hell. I want you to get back to Zeffir."

"No. I stay and perform my function."

I glared up at him. Damn, I did not want to have to pull rank on the man who had become my friend. "It will take you five minutes to go and return. With Eve. Or PT, if you can't find her."

Evard jerked his chin once. "Cover me."

I looked through the viewing port. One guard circled closer, and I sprang onto him. My weight carried him down, and my fingers at his neck did the rest. The blur of orange at the corner of my eye meant Evard was on his way.

A scuffle broke out—Quetta had left her Lacuna. I scrambled up to help her—

Whack! The blow bent me double, and a gripping hand accessed my keypad. I bucked and rolled, cursing my stupidity at not guarding my weak point. I found my face staring at me.

"You!" I snarled at Impostor Quinn. "How dare you steal my face?"

I lunged for his keypad.

We tumbled across the floor, grappling for position. He grunted, "I needed to be you worse than you did." His hand landed on my neck again.

He poked several keys before I shook him off and gained my feet, staying low as I checked my function. Nothing lost. I sprang and grabbed him, but he muscled from my grasp. In addition to my injury, my impostor was bigger than I was. I aged up to gain some bulk, but it didn't match his.

He smirked. "Sorry, you don't share *my* DNA, so

you'll never have the body I do. Nor the temperament to succeed. If that damned Docgan hadn't trailed you everywhere, you'd have been long gone."

Fury built inside me, an emotion that wouldn't serve well in a fight. Since I couldn't overpower him physically, I had to remain logical to see my advantage. I stepped back and slipped into Lacuna.

He snatched my arm and came with me. "You do have nice skills," he said smoothly. "Care to share them with our cause?"

I dissolved the barrier, and we reemerged circling each other. Though I knew he planned to become Schiftan's Premier, I wanted to prod him into revealing more. "Which is?"

"Growing our own little group of immortals."

If he controlled the crystals, they'd only be slaves serving his eternal 'torg lifetime. Forget that. I tackled him and slapped a hand to his neck. My fingers flew...on nothing. There was no keypad. *What the hell is going on here?*

Impostor Quinn pinned me to the wall and laughed. "Discover something? Like how we were never like you, just copycats." He studied me for a reaction.

A copy? Then we were clones—and he must be one who was still fully human. How, dammit? How had this happened when the Docga were supposed to be guarding my electronic ass?

He sneered at my sour look. "How did you think I passed for you—lucky chance? That blood you gave—at the tip of my knife—was the godsend that allowed me to use the talents the clever Docga never suspected when they leased our land." His face shifted.

Not older, or younger, but to a completely different man—a young man I recognized.

Javion Feldfine.

"Remember me? Trainee pilot, thankful recipient of a big-time transporter tour."

Javion and I had bonded over aeronautics. His words slammed me. Hard. I wrestled against his hold, but under Javion's sneer, another memory slid neatly into place. This face had been in exactly the same position—with exactly the same look on it—when I'd last seen it. Right before I'd nearly died.

"The knife," I gasped. "*You* stabbed me in the bar."

He smirked. "And *you*, my buddy, didn't die. You might have noticed me if your bug-eyes weren't on Director Feldfine your entire R&R. Because after we'd pumped you for information, the lovely Myriah was done being your"—his voice dropped to a purr—"lover."

Pain shot through my head, but this time that memory also surfaced, and the hurt shifted to my chest. I'd seen *them* together when I'd gone to say good-bye, and not like brother and sister. Lovers. I was sure they hadn't noticed me in their passion. But right after, he'd appeared in the bar's back hall, shoved me, swung the knife—

"Caught on, have you? My woman does what it takes to support the real me, Javion *Lystlund*, candidate for the Advancement Party of Schiftan. We've progressed further than any other Schiftani candidate in improving our people's lives. Immortality, combined with our ability to change shape..." He smiled, and it wasn't the smile an old acquaintance gives another.

Damn.

"Of course," Javion said, "collecting your blood sample was nothing compared to Myriah's work to draw you in and procure the minister positions we'd trained so long to hold. I can't tell you how annoying it was to stand aside while Myriah did her little *job* on you."

Javion shifted again, back to Impostor Quinn. He pressed his bulk into me, his hands fighting mine for position.

"Bad luck for me you were such a wily opponent. If my aim had been truer, your team would have found you dead. Like Myriah left Quaene."

Myriah was Javion's accomplice here, too, on Aarde. She was the Blackguard in the costume—and because Myriah wasn't 'torg, she couldn't adopt the polymer.

It was too late for Quaene, but I could save Eve, everyone she loved and their planet. I had to rectify my mistakes. The whole stinking scheme made me madder, giving me strength to hold him off. We locked arms, our faces inches apart.

He rasped, "I may not be as good at hand-to-hand, but my skill in electronics is superior. While Myriah used her physical science training to set up crystal harvesting, I've *recruited* 'torgs to help. Together, we make a fine team, don't you think?" He turned his head.

I followed his gaze. For the first time, I noticed the

silence. Not a good silence. Quetta was gone, a guard positioned in front of the door to her room. A step before him stood Quala.

Her features shifted from sharp to round, her small mouth becoming full lips. They parted in a broad smile. Not to an older version of herself, but to that of a completely different woman.

I winced. Myriah Feldfine's familiar face ricocheted painfully around my brain in a flood of R&R memories. She'd seduced me, but I'd fallen for the attractive woman, totally taken by her attention, conveniently forgetting I was breaking a Docga policy.

"I'm grateful to have the luscious bit of woman back as mine." Impostor Quinn wrenched his arm from my grasp and clamped it on my keypad. I twisted, but couldn't escape his hold.

He frowned and muttered, "Wrong sequence?" His fingers flew over my keys.

I bunched my muscles to throw him off—then froze. Not because of what he was doing to me. No, quite to the contrary—because of what he *wasn't* doing to me. Nothing he did made a difference to my function. And yet, when I stilled, Impostor Quinn acted as if he'd succeeded.

"There." He shot a triumphant glance to Myriah. "He's completely under our control, the perfect bait to bring in the last Biosphere Corps minister."

FORTY-NINE

EVE

Zeffir Island

Snow swirled down our street, its normal white re-
flecting yellow from the goud-laden clouds. Taior's
crew must have almost finished. I ran for Passages.

Propped on the table in the center aisle was a note.
Evard's scrawl read: *I've taken PT to Dome. Eve, if you
find this, get to Quetta. She's with us.*

My heartbeat sped up. Quinn needed me. I had to
change the situation, for him, for me and for Aarde.

My gaze fell on the thing under Evard's paper—
Quil's abandoned cuff.

I fingered the two short crystals. Tristam had re-
marked on the rarity of a stranger acquiring two at
once. No wonder we'd all accepted him so quickly.
What fools we'd been. Where was he? Probably far
from here. I slipped the armband into a pocket on my
belt in case I needed extra goud.

Evard had just used the system, so I should be able
to follow him with the goud. I opened myself to my
crystal, took a deep breath and put on my helmet.
Glowing words swam before my eyes. I intoned the key
titles, and the corridor blurred its opening.

The bookcases shifted to trees, and I found myself on Dome's plaza—but not within the guarded Conducer. Instead, I stood on a walled garden bed, half hidden between two old trees. Below and around me was noise and movement. Hundreds of 'torgs crowded onto the plaza, raising the temperature to an uncomfortable swelter.

Outrage flooded me. Despair. Fear. I didn't have to speak to anyone for the problem to become clear: They'd reported with their equipment, but had been locked out. Locked out of Dome and locked out of returning to their Posts.

Hoping the flux of bodies would disguise me, I jumped off the wall.

Someone shrieked, and everyone in the vicinity rounded on me, each face rapidly morphing to anger. One shout of "Stop her!" sent me jumping back onto the wall, my sword clutched in one hand, my dagger in the other.

The few who had stepped forward flinched back.

"Freeze," I boomed in my best imitation of Evard.

They did, for a moment, but nervous twitching rippled across my growing audience. Their murmured words escalated—

That's a minister's Blackguard...

...five could take a stunner...

...use her for leverage...

The snatches of risky opinions meant the situation was bad. People were on edge. Anything could happen. I had to get to Quinn before it did.

"You there." I motioned to a woman who seemed to still have her wits about her. "How long have you been here?"

"Yesterday morning, but for others, it's been since the evening before."

A man snarled, "You should know. You're just one of those rotten—"

In a flash, I leaped to his side, stunned him and returned to the wall. People skirted away, their eyes wide and fearful. My actions would have horrified me a week ago.

I cleared my throat. "Your cooperation is appreciated." I nodded to the woman. "Please continue. You can't get in?"

"N-not ex-exactly. 'Torgs don't *want* in, since word filtered out we're being deactivated."

Splendid. How was I to gain their help when I appeared to be on the side issuing our version of death? I nodded encouragingly—with my gift—and she continued.

"Things got ugly, and there was a fight. The guards locked the gate. That's when someone discovered the Conducers had been reprogrammed for one-way travel *in*. Once you're here, you can't get out. But a man came in who insisted he can fix it."

"Where is he now?"

"Don't tell her," came a shout from the gathering crowd.

A wave of my sword silenced the dissenter and got me the answer. "The guy huddled in that pack near the gate."

The added height of the wall gave me a good view of the group. The man in the center had damaged our plans, but my crystal's hum trounced my groan. I had to get to Quil.

I made eye contact with the nearest 'torgs and emitted my honest and helpful feelings.

"I don't want to hurt anyone. I want to get into Dome and stop the deactivations. The native people need our help. Who can get me over to that man who can fix the Conducer?"

Ten hands went up.

"Thank you. Please move to my right, and the rest of you move to the far perimeter of the dome, away from us and the gate." It took seconds for most to do as I directed. I gave the resisting few a hard glare and a moment's pause before I stepped off the wall and stunned them.

My volunteer helpers eyed me, a few edging back.

"Anyone else want to challenge me? No? Excellent. Clear a walkway." They hustled people and possessions out of the way. Word reached the five men just as I strode up to Quil.

His arm-crossed stance was meant to threaten, but when I lifted my helmet, his eyes widened. He quickly covered his surprise. "Eve. Fancy meeting you here."

"I never would have guessed it either." Light manner, no hostility, but I needed a sense of his attitude. I'd rather have his help and wrestle with his desertion later. I stepped closer. A gutsy pluckiness wafted from him. While not outright bravery, this was better than I'd expected. "What in the name of the Golden Waters are you doing?"

He jerked his head sideways, and we stepped aside from the group.

"I made a mistake." He rolled his eyes. "Understatement, I know. My hotheadedness has landed me in trouble before, but never this bad. It sank in this morning when I field-checked the hornwort levels myself, something any decent minister should do. I cross-leaped—"

Right, with skills and files Quaene had given them for the mission he'd deserted.

He raised a finger. "Hear me out."

I had to forgive and forget. At least until we were out of this.

"Before checking the Minneri Pools near here, I leaped from Osster on the other side of Aarde, to Torrent Falls in Breccia's northern latitudes, then to Marra on the Pucco continent." He shook his head. "Those springs were a favorite of mine seventy years ago, the first we cleaned up. Now hornworts cover the rocks, spread thick over any surface that gets a daily tidal fluctuation, and every one spiked with a nub horn growing into a spore capsule. The Aardites within the range of those Bounded Winds will lose it all. We will lose..."

He briefly closed his eyes, and I detected a wave of hopelessness before he sighed. "It's difficult, but I'll come to accept that loving Evangeline is futile. So that leaves me...here. I have to hand it to Quaene. Without her perseverance with Quinn and I, we wouldn't have a chance to save Aarde. I have to do this for her."

"Thank you," I whispered.

He cracked a wry smile. "I can't believe I'm actually rooting for the little volcanic planet. And as much as I hate to admit it, Quinn works as hard as he plays. I can't fault him when he's also followed every lead and nailed the source of the problem. An entire Biological Resources team with years of lab data overlooked the delicate balance between an element and a dangerous plant."

His features shifted to somber. "Running out on my run-mates a second time is worse than other mistakes I've made, including the pod wreck that originally killed me. If I don't make all this right somehow, I've nothing to live for."

This change of heart didn't surprise me. I'd seen how readily he shifted moods. But would he hold his current temper long enough for us to get to Quinn and help? I had no choice. I needed him.

I hit Quil with an emote of confidence. "Or you could consider your mistakes successes. Dying at a time when you were needed here and leaving so the rogues didn't deactivate you. Who knows? Maybe we'll discover your desertion also has a good side. Can we work together?"

"Can we? Word is you kick ass."

"Only if you stand in my way."

Quil extended his hand. To free one of my hands, I slipped the dagger into its sheath and in the process brushed my cuff pouch. Ah. There *had* been a reason to bring his armband. I retrieved it and held it out. "Care to rejoin?"

Excitement flashed over his face before doubt clouded it. "You think I'll be accepted?"

"I'll give you a good word."

He fitted the cuff over his wrist and pushed it up his forearm. Then we shook hands and rejoined our groups. Quil grinned at them. "Mates, I think we can go with a more straightforward approach, since we have the services of a Blackguard on our side."

The plan had been to storm the gate, but it shifted to me pretending to take them in, at sword point.

"I'm all for it," said a man, his tone anxious. "I need to find out what happened to the rest of my triad."

A returning triad separated? I looked at the guy questioningly, and he blushed. "I got delayed by a, uh, native who needed help."

Looked like I wasn't the only one who had indulged in a native-electorg alliance. "Right, after we change the Conducer controls, go help other 'torgs. Are we in agreement?"

We made a commotion, I issued a few loud commands, everyone fell into line and I marched them at sword point through the parting crowd, my stunner palmed in my other hand. It *might* have some effect on regular guards if I used it against bare skin.

We approached the imposing building's closed entrance doors. Despite the turmoil, only two guards manned the guardhouse. A bulky, older man—who had shed his helmet—was seated at the control panel in the cramped booth. The lanky, helmeted one stood before the doorway with his weapon drawn. His emotions jumped, divided between putting up a good front and wanting to be safely inside. When he opened his mouth to order me to halt, he had to form the words three times before he got them out. Petrified.

Once more, I exuded confidence. "I slipped out the back and rounded up the ringleaders. Open the gate so I can take them to—" D'dair, what did they call it?

A SECURE—

"A secure holding area."

He turned to confer with the older guard, and I whipped my stunner to his bare neck. He stumbled. I caught him around the chest, squeezing tight enough to stop speech.

"This guard has fainted." I wrestled him forward as my shield. "How long has he been on duty? Get him inside immediately."

The supervising guard rose. "Are you nuts?" he barked. "It's a madhouse in there. Ain't nobody getting me to open that gate." His gaze shifted up and to the left.

Aha. A nondescript button was mounted an arm's length up the wall, where it wouldn't be hit by mistake. The gate control.

I let my gaze linger a second too long. He lunged to block me. I thrust the other guard at him, and they stumbled together. I tripped closer to the button, but got knocked aside. The young guard collapsed with a gasp and the older straightened. My arm swung automatically, carrying the stun sword into his muscular chest. The blow bounced up under his chin, and sparks coursed over his unprotected skin. Any longer and he might have succumbed, but with a roar, the man jerked and struck out. My weapon flew at me. I shut down the jolting current.

He squashed me against the control panel. Pain shot through my flattening rib cage.

"Just who the hell are you?" His hot breath streamed under my helmet. "I'm gonna have your circuits on my lapels by the end of the day."

No. My arms wouldn't move, but my finger did. I flicked on the stunner and rammed my knee up at the same time. The shock budged him enough to catch my breath and push. I lodged the sword under his chin again and the bigger man faltered. I kneed him out of my way, and by some miracle, I smashed the gate button with the sword blade.

I swung around, tensed to deliver another punch, but the guard buckled to the floor beside his partner. "I'll keep my circuits where they are, thanks."

The gate's broad doors opened, and electorgs swarmed from the building. My dutiful volunteers broke rank and ran with the crowd streaming onto the plaza. I didn't blame them. I would have taken a minute to reconnoiter if Quil hadn't yanked me out of the gatehouse.

"Eve? You know the way?"

We shoved through the throng. "Where did they get

the information about the deactivations?" Quil yelled.

A man stopped midstride. "We *were* deactivated. Then some inside 'torgs fed the guards something that had them vomiting within minutes and reactivated us. With everyone working together, we managed to take over these bottom two levels. The only thing stopping us from leaving was the gate control. We're getting the hell out of here—back to our Posts where the natives can protect us."

We didn't bother to tell him the Conducers were down. In their haste, most 'torgs missed that I was a guard, but a few saw me and peeled away, allowing us to plow forward.

Quil noticed. "Sweet. I had no idea that outfit commanded so much respect."

I spared a look at him. "You know, the ministers' bodyguards won't be as easy to take down as the gate guards."

"How so?" Quil asked.

"Class 1's aren't affected by stunner volts. They're my peers, with the same performance functions. Can you access your function for something to help us stop them?"

"It's been a while. Those weird sub-vision messages always interrupted my work, so I've kept them turned off." A faraway look came over his face. I guided us through the thinning crowd, aware of the message flashing in my mind.

RETURN TO MINISTER COMMENCED. PROCEED ACCORDING TO DIRECTIONAL MAP. ETA: 5.3

MINUTES.

I didn't have time to open the map before we came to the main bank of elevators.

"They'll be locked down," Quil muttered. "We'll have to find the stairs. But I might have the solution. I can disengage a Class 1's functions."

I had to hope the same wouldn't happen to me. "Good enough. The ministers' floor—the fifth—will probably be guarded. We'd be better off teaming up with these insider 'torgs. If they haven't left already."

"How do we find them? Who would be smart enough to serve the guards laced food?"

Serving food. "Charlotte."

"Huh?"

"A girl I met in the kitchen. Long story, but her run-mate is a guard. Her lover, as well. I bet she was trying to get everyone out of this mess."

Quil grinned. "See? Some people will go to worse lengths than I did for love. Where will we find your Charlotte?"

"Kitchen. This way."

The kitchen corridor was clear. Still, we slowed and crept the last twenty feet. The door was closed, paper over the window. I could hear voices, but was Charlotte inside? If she wasn't there, this plan was of no use.

If only Quinn were here now. Last time, we'd hidden right here. If he was here now... I loitered long enough for Quinn to signal me. Finally, I jerked my chin to the kitchen door, and at Quil's nod of readiness, I knocked.

"What do you want?" someone shouted.

I didn't bother trying to explain. "Bring Charlotte!" I shouted. The curly-haired brunette appeared in the window. I lifted my helmet to show her my face, and we were in.

A dozen workers—including the supervisor, Mr. Wellsey—surrounded us, each bearing a sharp knife or cleaver. Quil was like glue to my quivering side. D'dair. Didn't he realize I needed space in case I had to pull my sword?

"Easy, Eve," he whispered, and a stream of goud zinged my ring. "We're facing them, people to people. Not guard to subordinates. I've learned a few things from my peer interaction lessons."

He was right. I removed my helmet and distanced myself from my guard function. Trepidation emanated from the other 'torgs. Most were probably new, in entry positions like they'd thought I was the first time I came here. Only Charlotte and Mr. Wellsey had any confidence.

"I tell you, she's one of us," Charlotte said again.

I dipped my head encouragingly. "I think we have this crew to thank for the rebellion against the deactivations, which helped us break through the gate. Rumor has it the food made people sick."

Exclamations about their coup began, but I waved my hand for silence. "Do you think you can do that again? We've got to get up to Level Five to confront the ministers and stop them from stealing minerals from G47."

Charlotte snorted. "Are you kidding? They realized

we did it. Minister Quinn is furious. Food service has been shut down, and every kitchen 'torg is slated for deactivation."

As if he wouldn't have done it anyway, the bastard. Quil and I would have to devise another—

"But we've got lots of ideas in our apron pockets," Charlotte said. "We'll get you to Level Five, won't we, guys?"

In no time, we rode the elevator to the top. The doors opened to three guards wielding stun swords, but plucky Charlotte sang out, "Just me." She and Mr. Wellsey stepped forward, each holding up a tray of chocolate-chip cookies arranged on white doilies.

The guards' stunners flared. The treats went flying, along with a layer of flour that coated their helmets. Two of them staggered back, blinded. I tackled the third in the gut, gritting my teeth against the jarring sting along my side as we slammed into the wall. Polymer smoke filled my nostrils.

"Would you hurry up?" I growled at Quil, who was angling a hand to the man's neck.

"Done," he panted and jumped away.

I let go of the slumping guard, only to career sideways when another—powdery-white—barreled into me. He carried me down with a stunner held to my back. Sparks snapped and singed my suit—

Armor repairs in progress.

I shoved and rolled, scrambling to gain the upper hand as we tumbled across the floor.

"Come on, Eve. You nearly have him," Quil cheered

and sent another burst of encouraging goud.

Goud. An image of Evangeline encased in yellow popped into my mind. My goud flashed over the guard, coating him the same way. The Blackguard's suit shimmered yellow one second and then dulled the next, until the man lay still over me, every inch of him covered in minute crystals.

Quil's awestruck face loomed above us. "Whoa."

I heaved my opponent aside and leaped to my feet in time to ram the last guard away from Quil. His sword flew through the air as we crashed into the wall, both of us coated yellow before he froze and dropped.

This time, Quil peered at me instead of the guard. "Why didn't you say you could—"

"That was utterly cool!" A gleeful Charlotte danced up. "I've never seen any of the others do that. Is it a special function you received from that new young minister?"

"Something like that." I leaned against the wall to catch my breath. Particles of flour floated around the coated guards and Mr. Wellsey, who was out cold. "What happened?"

"He blocked the last guard while you fought." Charlotte knelt by her boss' head and stroked his brow. "I didn't realize the meek little man had it in him."

I checked his pulse. Still strong. "We surprise ourselves sometimes. Can you take care of him while we continue on?"

Quil and I dragged him into the elevator. As the door closed, Charlotte said, "I'll get Charlie and Avery from guarding the transport bay. No harm now with the command changing."

Nice of her, but we couldn't wait. I grabbed Quil by the elbow and tucked him slightly behind me as we strode along the wide granite hallway.

Proceed to Minster's side. ETA: 42 seconds.

"So, er, thanks," Quil said. "I guess I wasn't prepared for things to get quite so physical. Or to move so fast."

"*Minister* Quil, you're not supposed to be engaged in a fight. But if the opportunity arises again, I won't refuse a little help."

"Got it. Not saying I can keep up, but I'll jump in. You familiar with the layout up here?"

"We're approaching the female ministers' rooms on the right." I opened my senses and felt around for anyone present. "This floor is deserted." I explained how I knew. "I suppose they've gone to the lead minister's suite on Level Six. The stairway is behind this locked door. Can you detect differences in electrical impulses?" I nodded to the knob.

Quil grasped it and turned. "Not locked."

"D'dair," I muttered. "They're expecting us."

We ascended the stairs.

Proceed to Minster's side. ETA: 15 seconds.

A variety of emotions assaulted me as I scaled the last riser. I stopped Quil with the flat of my hand and advanced a step on my own. Ten feet ahead, a hand appeared in thin air and waved.

Blessed Waters. I linked arms with Quil, hissed, "Keep your mouth shut," and propelled him forward. Steps later, the hand grabbed my arm, and I felt myself break apart.

"What"—Quil spoke as I pulled him after me—"the hell?"

"Precisely," snarled a familiar Tarni accent. "What the hell are *you* doing here?"

FIFTY

EVE

Evard shoved me behind him. He had Quil in an armlock before my rear hit the Lacuna floor. PT's furry body jumped between the men and me, nearly knocking me senseless. The wolfhound circled Quil twice before sitting in front of him, eyes glaring, lips curled back to show an impressive array of teeth.

"Start talking, mister," Evard snarled at Quil.

"D'dair, ease up." I got to my feet. "He's on our side. We met on the plaza and fought our way in. What are you doing here? Is Quinn all right?"

"I can't answer that affirmatively. Good that you and Quinn took advantage of last night's interlude and screwed each other silly."

"Evard," I snapped.

He let go of Quil. "Sorry. You understand I'm making sure Evy was safe."

"Humph." He straightened his clothing. "Answer her. Why aren't you with Quinn?"

"Doing what I was told and cursing the bloody mess the whole thing has become."

That's when I noticed Evard looked ill, and his emotions...stretched to the breaking point. "Evard? What's happened?"

"Hate to say it, but I should never have let on that I mastered the cross-leap. It's gotten me separated from Quinn and Minister Quetta." Evard relayed that Quala and Impostor Quinn were in cahoots. "We tracked them up here, planning to storm the room." He shrugged and nodded deferentially to Quil. "What do you want us to do?"

He shrugged back. "My guess is as good as yours. At this point, storming the room sounds like a plan."

"It's an office," I mused, recalling the room. "Pretty spare—a desk against the back window. A table of rocks to the right of the door."

Quil said, "Should we count on this door also being unlocked?"

"Probably," I answered. "Evard? You said they didn't see you?"

"Right you are, my revered run-mate. I should remain hidden."

PT rumbled something to which both men nodded.

"He will stay with me in Lacuna. Are we ready?"

We exited, crept to the office, and once Evard and PT hid, I held my sword before us and simply opened the door.

Across the room, four ministers stared from behind the desk. My gaze shot to Quinn. *Alive.* Quetta, too, pale but strangely less beleaguered than before. They stood, unrestrained, at bookend positions on the wide desk's corners. Yet, something besides Quinn's torn jumpsuit looked different. Then it hit me. They scowled, a look more fitting for reprobate guards than captured leaders.

In contrast, the impeccably dressed Impostor Quinn sat in his high-backed chair nodding serenely, his fingers tented before his chin. Standing to his left, Minister Quala smiled, a smug curve to her lips. An act staged to counterbalance the ministers who we—or Quil, because that's at whom the rogue gazed—knew.

"*Bloody hyphae*," breathed Evard from behind me.

Quinn and Quetta moved, raising swords that flared to life.

"They've been converted," Evard whispered. "We'll have to take out our ministers to rescue them."

Again, exactly my thoughts. Evard and I had been together far too long. Suppressing my serious concern that we'd not be together much longer, I fought to maintain a steady, bodyguard-like stance. Heightened emotions swirled through the room. As I would expect, determination flowed foremost among them, as well as self-righteousness, some fear and, oddly, a spike of pride.

Impostor Quinn rose and leaned forward on his desk. I registered the absolute replication of his handsome features when his confident gaze lit briefly on me.

"Welcome, Quil. We've been expecting you to join us."

"Thanks," he said, intoning more sarcasm than was necessary.

"Ask your guard to wait in the hall if you wish to keep her. She looks fit for all types of service, so I expect you do."

That raised my hackles. And someone else's, but the air brimmed with emotion, masking whose. Quinn's and Quetta's faces remained stony, giving me no clue to their allegiance. I had to go with Evard's deduction that they'd been converted.

Quil pulled me back to where we'd exited Lacuna. Behind us, Evard hissed, "Eve, have you got an emotional reading? Whom do I go for?"

I turned, blocked by Quil shuffling on the threshold. "Difficult to tell. Remove Quinn and Quetta, then deal with the impostors? You take her, and I'll—"

"Settled?" asked Impostor Quinn.

Quil muttered to us, "Three on four? Seems fair with the two of you."

Instantly, a feeling of raw envy rippled across the room, but with a surge of resolve, Quil stepped forward. "You traitor!"

Blessed Waters! I couldn't let this minister get killed either. I dove and caught him mid-leap. He tumbled, snagging my stun sword. Current pulsed through us.

"*Hell!*" he choked and thrashed.

I twisted aside, dropping my sword and losing my helmet as his head slammed into the desk.

ALERT!

A scramble of bodies came at me, and I grabbed my ankle dagger.

In a flash of coral, Evard cut past and grabbed Quetta. Quala rammed him, but couldn't stop Evard's bulk. He shoved Quetta from the room. They plowed into the far wall with a *whack*.

Surprise blossomed over Impostor Quinn's and Quala's faces, but not Quinn's at the rogue's back. I had no idea whose side he was on and no time to guess as Quala wheeled toward me.

"You interfering synapse of inferior function," she cried. "When I get my hands on you, you'll only be fit for kitchen work!"

"After all I've done for you?" Charlotte stood rigid in the doorway. "Why, that's just plain rude. I'll have you know, we like our function. Do something, Avery." A hand grasped her shoulder, and Charlotte disappeared.

Impostor Quinn barked, "Quinn, get them," and both Quinn and Quala moved forward.

Stay back, I willed him, seeing Quala's short sword swipe for my throat. I blocked with my smaller dagger. Metal hit metal, and I staggered. Her weapon arced for another swing. Desperate, I shot goud from my hand. Thick yellow streams hit, then crystallized over her. She fell stiffly against the desk, her sword held aloft.

Impostor Quinn's jaw dropped. My Quinn reached for the rogue, but the man lurched from his stupor. He snatched Quala's sword, cracking the crystal-like glass, and turned to me in unbridled rage.

I threw my dagger, willing goud with it. The golden mass sailed wide of his shoulder as he swung the sword. *No!* I leaped aside, raising my arm over my helmet-less head a heartbeat before the blade hit my forearm. Pain radiated through it, and I launched my body at him. We slammed to the floor. I twisted to gain the upper hand, raised a fist to punch, to block, to...

Beneath me lay not one, but two men. Two men who would look alike, except golden crystals coated one whose mouth was open, frozen in a silent scream.

"Eve?" Quinn pushed aside Impostor Quinn, his movement snapping a fine strand of goud running from his ear cuff. Slivers of yellow crystal dropped to his beard. He knelt by me. "Are you okay?"

His cuff was empty. He had coated the impostor? No, he didn't have that kind of goud reserve. I must have. I lifted my hand. An empty osmium band circled my finger.

My crystal was gone.

The room spun, until strong hands caught me.

"Stay with me, Eve," Quinn murmured. "You're safe." His deep, rhythmic voice stilled the rushing in my ears. "He's dead, thanks to the dagger you threw."

"I m-missed," I hiccupped into his neck.

He levered his look-alike off the floor enough for me to see my dagger embedded in his back. "I didn't."

FIFTY-ONE

QUINN

Impostor Quinn was dead, but Eve was safe in my arms. That's what mattered. I'd never been so glad to see anyone in my life—or as frightened. I held her tenderly, wiping her tears and helping get her injured arm as comfortable as possible. "I'm sorry I had no way to tell you I was still on your side."

"I thought I was going to have to hurt you," she mumbled. "Evard said so, too. I tried to read you, but things moved too quickly."

"Quickly? Ha." A laugh burst from me. "Waiting for Impostor Quinn—or, rather, Javion Lystlund's—game to play out tested my limits. Seeing Quil whispering in your ear made me want to knock him flat. When I finally could have stopped Javion, you sent one clear message. You wanted me safe, out of the action. I hesitated, and it was enough for him to hurt you." I nodded to the arm she cradled.

Her eyes fluttered closed. "It'll be fine."

A scuffle tumbled through the doorway. "Let me at her!" Quetta's arm shot around Evard's orange-coated figure, and she hit his rear with the broad side of her activated stun sword.

He yelped as sparks sizzled over his coat. "I tell you,

woman, you'll feel differently when you have your proper senses back."

"Evard!" I eased Eve to a chair and scrambled over to them. "Quetta is herself. The fight's over, let her go."

"*Great Grünmann*, thank you." He released her and sagged to the wall, swatting at his smoking coattails while Quetta stumbled forward and proceeded to smack Quala with the sword.

"Apparently, repeated stunner jolts do have an effect on us," said a bleary-eyed Evard. "Wonder what it's like for Quala covered in goud?"

"I don't think it's wise to find out." I reached Quetta in two quick strides, took the sword from her and gently guided the shaky minister to a chair.

"This woman killed the real Quala," she cried, her eyes flashing.

Behind me, Eve gasped.

Evard swore. "Killed her? Not just holding her captive at Reboot—"

"No. This woman gloated about Quala's murder, threatening me with the same." Quetta's fist slammed the chair arm.

"Poor woman. Someone slap me if I complain about my lot again." Quil leaned against the desk, his hand pressed to a bloodied spot on his head. He must have hit something when he fell. "Good to see you again, Quetta. Who the hell is this, then?"

"I have no idea, but what gall," Quetta spat. "To think I wouldn't learn her real identity and bring her to galaxy trial." She leaned back and closed her eyes.

"Perhaps being drugged was a blessing. Imagine, a Docga subject murdered."

The word *murder* echoed in the hall. Quetta didn't know this was Myriah. If Quaene and Quil had known my history with the Reboot liaison, surely she did as well. My former lover wouldn't get away with it, but we couldn't discuss the matter yet. People had appeared at the door, guards, staff...

Our staff. I glanced around at Evard barely standing, Eve and Quil still sitting near the dead Javion. "We'll see to it," I murmured. "But please, we have other business now. We must present the semblance of leaders to our staff."

"They are good people, once we weed out the others he's drugged." Quetta drew a breath and eyed me. "Though my heart is willing, I do not have the reserves to handle this. If you and Quil would be so kind as to take charge?"

I nodded. "Evard is our guard, by the way."

She cast him a genteel smile. "My apologies. You're welcome to the extra sword, if you think it'll be useful."

He grinned at her and accepted the sword I offered. "It just might."

We turned our attention to the 'torgs at the door. I recognized the brunette—Charlotte, Eve had told me was her name—but the guard behind her made me thankful Evard had the swords.

At my wave, Charlotte strode in. "Thank goodness, the right people are standing. I've sent Avery for help, but this shouldn't wait." She dropped beside Quil, popped open a first aid kit and tore into a gauze pad that she pressed to his temple.

"Eh?" His eyes widened at the pretty brunette's attentions.

Evard chuckled, and Eve threw Quil a faint smile. Obviously, he'd regained her good graces, so I might as well try to accept him. I eased Eve up and into a chair. She tried to hide her grimace, but the arm hurt.

Quil lifted his chin to her. "I don't get it. How did you know he was still on our side?"

"I didn't exactly," Eve said, "but my bodyguard function told me to protect him. After that, I just hoped *his* function hadn't been messed with."

I cleared my throat and gave a nod toward Charlotte. "How's his cut, Charlotte?"

"Deep, sir." She finished applying a bandage. "Shall I go for the med-tech?"

"Please, and ask for a stretcher for Eve." My lovely bodyguard made a protest, but I gave her a gentle squeeze and left my hand on her shoulder. "And perhaps one for Minister Quetta?"

"Minister Quetta is fine, if she can remain in this chair," she said. "It's good to be up and about, a blessing for which I owe a deep gratitude to this young lady. Charlotte, dear, don't be long now. I would feel better if you were in attendance."

I added, "But would you check on that other help from...Avery, was it?"

Charlotte smiled and then winked at Eve. "Yes, sir, Minister."

She left. While Evard helped Quil into another chair, I knelt next to Quetta. "I have bad news. Quaene has died."

She closed her eyes again. "I suspected as much. I could think of no other reason for her not to be with you. The story of how can wait. Please fill us in on these impostors."

All eyes turned to me. I drew a breath to level my tone. "Quala turned on us, alerting my look-alike, who revealed himself to be Javion Lystlund. While we fought, Javion flaunted my mistakes on W234, particularly with Myriah."

"Myriah?" Eve and Evard echoed. Quil groaned, and Quetta's lips formed an O.

I gestured to the fallen Quala. "Myriah Feldfine, a Schiftani, who, like Javion, used blood they stole from Quala and me to masquerade as us." I swallowed hard. I had to come clean on everything. "She befriended me during my R&R to infiltrate the Docga's mission, along with Javion, who posed as her brother. Quil was right." I named him, but my gaze darted to Eve, whose opinion meant more now. "I exposed us. I got involved with a native, ignoring the explicit Docga policy."

I waited for the barrage of allegations. Instead, Quil simply said, "Blood he collected when he stabbed you."

His tone of sympathy made confession easier. "He intended to kill me—probably when I went to tell Myriah good-bye after the E-IV conversions—but I waltzed into her place earlier than expected. Javion was...with her. I left, thinking they hadn't seen me."

Eve snapped her fingers. "The memories you told me—these are the people, and the incident, that made you distrust everyone?"

I shrugged. "Learning she'd played me for a fool me was a blow to my ego that I wanted to totally forget. I was so hurt and betrayed seeing them at Myriah's apartment, I couldn't remember either that or the knifing after nearly dying from it.

"I bet that's what happened to Quala. Perhaps the *friend* she left the bar with was Javion who'd shifted to another disguise from his arsenal. With the concern over my stabbing and security breaches, no one paid any attention to Quala or the man she'd stowed away. They couldn't get to me on the transport, because I bunked with PT to avoid Quil. So he posed as a crew member to try and get me in the confusion of arriving. Then my head injury scrambled everything."

Quil grunted in agreement.

"For weeks, I considered myself a complete sucker, and the feeling returned tenfold while Javion bragged. He's a politician. Can you imagine what he could have done as the immortal leader of a planet of shapeshifters?"

"A close call," Quetta said.

"Thanks to Quaene, the galaxy dodged it. She never gave up on me."

PT rumbled, and Evard translated, "The Schiftani have attempted an unacceptable alteration to a society, no matter how advanced they *think* they are. Docga policy on this is strict. It's...unforgivable." Evard cast a worried look at me. "He plans, however, to speak strongly on your behalf at the investigation."

Quil cleared his throat. "We'll insist the Docga look into how an apparently benign population hid a dangerous skill so well we put a port-of-call's management in their hands. But I'm also interested in how you managed to keep your function when Javion attacked you."

"A simple bluff, a result of my own hesitation. When I didn't succumb to his control, he acted surprised, so I pretended to give in. He bought it—so completely that he made the mistake of leaving Quetta and me next to each other. When they weren't looking, I released her."

"I nearly gave the game away," she said. "Then Quinn moaned about his sword cut, and it distracted them. I got my wits about me while Quala patched up his chest—"

"Cut?" With surprising swiftness, Eve stood and gasped at the bloody slice in my jumpsuit. I tried to brush her off, but she lifted the bandage. "Blessed Waters, this could have been fatal."

"It wasn't."

"A puncture like that...any lower and your lung—"

She faltered, and I caught her around the waist. "Leave it to the med-tech, Eve."

"She's looking pale again," Evard said.

Quetta gave Eve a once-over. "She needs medical attention. We've got to secure command of this facility to get it."

"Help is here." Quil rose and ushered Charlotte inside.

"Excuse me, Minister," Charlotte said. "May I make a suggestion?" Quetta nodded. "It's simple. Send all those other 'torgs home. That's what they want. That's what we want. Once they're out, you get a few guards like Charlie and Avery here"—she gestured to the two Blackguards speaking to Quil—"to root out those who will support you, and the Dome 'torgs will spread the word. Meanwhile, let me put Eve in the infirmary. She can barely stand."

It was true. With Charlotte's help, I lowered her to the chair again.

Quil hustled up. "Quinn? These guards say the situation downstairs is rather desperate. If we don't do something quick, we may not have a building left from which to administer. I'm leaving with one to open the Conducer controls. Can you smooth things down there?"

Blessed— "Be right there. Sorry, Eve, I—"

"I understand." Her arm tightened briefly and released me.

I didn't want to leave her, but more 'torgs had appeared at the door, including the med-techs. I waved them over. I kissed Eve's temple and took a last long breath of her lilac scent. "Take care of yourself."

I turned, and she called, "Med-tech? See to Quinn's chest, please."

I ignored the man opening my bloodied bandage and gestured Evard to my side. "We must resume contact with the Zeffirites. The other labs must be checked and the return of the boxed Aeroport crystals arranged.

From the little we've gleaned of the element's effect on hornwort growth, we may be able to disperse the crystals to interrupt the maturing sporophyte stage. Can you take charge of this portion of our operation?"

"Me? I..." His gaze shot to Eve, who smiled. "I'd be honored."

FIFTY-TWO

EVE

Zeffir Island

Days later, I couldn't say what happened after they helped me onto the stretcher. I woke up in the infirmary with my armor removed and my function returned to research. A surprising sense of loss swamped my emotions, one that even the sight of my reformed crystal did little to soften.

According to Evard, when he'd sought out the Zeffirites, Sabein's first request was to see me. She presided over the removal of my goud from the crystallized shifters. Myriah recovered, just as Evangeline had. Dome security held her, along with the body of Javion, awaiting the arrival of the Docga contingent, due ten days hence. Quil restored the communications satellite, putting PT, the ministers and any Aardite leaders who wished to be, in contact with the Docga. They locked down the Schiftan R&R facility while they scoured it for other infiltrators. Rumor was that it, and other alien ports of call on the planet, would close in a boycott over the Schiftanis' concealment of their shifting ability.

Evard, Sabein and PT escorted me back to Passages

and insisted I rest on our sitting room couch. While Evard adjusted the gas flames in the fireplace, Sabein wrapped me in one of her afghans.

"I'm not an invalid. They repaired my broken arm." I held it out to her. "Perfectly healed, thanks to PT's E-IV technology. Though I do appreciate your concern."

She sat beside me and ran her fingers over my unblemished arm, her study ending with a shake of her head. "Take advantage of it for a few days, my friend. People fretted about you, missed you. The community wasn't the same when we returned without you."

"Well, you don't need to worry about that happening again," I murmured.

"Nor many other things, according to your Quinn."

My Quinn? The only contact I'd had with Quinn was through Evard. Evard telling me I could go home to Zeffir, my now-permanent Post. Evard rattling on about the extensive planet-wide cross-leap trip that took Quinn off to check for hornwort in every puddle of thermal water on Aarde. Evard describing how Biological Resources now had the manpower—and torches—to destroy the plants, and that he and Quinn planned more trips to talk to city-state leaders... I lost track. "*But then*," Evard had assured me, "Quinn will have more time."

More time for what?

Sabein's warm fingers clasped my left hand. My right moved automatically to cover my crystal and stroke it. "I know. Let it go, or my emotions will be my undoing."

"Exactly." She rose and kissed my forehead. "You

have other concerns." She gestured to PT standing at my knee and left.

Evard knelt beside the Docgan. "It's about Evangeline."

"Yes, I..." Tears filled my eyes and threatened to overflow. I wiped them away, and with my hand to the wolfhound's shoulder, I opened my gift to the Docgan's message—one I understood through emotional intent, rather than the direct words Evard and Evangeline heard.

PT had spoken with his supervisors after communications had resumed at Dome, relaying his observations of Evangeline's status. They valued her contributions to Zeffir's husbandry, but wanted to explore how to help her fulfill her soul. He'd given Evangeline the options, but PT was worried about me. His meaning was kind, but insistent. Evangeline had to make up her own mind about her future. Could I contain my emotions and my goud influence?

I met the steady gaze of his amber eyes. "I'll step back. I'll allow her to make her choices as she sees fit."

With a nod, PT left, no doubt to find Evangeline. Mylta served our favorite foods. Over bowls of steaming goat stew, potato salad and chocolate cake, Evard regaled me with his techie fascination in his new functions. I was sipping tea when Evangeline wandered in with PT.

She'd dropped her age and left her brown hair hanging loose for the first time in ages. As I'd always suspected, seeing her younger self was very nearly like looking in a mirror. Yet, her tanned features were pinched and her gray eyes clouded.

She bent and gave me a hug, then settled on the couch beside me.

Evard poured her a cup of tea and murmured an excuse to leave.

"Don't go." She gave him a weak smile. "You're family, and I've been waiting to talk to both of you."

Evard raised a brow to me, and when I nodded, he resumed his seat in the chair next to us.

PT leaned into Evangeline's leg. Her fingers curled into his fur. "I don't want you to think I'm not grateful for asking the Docga to accept me despite being only a child. I am. PT has explained why I feel out of sync with people. It's a growth stage I missed."

Apologizing again wouldn't solve the problem, but I did it anyway, and Evangeline and Evard reminded me that we wouldn't be having this conversation if I hadn't done what I had. As if that settled matters, she picked up her tea.

There had to be more. I clasped my hands together and waited.

Evangeline blew across the top of her tea, sipped it and then set the cup in its saucer with a clink. She looked between the two of us and forced a smile. "I can't go on like this."

My eyes blurred. I couldn't breathe. Blessed Waters, she'd decided to have the Docga deactivate her. Evard moved to my side, his large hand kneading my shoulder and drawing me back. "Give her a chance to tell us,

Evy, before you anticipate the worst."

Evangeline frowned. "The worst? What would—oh!" She wrapped her hands around mine. "I do *not* want to die. Though, PT says the surgery would be risky." Her voice broke on the last word, but she rushed on. "I'm willing to chance it. I need to find out who I am, what I can be. I've asked to have my electronics removed. I want to be human again, to live the life I missed."

Her determination flowed so strongly that I didn't need my gift to detect it.

Evangeline smiled and gave one of her rare nervous giggles. "I want my childhood back. I want the gradual and happy experience of growing into myself."

Childhood? Reverse her aging...how...I couldn't even imagine...

"Hold it together, Evy," Evard rumbled, his voice hoarse. "I see her point."

Evangeline bit her lip and fixed a glassy gaze on me. "The Docga have agreed to the request, and I have a place with the Zeffirites, though they don't know the details. I'd like to keep the age reversal quiet, in case...just in case." She wiped an eye. "That leaves one last arrangement. Who would raise me?"

Turn the rearing of my little sister over to someone else? "I will, of course. But the risk—"

"Whatever it will be is worth it to me." She threw herself into my arms. "Thank you, Eve! Thank you so much."

Ten long days later, the Docga contingency arrived at Dome to evaluate Aarde's disrupted affairs, and PT

452 | LAUREL WANROW

escorted two wolfhounds to Zeffir. Evard and I watched them walk with Evangeline up the hill to the hot springs. "The best pro-techs the Docga have, Evy. Evangeline is going to be fine."

But things weren't fine.

The odds of her surviving the risky surgery weren't available. An age-reversal surgery of the type she'd requested had never been done before.

"Academically," Evard explained, after he'd conversed with the pro-techs, "they believe they can do it. They have the process defined through the crystalline structure that amalgamates with the cellular structure." He dared a smile. "You know as well as I do, my dear girl, that with Aarde's goud, anything to do with life and aging is feasible."

"It wasn't for Pier," I muttered.

"Different situation." He eyed me and scooted closer on the couch to throw an arm around me. "It's not just the goud, it's what they can do with the electronics. The functions will provide life support until the last piece is removed from her—"

"Stop." I urged a wash of goud over me to halt my shaking. "She's the first. They don't really know what will happen."

"True," he whispered. "It's still experimental."

But Evangeline was a grown woman, and she'd made her choice, one that found the three of us back at the Dome medical wing two weeks after what the Aardites called The Second Shift of Command.

Evard hugged Evangeline and slipped away to give

us some privacy. I held her by the shoulders for a last long look. She'd aged to the youngest age she could, eighteen. Her hair and eyes matched mine, but her face was shining with anticipation.

Mine sagged with worry. "You look fabulous," I said. "Are you sure you don't wish to retain some years? A young woman's age? You've been much happier since learning the truth."

"Are you backing out?"

"Of course not. But the risks are—"

"Overshadowing any happiness you can have for me." She touched her forehead to mine and giggled. "Eve, I've never been more sure about anything in my fifty years on Aarde." She kissed me, and we hugged. "Now tell me good-bye."

I mumbled it out and managed to wait until she disappeared through the door before my tears escaped. Lowering myself to a couch, I fumbled for the handkerchief I'd stashed in the pocket of my skirt. A wad of tissue was pressed into my hand. I covered my face and said a broken, "Thanks," hoping Evard might keep his upbeat outlook to himself so I could cry in peace.

"You're welcome."

The deep voice was different. Quinn. He was here?

I wiped my face and stared at him, his brown eyes, the strong planes of his rugged face above the clipped curls of his beard. He still sported the hairstyle Sabein had given him—when? Two weeks ago? The length tapered neatly above the dark green collar of his pressed minister's suit. He had the air of a man secure in his

454 | LAUREL WANROW

position. Comfortable with himself and his role. Everything about him was the man I knew, and yet, one I no
longer did.

"Sorry I'm late. She went in already?" He smiled hesitantly. "May I sit with you?"

I nodded. What could I say? I supposed we had a lot
to talk about. He'd been occupied with establishing the
new regime. I'd been occupied with Evangeline's decision. But his absence hurt.

I'd expected at least a visit. Or a note. But nothing
had come, only messages via Evard that Quinn supported Evangeline's request. And, of course, the daily Dome
reports, which had been addressed to me since the start
of their command. Evangeline had officially given up
her position, and Evard spent most of his time at headquarters, so I was the de facto lead. I *had* received
Quinn's signed official orders designating Zeffir as my
permanent Post. Which should have made me happy,
except for one tiny problem.

My tears renewed themselves with vigor, and Quinn
filled my hands with fresh tissues. Why did I have to
lose control now? But I let go and gave in to the
warmth and comforting embrace of the man I missed
so much.

FIFTY-THREE

QUINN

Eve fell asleep in my arms. Thank the Golden Waters. Now I could stare without her asking why and feel my emotions without her knowing. I dipped my nose as close as I dared to where her fine hair lay tucked behind her ear. Ahh, she smelled more lilac than leather. My Eve hadn't spent much time handling books lately.

She shifted her shoulders and sank her weight into my side. I tightened my embrace with her movements and cuddled her close.

The waiting room door opened. Evard caught my eye and hesitated when his gaze lit on Eve. I waved him in, and he took a seat, his grin stretching from ear to ear.

"Good to see you relaxing at last," he whispered, "but even better to see the two of you together again."

I shook my head.

"What? You haven't told her?"

"What is there to tell? We've spent the last ten days on the road or holed up in that office, and for what? The Docgans are taking their sweet time checking and rechecking the proposal we killed ourselves preparing before they landed."

"*Grünmann,* man. I feel your frustration, but we've made great progress. Here's the latest." He held up his porta-scan, its screen cued to the status report I checked a dozen times a day. The update read another goud enclave and two city-states had signed off with the Docga.

I rolled my eyes. Some coalition we were forming.

"Okay, it's slow, but it's progress. What do we have to hurry for? No one's going anywhere." His voice rose, and Eve shifted in response. He leaned in to whisper, "The Docga *like* the idea. The gentle blokes never imagined interest in this quiet planet would lead to repeated theft and the loss of life. They're all for 'torg recruits protecting the very planet that sustains us, as long as it's done properly."

I had to keep reminding myself this was for *us,* too. The Docga had perfected the electorg system with the Aardites' gift of goudrogen crystals.

"Let them revisit all the 'torg leads and the Aardite leaders to verify our scheme. I, for one, never thought we'd see the day B-runs would be consulted in planning matters and given the option of *applying* for positions. Including them and native leaders in the administration is key to restructuring G47's Biosphere Corps administration, with power checks and balances to safeguard the planet against another coup. In light of the hornworts' near-fatal outbreak, how can the Docga refuse?"

How could they refuse? Only in a hundred details they could nitpick until the galaxy imploded. I opened my mouth, then bit off the retort. Evard had more than stood by me this week and a half, he'd been a godsend in interacting with electorgs and Aardites both. My frustration came from lack of sleep—and lack of Eve—and I couldn't take it out on him.

"*Grünmann*, with the resource we're protecting known to the leadership team, it's going to be far easier to monitor. For the Aardite goud users and for us."

"Agreed, once we get a handle on the unique ecological interactions. It's a great proposal, and I think better of them for their careful analysis." Eve would love to hear the plans for better representation for B-runs. But to give her the details prematurely, including details of my plans, when those could still fall through... "She did fight as hard as anyone to save this planet's life for her friends and children."

He snorted. "That's only part of why she followed you to Dome, and you know it."

Was I as important to protect as they were? I pulled Eve closer. "I never had the chance to ask."

Evard shook his head. "Your call. It's your relationship. Or not." He settled back in his chair and waved the porta. "Still planning to meet them out at Te'eg this afternoon?"

I nodded, and he started tapping. The Te'egites had been hard to pin down. I couldn't miss it. But I'd wrangled this window to be here for Eve, and that was what I was going to do.

I sank my head to rest against hers, inhaled and allowed myself to revel in the simple pleasure of having her beside me, feeling the slow, steady breathing of her sleep state. During the long days of cross-leaping about the planet, I'd fantasized about holding her again. The handful of times I'd held her in the tough days we'd shared were still the highlights of my memories.

I had so few.

I'd read my previous assignment reports in hopes of triggering more recall, but none came. A Docgan specialist confirmed that the little I'd regained would likely be all I'd get. I'd happily put my frustrating past aside for a future with Eve, but did *she* want me in *her* life?

I shook my head and sent up a prayer to whichever deity I may or may not have followed during my organic years. Evard saw my movement and checked his pocket watch.

"Thirty minutes," he said. "By now, they'll have Evangeline in a suspended state and be reworking her molecules through a goud infusion. If that goes well and she remains stable, the electronics will be disconnected. Then, one by one, the components will be dissolved and flushed from her, also via some technique involving goud. I wish I understood it better."

My innards roiled. "I don't." Thank the Waters I hadn't had the time to figure the odds on the complex surgery. Now was not the time to dwell on my selfish desire to see Eve—to be allowed a place in her life—when Evangeline's life was either over or beginning anew as a Zeffirite.

I should back off, give Eve and Evangeline time to reestablish their sibling bond. What type of relationship would they develop over the coming years and decades? For Eve's sake, I hoped it'd be as close as the one Gwyn and Tristam shared.

My precious minutes for holding Eve ticked by. I must have dozed. When the door opened and the Docgan cleared his throat, hours had passed. Evard was gone. The wolfhound looked pointedly at Eve, and for once I felt a twinge of regret I couldn't understand the Docga language because of whatever I'd done to render my E-IV system unable to hold a reset, even after diagnostics by the visiting specialists.

"Eve? The surgeon is here." I eased her upright, but kept an arm around her.

Shakily, she extended a hand to touch the wolfhound's shoulder. "Is she...?" With a sigh of relief, she repeated, "She made it. Evangeline's alive." Tears streamed down her cheeks.

I grabbed tissues from the box and handed them to her as the Docgan rumbled something more. I got to my feet with Eve, but when she followed him to the door, I hung back.

She looked around, bleary-eyed and weary. She was such a beautiful and loving woman. Not being free to take her in my arms and stay tore at my heart. I shoved my hands deep into my pockets to steady myself.

"She's asking for me." Eve clenched her hands together and rubbed the golden crystal that had reformed on her ring, but nothing emanated from it, or her. "Would you like to see her?"

I took her arm and followed the Docgan through the medical wing to a room. A smiling nurse met us at the door. "Keep things quiet, please. If she closes her eyes, let her sleep. Her organic system will need it." Then she stepped aside, and Eve rushed past.

"Thanks." My gaze went to Eve bending to kiss—

A child?

I stumbled to a halt and stared at the pale girl with fine brown hair whose small hand covered Eve's. "Please don't cry," she said, and the familiar shy voice cleared my confusion.

Evangeline.

"I'm trying not to," Eve said with a half-hiccupping laugh, "but I can't seem to stop. I'd never forgotten, but without a picture..." Her finger traced the little girl's cheek. "I'm so happy to see you again," she whispered, and the girl smiled.

Evangeline *was* a child. No wonder Evard's manner had contained an edge of graveness each time we'd discussed the impending surgery. Blessed Waters, these weeks for Eve must have been worse than my own. And I hadn't been around to offer any support. I squeezed her shoulder. Lame, but it was too late for anything else.

Evangeline noticed. Her eyes lit up, and she smiled at me as well. "Minister Quinn. Are you surprised?"

I managed a nod, my gaze fixed on the delicate pixie face that was a rounder, softer—and happier—version of the older Evangeline.

"She's—" Eve drew a shuddering breath. "Four years older than when we died. Nine. She wanted to be the same age as the other Zeffirite children."

"Excuse me," said the nurse from the door. "A tall, blond gentleman is at the desk insisting on admittance."

"Evard," we said in unison, and Evangeline added, "Oh, please let him in."

"We'd like to keep it to two visitors at a time for today," the nurse said.

I assured her I'd be right out, and she left. Stepping closer, I said to Evangeline, "I hope to hear the story of this one day, but in the meantime, you do everything your"—my gaze darted to Eve—"sister says to speed your recovery, young lady."

Evangeline nodded and giggled.

Giggled?

Eve accompanied me to the door. "Thanks for coming to sit with me," she murmured. She wiped the tears from her cheeks and seemed to want to say more as she wavered beside me, but didn't.

Neither could I. Not now. I gripped her elbow and whispered, "I don't know much about this family stuff, but my instincts tell me this is a time for you two. Take care of her." I kissed her cheek and slipped through the door before I broke every promise I'd made not to hurt her.

FIFTY-FOUR

EVE

Zeffir Island

"Eve, thinking he's dropped you is a fool-ass thing to believe. I thought after you finally broke your celibacy and had a jolly time with Quinn, you'd be ready to see more of him."

I was, but I didn't want to tell Evard that. Although, in the two weeks since Evangeline's surgery, he hadn't been around much to tease me about it. Neither would I tell my longtime friend that on top of giving up the hope of connecting again with *my minister*, the change in our triad dynamics made the long days following my return to Zeffir lonelier than the previous few decades without Pier.

I leaned against the counter in our office and crossed my arms. "I have a child to raise now. You can't tell me that didn't throw him off. I saw his face."

Evard selected another file from our database to add to his porta-scan and then looked up. "He's head over heels for you. I should know. I'm his closest adviser."

"No," I whispered. "Even if he doesn't like the idea of a child in my life, there's nothing in the future for us. E-run and B-run electorgs don't move in the same circles."

His eyes turned doleful, the way they did when Quaene's name came up, and I wanted to smack myself. One night he'd told me he thought it'd be ages before he'd even *date* again.

"Sorry. I didn't mean to—"

"If she'd lived, we would have found a way to make it work. Officially. Like Quinn will." He selected another file. "That man has rule-breaking issues to rectify that are bigger than yours."

He did. And I was steering clear of his past, trying not to add to it. "You're forgetting mine have names."

"But you haven't been called in."

They were probably giving me a little time after Evangeline's surgery before serving notice of the official review Quaene had predicted weeks ago. "I'm sure a few other matters in the running of G47 are higher on the list than my thirty year old indiscretion."

"My fair nym—"

"Don't call me a nymph."

"—dear, it's not being viewed as an indiscretion. They find it quite interesting you circumvented their sterility measures." He lifted a brow to me before turning to shut down his computer and pack away the porta-scan. "Right-o, I have the fungal report Evangeline was to have submitted before all this happened."

"You spending the night at Dome again?"

"Maybe longer. I've found a temp 'torg to fill in. He'll be here today."

"Just one? With Evangeline reverted to non-electorg

and you gone half the time, I should think a request for two replacements for Zeffir would be granted."

"See how this one works out and then decide. Come on, I want to say good-bye to Evangeline before I go."

We found her, trousers muddy and one braid coming undone, in the back garden feeding two goat kids the scraps from Mylta's lunch. One gobbled the carrot peelings from her fingers, while the second nibbled at the new bracelet Tristam had made for her. Its line of five yellow crystals sparkled warmly in the bright sun, but a cool breeze whipped by, reminding me it was only the beginning of March.

I called, "Evangeline, you should have on a sweater."

She ran up to us. "Oh, Evy, you worry too much."

"Eve, leave her be. How's my girl?" Evard swung her high, and Evangeline giggled as he hugged her.

"Uncle Evard, aren't Buttercup and Princess the best-looking milk goats we've ever had?"

"Right, they are. I can't wait to sample their cheese, though I bet you forget to milk them with all the pets you've taken on. You have been one busy girl."

"It's because I have so many years to make up for."

She laughed, and he joined her. "You do, and I shan't keep you from them. Bye, love. Be good for your sister." He put her down.

"I always am, aren't I?" she said.

My heart flipped at the coy reference to our past— the five years of which she now had a child's vague memory. "The best." I bent for a kiss before seeing Evard back to the house. We hugged good-bye on the back porch.

"The new guy should be here soon," he said.

"I'll stick around and show him around town as I run errands. What's his name?"

Evard scrunched up his face. "Can't remember. But you'll know him—the only stranger in town. Good day, my dear." He lifted his hand in a two-finger salute above a broad grin and entered the bookshop to travel back through the Conducer.

With Mylta in the kitchen to call me when the new 'torg arrived, I waited in the garden and watched Evangeline tend to her goats, chickens and geese. Having this many animals in the yard would wear it bare before May rolled around. Idly, I wondered what Pier had done to keep the grass growing when the children were young.

The back door opened, and I turned to greet the newcomer.

My heart leaped. Instead of the temp, Quinn walked out.

Was he here to see me? Oh, no...probably to tell me I finally had to report in. If I had to be gone for an extended time, who would care for Evangeline? I supposed I could ask Gwyn.

"Hello." He ambled over with his hands stuffed into his pockets, making him look nothing like one of the planet's ministers.

I rose from the bench and went to meet him. It wasn't just the hesitant walk, but his clothes. Unlike when I'd seen him at the surgery, Quinn wore a cotton shirt and canvas trousers, looking the same as he had while he lived on Zeffir weeks ago. Perhaps this wasn't an official visit. "So what brings you here?"

"A number of things. How's she doing?" He inclined his head to Evangeline.

"Fine. Her healing was immediate, thanks to the Docga's advances with the goud. So Evangeline's physical therapy has focused on getting her coordination adjusted to the smaller body. She is determined to prove through every activity possible that she's agile enough to go horseback riding with Perry, but..." I shrugged.

Quinn stared to the far corner where my ambitious sister had finished mucking out the goat shed and was now installing fresh straw. "Better safe than sorry. Does she—" His gaze shifted to me, and his voice dropped. "I suppose this might fall into the realm of too personal, but I've been wondering. Does she remember?"

I grimaced. "Oh, yes. Though she never directly says, poignant remarks litter her conversations. Her memory retention was the biggest point of debate for our arrangement. She had lost so much already, she wasn't about to lose the experiences of her last fifty years. The surgeons were even able to unlock the previous five. It's as if—" I struggled to forestall the tears that still came when thinking about this miracle. "I've regained my human family."

"I'm happy for you. For both of you."

The words were somehow strained, but I didn't pry to discover why. It had become my habit during my "off hours" to keep my gift closed down to focus on

Evangeline without intruding on her emerging feelings. As far as using the gift for personal insights... I eyed Quinn. No, I didn't dare tread that ground.

He said, "I'm going to have a look at the house next to Cyrem's. Care to join me?"

"Uh..." What was I supposed to say? I knew what the house two doors away looked like. "I better not. I'm waiting for a temp 'torg Evard has arranged to fill in."

Quinn grinned sheepishly. "Then you can see the house. That would be me. The temp."

"You?"

"Yeah. I wanted to tell you myself, so I'm sure Evard put a spin on it, as only he can."

I crossed my arms to hold my jumping stomach in place. "What's going on, Quinn? A minister can't live out here."

"I'm on...a break."

"What—oh, no. Is this because of me, us, um, what we did? Oh, Blessed Waters, did all that come out in a private dismissal rather than a hearing? Because I'll—"

Two fingers covered my lips and a strong hand gripped my elbow. "Shh. Eve, it's not anything to do with us. You're not going anywhere, as I promised."

I studied his forthright gaze, the set of his jaw, his reassuring smile.

He nodded. "Because Evangeline is no longer a 'torg, she has to be on Zeffir to take the Waters. I heard the moons moved into conjunction this week."

His hand on my arm was warm and secure, and I found myself focusing on the feel of it too much. I sucked in a breath and muttered, "Yes, and it helped, especially for Evangeline. Her crystal reformed to acknowledge her new being." Splendid, just what Quinn came here to find—me an emotional basket case. "Sorry, things are a little in disorder. With half the town leaders gone working with other enclaves and the goudrogen-hornwort balance, people are coming to me."

"So Evard said when he made the request for help."

"Then why are you here instead of a temp?" D'dair, that didn't sound right. I dragged in another breath. "I didn't mean... Sorry." I stepped back, but Quinn laughed and drew me closer. I resisted only a moment before I found myself burrowing into the warmth of his chest.

It felt good. D'dair. It felt *wonderful*. And I hadn't a bloody clue why the man was here. Did it matter? It would when he left. The horrible loneliness would start again, and I couldn't take—

A little throat clearing came from behind me, and I shoved off of Quinn. Evangeline stared up at us, her eyes twinkling merrily and an impish smile on her lips.

"Good morning, Minister Quinn. Good to see you back on Zeffir. Evy, I'm finished with the animals here. Mylta's brother asked if I could stop in to decide which of his stock of new kids to keep versus which to ship out. Afterwards, I thought I'd go to Perry's to help brush down the horses. I'll get my sweater first."

By the Waters, Evangeline had her mix of adult responsibilities—which the Zeffirites still called upon her for—and her childhood activities under better organization than I had my own straightforward roles. "Please be back for lunch."

Her gaze shifted between the two of us. "No, I think I better have lunch at Gwyn's. It's nearly time for Mylta to leave, and I can see the two of you have lots to talk about. Alone." She skipped inside before I could get out a reply.

"Yep, she's right. Lots to talk about." Quinn stuffed his hands back into his pockets.

I clasped my hands and searched for a safe topic. "Sabein is pleased by the lengths you've gone to solicit everyone's opinions, native and electorg."

"We're making it permanent."

"H-how do you mean?"

"Native Aardites and B-runs will hold positions on the leadership team, along with the experienced E-IV runs. It'll kill Evard not to break the news himself, but he's been asked to serve as a minister, as has Taior."

"But the Docga—"

"Approved. Two days ago, they approved our team leadership proposal. Then as part of it, they finalized private meetings with Quetta, Quil and I. Quetta is back on her feet and almost up to full-time work. Charlotte, our new office manager, keeps a watch on her stamina."

I smiled. Of course Charlotte would. "Quil's staying? I knew he requested pure tech work."

"He's got it. Hell, Javion messed with everything electronic, from jumbling the data-filing system, to re-programming dozens of 'torgs, to those weird quarters' locks with the mysterious extra plate. The Docgans told

Quil he'd had his break and to get on it with a smile."
Quinn rolled his eyes. "I'd predict he'd eke it out to the
five-year minister term, but that's gone, too."

"What?" My heart began beating very fast. "No shuffling out ministers anymore?"

"Nope, the three of us are here to stay."

My heart started to soar, then I remembered. "Except you're on break."

He drew a breath. "I'm lucky not to get deactivated
after my infractions with Myriah. I had to come clean
about *everything*," he said pointedly. "Everything I recall, that is. Luckily, they view saving the planet as
compensation for those violations and, coupled with
my injury, are giving me time to recuperate before resuming my minister position officially."

Did he mean—this was too much to hope for. I tried
for a light tone. "You'll take up fishing, like Quil did?"

He laughed. "No." His hand rose, and he fingered his
crystal ear cuff. "The Docgans agree the goud has a
strong affinity for me and accepted my proposal to
study the goud conduit system. I'll suggest changes to
the Conducer or other travel systems on planets the
Docga assist."

Other planets—no. My stomach wrenched. "That
means you'll travel?"

"It does. But only on Aarde. They're finding me an
apprentice to implement the applications elsewhere.
After my exhaustive tour of Aarde, I found someplace
I'd rather live." Quinn's hand dropped from his ear, revealing an intense glow deep in his amber crystal.

I swallowed. "Here on Zeffir?"

"Yep." He stepped to a hair's distance from me. "And someone I'd rather be with." His hand came to rest on my hip. His crystal flared to life, and a humming emanated from it. The goud pulsed, but Quinn held it in place and stared at me intently. "I love you, Eve. Would it be okay if I live here, close to you and Evangeline?"

I searched his face. "Really, you're including Evangeline, too? Raising a child is—"

His fingertips sealed my lips. "Exactly what I meant. I'll give parenting a shot. If you trust me, that is."

"I do." I kissed his fingers and released my hold on my goud. But instead of my ring crystal responding, the one on my belly began to vibrate. Of all the—*fine*. The goud was asking another question, making it ultra clear to Quinn just what moving to Zeffir involved.

He leaned in and brushed my mouth with a kiss.

With a sigh, I wrapped my arms around his neck, whispered, "I love you, too," against his mouth and pulled him closer for more. His hand slid to the purring crystal. Our lips demanded more, and a delicious warmth crept through my middle.

Quinn lifted his head. "Eve? What does this mean?" He brought his hand up between us. On the back of his left middle finger was a glowing crystal.

I patted my belly. The crystal was...on Quinn now. "Oh."

"Oh?" He frowned. "I am *not* going to have a baby."

"No... The fertility crystals do that..." It had to mean the same thing.

"Eve?"

"They go from the woman and adhere to the man after the mating results in fertilization."

"So when we..."

I shook my head. "The fertility period hasn't started yet. This one must be for...Evangeline."

His gaze dropped to the crystal, and he stared for the longest time.

I held my breath. Nine years was a long time to say yes to when he hadn't even spent an hour with my little sister.

Finally, Quinn raised his head. His fingertips traced my tight jaw before stroking up into my hair. "I was scared you wouldn't want me."

"I thought you'd never come back."

He chuckled. "Are you kidding? I was the most impatient 'torg on the team. The most demanding, the most *frustrated*..." His arms tightened around me. "I am so incredibly happy you want me to share your life."

The smell of musky woods enveloped me with the force of a thunderstorm. In a flash of golden light, we moved closer. Our particles overlapped, swirled and swelled, then brought us together in a way I wanted more than anything.

Forever.

ACKNOWLEDGMENTS

Passages is the sixth manuscript I wrote. It's the one that has given me the most validation as a writer, just when I needed it. Several times.

In 2009, this novel was my first sci-fi, so I turned to Romance Writers of America's fantasy chapter—FF&P—to finesse it through the MudPuddle critique group. Among many readers, Bart, Brenda, Jean, Kate, Lori and Alison gave it reads. *Passages* finaled in FF&P's On the Far Side contest and the Kiss of Death (mystery/suspense) chapter's Daphne du Maurier contest.

But I was still growing as a writer. A huge thanks goes to my writing partner, Michelle, for helping me revise the novel to win the paranormal category of the NJRW's 2012 Put Your Heart in a Book contest.

Special thanks go to Karen for insisting I write as myself, and to Connie, one of my early judges, for asking about the novel's status *years* after the contest.

Through CritiqueCircle.com, *Passages* led me to meet Jason, Andy and John. Thank you for your help!

A year later, more rounds of revisions with Michelle, Jason, Marta and Lindsay brought the novel to its present version. These folks have my complete gratitude.

ABOUT THE AUTHOR

Before kids, Laurel Wanrow studied and worked as a naturalist—someone who leads wildflower walks and answers calls about the snake that wandered into your garage. During a stint of homeschooling, she turned her writing skills to fiction to share her love of the land, magical characters and fantastical settings.

She's the author of *The Luminated Threads* series, a Victorian historical fantasy mixing witches, shapeshifters and a sweet romance in a secret corner of England, and *The Windborne*, a nature-focused YA series set in our world.

When not living in her fantasy worlds, Laurel camps, hunts fossils, and argues with her husband and two new adult kids over whose turn it is to clean house. Though they live on the East Coast, a cherished family cabin in the Colorado Rockies holds Laurel's heart.

Visit her website at www.laurelwanrow.com.